THE
BOOK
THAT
BROKE
THE
WORLD

THE
BOOK
THAT
BROKE
THE
WORLD

BOOK TWO OF
THE LIBRARY TRILOGY

MARK LAWRENCE

HARPER
Voyager

Harper*Voyager*
An imprint of
HarperCollins*Publishers* Ltd
1 London Bridge Street
London SE1 9GF

www.harpercollins.co.uk

HarperCollins*Publishers*
Macken House
39/40 Mayor Street Upper
Dublin 1
D01 C9W8
Ireland

First published by HarperCollins*Publishers* 2024

3

Typeset in Adobe Caslon Pro by Palimpsest Book Production Ltd,
Falkirk, Stirlingshire

Printed and bound in the UK using 100% renewable electricity by CPI Group (UK) Ltd

To my friend Sherrina, who didn't get to finish this story.

The Story So Far

For those of you who have had to wait a while for this book I provide brief catch-up notes to Book Two, so your memories may be refreshed, and I can avoid the awkwardness of having to have characters tell each other things they already know for your benefit.

Here I carry forward only what is of importance to the tale that follows.

- The library is effectively eternal and infinite. It reaches into many worlds and contains a truly vast collection of books (or the equivalent) from a great many species, spanning all periods of history. It comprises square chambers two miles on each side and is staffed by gleaming white assistants that stock and restock the books. The door from one chamber to the next opens for every member of some species and not for those of others. The further you travel from an entrance keyed to one particular species the rarer doors they can open become.

- The Exchange is an in-between kind of place whose appearance is partly shaped by the expectations of those visiting it. The Exchange can change the appearance of others to suit visitors' expectations and it makes the speech of everyone in it understandable to everyone else.

- The Exchange contains many doors. Those doors lead to the past, present, and future, and to different worlds. The furthest forward time a person visits becomes their present. If a person leaves the Exchange by a door that leads to their past then they appear there as a ghost, invisible to the people of that time and unable to touch anything or communicate with anyone. They will regain their normal form in the Exchange and in any place in their present or future. Left to its own devices the Exchange brings things together and creates coincidences.

- The Mechanism is a small building into which a single person can take a single book. It will then allow them to experience and interrogate the book as if they were walking through the world in which it's set or talk to the author with the advantage of all manner of solid illusions to illustrate the text.

- Escapes appear to be spirits of some kind that can take physical form. They escape from the Mechanism and seem to be the result of damage to it. They tend to attack whatever's in front of them. It seems that Mayland can direct their appearance in the Exchange and has done so in the past when people started to look for him.

- There are many mythologies concerning the library's creation. All of them are true. The one that is used by Livira, Evar, and the others in order to make sense of the situation concerns two brothers: Irad, who created the library, and Jaspeth, who wants to destroy it. The current library is an imperfect compromise resulting from a fragile peace between the two brothers. A low-level war between the brothers' proxies has been flaring back and forth across history. It appears to be coming to a head again in the here and now. In the library's war Yute is championing the current compromise. Mayland appears to have sided with Jaspeth and wants to destroy the library.

The main characters we have already met in this story are:

Livira: a human from a settlement on the Dust, now a librarian aged around twenty. She spent about two hundred years trapped inside an assistant (known as the Assistant) that raised five canith children trapped in a library chamber. Currently she is a ghost after her assistant body was destroyed by large insectoids known as skeer.

Malar: a human former soldier in his late forties, a very skilled warrior who cares about Livira. He spent around two hundred years trapped inside an assistant (known as the Soldier) and raised the canith children with the Assistant. Currently a ghost after his assistant body was destroyed by skeer.

Evar: a canith in his early twenties who spent a decade in the Mechanism with Livira's book. Last seen failing to save the assistant in which Livira was trapped from being destroyed by skeer. Thinks Livira is dead.

Clovis: raised as Evar's sister. Dedicated to the arts of war. Hates humans for slaughtering all her people in the library chamber when she was a child. Clovis escaped into the Mechanism.

Starval: raised as Evar's brother. Dedicated to the arts of stealth and assassination.

Kerrol: raised as Evar's brother. Specializes in understanding and manipulating others.

Mayland: raised as Evar's brother. Thought to be dead but turned out to have escaped the chamber a year before Evar did. Specializes in history.

Arpix: male librarian, early twenties, companion to Livira, studious and serious.

Meelan: male library trainee, early twenties, companion to Livira, rich, intense, loyal. Brother to Leetar, who joined the diplomatic corps under Lord Algar.

Jella: female bookbinder, early twenties, companion to Livira, timid, kindly.

Carlotte: female house-reader, early twenties, companion to Livira, vivacious, adventurous.

Yute: deputy head librarian, former assistant, married to now-deceased head librarian Yamala (who was killed by Mayland). Has been in semi-human form for around a thousand years. Had a ten-year-old daughter who went missing in the library about a decade ago.

Lord Algar: one-eyed nobleman who has tried to put an end to Livira's career at every stage. Has employed assassins to kill her in the past.

King Oanold: ruler of the now destroyed Crath City. Stirred up hatred against the peoples who live on the Dust (including Livira) for political ends.

Salamonda: Yute's housekeeper and cook. A woman in her late fifties.

Wentworth: Yute's cat. The size of a largish dog.

Book One ended with Evar understanding that Livira was the love of his life and had been trapped in the Assistant for the whole of it. He runs to save her but is too late, discovering the Assistant and the Soldier destroyed by skeer.

The door to the chamber is open for the first time in two hundred years. Evar lets his sister Clovis and brother Kerrol lead him through.

Livira and Malar survive the destruction of their assistant prisons but are now in ghost form following Evar, unable to interact with him.

Mayland and Starval were last seen in the Exchange as Escapes drove everyone from it.

Yute was last seen directing the exodus from the Exchange of around two hundred soldiers and a few dozen civilians who had survived the destruction of Crath City by the canith, then escaped the fire in the library that started during fighting between the canith and the soldiers. The civilians included several of Livira's childhood friends including Neera and Katrin; also Leetar (Meelan's sister), and Lord Algar.

Arpix, Meelan, Jella, and Salamonda escaped the library fire through a portal Livira hurriedly made for them. They were accompanied by half a dozen bookbinders and Jost, a senior librarian.

Carlotte escaped the library fire through the pool in Evar's chamber just after Livira (in assistant form) first created it.

The greater tragedy of our world is not the victims of cruelty, but that so many of those victims would, given the opportunity, stand in the shoes of their oppressors and wield the same whip with equal enthusiasm.

Excavating Crath, *by Anthony Robinson*

CHAPTER 1

Celcha

Being able to see the walls of your prison is a luxury that few are afforded. Make no mistake though: every one of us is trapped.

This was the slaver's wisdom, and he was given to sharing it. The palisade around the Arthran dig site had seen better days and had probably been unimpressive on the day it was finished, but its presence, Myles Carstar maintained, allowed a concrete focus for the restless dissatisfaction that would otherwise turn inwards and chew away at a person, or even an animal, from the inside.

Celcha wondered whether the slaver should in fact be called a slaver since it was other sabbers who went about the world hunting people down and bringing them from the wilds in chains. Whereas Myles Carstar simply set them to their tasks and enforced the law. Celcha's brother, who had an unhealthy interest in words, claimed that you could be a slaver simply by owning slaves – the business of riding them down and beating the fight out of them with iron-rod staves was not a necessary qualification. And in any case, Myles Carstar did more than handing out duties and assigning the official cruelties – he also made slaves of those new arrivals who rather than entering the dig site by the gates, wailing behind the trackers' horses, came the second way, also wailing.

The second route onto Arthran Plateau, the one Celcha and her brother had taken, was by far the shorter journey. It still took the best part of a year, though, before the newest slave was dragged out from between their mother's thighs to join the workforce.

Celcha's brother felt that the babies were born free and deprived of their liberty only when Myles Carstar set the first manacle around their bloody little wrist. Celcha thought that they were slaves from the moment they emerged, and perhaps before, but that it really didn't matter either way – they were as screwed as the rest of them.

The first official cruelty involved a flexible steel cane with which between five and fifty lashes were delivered. The scale of horror inflicted escalated rapidly through the second to sixth cruelty, moving through peelings, amputations, and the removal of an eye. By the time she was ten Celcha had seen all but the seventh – death by slow fire – enacted in the main yard, and had endured the first herself, bearing five long scars wrapped around her shoulders, side, and hip.

Celcha had been the youngest in memory to bear the steel lash. Casual beatings were common at any age, but until Myles Carstar assigned ten lashes to her brother, Hellet, she had been the youngest to receive an official cruelty.

By the time of her brother's crime Celcha had worn her scars for five years and the sting of them as she moved still echoed with the vastly greater pain of their delivery. How Hellet, a little younger and far frailer than she had been, would withstand twice as many blows she'd had no idea.

The truth turned out to be that he didn't withstand them. The agony broke him. The agony or perhaps the humiliation, for he'd always had that small pride to him. The sort that comes to those who aren't just a little cleverer than their brethren but stand head and shoulders above them, so much so that simply hiding it can become a full-time occupation.

Hellet's crime, the one that earned him the official cruelty, had been curiosity. He had looked inside a book. What had truly broken him, however, was pride. Not the bold, swaggering pride of the slavers but that quiet, confident sense of self-worth which no slave can afford to keep. The cane had divided his flesh, but it was his own pride that provided the anvil over which his spirit and mind were broken. Pride can endure pain, but it can't survive the body's inevitable reaction to pain: the screams, the soiled legs, the begging, and the crying, all of it before an audience.

The worst part of it was that it had all been Celcha's fault. She had been the one to haul the filthy object from the layer of dried mud, having first torn into it with her pick. She hadn't known what it was, but the curiosity in her fingers made her prise the stiff pages apart and hold the book up to the lamp flame. The overseers seldom came to the dig face, not wishing to suffer the dust and the stench of bodies, but one came that day, that moment, his footsteps unheard beneath the rise and fall of nearby hammers.

An instant before the overseer had rounded the corner Hellet had snatched the book from Celcha's hands. He said later that he didn't know the slaver was coming. He said it was bad luck. Bad timing. Celcha didn't believe him. She'd seen the fear on his face. And she couldn't save him. To admit her guilt wouldn't erase his. It would merely have earned them two cruelties rather than one.

Myles Carstar maintained a fiction that the slaves were not only a different species but were morally, functionally, and spiritually no different to any other animal in service to the sabbers. No different to the sheep whose wool might clothe the sabbers and whose meat might feed them. To their slavemaster, the sabber who had first set the manacle on Celcha's wrist, the greatest sin was to deny this fiction in any manner, be it in deed, or merely by attitude. A slave who wanted to live had to pretend to be part of the herd, exhibiting only the minimum intelligence required to execute their tasks. And Myles Carstar, seeing before him year after year exactly what he wanted to, perhaps even believed that lie he had cut into their flesh.

It was during the allowed week of recovery that Celcha came to understand that they'd broken Hellet. Their father had stitched the boy's flesh back together, in much the same way that he stitched his jacket with each new tear. But the steel lash had fractured Hellet in ways beyond the skill of any seamstress to repair.

She had watched Hellet lying on the bloodstained pallet in the airless barracks where the slaves slept. During the long nights he would lie without turning, locked in place by his torn flesh, only his jaw moving as he chewed his pain and muttered, talking the whole night through, his voice just above the threshold of hearing but below that of comprehension.

It wasn't until the week had run its course, and Hellet stood like the oldest of men to join the long line of unwashed bodies that led to the pits, that Celcha realized that her brother wasn't talking to himself. She stood behind him in the queue, watching, ready to catch him should he accept the fall on whose edge he seemed to be teetering. She stood close enough to see that the twitch in his eyes wasn't a twitch. He was watching something that she couldn't see. And listening. Always listening.

'Another day, another dollar.' Celcha rolled from her pallet as the clanging of the morning bell faded. They called it a bell, though Hellet said that bells were hollow and typically not just a twisted bar of metal to rattle a stick in. Celcha didn't much care about bells or dollars, neither of which she'd ever seen, but her father had always woken with the phrase on his tongue, and repeating it felt as if she was keeping him among them in some small way. She didn't think he'd ever seen a dollar either, though he had been sold for seven of them so perhaps he saw them change hands on that day, years back, before he'd been brought to Arthran to dig and die.

Hellet lined up behind Celcha. Both of them had grown into their scars. Ten more years had seen Hellet grow taller than her. Taller and wider than everyone in the long shack where nearly two hundred slaves slept elbow to elbow, breathing in each other's stink. Myles Carstar was still a head taller than Hellet, however, and he was the shortest of the sabbers, dwarfed by the guards, though the guards looked up to him in every way that counted. Celcha liked to think that Hellet could set Myles Carstar on his backside despite his height, knock him down then lift him up with arms strengthened by a lifetime of digging, and break his spine across his knee.

Not that violence was the answer to the slavers. Experience had shown that the sabbers would meet any resistance with greater aggression, and that they were far better qualified in the arts of war even if they hadn't had weaponry at their disposal that made a mockery of what either the slaves or the free people still out in the wilds could bring to bear.

Violence certainly wasn't Hellet's answer. Curiosity had earned him his lashes just as curiosity had earned Celcha hers. Hellet might be notable among the labour force for his size, but his intelligence was what really marked him out. Celcha had a quick mind, but Hellet's was lightning. Even though he'd been exposed to an official cruelty for seeming to have looked inside one of the dusty books they'd excavated, he'd taught himself to read, not from books but by tracing the lines carved into the oldest markers out by the palisade where shallow graves were scraped into the dried mud.

These days the dead got nothing to indicate where they lay. Celcha found their father's spot by memory and sometimes dreamed that she'd forgotten the place and had for months been speaking her words to the wrong patch of barren ground. In the old days though it seemed as if reading hadn't been considered such a sin among slaves, and the people brought in off the plains had often set the names of the dead above their graves, along with a few words about their lives.

Celcha didn't know how Hellet had learned to read from such a meagre source. She would have liked to read too, but she could already read the lesson she'd learned years before. It lay written in the hairless scars that divided her brother's back into a map of the awful places such curiosity would take her. Fear kept her in her place, breeding an anger that she turned in on herself.

The mouth of the current entrance to the dig lay outside the palisade. This offered no particular opportunity for escape. The weathered fence had never been what kept the slaves at their tasks, any more than the single manacle they all wore did. Both were more symbolic than practical. What held them was that the world outside was harsh and unknown and owned by others who saw their lives as nothing but an opportunity for profit.

Just beyond the palisade the head and one shoulder of some long-forgotten sabber queen emerged from the hard-baked ground at a drunken angle. Why she hadn't been broken up and carted away, Celcha wasn't sure. Perhaps it was the hardness of the stone, as witnessed by the failure of uncountable dust storms across untold centuries to do much more than soften her features. Even the fall of the city seemed to have done nothing but chip a little off her prominent nose. One of the older slaves claimed the monument to be a full body statue and that decades earlier he had excavated around her toes, far below ground.

From the rise that the slave line crested before being swallowed below ground Celcha could see a great salt-edged lake shimmering in the eastern heat, and to the west, a mountain behind which others crowded. Hellet said that the fruits of their labour flowed towards the mountain, in whose arms a city lay cradled. In the times when Myles Carstar was not at the dig site the city was where he went.

Celcha had spent most of her life below ground. The Arthran Plateau had somehow swallowed another city, deep enough that the majority of it had to be excavated through tunnelling, though in places the slaves had long ago dug vast craters exposing streets and houses. None of that remained. The stone had been carted away and time had worn that great work of digging into smooth depressions that would one day pass unnoticed, carrying with them all memory of the lives spent shovelling away the soil in search of a less-forgotten people.

Celcha took a shovel and a pick from the tool hoppers by the tunnel mouth. Two sabber guards watched over them, always disapproving, displeased by the sight of a potential weapon in the hands of any slave. Hellet took only a pick. The overseers said his strength was wasted on shovelling.

'And how's Maybe today?' Celcha asked.

Hellet grunted. Since the angel had appeared it had been hard to get anything out of him. It had taken years for him even to admit to seeing the angel, longer before he named it to her. He wasn't sure about the name. Angels, he said, were hard to hear, and the language that spilled from their tongues wasn't the one the slaves spoke. Similar, but not the same.

Celcha would have dismissed Hellet's claims as the products of a fractured mind but for three things. Firstly, he was her brother. Secondly, whilst others said that sense was apt to leak from a cracked brain, she wondered if the fissures might not also allow new things to leak *in*. Thirdly, and most importantly – though it shamed her to say it – when she looked where Hellet looked, she had begun to see glimmers. Golden glimmers, hints, slices of understanding, almost fractures themselves, as if her vision had on occasion offered her fragments of another truth.

She couldn't hear the angel, not like her brother could; she couldn't see it either, not properly, but over months the glimpses built into something, piece by piece, taller than the tallest sabber, built like a man, arms and legs in the right number and similar proportions. Hellet said that the angel called itself Maybe and that through the long nights it filled his dreams with unease and promises of a greater destiny, one that made him feel smaller even than standing beneath the vast star-scattered arc of the sky. That sky lay hidden today, veiled by the dust that blew in whenever the wind came from any direction but west.

'Ready to dig some dirt?' The overseer for Celcha's group today was Kerns, the worst of the lot. 'Of course you are, you filthy animals.' His cane flickered out, landing across Hellet's broad shoulders. Hellet grunted. If he held out, Kerns would just beat him until he showed some sign of weakness. Celcha tried not to hate the sabbers. Her father had always told her, 'We aren't the ones that hate.' But it was hard. She couldn't let it out and she couldn't let it go. Sometimes she felt that holding onto all that anger had condensed it into a poison that ran through her veins, doing her more harm than the official cruelties that would follow if she gave it a target. Hellet on the other hand seemed to bear no malice. As if the thought had never even occurred to him. As if the sabbers were nothing more than weather, their offences no more personal than a tornado off the Dust or one of the lightning strikes which came with the rain that would fall once or twice each year.

In chamber seventy-nine the work party split into groups of five, each of which followed a different tunnel. Kerns remained in the junction chamber with his lantern to oversee what might be brought up. Hellet led Celcha and three others down the rightmost tunnel.

Celcha held the group's small oil lamp whose meagre light served to minimize injuries from swinging picks and stray shovels.

'We're going to find something today,' Hellet said.

Hellet so rarely offered an opinion that doing so proved enough to make the others miss a pace. Of all of them only Celcha knew that this must be something Maybe had told her brother. It felt as if Maybe had been steering Hellet for years, and he in turn had steered the digging, moving the sabbers with imperceptible nudges, aiming the excavation ever more to the south.

Most of what they brought to the surface was shaped stone and carts loaded with rockcrete chunks. Less frequently they dragged out pieces of wood from the unwilling bone-dry clays, or hunks of rusting metal, or stranger materials for which they had no name other than the sabbers' coverall term 'plasteek'. All of it was seemingly worth the lives of slaves. All of it could be taken to the city and repurposed. Hellet said that the world had been squeezed dry long ago and that there was almost nothing that had been thrown away in past millennia, or covered by catastrophe, that was not now worth digging up. Especially if someone else was doing the digging.

At the end of the tunnel Hellet and Farga went ahead with their picks to continue digging out the current wall, leaving Celcha and the others to carry on loading rubble from the previous day into the cart.

Celcha hesitated as the others started work. She watched the shadows flicker across Hellet's back, the interplay of light, muscle, and scar. Many of the slaves feared her brother for his size, his silence, and the way he looked past them, his black eyes following things that weren't there. Celcha still saw the broken child, the boy whose sacrifice had opened his flesh to the bone. The boy who had nursed an injured tunnel rat to health and kept its company until age claimed it. Who had laughed and sung and danced. Her father had loved that child with his whole heart. Celcha had always sensed a thread of duty running through the care he'd turned her way, a degree of reservation. Perhaps she reminded him too sharply of their mother, the woman he said she so resembled. What had always surprised Celcha was not the uneven division of their father's love but the fact that she could never hate Hellet for the size of his share. Instead of their father's death unleashing that resentment, it had, if anything, prompted her to take on the mantle of loving Hellet. She was jealous of the angel though. Wary of him. Even now as the golden sparkle of him crackled across her vision, shedding a light that none but she and Hellet could see, she worried why it was that he haunted her brother and what he was aiming him towards.

They laboured in the heat and dust and din, Celcha bending her back to the task of loading the sharp-edged 'crete chunks. The tempo of Hellet's blows seemed almost to outpace her heart. At times Farga would just stand back in amazement, giving Hellet more room to swing, and even without Farga hewing at the rockcrete wall the rubble mounded up faster than the three of them could load it.

Celcha turned from tumbling a chunk into the cart. 'Brother . . .' She wanted him to stop, to rest a moment, take some water. Hellet didn't hear her. She doubted he'd have paused even if he did. His attack on the wall proceeded at frenzied pace though it wasn't a frenzy – each blow landed with precision to match its power. Years of hewing at ancient walls builds an understanding of their structure and weaknesses for which Hellet's genius was not required, just his appetite for destruction.

The void beyond had been announcing itself for some while in the resonance that answered Hellet's blows. When he breached it, they all knew it in the moment that the pick struck. A change in the quality of the sound, followed by the scatter of fragments inwards rather than outwards. With seven or eight more powerful blows Hellet opened a gap wide enough for a child to crawl through. Celcha advanced, holding her trembling flame high. The rest of them crowded at her shoulders, all save Hellet. He fell back, panting, dust coating his fur. He slumped against the opposite wall and slid down to his haunches, seemingly uninterested in what his labours had exposed.

For several long moments all that the oil lamp's light revealed was dust, hanging in lazy veils, settling only as the violence that set it loose receded into memory. Most chambers in the buried city had collapsed long ago, their roofs perhaps consumed in the inferno that had blackened so many of its structures, or simply crushed beneath the weight of years. Hellet said that the place had been covered swiftly in some sudden event. Maybe a great act of destruction nearby had raised a dust cloud much the same as the one obscuring Celcha's view, only far greater, and it had settled to bury the city fathoms deep. In any case, intact rooms were a rarity.

The book that had drawn Hellet into the crime that had earned him his lacerations had been dug out from a layer of dust that infrequent rains had turned to clay and the years were fashioning into mudstone. It had been a sorry thing, barely recognizable to the elder who had been with them. Celcha had had to prise one stiff page from the next, and the text upon them had been so faded and so stained that even the most practised reader might have struggled to extract sense from it.

The thinning veils of dust now revealed a large chamber where row upon row of ancient shelves owned the floorspace, each of them taller than a sabber and stretching beyond the reach of the lamp's glow. Many had collapsed under their burdens, but a great number still stood, withstanding the weight of the books lined along them. Score upon score. Hundreds. Thousands maybe.

'What is it?' Farga gasped, clutching his pick as if it were a lifeline.

Hellet didn't look up.

Celcha turned from the hole and crouched beside her brother. She repeated Farga's question. 'What is it?'

Hellet raised his gaze though not his head, his black eyes glittering through the curtain of his fur. 'A means to an end.'

It's remarkable how seldom visions are unremarkable.
Or might it be that the great majority of our days are
populated with visions that are simply too pedestrian
to be called into question? How many of us have an
acquaintance that is entirely fictional and who we
will go to our graves believing to have been real?

The Unremarked, *by Markus McMarkle*

CHAPTER 2

Celcha

The second angel called itself Starve. He came after Kerns had
fetched Raddock, and after Raddock had fetched Myles Carstar,
but before the first cartload of books was hauled to the surface.

Celcha saw Starve even less clearly than she saw Maybe. Both
were indistinct, more easily seen from the corner of her eye than
when staring straight at them. He moved more than Maybe did.
He prowled. Always watching. It was Starve who noticed she could
see him. Maybe had seldom glanced her way and never shown any
interest. Starve circled her, moved his extended finger before her
eyes, and watched her watch his progress. He spoke to her too,
though she heard nothing, or rather she heard a new kind of silence
when his lips moved, as if what he said didn't reach her but instead
stopped any other small noise from doing so.

They all got an extra ration that night. Not just Hellet's group
but the whole shack. And Myles Carstar patted Hellet on the
shoulder, almost stroking him as if he were one of the dogs that
haunted the outskirts of the camp.

'You did well today, boy.'

Hellet gave the grateful twist of his mouth that was expected of him.

'Who would have thought that you of all my herd would be the one to find more books?' The slavemaster's teeth showed at his own joke, fingers idly tracing the scars that crisscrossed Hellet's shoulder. 'I'll wager you were scared to even touch them.'

Hellet let his head fall. 'Hellet was. Yes, sir.'

Myles Carstar nodded, his sharp eyes flicking towards Celcha, who lowered her head, unable to match Hellet's acting. The slaves rarely spoke around the sabbers, particularly around the slavemaster. He preferred to hear grunts and growls, and what kept his mood good was good for them too. 'Do you want a she-slave or more food?'

'Hellet want food.'

When answering the slavemaster, you said your name first. He pretended it was because they all looked the same to him, but the real reason was to make children of them. You spoke like a small child too, no matter your age. None of them were supposed to be equal to the language of the masters. To speak it too well would be arrogance and that would earn an official cruelty faster than stealing or getting into a fight – those things were at least expected of a slave.

Myles Carstar did some sabber thing with his mouth that meant amusement. 'Not a she-slave? You've grown big. We need more big slaves.'

'Hellet want food, please.' Hellet looked down, humble, trembling with the correct amount of fear at daring a choice even when choice was offered.

The slavemaster laughed and ruffled Hellet's head with a thin-fingered hand. 'Food it is.'

Celcha and Hellet had both determined long ago never to breed. Few children born into the Arthran dig would choose to produce their own replacements. Slaves had no say in the matter, of course. As livestock, they did what they were told. But Hellet knew ways to ensure such enforced unions bore no fruit. He said Maybe had told him how to find the plants required to make the paste. Bitter stuff that made you ill for days. Celcha considered it the only good thing the angel had done for them.

When they locked the shack door, Hellet sank into his sleep without a murmur. He lay so quiet that Celcha, wide awake and a thousand miles from dreaming, worried he might have died. Hellet never rested well. But that night he slept like the righteous. And far below him the ancient chamber waited for them, thick with secrets that they would never be allowed to know.

Dawn brought them a day much the same as any other save that instead of hauling rubble they were hauling books, and they got three overseers in place of one, two of them doing their overseeing in the newly broached chamber. The work carried on without breaks, the task of emptying the shelves apparently an urgent one, as if the slavemaster feared the buried city might recognize its oversight in not collapsing the ceiling above the books and have it come tumbling down post-haste.

Change arrived on the second day.

Around noon, beneath a blazing sun, a carriage jolted its way through the palisade gates. Not a drab covered wagon of the sort used to bring in food and tools but a work of art on wheels, lacquered sides dark as night skies, impossibly skinny wheels, and drawn by horses with glossy hides and flowing manes rather than the stumbling beasts that dragged the products of the dig to the city and rarely looked more than three trips from the cooking pot. Two sabbers in gleaming armour rode behind the carriage, their ornate helms styled to resemble howling wolves.

Celcha saw all this over the top of the cart she'd pushed with Stana and Cherl up the long incline from the chamber and out into the dizzying brightness of the day.

'No! No! No! No! No!' The elderly female sabber emerged from the carriage before its wheels had stopped rolling. She came towards them in a swirl of crimson robes, astonishingly vivid in the dull grey camp. 'No!'

Kerns, who was bringing up the rear, cracked his cane across Celcha's shoulders as if it were a given that she was the source of their visitor's displeasure.

The female came right at them, laying her skinny, withered hands – too delicate for any serious work – on the cart's front as if she might actually be able to stop it by herself. 'Who has done this?'

She looked around the yard, eyes sliding over Celcha, Stana, and Cherl as if they could no more be responsible for whatever offence had been committed than the cart itself. She fixed Kerns with the heat of her stare.

The overseer stepped uneasily around the cart as the two guards dismounted. 'We're following orders, librarian.' Kerns kept his head down, all his customary malice gone from him like water spilled from a cup.

The librarian's sharp gaze cut to Myles Carstar's office, a large stone-built structure not far from the gates. 'Whose orders?'

'Mine, my lady.' Myles Carstar came from the direction of the slave shacks, unseen until he was almost among them. Even he seemed flustered by the librarian's arrival, humble, when for all Celcha's life he had been defined by his arrogance. An arrogance that ran so deep he hardly needed to express it, any more than an upright man needed to show you his bones. 'The books we've brought up are in the sorting hall, out of the sun, safe from any rain.' He glanced towards the building in question, making a strained chuckle at the idea the books might get wet even without a roof. Rain might be more common than the discovery of books, but not a lot more.

'And the indexing has been preserved?' the librarian snapped.

'The what now?' Myles Carstar peered at the old woman as if she had spoken in a language other than his own.

'Did it not occur to you' – the librarian advanced on the slave-master, and to Celcha's astonishment the man retreated with a nervous swallowing – 'that the arrangement of these books *on the shelves* encoded information of great value? Information that is almost certainly wholly lost in the ugly heap you've doubtless created in this storage shed of yours?'

Myles Carstar had always styled himself as the intellectual super-ior of his staff, cutting down larger men, and some larger women too, with deft twists of the verbal knife, belittling them with refer-ences beyond the scope of their education. Just as he cast the slaves into the role of animals, he portrayed the overseers in his employ as unruly and rather dim children. The official cruelties exacted upon Hellet and Celcha had been to ensure that they conformed to the slavemaster's view of what they were.

To see that same man now robbed of his power was a revelation to Celcha. She understood in one moment the sudden change that can be wrought in the appearance of an object simply by changing the angle from which you illuminate it. The librarian had cast the slaver in a new light. And she realized that although his discomfort was only a small revenge for all that he had done to her, her family, and her people . . . she liked the taste of it and wanted more.

'Well?' The old sabber woman lifted her hands from the cart and tilted her palms upwards. 'Show me the shambles.' She turned towards another cart rumbling in through the gates, pushed by Hellet and Farga, loaded with books. 'And for the love of all the gods of canith and men stop bringing up more!' Without waiting, she began to walk towards the hall, her two guards falling in behind her. The slaver moved reluctantly to follow. They wouldn't find any order in what had been brought up. Care had been taken to preserve the wellbeing of the leather-bound tomes as they were loaded and unloaded, but their arrangement on the shelves had been lost in the process.

'You won't find what you're looking for.'

For a long moment even Celcha wasn't sure who had spoken. She hoped to the heavens that it hadn't been her, but it had been the voice of a slave. The slaves spoke the slavers' language but they spoke it with different mouths, different chests, the words never sounded quite the same as they did from a sabber's tongue. More importantly though, they spoke it in a different tone. All of the overseers, and Myles Carstar in particular, placed a great deal of importance on tone. A slave must never contradict a master, that was obvious, but more than that: a slave's voice must never show confidence, let alone arrogance. Even certainty was dangerous. Hesitant and timid was the way. Intelligence was dangerous too, perhaps more so than disobedience. A slave must sound as stupid as their master imagined them to be, or more accurately, as their master wanted them to be. They must show their belly by willingly entering into the pantomime that both sides knew to be a lie, and speak as if every one of them were the village idiot.

Hellet's voice broke all of Myles Carstar's unspoken rules at a stroke. Celcha wasn't sure if the slaver would properly understand what he was sentencing her brother for but she was certain that the penalty would be the third of the cruelties at the very least, perhaps even the fifth given the audience before which Hellet had disgraced himself.

The librarian stopped in that moment of stillness and rotated towards Hellet. Something golden sparkled briefly between them but for once Hellet's eyes didn't track it, remaining fixed upon the elder before him instead. Celcha had seen Kerns take a slave's eye before, at Myles Carstar's behest. The fourth official cruelty was a slow process, carried out with mechanical precision on the punishment platform behind the tool sheds. Sudden nausea swamped her as she imagined the same procedure with Hellet as the victim.

'What did you say?' The librarian pinned Hellet with a gaze that had a measure of curiosity in it where Myles Carstar's held only contempt and a cold anger.

What did you say? She had heard what Hellet said. Everyone had. She was challenging him to say it again. To dig his hole deeper when it was already deep enough to be his grave.

'You won't find what you're looking for.' Hellet repeated himself without elaboration.

Kerns's cane exploded across Hellet's shoulders, the blow hard enough to fracture the wire-wood. Hellet gave no reaction at all, not a flinch, not a grunt, as if all the faked submissions over the years had combined to nullify what must be excruciating pain.

The librarian waved Kerns back, an annoyance, her blue eyes fixed on Hellet. 'If you were insane, you wouldn't have survived this long. So, there's an implicit promise here. You have what I want.'

'I can recreate the ordering on the shelves.' Hellet rolled his shoulders, finally acknowledging the blow.

'Show me.' The librarian extended her arm, indicating that Hellet should precede her.

The air around Hellet glimmered and he turned his face towards Celcha. 'I'll need my sister. She memorized part of the layout,' he lied.

Two emotions split Celcha in that moment. The first was a cold, selfish terror at being roped into Hellet's fatal hubris. Whatever head-patting the librarian might reward him with would provide no protection from Myles Carstar's revenge. Celcha had had a lifetime to observe the slavemaster, and she was certain that whilst physically attacking him would earn a gruesome death, it would be less horrific than the one that humiliating him would bring.

The second, competing emotion was pride, something no slave could afford to have flowing through their veins. Pride in her brother's action, and the other kind of pride, that of self-worth, pride at being named by him as co-conspirator. Even if it wasn't true. Even if it could get her killed. Because so often since the lashing that broke him, Hellet had seemed to consider her part of the scenery, little different from those others who laboured beside him in the flame's flicker. The fact that she loved him and sought at every turn to protect him went unnoticed, or so she'd thought in the long years since the collapse of the tunnel that had buried their father.

They entered the wide loading hall, all of them following Hellet. Outside, even the forgotten slaves edged closer, hoping to see what would happen. The place smelled of dry rot and roofing tar. The day's brightness fingered in through narrow slits high in the walls, turning dust motes to gold.

In the space freshly cleared of rockcrete mounds, several thousand books sat in hip-high stacks, all of them thick with dust that had recorded every recent contact, the mark of a hand there, a finger graze here. The books had brought their own scent to the hall, one that Celcha was not familiar with, complex, old, and dead. There was, it had to be said, something of the mustiness of a dried-out corpse about them. Unsurprising really, given that Hellet had told her both the coverings and in many cases the pages themselves were made from the skins of animals.

Hellet moved around the stacks, occasionally placing a small stone from the handful he'd scooped up in the yard. The air around him glimmered with Maybe's sparkle. Starve prowled the perimeter, occasionally circling Celcha.

The slavemaster and the three overseers who had joined him watched Hellet like the hawk watches the hare. Hellet ignored them. He set single stones here and there on top of various stacks, some close together, some far apart. From time to time, he looked towards Celcha as if for confirmation, and under the pressure of his stare she would nod.

At last, Hellet turned to face the librarian. 'The marked stacks come from the first shelf of the set closest to the breach.'

'You're going to trust the word of a slave?' Myles Carstar managed to look astonished and disgusted at the same time.

'No,' the librarian said. 'I'm going to put that word to the test.'

She lifted the top two books from the first stack Hellet had marked and studied their spines before returning them to their place. She moved to the second stack and leafed through the topmost book. Going to the last stack she motioned one of her guards to her and had him lift all but the bottom book then pass that one to her. The woman opened the tome to the middle pages, resting it in her arms, and scanned the text. 'The subject matter is related in all of these books. They came from the same shelf.' She turned to Hellet. 'Show these men how to arrange the stacks to reflect the shelving.'

In one fell swoop the librarian reversed the order of the world. A slave became the overseer. It proved a step too far for Myles Carstar. His pink, hairless skin flushed deep red, and a tremble found its way into both his hands and his voice. 'I'll bring some slaves in.'

'No.' The librarian shook her head. 'I need the chamber emptied quickly and efficiently. You will ensure that the rest of the books are arranged shelf by shelf as they're brought up. I want a map of the shelving in the chamber and to be able to identify where each book came from. That's something you can supervise? Or do I need to bring a junior from the library to go . . . below?' She said this last word with a shudder. The tunnels and their darkness and dirt were physically beneath her, but socially they lay much deeper than that.

And so, Hellet was left to oversee the overseers, which he did as if he'd been born to it. Celcha returned to the depths with the fuming slavemaster, coming back to the hall periodically, pushing carts of books, all now meticulously noted in Myles Carstar's ledger. On each return, Hellet would consult her about details of the ordering, maintaining the fiction that she was a necessary part of the exercise.

Whilst the sight of Kerns and the others labouring under Hellet's direction afforded Celcha great satisfaction, she knew that the daggers in their stares would be actual blades planted in her brother's flesh as soon as the librarian went on her way. As such, Celcha loaded books and pushed carts all in the certainty that if she was lucky this would be her last day, but that it was more likely her final hours lay several days hence after a period of sanctioned torture that would feel like an eternity.

Whatever consequences were coming, it turned out that they would have to wait another day at least. By the time a moonless night swallowed the plains, the chamber still held about a quarter of its original contents. The slavemaster was keen that the labour continue till dawn if that was what it took; and if the slaves assigned to the job died of exhaustion, it was a price worth paying. The librarian disagreed. Organizing the books in the loading hall would require a good many lanterns if they worked on into the night, and the risk of fire was too great. Besides, she wanted to sleep. Myles Carstar offered her his quarters, but she preferred the bone-jolting carriage journey back to the city, a slight that left the slavemaster fuming as the librarian and her guards clattered out through the compound's gates.

In the blindness of the slave shack, Celcha huddled beside her brother's broad frame, more terrified of the slavers' revenge now that her mind had nothing to divert it from such thoughts.

'Hellet?' She poked his back and whispered his name again. 'Hellet?'

A low grunt.

'Why are you doing this? They're going to kill us.' Part of her already knew. His mind had broken years ago, and it was amazing that his madness had taken this long to kill him. The only surprise was that it had killed her too. Hellet's silence seemed to confirm it. She seized on the one thing offering hope that there might be more to this. The angel. Angels now. 'This new angel – Starve – what does it want?'

Hellet rolled slowly to face her, drawing sleepy grumbles from their neighbours. 'It's the angel of death.'

Celcha's last fragile hope shattered. He'd come to watch them die. And Hellet had given him just what he wanted. She turned away, stifling a despairing sob.

'No. You don't understand.' Hellet's big hand covered her shoulder. 'Starve's here to show me how to kill them.'

'Kill Myles Carstar?' Celcha hissed, horrified.

'All of them.'

'The overseers as well?'

'All. Of. Them.'

Every loss of consequence creates within us a cavity in which that ache makes a home. An empty space full of sorrow. A void in which silent screams can echo, and unshed tears may pool. Some losses are so great they hollow us. We are cored. Nothing but skin wrapped around the hurt we've become.

Grasping the Tiara (Beauty Pageants for
Children, Volume 6), *by Anne Summer*

CHAPTER 3

Evar

Evar hardly noticed the skeer in the doorway though he passed within five yards of it. The creature – whose presence prevented the door from re-forming – stood motionless and if it tracked him with all or any of its many bead-black eyes, there was no way to tell. Evar hurried after Clovis and Kerrol, entering, for the first time in the flesh, a library chamber other than the one he'd been born into.

'Find my girl?' Evar grabbed his brother's shoulder, spinning him around. 'What did you mean by that?' Kerrol's departing words had been "I know where to find your girl." Livira had been imprisoned in the Assistant for centuries, so the problem wasn't one of 'finding'. The Assistant was easy to find. Her shattered body lay not far from the Soldier's, back among the corpses of the dozens of skeer that had died trying to destroy them. The skeer had succeeded, albeit at great cost, achieving what Evar had thought impossible.

There had been among those broken pieces no trace of the human Evar had fallen in love with. No sign that Livira had ever been trapped in that ivory statue. No sign of her companion Malar either amid the shattered remains of the Soldier. 'Speak!'

Kerrol twisted free and raised his hands apologetically. None of his unparalleled skills at reading people were required to understand how close to the edge Evar stood. 'I'm sorry for your loss, brother.'

'You said you could find her!' Evar snapped, unwilling to let go of the offered hope but also unwilling to believe it.

'I needed you to come with us.' Kerrol lowered his gaze. 'Couldn't leave you there for the next skeer that happened by.'

Evar wasn't aware he'd swung for Kerrol until Clovis caught his wrist and pulled the blow aside. 'Enough!' She pushed between them. Kerrol stepped back, unruffled, as if he'd anticipated both the attack and their sister coming to his aid.

'You don't even know!' Evar shouted at both of them. 'You don't even know . . .' He jerked his arm free of Clovis's grip. 'Livira *was* the Assistant!' He tried to stop shouting, tried to steady his voice, but it kept breaking around surfacing emotion. 'Her spirit. Her ghost. It entered the Assistant centuries ago. She was trapped in there ever since. The other one, Malar, was trapped in the Soldier. Until . . .'

Clovis stepped back, frowning, minute shakes of her head to express her disbelief. 'No.'

'He certainly thinks it's true,' Kerrol observed.

'IT IS TRUE!' With effort, Evar reeled in his anger. 'It's true. They raised us. Two humans trapped in assistants raised you, Clovis.'

Clovis shook her head more fiercely, but when she opened her mouth to deny it, no words came.

'I wasn't lying.' Kerrol drew Evar's attention to himself. 'Misleading perhaps. I know your human's in that book. Take it to the Mechanism and you'll be together again, in a manner of speaking. It will help.'

'I don't have the book,' Evar growled. He wasn't even sure if there was a book any more.

'So, what we need is an assistant to tell us where it is,' Kerrol said. 'And whilst I don't know where to find one of those with any great precision, I do know that it will be out here and not back in there.' He waved at hand at the corridor leading back to their chamber. 'Plus, if that skeer decides to move, any of us still in there may well be trapped for another two hundred years.'

Evar's shoulders slumped, his anger diffused. He couldn't feel aggrieved against Kerrol, even though he was sure he'd been expertly manipulated.

Clovis shook her head a final time. 'Come on.' She led off along the wall. 'And quietly. This is skeer territory. There'll be more of the bastards coming. Lots more.'

Evar refused to be led away. 'Where's Starval?' He looked back at the corridor. He wasn't leaving Starval behind.

'With Mayland,' Kerrol said. 'I saw them both go into a different pool.'

'Mayland . . .' Evar still hadn't come to terms with the idea that Mayland hadn't died, he'd just left, and had been in and out of the Exchange all this time they'd been mourning him. 'Why did Starval—'

'I don't know.' The pain of the admission ran through Kerrol's words.

'Enough!' Clovis said. 'Come on!'

'Where are we going?' Evar finally allowed himself to be led, and fell in behind her.

'Outside. I can't fight them all by myself. I'm good . . . but not that good. We need warriors.'

If it wasn't for needing to find Livira's book Evar would have asked why they should fight the skeer at all. He wouldn't have cared if they claimed the library while there was a whole world out there to explore with Livira. Instead, he asked, 'And you know the way, do you?'

'I know that staying still is not the way to the outside,' Clovis said, 'and that if we walk in a straight line for long enough, we're bound to reach the edge at some point.'

'At some point.' Evar nodded. Clovis didn't yet understand quite how large the library was. If they chose the wrong direction, they might walk until they got old and still not find the other side.

Evar trudged behind Kerrol, who in turn followed Clovis. They had no food, no water, and doubtless they would find – or be found by – more skeer long before they met an assistant. Bound tightly in thoughts of Livira, Evar couldn't find the space to care about his own prospects. He'd spent a lifetime trapped with the one he had come to need most, and hadn't known it. Instead, he'd bent his whole being towards escape. And here he was, trailing through the great beyond, discovering it to be no different to the place he'd come to despise. No different, except that it lacked her. How many people, Evar wondered, had spent their youth, their whole lives, battering at locked doors, only to find – if they ever managed to open them – that there was nothing on the other side they couldn't have found on their own side? When they were children, the Assistant had often told them a tale that seemed to capture this 'wisdom' in a handful of lines, a tale about three goats wanting to cross a bridge. The lesson had sailed above Evar's head. Mayland had noted that the same mythology pierced a thousand cultures like a spear driven through sentience of every kind, perhaps even that of goats. And still, despite it all, Evar had pounded on his door.

And that was where, in the end, he'd found her. That was where his extravagant race to 'save' her had ended. Before his precious door. She'd even been the one to open it for him. When he'd finally understood the riddle of the book, understood that Livira had been locked away in the Assistant's flesh for all these lifetimes, and started to run back to find her . . . what had he expected? He'd been so focused on getting there in time that he'd given no thought to what would happen next. Had he believed he could haul the girl bodily from the Assistant's flesh? It hadn't been her body that had gone into the Assistant, it had been her ghost. But the blood and bone of her, where had that gone? Those had vanished when she went from the now into the past through that portal in the wood between. The whole thing made his head hurt, even without considering the book – Livira's book – which had somehow eaten its own tail and existed looping around two centuries in the past, like an infinity sign burned through the years. None of it—

'Evar!'

Evar startled out of his thoughts. 'What?'

'This.' Clovis held up a plate of skeer armour, almost large enough to cover her chest. It looked strangely weathered, like the wooden doors in the city's poorest quarter, porous and weakened by age. 'They shed them from time to time.'

Looking around, Evar saw that the shelving had driven them from following the chamber wall and that they were in a long aisle that vanished into the distance in both directions, shelves rising above them for several times his height. A ladder on broken wheels leaned across the gap ahead of them.

'They're close.' Clovis sniffed the air.

Evar pushed his selfishness aside. He might not be overly bothered right now if his misery saw him sleepwalking into a fatal encounter, but his siblings would share that fate. In the absence of Starval he was the expert on concealment and evasion. Clovis would come into her own if they came face to face with the skeer, but it would be better if that didn't happen.

'They can probably scent us too.' Evar scanned the shelves. He pulled a couple of books from shoulder level, opened them both, then discarded them. 'Keep your eyes open for anything written in Carcasan. The more substantial tomes. They'll be written on tweel vellum.' Evar didn't know what tweels smelled like in life; however, their cured skins carried a gentle but penetrating reek. Wrapping a person's feet in a few pages and secreting loose leaves around their body would confuse the nose of even the best hunting dog.

Evar took hold of the ladder. 'I'll go up and have a scout around.'

Clovis caught his arm. 'Keep your mind on what you're doing. Daydreaming about your sabber-girl will get us all k—'

'I'm focused.' Evar pulled free and began to climb.

From on high the chamber presented itself very differently. The shelf tops resembled banding across rolling hills or the swells of some alien ocean. In places they were completely level with each other; elsewhere their heights jiggled around some common mean, but generally they grew or shrank gradually, creating slopes. Where the height changed dramatically from one aisle to the next a cliff face formed. These were rare but drew the eye.

Evar stayed on the ladder for a long time, raising his head above the shelf top just enough to see. At last, convinced that no skeer had dared the heights, he moved from the ladder to the top boards in one fluid motion, keeping low. Something towards the middle of the chamber had caught his eye but he'd needed more elevation to understand it. Even now he lacked the required height. He stood up tall, ignoring his sister's hiss of caution.

In a great bowl formed by the increasing shortness of the shelves sat something much larger than any living creature Evar had seen. Not that it was alive – but it appeared to have been modelled on a beast that struck a chord in Evar's memory. Crouched as it was, knees to chest, head down, thick over-long arms wrapping its legs, the thing was almost spherical. It seemed to be fashioned from metal plates, steel, bronze, and brass, and decorating every limb was long golden fur, so cunningly cast into the metal that it truly looked like a shaggy pelt.

To Evar, the strangest thing about it was not its size or the manner of its construction but the fact that he recognized the creature on which the titan had been modelled. He had seen its much smaller cousins when he had tried his first and only off-world portal. It had taken him to a library where the air itself had been poison, driving Livira back immediately. Only the fact that he'd been a ghost there had allowed him time to look around. But those creatures had been half his height.

'What is it?' Clovis's hiss came from ankle level. 'What do you see?'

Evar motioned her to silence. Unnervingly, despite being at least a quarter of a mile away, the mechanical being raised its head and looked in their direction. It unclasped the hands around its knees, each sporting a blade-like claw that jutted from the back. The great blunt head tilted left, then right. The faint popping sounds reaching Evar must have been loud retorts as ancient joints unlocked. He could see that, inexplicably, the golem bore a single dull iron manacle around its left wrist. A band of metal that would have encircled Evar, Clovis, *and* Kerrol if they stood close together.

'Oh crap.' Evar didn't know how he knew the thing wanted him dead. But he did know it.

The roar lagged behind the opening of the golem's tooth-lined mouth, but when it arrived it shook the air. Evar was already sliding down the ladder with Clovis barely keeping ahead of him.

Kerrol looked at the pair of them expectantly.

'We need to run,' Evar said. 'Now!'

*An execution brings with it moments of great focus
and decisions of consequence. It's a time for reflection.
So grab that mirror! How much neck do you dare to
bare? This reign of terror the word is 'lace'. We're seeing
big ruffs for the ladies, frothy jabots for the lords.*

Dressing for the Guillotine, *by Madame Gâteaux*

CHAPTER 4

Celcha

Celcha woke before the bell on what was certain to be the last day of her life. The remaining books would be emptied from the chamber. The librarian would depart to the city for the last time. Hellet would be left with Myles Carstar and the consequences of his behaviour. The slavemaster's fury at his humiliation would not be satisfied with only Hellet's torture and death. Celcha would suffer the same fate.

Celcha left the shack in Hellet's wake, her mind filled with means of escape. Not out into the stark desert beyond the palisade – that would only afford the slavers the thrill of a chase – but a cleaner escape into death. Given some rope and a few minutes of privacy she could—

'It will be all right, sister.' Hellet turned and covered her hands in his, his rough palms covering the claw scars along the back of each where her blades would grow if the slavers hadn't torn them out in her third year and cauterized the wounds with hot iron.

'How will it be all right?'

Raised voices from outside stopped Hellet from replying. The sabbers always rose early. It wasn't out of kindness they let the slaves sleep longer. The simple mechanics of it were that sabbers needed less time in their beds, and that if they forced the slaves to match them, in a matter of weeks the slaves went mad and died.

'—any other pair!' That was Myles Carstar, his voice shaking with restrained outrage.

'I don't require any other pair.' The librarian, imperious, unimpressed by the slavemaster's protests. 'I require those two.'

As Celcha and Hellet shuffled blinking from the shack's shadows into the sunlight the librarian singled them out from the line. 'Those two, just so there's no doubt.'

'They'll be nothing but trouble for you, ma'am.' Myles Carstar retreated into politeness, though to look at his face Celcha thought that without the librarian's two guards gleaming in their armour he might have beaten the old woman to death. 'They've both been disciplined for curiosity. Without strict supervision, who knows what they'll do next. You need chains, gates, proper discipline . . .'

Hellet kept his head down and Celcha followed his example, reluctantly tearing her gaze away from the slavemaster's distress. She felt as if she were in a dream and she wasn't going to accept any of it as real until she was actually walking away from the dig in her brother's company.

'Curiosity is a necessary qualification, Mr Carstar. We will be turning a liability into an asset. The library will compensate you at above market rates.' She turned towards the loading hall and the small convoy of unusually smart wagons lined up beside it. 'Now, if you'll be so good as to direct your workforce to the task, we should be able to finish this business before noon.'

And so it was that on a hot autumn day, after over twenty years spent digging out the ruins of a dead city, Celcha and her brother walked away from the place in which they had been destined to die. They followed the last of seven book-laden wagons out of the compound, leaving everything they'd ever known, leaving the dead city behind them.

Myles Carstar did not emerge from his office to see them leave, and the overseers drove all the slaves below ground so that none would witness Celcha's departure. Even so, there wasn't anyone in the Arthran dig, slave or slaver, who didn't know that the pair of them, brother and sister, had escaped from beneath Myles Carstar's rage and left him humiliated in their wake.

Hellet and Celcha took nothing of their own with them. They had owned nothing. But in her hands Celcha carried several dozen tiny wooden figures – nootki in the old tongue – whittled against the slavers' will and beneath their notice. Many of the slaves, the ones who followed tradition, made these figures, just one each, allegedly in their own image, though it was hard to tell on such a small scale. When a slave died, they were buried by the fence, unless they'd died during a cruelty, in which case their corpses were given to the dogs. The dead were always buried on the inside of the palisade, as Myles Carstar wanted to make it clear they hadn't gone free, even in death. The figure they had carved was then returned to the shack and hidden in the rafters or some other suitable nook, so that their spirit would remain with the group, watching over the young, comforting the bereaved.

These were the figures that Celcha had been entrusted with, their owners knowing that they themselves would never leave the Arthran dig, and choosing to set their nootki in Celcha's care so that some small part of themselves might go with her and witness the wider world.

It took shockingly little time before Celcha had gone further from the shack in which she'd been born than she had ever gone before. The dusty, rock-strewn world didn't care, Hellet didn't seem to notice, but Celcha did, turning briefly to look back on the compound, its low roofs, its weathered fences, and thinking in that moment how very small it all was and how awful that so many lives were eaten up there, ground into nothing for the greed of others. She turned from it and followed her brother's broad, scarred back, wiping away hot tears. Not of sorrow, nor of joy at her salvation, but of anger.

Celcha's first surprise was how big the world was. She had, of course, gazed on the lake to the east and the mountains to the west, but a life lived entirely within a few hundred yards of your birthplace fails to educate the eye in the matter of distances. She had understood that the lake and the mountains were both bigger and further away than they seemed, but she had not understood how much bigger and how much further away.

Celcha knew herself to possess both strength and endurance. These were the qualities that the slavers most valued. Her legs, however, had never been used to walk a great distance. She hurried along behind Hellet, finding that the horses pulled the wagons faster than she would have chosen to march. The mountains at which they were aimed seemed to come no closer though, no matter how far the road took Celcha, as if they were shuffling away at much the same pace as she advanced.

To distract from the growing fatigue in her legs, Celcha focused on thoughts of the city itself. The slaves weren't wholly ignorant about it. In the past, though not in Celcha's time, city slaves guilty of minor infractions such as being surplus to requirement, old, or injured, had been sent to work out their remaining days in the Arthran tunnels. The stories they brought with them were astounding, though Celcha suspected that they had been embellished over the years. The tales said that there were not one but two kinds of sabber living in the city, two species with a long history of warfare behind them, finally joined in a truce that had become an enduring peace. That in itself sounded like a miracle. Moreover, the stories had it that the second sabber race was even larger and even more warlike than the ones who ran the dig site.

The wagons rattled down from the Arthran Plateau and across an arid plain. Celcha and Hellet, walking at the rear, turned grey with the dust raised by seven sets of wheels and the hooves of a score of horses. A sabber rode towards the rear of the column, occasionally glancing their way, though far from vigilant. Escape wasn't on Celcha's mind, however – this *was* escape. Whatever the librarian had planned for them, it was hard to imagine that it would be worse than wandering aimlessly in the surrounding wasteland until death found them.

The librarian rode in her carriage ahead of the creaking wagons. Celcha had to imagine that the sleek horses pulling it must have fairly flown across the intervening distance to have the old woman there before the slaves woke that morning. The ganar slept late, but not *that* late.

Gradually Celcha started to catch up with her shadow. The prenoon sun had thrown it before her to point the way. By noon it puddled around her feet, and as more miles passed it trailed behind her as if reluctant to journey further. Celcha continually readjusted her sense of scale as the hours passed and the mountains reluctantly began to grow larger. Even so, when Hellet raised his arm to point at the foot of the nearest mountain and said, 'Krath,' Celcha took a long time to understand what she was looking at. She had heard that the city of Krath had walls so tall that someone falling from them had time to scream, draw breath, and scream again before they hit the ground. So wide that many defenders could walk abreast along their thickness. The small dark line at the foot of the closest mountain couldn't be that wall. It would mean that the mountain was so vast as to defy all sense.

And yet, mile by mile, the line grew into a wall. And by the time they reached the gates, Celcha had to crane her neck to see the serrated line of the battlements against the bright steel of the sky.

Hellet had made no complaints, not about the unaccustomed miles or eating dust the whole way. 'Krath' had been his first word of the journey and his only word until they passed through the gates. Once inside the city there were innumerable amazements to capture Celcha's attention, but the fact that her brother started to talk and said more in the next half-hour than he had in the previous six months was perhaps what amazed her most.

'The canith are faster and stronger than the humans.' In the crowd just beyond the gates the canith towered above the humans, head and shoulders taller in many cases, just as most humans towered above Celcha and overtopped even Hellet's unusual height. All three species had more in common physically than differences. Size was the most obvious dissimilarity. Celcha was used to the humans' nakedness and their need to cover it with cloth. Even the hair on their heads often looked thin compared to the golden pelt she shared with all other ganar. The canith's manes were impressive but faded to a short bristling fur that could go unnoticed, particularly on their arms and hands. At first glance their faces had something canine about them, though closer observation showed this to be a passing similarity rather than some shared fundamental.

'The canith owned this city too. For a century here and there.' The air to either side of Hellet glimmered, Maybe and Starve flanking his advance along the broad streets. 'Swapping it back and forth with the humans. Nobody's sure who first built it.' He paused to shake out some of the dust from his pelt. 'There's a lesson there. Size and speed aren't what really matter. The big child might push the smaller one over, but when we're grown . . .' He tapped his forehead. 'It's this and what we do with it that matters.' A stone hit Hellet's shoulder, but he didn't look for whoever had thrown it. Instead, he turned the other way as a child shouted, 'They caught another hairy!' and other children laughed. Hellet gazed up at the tenements rising four and five storeys above them. 'Brains, not brawn. They know this too – the canith and the humans – under the mockery and cruelty and abuse, they know it. It's why they clamp down so hard on us.'

'This is what Maybe's been whispering to you all this time?' Celcha asked.

'Some of it. Some I understood by myself even before he told me. Maybe can see the past like he's turning the pages of a book. He knows the history of our people. We've built cities too – greater ones than this. We've fought to defend them. They say that the ganar are slow to anger but they hold on to it. Our enemies say we don't fight fair, as if any sane creature would fight fair against an opponent twice their size. Fairness is something others try to impose at the surface level once they've fixed all the foundations in their favour.'

Celcha shook her head, torn between the strangeness all around her and the strangeness of her brother, who appeared to have been tutored by ghosts or angels in matters of a past lost to the memory of even the oldest slave. They followed the wagons, no longer in a dust cloud. The ghosts were slightly clearer here in the light of day than down in the tunnels of Arthran. She'd expected them to fade in the sun, but they'd done the opposite. Maybe was the taller by quite some margin, and the easier to see. In the sunlight he could almost be a canith . . .

The city lay in a valley between two great arms of the mountain and climbed the slope towards the impossible sky-scraping heights that loomed above them, making even the towers and temples seem small. As the main street led them higher, the buildings became still more grand. Celcha had never seen or imagined anything like it. The dig site held only the most utilitarian of structures: boxes in which to keep things. The buried city had always hinted at more, but it was hard to appreciate grandeur when you were hewing it from the ground one lump at a time. Here, there were soaring works of art in solid stone on every side.

The wagons clattered ever upwards, over stone-paved streets. As the gradient steepened, the path wound back and forth, softening the slope for the horses, each zig and zag gaining elevation and expanding the view back over the city. The carpet of canith and humanity spread further than Celcha had been able to understand from outside the wall or from within the shadowed valleys of its streets. From up on the slopes, where the houses began to thin and the raw bedrock started to reassert itself, Celcha could see that there must be not the thousands she had imagined but tens of thousands of citizens, a hundred thousand even.

The sun burned red, peering from the shoulder of the mountain. As Celcha passed a tall pole standing by the roadside, the top of it burst into brilliance. Hellet caught her arm when she startled away. The horses carried on with barely a snort. Back along the winding street they'd travelled, more of the poles lit, the bright yellow flames held inside glass boxes. Celcha hadn't even noticed them – there'd been so much else to see.

'Street lighting,' Hellet said. 'So they can see where they're going at night.'

The ganar slept at night. The idea of having the way lit for anyone to wander seemed extraordinary to Celcha. Just thinking about it made her yawn mightily.

'They have these lights in their homes too. The lights burn the same kind of gas that they use to cook with and for heat,' Hellet said.

Celcha walked on in silence, watching the illumination spread. It almost seemed that Hellet had been here before. If Celcha had pointed to a random house and asked who lived there she wouldn't have been surprised if Hellet told her.

✦ ✦ ✦

The wagons left the houses behind and stopped shortly afterwards on a steep road that led up towards the head of a howling wolf carved into the mountainside. A wolf whose mouth stood wide enough to devour them whole.

The guard who had ridden at the back dismounted and pointed towards the entrance. 'Go help with the unloading.' Hellet chose that moment to yawn hugely, showing all his big square teeth. 'None of that.' The guardsman shook his head. 'Sleep comes afterwards. One late night won't kill you.'

It took remarkably little sleep deprivation to cause a ganar to fall unconscious, but even so neither of them protested. For the first time since passing through the gates, yawns notwithstanding, Hellet seemed as excited as Celcha to see what lay ahead.

Librarians in crimson robes, both human and canith, came out onto the stone platform before the entrance to watch the books being unloaded by underlings uniformed in black. Although the physical labour seemed to be beneath them, many of the librarians were unable to maintain their air of aloofness and stand back watching. Instead, they broke ranks and came forward to pick at the loads being carried into the wolf's jaws.

Celcha and Hellet joined in with the effort, working alongside humans and canith for the first time. They unloaded the wagons and set the books inside the wolf's mouth where other library staff took them off in wheeled shelving units at a much slower rate. Celcha wondered why there were no other slaves doing the work. The staff paid her and her brother little attention but there was none of the overt hostility that she'd sensed in the streets, and certainly none of the murderous rage that even the suggestion of human labouring beside ganar would have evoked back at the dig site.

Books were easier to load and unload than the material Celcha normally worked with. They were lighter, blunter, and had regular, stackable shapes. She found the labour easy, the only difficulty being that she very much wanted to be asleep. Also, it was hard to handle the books with sufficient care that one of the onlooking librarians didn't wince or scold. Hellet seemed to be making a better job of it.

Celcha had both arms out and had received most of a double armful of books when the black-tunicked woman loading the volumes onto her stopped in mid-action. Everyone stopped. The murmur of conversation around the task vanished. Awkwardly, Celcha shuffled herself around to peer past her burden in the direction everyone else was looking.

On the stone platform before the wolf's head, somebody new had come to join the librarians. Although built on similar lines to all three, this newcomer was neither canith, human, nor ganar. Tall as a human, unclothed like the ganar, with the confidence of a canith. If the creature hadn't been moving Celcha would have assumed it was a statue, carved from a stone she'd never seen before, white and gleaming like a tooth. The most unnatural thing about it, apart from the texture and uniformity of its flesh, was the lack of detail, everything smooth, without wrinkle, hair, claw, or colour. She couldn't even see if it had eyes or nostrils or tell if its mouth could open. In many ways he – she felt it was a he – reminded her of the nootki she'd tied into her pelt for safekeeping. More of a suggestion or reminder of the original than an accurate representation.

The new arrival took a place among the librarians in their crimson robes and, looking down at the wagons, lapsed into the immobility that Celcha had expected from it all along. It stood stiller than sculpture. Watching. Or dead. The librarians around the creature seemed unable to look away, though it was surprise and deference that reflected on their faces rather than fear.

'What's an assistant doing out here?' someone muttered behind Celcha.

'Never seen one before. Not even in the library.' Another astonished mutter.

Hellet provided the signal to return to work. He walked past Celcha with a load of books, unconcerned, as if nothing had happened. Celcha started to follow him. Nobody had told them to stop, after all. For a slave, unilaterally deciding to take a rest could have horrific consequences. The rest of the workforce took the cue and a moment later everyone was back to what they'd been doing.

Hellet's arrival at the platform and careful negotiation of the steps caused the second astonishment, shutting down conversation and activity just as effectively as the first. The assistant walked towards Celcha's brother, blocking his path. Several librarians had done the same thing as evening had darkened towards dusk, but the assistant didn't take a book for inspection.

'Your name?' he asked in a voice free of inflection.

'Hellet.'

The assistant looked to Hellet's left and right, resting his gaze briefly on Starve and Maybe. 'Welcome to the library, Hellet.' He stood aside and Hellet carried on his way.

The stillness and silence persisted this time, but Celcha felt more compulsion to follow her brother than to stand staring with the rest. She climbed the steps to the platform with great care, not wishing to find out what punishment would be earned by dropping books.

The assistant moved to intercept her. 'Your name?'

'Celcha.' Her mouth struggled to say 'master' but she wouldn't let it. Hellet hadn't said it, and following him had got her this far. An insane desire to ask the assistant's name in turn took possession of her, so much so that simply fighting it off made her tremble with the effort.

'Welcome to the library, Celcha.' The assistant turned away and walked back towards the wolf's head entrance.

As he left, Celcha saw the golden sparkle of one of the angels approaching from the direction Hellet had gone in. Maybe, the one she could see better – in fact she saw him better than ever before. He looked for all the world like a canith.

Maybe came to her side, bent low, and whispered in her ear. 'Himma-calling Yute.'

It is one thing to live a life contingent on necessary evils. And another to be one of those evils. To be suffered is, in and of itself, another form of suffering.

Accountancy for Beginners, *by Murray Humphreys*

CHAPTER 5

Celcha

Yute was the first name Celcha learned at the library and the only one she never heard used. The librarian who had acquired Celcha and Hellet from the Arthran dig was named Sellna Smith, though Celcha doubted there had been any metalworkers in the woman's family for generations. Celcha was to call her Librarian or, when the need to be more specific arose, Librarian Sellna.

The woman was old for a human, who, compared to the ganar, lived relatively brief lives, and quite senior, though three other librarians stood between her and the head librarian who was, it turned out, cousin to the queen who ruled not only the city but everything that might be seen from the mountaintop and more beyond.

Librarian Sellna took it upon herself to explain Celcha and Hellet's duties to them. She spoke more slowly when addressing the siblings and offered them a similar level of respect to that which she'd shown Myles Carstar. She wore a brittle smile at such times and struggled to hide flashes of displeasure when Hellet accepted this limited courtesy as his due rather than simpering beneath small but unaccustomed kindnesses.

The library, Sellna told them, was very old and the trick to opening its doors had been partially forgotten. There were many doors that would yield to the touch of a human, or to that of a canith. Others, however, particularly further out from the entrance, would not. And some of these had in the past been shown to open for ganar. The library had employed two ganar whose main job was to accompany librarians in and out of these chambers, or occasionally on expeditions into new areas. Sadly – at this point Sellna paused and made her face sad in the way of humans – both these ganar had been killed in an unusual accident just prior to Sellna's visit to the dig site.

Celcha and her brother were given a room within the mountain, all to themselves. A rectangular room that still smelled of the ganar who had lived there until recently.

Celcha peered in. 'It's big.'

'Hmmm.' Hellet shrugged.

'It's just us?' Celcha still felt wary addressing the librarian.

'Just you.' Librarian Sellna paused before she left them at the door, seeming to struggle with something. At last she spoke, drawing the words slowly over her teeth. 'The assistant that spoke to you at the entrance . . . That was not . . . usual. It's very rare to see an assistant. I've never seen one outside the main library. And they might sometimes answer questions, but they don't talk—' She shook her head and started again. 'Why did he speak to you? What do you know about this?'

Celcha answered honestly. 'I don't know. I've never seen an assistant before.'

The librarian had frowned. 'This is a very old place, very important. We don't like surprises here.'

'You weren't surprised when our predecessors died?' Hellet asked.

The librarian's face twitched towards annoyance, perhaps anger, quickly erased. 'I was. I didn't like it.'

It was when the pair of them were in this room and finally alone that Hellet expanded on what Sellna had said. The library's doors could only be opened by willing individuals. A grim history of attempted coercion had, according to Maybe, been unsuccessful, leading to the librarians selecting naturally curious candidates and taking pains to treat them well.

✦ ✦ ✦

So it was that library life replaced the arduous monotony of the Arthran dig. Celcha and Hellet were free to wander, though they were told not to go down into the city. They were fed the same as the librarians and their staff, in the same hall, though at a table by themselves. They were warned against eating fruit. Apples, although they looked and smelled delicious, had, in the past, made ganar violently ill.

Opening books wasn't punished with cruelties, official or unofficial. In fact, they were encouraged to take some of the precious objects back to their room. Librarian Sellna clearly wanted them to be interested in what lay on the far side of the doors only they could open.

A trainee librarian was even appointed to see if either of them could be taught to read. Apparently, their predecessors had become almost competent in modern Eursian, though neither had mastered writing. Their tutor, a young canith male called Ablesan, even explained to them why they needed so much sleep. It was an education that Celcha had already acquired at a simpler level through the ganar slaves' oral tradition of myths and tales, and at a more complex level from Hellet's account, which he in turn had received from Maybe. Ablesan's version was predicated on the notion that any creature barely reaching his hip would be incapable of advanced thinking.

'Your distant ancestors were brought here from another world. Somewhere you could never walk to no matter how far you went. Like the moons.'

In fact, the first ganar had arrived in their own ships in search of resources and trade, having made the voyage of their own volition. And their home wasn't 'like the moons'. They came from the larger moon, Attamast.

'Your world has long nights and short days.'

This was untrue. The truth, according the Hellet's recent studies, was that Attamast had a permanent axial tilt such that some latitudes had long nights and short days, whereas others had short nights and long days. The habitable parts had long nights. There were other complications to do with tidal locking and planetary eclipses, but those were the bones of the matter. That and the fact that whilst you could easily go out during an Attamast night you wouldn't survive more than an hour before the darkness ate you. Evolution had favoured ganar who went to bed when the sun did – and stayed there. Celcha wasn't sure how much of the mechanics she understood, but the 'stay in bed' bit seemed very clear.

Ablesan neglected to mention that Attamast had an atmosphere poisonous to canith, humans, and pretty much everything else on the planet. Fortunately, the ganar didn't need those poisonous components to live but it did mean that they found the air in this world rather thin and incapable of sustaining the strength and stamina that they enjoyed in their true home.

Celcha's first journey into the library was with librarians Sternus and Markeet, accompanied by a small band of the youngest trainees. Sellna, it turned out, rarely ventured into the chambers any more because of the frailty that accompanied her advancing years. Her appearance at the dig site was testimony to her excitement at the discovery of books outside the library. And perhaps to the librarians' need for a new pair of ganar.

The novelty of chambers two miles on each side and ceilings that might as well be skies took some while to sink in. Marching along aisles that were effectively deep, book-lined trenches might have given many ganar claustrophobia. Each year some of the children raised at the dig site were sent to the city as their species' intolerance for confinement flowered within them. Sent to the city, or just killed. Frequently, Myles Carstar's efforts to determine whether these were borderline cases that might be trained out of their native distrust of tunnels ended up with 'encouragements' that proved fatal.

In any event, Celcha and Hellet's years below ground meant that the library's aisles held no fears for them. Celcha's first encounter with books had been a singular example resulting in tragedy – the cruelty that had broken her brother. Her second encounter had been with many books, and it had led her to escape the dig site. This third encounter appeared to be with all the rest – an infinity of books – and Celcha had no idea what it might lead to.

✦ ✦ ✦

The trainees took to Celcha much more than they did to Hellet. She was as short as the smallest of them and her scars less unsettling than her brother's – fewer and better covered by her pelt. Most of the trainees appeared to look upon her as a pet of sorts, which although it was a kinder relationship than the one Myles Carstar had imposed upon her was still one that cast her into the role of an animal. Several of them stroked her fur without permission – though even the act of asking permission for such an invasion would have felt wrong to Celcha. Such things are invited not requested.

One girl, Lutna, a child of eleven, skinny in her black tunic, showed a closer interest, asking questions as they trekked past endless rows of shelving.

'What are these?' Lutna touched her own hair rather than Celcha's to indicate the nootka hanging from small braids around her neck and shoulders.

'A kind of hope.' Celcha had never really understood the practice herself and had no plans to make her own, but she had been moved more deeply than she had thought possible when so many of the slaves had pressed the tiny carvings upon her.

'They're pretty. Did you make them?'

'No. Each one was made by a different person. We make only one each.'

Lutna looked surprised and peered for a closer look. 'Can I touch one?'

'No.'

The girl nodded and pushed her hands into the pockets of her tunic.

A boy behind them snorted. 'Not much to them for a life's work.'

Celcha didn't answer. Her father had made a collection of pebbles, a dozen or so, over the course of his life, a span of at least two centuries. He had polished them with his fingertips at night, shining them until they almost glowed. They had been his joy. In that place of hunger, pain and sorrow where they had nothing but the tunnels and the shack and endless work in the dusty flickering shadows, he had poured himself into twelve shiny pebbles and found some small measure of contentment in their presence. An overseer had seen them and taken them from him. It hadn't even been an act of particular cruelty or malice, just casual nastiness: the human had no idea that Celcha's father had counted those small stones through his fingers since before the man's great-grandfather was born.

The boy, offended by Celcha's silence, started to repeat himself. 'I said—'

'No,' Celcha said. 'It's not much.'

She bowed her head. She had been waiting. Waiting since they'd arrived at the library and begun to enjoy good food, light, cleanliness, education, and some measure of freedom. Waiting for the anger she'd lived with all her life to start to leave her, to fade away, to cool towards something that didn't burn her. But walking beside Lutna, who had been friendly and seemed willing to treat her as an equal, Celcha came to understand something.

Her anger had never been a flame, quick to catch, ready to become violent in response to some new indignity. There was no hidden threshold over which she couldn't be pushed without consequence. She had already been pushed far beyond any such boundary. Her anger was the implacable heat of a planetary core. It wasn't going away, ever. The wounds had been struck too deep and too early for forgiveness to be an option. Lutna might be nice, the boy behind her might be mean: it made no difference. They were pieces in the machine that had devoured her.

Celcha had always thought that Hellet was the one they broke. That the cruelty administered to him had cracked his mind. She understood now that her brother had been the sane one. He had said they were going to kill them all. The librarian thought she was going to make allies of the siblings. She thought that bringing them to the city and showing them plenty, bringing them to the library and showing them possibility, would be gifts that would earn gratitude and service.

Somehow the opposite had happened. Celcha's anger had deepened. Showing her what her life could have been and could now be didn't erase what it *had* been. It simply set the crimes that had been committed against her in new context, one that made her tremble with an outrage she was wise enough not to show. Yet.

Every notable toymaker puts a piece of her soul into each creation. The love with which it was crafted can be seen in every line. But even the cheapest toy, die-stamped and disgorged from mechanical bowels on conveyor belts, has a place where a child might hang their heart. The power of a fresh imagination is such that the meanest vessel can hold miracles.

Clockwork Dreams, *by P. K. Richard*

CHAPTER 6

Evar

Evar ran, chased by his brother and sister. There hadn't been time to explain to Clovis or Kerrol what it was exactly that was ploughing towards them. The sound of ancient shelves exploding into splintered wood and of books falling by the ton was sufficient motivation for both of them to follow him.

They had crept into the chamber hoping to avoid any encounter with the deadly skeer who held sway over this part of the library, never imagining they would leave it pursued by a mechanical beast that could squash a skeer warrior flat beneath a single foot. The thing had clearly not moved in an age – the very shelves themselves had been built around it as if it were an immobile fixture.

'What is it?' Clovis caught up with Evar as he skidded around a corner into an aisle heading roughly in the direction of the nearest chamber exit. Apparently, she still had enough breath for questions.

The broken body of a skeer hit the top of the shelves just ahead of them, making the whole structure shudder, and ricocheted down to the floor a few dozen yards away.

'It does that,' Evar managed, sprinting on. He vaulted the skeer's twitching carcass ahead of Clovis.

For now, it seemed sufficient answer for Clovis. They ran with purpose. The thunderous destruction behind them seemed to be gaining, but slowly. They might make it to the tunnel that joined the chamber to the next one. Evar's main hope – apart from getting there first – was that the construct either couldn't open the door or would be too large to fit through it.

The chamber wall loomed ever closer but there seemed no end to the shelving lined up in their way at increasingly unhelpful angles. Behind them the thunder of destruction swelled, and Evar could imagine the construct just one fragile wall of books and wood away.

'Up!' Clovis elbowed past him and scrambled up a ladder.

By the time Evar reached the top his sister was already away, leaping from shelf top to shelf top. A backwards glance as he reached down the ladder for Kerrol's hand showed the metal beast barrelling through shelves that reached to its shoulders, destroying one after another with swings of its arms, leaving clouds of loose pages swirling in its wake.

At least a dozen skeer were clinging to the thing, anchoring themselves on the armour plates that made its body, and pounding away at it, their efforts lost in the general din. Evar didn't fancy their chances, but he had to admire their bravery.

'Come on.' He hauled Kerrol up and started after Clovis.

Evar crossed the next twenty aisles in twenty leaping strides, all of them on the edge of control, with a potentially fatal plunge waiting for him if he missed his footing. Ahead, just shy of the wall, Clovis had stopped and turned. Evar barely kept himself from falling in his effort to halt beside her.

He looked back and his heart went cold. 'Where's Kerrol?' The mechanical giant was barely fifty yards away, ignoring the skeer still clinging to it, hammering its way through the shelves in an orgy of destruction.

Kerrol's absence explained itself. He'd missed his footing and fallen. Evar gathered himself to start leaping back. Clovis grabbed his arm. 'It already passed him by. It's not after Kerrol.'

'The skeer will be!' Evar shouted above the crashing, but Clovis had already gone, aimed towards the exit.

Evar reached the last set of shelves and scrambled down before dropping the remaining twenty feet. He could see Clovis running down the corridor that stretched two hundred yards to the next chamber. The white door that sealed it halfway along was sixty feet high and as wide as the corridor. If it didn't open for them, they'd be stuck in the corridor, and if the beast chasing them could follow on in then it would pound them both to mush. The thing was big, but so was the corridor. Evar's best guess was that it would be able to squeeze through.

'Shit . . .' He sprinted after Clovis.

Evar got about halfway to the door before Clovis bounced off it. 'Shit.'

He turned in time to see the last wall of shelving explode. 'Shit!'

Another swing of the construct's arm cleared the remnants, and without warning a large object came flying out of the swirling cloud of pages. Evar barely threw himself aside in time as the bleached white body of a skeer sailed past him. It tumbled in a rough ball shape, wedge of a head over six sets of heels, still travelling at speed as it reached Clovis. It rolled on without interruption, the great expanse of the door not even managing to dissolve completely before the creature was through.

'Come on!' Clovis stepped smartly into the newly emptied space and beckoned Evar urgently, holding back the door that the skeer had opened.

'Kerrol?' Evar looked towards the chamber. The metal beast filled the corridor's entrance, hunching to follow them, its armour scraping the ceiling, another skeer falling from its back.

'He'll find us!' Clovis shouted. 'Run!'

Evar ran. He sprinted after Clovis with the clatter and clang of their pursuer echoing all around them. The skeer that had rolled past Clovis found its feet and began to race away with a speed that, had it been turned in their direction, would have been frightening.

Evar was glad to see the skeer ahead of them running, glad that these insectoids could feel fear. The manner in which they had sacrificed themselves en masse to take down the Soldier had been unnerving. Somehow an enemy that knows terror in the face of overwhelming odds felt—

'What's it doing?' He managed to gasp the words as the skeer warrior came to a halt immediately upon entering the next chamber.

Clovis didn't manage a reply before the skeer answered for her. The insectoid released an extraordinary wail that emanated from its whole body, a shrill whistle riding over a deep penetrating throb. The skeer had run but only far enough to summon more reserves. Evar had to wonder if there was a limit to the number of lives skeer would throw at an enemy or if a sufficiently powerful foe could slaughter their whole nation simply by standing where it was and taking them on as they arrived.

Evar and Clovis sprinted past the howling skeer and on into a new chamber not dissimilar to the previous one. They climbed the first set of shelves, swarming up across the book-face, careless of damage, and started to bound across the tops, inches from a fall at every step.

They'd gone about a hundred yards when the skeer's howl stopped suddenly mid-flow. The creature had probably been squashed by the emerging construct.

'This thing—' Evar spoke each time he and Clovis made contact with a shelf top.

'—is just—'

'—going to—'

'—keep on—'

'—coming.'

Clovis didn't answer. The monster answered for her, smashing into the first set of shelves by the entrance behind them, pulverizing more timber, more books.

They bounded on, out into the thousands of acres before them, with no better plan than skimming over the surface until their stamina failed and fatigue sent them tumbling. For a time, they were able to slowly extend their lead, but it wouldn't last, not unless the construct ran out of whatever energy drove it. Twice Evar glimpsed skeer in the canyons beneath them, the creatures skittering towards the monster that they should be running away from. Perhaps they thought they could clog its mechanisms with their corpses . . .

Running along a lengthy stretch of shelf top that happened to head in the direction they were going – towards the opposite entrance – Evar skidded to a halt. Despite the ever-present crash of their pursuer Clovis somehow sensed her brother had ceased following and brought herself to a stop.

She hauled in a breath. 'What?'

'It's after . . .' Evar paused, panting. 'It's after me. Split up. I'll prove it.'

Clovis eyed him, her face inscrutable. 'OK.'

Evar had expected more of a fight – some token objection at least – but it was the answer he'd wanted. 'You head that way.' He pointed left, raising his voice over the approaching din. 'If it follows you then go back to the original course.'

Clovis sprang away and Evar, still struggling for a breath, stumbled back into a run.

By the time that Evar dropped from the last shelf into the clearing before the opposite corridor the gap had closed to what it had been at the start of his run, and narrowed past that. Evar didn't know if the door ahead of him was one that opened for canith, or for humans, or for skeer, or for some other species. What he did know was that, whether it opened for him or not, he wouldn't make it across the next chamber without the metal monster catching him.

He ran on, his rhythm starting to fail, limbs heavy with fatigue. When he bounced off the white plane of the door it was almost a relief. There was no reason to run any more. He'd forgotten why he was running in any case. He'd lost Livira. It felt melodramatic to say life felt hollow without her – they'd spent so little time knowingly in each other's company – but slumped against a door that wholly blocked the only way out, and with an implacable giant of steel, brass, and gold bearing down on him, it seemed like the best time for drama.

The skeer, Evar noted over his heaving chest, were less given to fatalism, or at least to the sort that involves giving up. The number of them clinging to the construct had doubled and their ichor ran down its armour plates. They'd done no noticeable damage, but the eight or nine of them clinging to the giant's legs were causing it to adopt a wading gait.

At the back of the advancing mass of metal and insectoid, glimpsed past the bodies hanging onto the construct's ankles, Evar saw Clovis, white sword in hand. The distance was too great to divine her expression, but her intent was clear enough. She was going to attack.

'Run! Leave me!' Evar's shout lost itself in the grinding approach. He stood, ready to fight. If he died sooner rather than later then Clovis would have no reason to throw herself into the fray.

The monster loomed over Evar, posture stooped, shoulders scraping the ceiling. Its face was neither savage nor bestial, closer to human than to canith, no teeth bared, its expression one of focused determination, eyes glowing hot and angry.

It reached for him, the blade on the back of its hand as thick as his arm and longer than his body. Evar readied himself, fear replaced by a sense of loss. He hoped Livira was waiting for him . . . somewhere.

The vast hand stopped. The whole construct froze. Even the crash of skeer hammering at its sides stopped. Evar gazed up at it in amazement. For a heartbeat he imagined that something he had done had halted the thing in its tracks – though beyond manifesting a fervent desire not to die he'd done nothing.

A glance to his side disabused Evar of the notion that he had suddenly acquired mind powers. The door had vanished and standing just behind and to the right of him was an assistant. An assistant in gleaming white enamel, not the ivory of *the* Assistant and the Soldier, both compromised by Livira and Malar's humanity respectively, not the grey or black of an assistant polluted by Escapes, but an assistant purely as Irad had presumably fashioned it millennia ago.

Why the construct and skeer should choose to stop in the midst of their attempted murdering just because an assistant had arrived, Evar was uncertain. The construct extended one finger towards Evar. A finger that was stubby in the context of its hands, though at the same time longer than Evar's arm. It said nothing but the implication was clear: *mine.*

'No.' The assistant seemed to speak in Evar's mother tongue but perhaps, as in the Exchange, words from an assistant's mouth could be universally understood.

A tremor ran through the huge construct, a vibration that grew until it could be heard as a buzzing of metal on metal. A skeer fell, landing badly. Another dropped closer to hand, untroubled by the impact. On seeing Evar, it advanced on him.

'No.' The assistant pointed back towards the chamber they'd so recently crossed. The skeer bathed Evar and the assistant in the black regard of its many eyes. It turned towards the construct and its fellow skeer, most of them climbing down now, one trapped against the knee joint by a mangled limb.

Four of them came forward to join the closest one that appeared to have staked a claim on Evar. A faint but varied hissing passed between them, and complex chemical taints filled the air. After a long pause the five of them backed away, turned, and began to retreat, taking the rest of their kind with them, including the trapped one who dropped down as they passed below, having chewed off its own leg.

Clovis and Kerrol slipped into the corridor as the skeer exited, keeping well clear of the insectoids. The construct, still trembling with what Evar took to be wrath, backed slowly away, metal squealing against stone or whatever it was that the library had been cut from. Clovis and Kerrol flattened themselves against the wall as it passed.

'Uh . . .' Evar turned away from the glower of the retreating construct and faced the assistant. '. . . thank you.'

The assistant made no reply. It watched him with entirely white eyes in an entirely white face. Evar's fatigue had caught up with him and continuing to stand had become difficult, but the shock and strangeness of the chase had run a strange trembling fire through his veins that wouldn't let him be still. He hugged himself, hands clasped to his upper arms. 'That thing – it hated me. It didn't care about the others . . .'

The assistant simply watched him.

Kerrol strode up, barging into the silence. 'Assistance from an assistant! I wouldn't have believed it this morning.' He looked Evar up and down, checking for injury. Evar was glad his brother had managed to escape from the previous chamber. A skeer must have been involved, since the door wouldn't open for canith.

Clovis arrived, sword in hand, still glancing back down the ichor-spattered corridor.

Kerrol turned from his inspection of Evar to the assistant. 'Let's push our luck, shall we? What's the way out of here? We want to reach the world. Somewhere with more people and fewer books.'

Without looking at Kerrol, the assistant pointed, his arm angled towards the corridor wall but in the general direction of the next chamber. It was a direction that a ghost could follow, and a bearing that Evar could use to navigate if he was careful.

'Are there many skeer out there?' Kerrol asked.

The assistant kept his gaze on Evar and said nothing.

'Why did you save me?' Evar asked.

The assistant said nothing.

'Come on.' Clovis took Evar's arm and bumped him into motion. 'If it wanted to tell us anything it would have.'

Evar let himself be led for a few paces then turned back towards the assistant, which had already started following the departed skeer. 'Wait. Are there any ghosts here? Do you see any ghosts?'

The assistant stopped and turned. 'Seeing ghosts is never a good thing, Evar Eventari. Hope that you never do. And under no circumstances speak to one.'

And with that he walked away, the questions Evar shouted after him echoing unanswered.

It's curious that ghosts, spectres, and spirits are so often depicted as transparent when no one is more opaque to the living than are the dead. Biographers offer keyholes through which the most famous may be viewed. Historians poke peepholes through the veil of years. For most though, we have nothing but what dust might sift down from the attic of memory.

All Our Yesterdays: An Undertaker's Guide, *by C. Haron*

CHAPTER 7

Livira

Livira and Malar followed Evar and his two siblings through the library. Livira hadn't any idea as to how she and Malar could regain their bodies, and lonely as it was wandering unseen and unheard by everyone but the soldier, she would rather do it close to Evar than in the wider solitude of the library. The aisles were generally so sparsely populated that most of the time you'd have to push through something solid to prove you were a ghost.

'So, we're just going to trudge after these three?' Malar scowled.

'We'll never find them again if we lose sight of them,' Livira said. 'They're not even headed in the right direction to get out.'

'They can't get out without a human helping them anyway, can they?'

Livira had forgotten that. She hoped Evar hadn't. Already she thought of him as the same as her, but the library didn't. 'There's a canith door to the outside not so far from here . . . Well, a few days. But they're not going the right way for that either . . .'

Malar spat. Or ghost-spat. She wondered briefly about the mechanics of ghost-spit before he pulled her from her thoughts. 'Better follow them. After all, this bitch has got my sword.'

'It's not your sword.' Livira gave him a hard stare.

'I had it for two hundred years and made better use of it than the previous owner.'

Livira huffed. 'My assistant made it. Yours just played with it. And she's not "this bitch" – you watched her grow and taught her to fight.'

'Clovis, then.' Malar grunted and scowled and looked as close to apologizing as she'd ever seen him. 'Still my sword.'

Livira walked on after Evar, steering clear of his sister. Livira was pretty confident of passing through most things and having them pass through her. The white blade, on the other hand, she didn't want to put to the test.

When Evar climbed the ladder Livira flew up alongside him. She saw the construct while Evar was still climbing. And it seemed to Livira that a faint tremble ran through the thing even before Evar showed himself above the shelf top.

When Evar ran, Livira ran with him, astonished by the single-minded violence of the chase. And when Evar slumped against the final door and faced his destruction, Livira faced it beside him, her hand running through his, sharing the depth of his emotion, an echoing sense of waste and loss.

Malar, on the other hand, went forward to meet the construct's advance on the trapped canith. The soldier ran at the closest ankle with a roar of frustration, sword swinging. When the blade passed through the body of one of the clinging skeer on the way, then bounced off the metal ankle beneath, Malar was so surprised that the construct's next step sent him flying.

The impact probably should have broken bones, but Malar rolled to a halt halfway into the corridor wall and got unsteadily to his feet, his survival implying some sort of muted contact, as if the construct was half real to ghosts.

Suddenly it occurred to Livira that perhaps the giant hadn't been chasing Evar at all, but had instead been going after her. As the thing's vast metal hand reached down for them Livira scrambled away from Evar, hoping to draw the clutching fingers after her.

Instead, the door beside them melted away and she found herself on her hands and knees at the feet of an assistant. She stood up slowly and watched amazed as the assistant sent the skeer away and then ordered the construct after them. The hot, angry light of the construct's eyes rested on Livira for a moment before it turned away, leaving her with the strong impression that unfinished business remained between them. Livira watched the thing clank off down the corridor while Evar and his siblings tried to get answers out of the assistant. They got about as much as might be expected, which was to say they got the direction to leave by and not much else.

Livira turned from the retreating construct to study the assistant that had stopped its rampage.

Evar's sister was leading him away towards the next chamber, but he shook her off and turned back towards the assistant. 'Wait. Are there any ghosts here? Do you see any ghosts?'

Livira remembered that yes, assistants could see ghosts. She stood in front of the assistant waving her arms. 'I'm here! We're both here! Tell him Livira's here!'

The assistant stopped and looked away from her, back at Evar. 'Seeing ghosts is never a good thing, Evar Eventari. Hope that you never do. And under no circumstances speak to one.'

'Wait . . . What? Don't tell him that!' Livira waved her hand in front of the assistant's blank white eyes.

Evar's shoulders slumped. Not in false drama, just by a fraction, and many might have missed it, but Livira saw his pain as he followed after his brother and sister. 'Tell him!'

Malar shook his head. 'These things are useless. And that's from someone who's spent two centuries on the inside.' He walked past them, headed after the canith, and Livira followed with a last exasperated glance at the assistant.

They got about five paces before something like an invisible chain pulled both of them up short. Livira felt herself being drawn backwards. The assistant, as it walked away in the opposite direction to Evar and his siblings, seemed to be dragging her and Malar after it.

'No!' Livira fought against the pull. 'Stop it!'

Malar leaned forward, grinding his teeth as he struggled to advance, but his feet found no traction and his progress continued smoothly backwards. Livira took to the air, flying as hard as she could in Evar's direction. The assistant didn't appear to notice. It towed her as a child might tow a kite.

For a short while longer Livira raged against the unseen leash until, having no effect whatsoever, she felt foolish and stopped. The assistant had reached the main chamber and paused to survey the broad channel of destruction carved through the aisles by the construct. They could see its metal back not that far off, returning along the same path, the occasional weakened section of shelving collapsing when nudged.

Livira positioned herself in front of the assistant once again. 'Why are you doing this? And why can't you see me?'

'I can see you.'

'You could see me all along!' Livira accused.

'Yes.'

'Why did you bring us here? Why didn't you let me speak to Evar?' Livira strode past the assistant, heading for the corridor. She got about six paces before the same force stopped her again. 'Let me go! I need to follow him.'

'How would that help?' The assistant's expression remained fixed and his voice even, but Livira's imagination painted a quizzical raised eyebrow on his enamel forehead. She didn't like his tone even if he didn't have a tone.

'What do you want?' Livira had a direction, and she could follow the canith fast enough to catch up with them. Best to placate the assistant, especially since defying him didn't seem to be an option.

The assistant tilted his head in a gesture far more human than Livira was used to seeing from such creatures. 'It is . . . dangerous and difficult . . . for a timeless being to speak of temporary things. You have written a wound into the world, broken ageless laws.' A white hand intercepted Livira's denial. 'There is a book that is also a loop. A book that has swallowed its own tale. It is a ring, a cycle, burning through the years, spreading cracks through time, fissures that reach into its past and future. And through those cracks things that have no business in the world of flesh can escape.'

'I don't know what—' But she did know. She had written a book and years later Evar had taken that volume into the Mechanism and been lost with it. His reunion with that book had triggered his search for her, leading him into the Exchange and back into time with her, carrying the book she hadn't written yet. Later – though the word 'later' was starting to lose its meaning – she'd come through the Exchange to his time carrying her earlier part-written version of the book – the same cover, same stolen pages, same ink. And somehow the two had fused into one, with their trails wrapped in and out of the portals of the Exchange in impossible knots. After that the book had plunged back into the past again in her hands to follow its course, back and forth, endlessly cycling through the years. It wasn't here in the now – she knew that much. Livira looked up from the tangle of her thoughts. 'The Escapes happen because of me? I broke the Mechanism?'

'You broke, or at least weakened, many things. Reason is fragile. Easy to fracture and hard to mend. Without reason, all things that matter fall apart.'

'How can I fix . . . everything?' Livira asked.

'You cannot fix it,' the assistant said, 'but the damage can be minimized.'

'How?'

'I . . . don't . . . know how.' The words seemed difficult for the assistant to say. 'You need to bring the book forward. To this now, this moving point that you and Evar share. You two joined the book. You sealed the loop.'

'I'm a ghost here,' Livira said, exasperated. 'I can't touch anything.'

'Returning with the book will restore your flesh. It's the fractures that keep you apart.'

'So, all I need is a portal.' Livira tried not to roll her eyes.

The assistant pointed behind her. A shimmering circle of light had sprung silently into being amid the wreckage of shelves and drifts of fallen books.

'But when I go to the time that the book is in, I'll be a ghost there too. It's going to make bringing anything back tricky. How's that going to work?'

'I don't know how. It might not work at all. Would you rather be a ghost now or then? Time doesn't care.'

Livira twisted her mouth, favouring the assistant with the hard stare that generally made people look away. The assistant gazed back, impassive as a wall.

Belatedly, Livira remembered the soldier. 'What do you think, Malar?' She turned, looking for him. 'Malar?'

She was just in time to see his back as he stepped through the portal and the light swallowed him.

A language may tell you more about the people who own it than do the things they use that language to say to you. We have in our collection no language without a word for anger. There are some few – some very few – with no word for revenge.

One Hundred Chambers, *by X'thon Qylar*

CHAPTER 8

Celcha

'Ahan'ah . . . mu-mutupk.'

Celcha, sitting with her back to the shelves, turned in surprise and looked up at the skinny child addressing her.

Lutna frowned. 'Did I get it right?'

'I don't know,' Celcha said. 'What are you trying to do?'

'AHan'ah mutuupk.' Lutna smiled nervously.

Celcha looked around at the rest of the trainees, most of them sitting down, making best use of the rest break that Librarian Markeet had called. The humans and canith had clustered together, away from the two ganar. None of them were paying her any attention. 'Are you unwell?'

Lutna looked put out. 'It's your language. *Ahan'ah mutuupk.* How are you?'

Celcha blinked. She never heard a ganar speak anything but the language they were speaking now, a tongue she'd recently learned was called modern Eursian. She knew a few words in the old tongue but they didn't sound like anything the girl had said. 'Ahanah mutupuk?'

'*Ahan'ahh mutuupk,*' Hellet said beside her. 'It means "are you well". It's a common ganar language, though not the one our ancestors spoke.'

Celcha didn't ask how Hellet knew or why he'd never thought

she might like to know. Maybe must have whispered it to him and, broken as he was, Hellet rarely looked up through the cracks of his inner world to see her and her needs. 'Where did you learn it?' She directed the question at Lutna.

Lutna looked down, rubbing the toe of her shoe on the floor.

'She probably learned it at the palace,' called over the pushy boy who had made fun of Celcha's nootka carvings.

'The palace?' Celcha asked.

'I don't live there,' Lutna held her hands up as if warding off a blow. 'I mean I didn't before here. Only visited. With my father. He's the fourth son of the queen's third daughter.'

'Princess!' the boy hissed. Librarian Sternus cuffed him wearily over the head.

Lutna aimed her back at the boy. 'I'm not really a princess. Not a proper one. But there were ganar at the palace. You know. Downstairs. They taught me a bit of their language. I've always been good at languages . . . I thought . . .'

'*Mutuupk*,' Hellet said, not looking up from his study of his claw scars. 'Your mouth is the wrong shape for the uu-sound. You're close enough to understand.'

'Everybody up!' Librarian Sternus clapped his hands. 'Four more chambers to go.'

The destination chosen for Celcha's first expedition into the library was the nearest ganar chamber. Most rooms could be accessed by four doors, those on the library's edge by three. Most doors could be opened only by one species. Most chambers could be accessed only by one species. A ganar chamber could be entered only with the help of a ganar.

If Myles Carstar had been told that the library held chambers where four square miles were given over to the ganar, he would have denied it. If it were proved to him, he would have burned the lot and committed murder if necessary to bury the knowledge that such a place had ever existed. He had constructed himself around the idea that ganar were his inferior in every way. Celcha would have enjoyed informing him that in some of those chambers it was next to impossible to find any book not written by a ganar.

They came at last to their destination. Or at least to the short corridor leading to it and to the final white door blocking their way. The many doors before this one had melted away before the trainees' touch. Markeet invited Lutna to try this one. She rapped her knuckles against the surface, unable to make a sound, and equally unable to pass through.

'And now.' Sternus extended his hand towards Celcha and her brother. 'If one of our honoured guests would like to see a chamber through which many of their kind have passed before?'

Hellet nodded for Celcha to do it. So often these days she felt as though she were not only the smaller, but younger sibling too.

She advanced slowly towards the immensity of the door, which was large enough for scores to enter abreast, and so high that she'd hardly be able to throw a stone to the top. The whole thing dissipated before her reaching fingers, not allowing her any sensation of contact.

Celcha advanced without seeking permission.

Hellet caught up with her. 'Once they're in they can't get out again without our permission. And nobody in the library can get in. They'd have to search the city for a slave who wanted to open the chamber for them.'

Celcha looked back to see the door re-form behind the last of the trainees, the irksome human boy whose name she'd learned was Kenton. For a moment she wanted to make them feel an echo of the terror she'd lived with all her life. None of these sabbers had set the manacle around her wrist, but it was still there. None of them had sent her down the tunnels, but parts of their houses were likely built of what her kind had recovered. None of them had administered the cruelties. Most of them were children. But they were clever children. They all knew that slaves worked beneath their feet in chains. They were part of the system. Part of the machine.

Hellet drew her attention forward with a snort. 'They're not enough. Think bigger, sister. Much bigger.'

The sight that greeted Celcha as she emerged from the tunnel put all thoughts of revenge to one side. The many rooms they had crossed to reach the ganar chamber had been filled with shelving.

Shelves of various designs, heights, spacing, and materials, in all manner of repair, some shrugging off the years, others collapsing beneath their weight. The ganar chamber presented something very different. A stone-block wall reached to the dizzying heights of the ceiling and curved to meet the chamber wall to either side of the corridor. Celcha stood in a vertical semi-circular shaft some thirty yards in radius, formed between the curving wall and chamber wall. A dozen doorways offered passage through the wall, with stone steps leading back and forth to visit the higher entrances. Far above the doors hundreds of windows stared down at her.

It seemed that instead of covering the floor of the chamber with shelving the ganar had filled the entire volume with some vast multi-roomed structure. That felt impossible. There would be sufficient accommodation for a nation; even the population of the largest city would be lost with such a volume.

'How far . . .' Celcha turned to the two librarians approaching behind her. 'It can't fill the whole space?'

'There are voids,' Sternus said. 'But it seems to be more full than not. We estimate that we've explored fewer than three in a hundred of the rooms.'

'But . . . how did they live here? There's no food. Can the chamber even be reached without humans and canith to open doors on the way?'

'All good questions.' Markeet came up on her other side, the larger and older of the two librarians, bulging belly tenting his crimson robes around his feet. 'We believe they traded books here, volumes of particular value gleaned from faraway chambers. It's possible that some of the population came and went by swift routes through the neighbouring rooms, using wheeled vehicles on tracks perhaps. But our scholars agree that food must have been grown here and consumed with very little delay between harvesting and the mouth in order that the assistants did not destroy it. It appears that assistants don't consider something to be food until it is dead, or at least picked.'

'I have read', said Hellet, 'that the library shuffles the chambers and everything in them. Less often than once in a lifetime. But that it is sufficient to move what might at one time have been the library's entrance chamber to some remove as distant as this.'

Markeet frowned. 'That's a rather fanciful story, best kept for children's books. But I have heard it before.' His frown deepened. 'The truth is that we have various theories and no certainties.'

'Why don't you know for sure? Isn't it written?' Celcha found herself eager to learn the languages of her own people – to study the books they left behind.

'Fire.' Sternus, blond-haired, short for a human, shuddered. 'A very long time ago. Almost none of the rooms in this chamber survived untouched. We find books hidden in small caches, but not often.'

'Why' – Hellet asked his first question of the whole journey – 'search in the labyrinth of a burned-out city for books when almost every step we've taken to get here has dozens of books within arm's reach?'

Sternus looked up at the high windows speculatively. 'The books uncovered here are often of considerable value to us.'

'And how many ganar tongues do you speak, librarian?' Hellet asked.

'Three.' The man frowned as if it was a number that troubled him rather than one he took pride in. He stared at Hellet, waiting for the next question, but Hellet looked away, craning his neck to study the heights.

When it became apparent that Hellet had no more to say, Markeet led them in through the nearest doorway. The next few hours were spent winding through corridors, climbing stairs, and finding paths through rooms that ranged from vaulted halls to small cubicles. Celcha tried to imagine the countless people who must have lived there, sleeping and eating in the many dwelling places. The windows in these homes often opened onto echoingly large voids, reaching down to the library floor in some places, false floors in others. With constant light everywhere it would have been easy to grow crops here: fruit trees; vines climbing the buildings. She tried to imagine it. The scale and complexity of it. The water that would have needed to be pumped in from outside the library.

The emptiness of the city grated on Celcha's nerves. The whole library was, of course, characterized by solitude, but these rooms were made for families: the halls and open squares ached for the crowds that had once thronged here. The fire and subsequent centuries had left little but scorched stone to record the passing of so many. The air around Hellet might sparkle with the presence of angels, but everywhere else it was ghosts that held sway. The phantoms of innumerable ganar taken from the world before their time.

Initially, they followed stair after stair, gaining height, passing through regions already picked clean. The taint of the great fire had long since left the air but memories of it haunted the empty halls: black drifts of char, banished to the corners where shadows would linger but for the pervasive library light, blocks of stone split by heat, scorch marks that the passage of many feet had not erased. Ancient soot blackened every ceiling.

The further they went, the darker the walls and floor became.

'In the unexplored chambers everything's black,' Sternus said. 'The mark of a librarian who has done their job here is that they'll come out looking like a trainee.'

A muted ripple of laughter went through the trainee ranks as they looked from the librarian's crimson to their own black tunics.

As the walls grew darker Markeet called a halt from place to place and sent the trainees out exploring, equipping each band of two or three with coloured chalk to mark their return paths, though their footprints should also serve. On the fourth such stop Lutna surprised everyone by asking to be in a three with Celcha and Hellet. The librarians, mildly amused, allowed it.

Celcha followed the other two, deep in her thoughts. Not looking for books or anything else. It was in this state of mind that she found the raven, or rather she glimpsed it from a window across the floor of a void that might once have been an orchard. It launched itself from a distant window on the far side, a brief explosion of glossy black wings, gaining height before being lost from view. Back at the dig the eldest slaves, some who had been there more than a century, held great store by the sight of ravens. They even had a peculiar arithmetic whereby the number of the birds seen together constituted a prediction. One was always sorrow.

'Come on!' Lutna called back.

It didn't take many choices of left or right, up or down before the other groups were out of earshot and a silence enfolded the ganar, broken only by the commentary of their human companion.

'I'm going to tell H'run and F'nort at the palace,' Lutna said. 'They're the ones that taught me to speak ganar. I mean, their language. I bet they've never heard about this place. They didn't say anything and they knew I was coming to the lib—'

'This city is a tomb,' Hellet cut across her. 'Many millions died here in the fire.' The air around him seethed and sparkled as Maybe and Starve circled him like prowling wolves. 'The remains that were not wholly consumed were heaped together when the survivors returned. They made a pyramid two hundred and fifty yards on each side and a hundred and sixty yards high, just of bones.'

'I didn't know.' Lutna looked down.

Hellet rolled his shoulders as he often did to ease the ache of his old scars. 'It is good that you show more interest in the ganar than your fellows do. But understand that your actions are neither a kindness nor reparation. They are a bandage applied to a cancer.' He waved a hand at the view from the nearest window, looking out across a void to countless windows on the opposite wall. 'This was the third and most recent ganar ascendance since the latest descent from Attamast. There have been earlier descents but information concerning those is scarce and patchy.'

'You came from the moon?' Lutna's eyes went round.

'Our ancestors did,' Celcha said, glad to know something about her people that the child did not.

'They will come again.' Hellet's voice was grim. 'Or one of our enemies will go there. It never ends well. One world always burns. Or both do.' He walked across the room and knelt beside the wall where a pile of rubble lay. He moved a few blocks, disturbing a small cloud of soot. There seemed to be a space in the wall at floor level, partly obscured. Hellet drew out first one book, then another, the fur of his arms black now. The first was large with gold foil decorating its embossed cover, the other much smaller with an ink-dark cover and the edges of its pages dyed black. This smaller book he placed in his satchel, offering Lutna a slow wink. Next, he stood, crossed back to them, and placed the larger book in Lutna's arms. 'Well done, you've found a treasure.'

✦ ✦ ✦

Of the two librarians it was Sternus, the younger one, who managed to disguise his excitement best, perhaps because he didn't fully appreciate the importance of the book Lutna presented them with. Markeet, in contrast, couldn't stop his cheeks spasming periodically with an alarmingly wide smile. Moreover, the older librarian began to sweat, and at such a rate that Celcha wondered if he'd reach the outer library half his current size, shrivelled beyond recognition.

The expedition ended abruptly and Markeet warned them all to be ready for a swifter return journey than the outwards one. Celcha, whilst she could imagine that the book was important, was unclear why the librarians were in such a hurry to get back. It wasn't as if someone was going to steal their prize from them.

On the retreat through the deserted warrens of the city Celcha lingered at the rear of the party with Hellet. 'It was Maybe that put those books there, wasn't it?' she hissed.

'I don't know.' Hellet shrugged. 'He knew they were there. That was enough.'

'Why though? What good does it do us?' *What good does it do him?* She wanted to ask that too, but Hellet grew uncommunicative if she ever questioned the angels' motivation. Even pointing out that from what she could see Maybe was definitely canith had set her adrift on his silence for a day. Starve she saw less well – he, or she, could be canith, or human, or something similar to them both.

'Goodwill is a currency that can be spent in many ways. We've opened an account with both librarians and with the princess.'

'She's not a princess.'

'Their queen has bounced her on her knee. It's close enough.'

They reached the bottom of the last flight of steps on weary legs and walked down a long corridor before emerging from the city. Behind its curving wall it had reminded Celcha of the towering ant nests and hanging beehives she'd seen illustrated in a book Tutor Ablesan had been teaching her to read from. As if it were an amalgamation of both, fashioned from stone.

Celcha's stomach rumbled as she crossed the ground between the city's wall and the corridor. Her last meal seemed a very long time ago, her stomach already accustomed to the librarians' plenty.

The sustenance offered by the centre circle of each chamber felt like a poor exchange for actual food. She was glad the searching had been cut short, but they still had a long walk home and would sleep a night on empty bellies before reaching the outer library.

The librarians led the way down the corridor, halting before the white door then turning to look expectantly at Hellet. Celcha noticed that both angels, who had been hanging around her brother ever since their arrival at the chamber, had vanished. Without acknowledging Sternus or Markeet, Hellet came forward and set his palm, still black with soot, to the door. Nothing happened.

Markeet's brow furrowed and, with his arms folded across the expanse of his belly, he swung his gaze to Celcha. 'You try it.' All command, no request.

Celcha joined her brother and set her hand to the door. Nothing.

'This is . . .' Sternus looked astonished.

'Bad,' Markeet supplied. 'It could be days before they come looking. And even if they bring more ganar . . . the door's not opening for them.'

'Try again,' Sternus urged.

Celcha looked pointedly at her hand still on the door. 'How long will we have to survive using the centre circle?'

Markeet and Sternus exchanged a look.

'This place is a maze,' Sternus said. 'It's hard enough finding the circle when it's just shelves hiding it.'

'You don't know where it is?' Celcha asked, horrified.

'It's not like we haven't looked . . .' The older librarian turned his gaze at the trainees as if considering how they might taste. 'But no. We haven't.'

'We'll starve,' the trainee Kenton wailed, all his sneering gone in an instant.

'No,' Hellet said, and for a moment Celcha thought he was offering comfort. 'Thirst will kill you long before that.'

There is, inside me, an unanswered ache, small but constant,
caused by no particular trial or tribulation, simply by the burden
of existence, the effort of holding aloft my own sky. Each of
us is Atlas and why some are crushed and others effortless is
a mystery whose answer will not translate into my tongue.

Existential, *by John Smith*

CHAPTER 9

Celcha

While the librarians, Markeet and Sternus, heatedly debated how to proceed, Celcha and Hellet waited by the door with the trainees. It didn't take long to catch the first whispered accusation, unsurprisingly from Kenton.

'They don't want to open it. That's why it's not opening.'

Angry glances sliced across them.

It was true that Celcha had thought maybe the librarians and their charges deserved at least a touch of worry, but she hadn't truly intended for the door to remain closed. And now, with her stomach growling, there was no ambiguity in her, she wanted the door open. Touching it yet again confirmed that this wasn't a case of mixed feelings getting in the way.

Markeet returned to the group. Sweat darkened the man's crimson robes beneath his arms. 'Come on then!' He herded the group to where Sternus waited at the entrance to the chamber. 'Right. Well, we're going to have to hunt for the centre circle. The circle will sustain everyone until they come for us.' The librarian's expression didn't inspire confidence. Seeing his own doubt reflected at him he tried to rally the trainees. 'I was on an expedition to find it . . . oh, fifteen years ago, so we won't just be chasing our tails. We can start—'

Celcha and the children turned their heads to follow the librarian's gaze back along the corridor. The white door had melted away. An assistant stood behind it.

A sigh of relief ran through the party. The assistants might not be overly helpful, but in a situation like this they wouldn't walk off and leave them trapped. They would help trapped explorers in the same sort of way that people happening across fledglings that had fallen from their nests would return them to safety.

Tutor Ablesan had told Celcha that nobody knew how many assistants served the library. Two at least, since one had a body suggesting a male frame whereas another had one that looked more female. From reported sightings it seemed that if there were only two they would have to travel very swiftly and with intention to deceive. Beyond that nothing could be said with certainty save that there were not many.

The assistant that had opened the door had the male form. Possibly it was Yute, the one who had greeted their arrival days earlier. After a shocked pause, Markeet thrust his book satchel at Sternus, the flap stretched around the prized tome with the gold lettering. He muttered two words to the younger man then went forward to speak with the assistant.

Markeet returned after only a few moments, looking perplexed. He frowned at Celcha and Hellet. 'The assistant wishes to speak with both of you.' After a short while staring at their immobility he fluttered his hands. 'Go!'

Hellet advanced towards the assistant and Celcha followed. Most would not have noticed it, especially not humans or canith, but Celcha saw the reluctance in her brother's steps.

'Assistant?' Celcha decided to take the lead. Hellet was nervous, and she was the older sibling. She was tired of him showing her the way.

'Walk with me.' The assistant turned his gleaming white back on them and paced away. Without looking to see that they were following, he began to speak. 'It's hard for the timeless to perceive the flow. Hard to see the change from this to that. Everything simply *is*. And yet, contrary to my nature, I struggle to do just that. I look into the current.' He raised a hand to clutch the back of his neck, a curiously alive gesture, at odds with the animated statue that he had first seemed. 'And it is difficult for the timely, those carried in the flow, bubbling to its surface, borne along, ultimately drowned in it, to see the crystalline glory of eternity, reflected and refracted through many dimensions, perfect in its imperfections. Language is also caught in the flow and everchanging. It lacks the capacity to exchange those experiences between us.'

'I . . . see,' Celcha lied. Ahead of them the white door grew closer. If they went through it, the librarians and trainees would be trapped with only a precious book and the dead metropolis for company.

'For many years I have watched the city that you came through to reach the library. Cities come and go at our gates. Growing from a scattering of huts, flourishing, falling into fire. Few last as long as this one has. And this is the first where canith and humans live together under lasting truce. It holds the first green shoot of the peace necessary for survival and advancement. It is, in the long march of years, a wonder.'

'Built on the backs of slaves,' Hellet growled.

'This brings me to compromise and the inherent imperfection of now. The city is a stepping-stone to something better. Something that is encoded into the structure of the library. I will . . . admit . . . to having interfered at times. Coaxed. Perhaps even guided . . .'

'Why are you interested in us?' Celcha asked. 'It offends the librarians when you single out a pair of slaves. It's the type of attention that could get us killed.'

'They don't kill you.' The assistant shook his head. 'My apologies, though. It is hard for me to see the world as something sliding by from known to unknown.' He touched his neck again. 'I talk to you because I can't see past you. You are turbulence in the flow. Cracks in the crystal. You, Hellet, in particular. There is no point in conversing with the others. I already know that I do not speak with them.'

He'd called them cracks. Celcha knew what had cracked her brother. The cruelty of humans, inflicted on a child. She ground her teeth and kept her silence. It was dangerous for a slave to show anger.

The assistant, seeing that she would not reply, carried on. 'Anomalies of your kind are very rare. The library draws them in but still they are rare. To find two together – is unheard of. You are dangerous. If left unchecked, you might start seeing ghosts. Or even worse, talking to them.'

Celcha resisted exchanging a glance with Hellet. 'Unchecked? You're planning to . . . check us?'

'You can serve the library as I do. Even for assistants there was a before.'

'As you do? You mean . . . all white and serious?'

The assistant inclined his head.

'Or?' asked Hellet. Celcha couldn't tell if her brother was asking about the consequences of defiance, or what the second choice was.

'Or . . .' The assistant shook his head. 'It's best to accept eternity. You'll never be bored, I promise.' He saw they were waiting for him to continue. 'Or, you can be repaired. You will no longer be cracks in time, no longer flaws in the crystal.'

'That sounds better,' Celcha muttered, then, louder, 'it always works?'

'It always works.' A nod of the head. 'You will no longer be a crack in time. You might, however, not be quite the same person you were before. You might not even be alive. You'll be whatever was necessary for you to no longer crack the world.'

It was the gentlest threat Celcha had ever received. Even the slavemaster would have been proud of it.

'Why wait to tell us all this now?' Hellet asked. 'Why not say it when we arrived?'

'I wasn't sure when you arrived. You weren't making that much turbulence in the flow. I thought maybe you were borderline cases. I wondered if there might be a compromise. But you're churning things up now. You're rocks in the stream.' He tilted his head, studying Hellet with blank white eyes. 'And you've found two books, I see. Interesting ones.'

Celcha didn't want to talk about books. 'You're telling us we're going to get turned into creepy statues like you, or have something done to us that might leave us dead or broken?' She started to say that it wasn't fair, but bit off the words. Less than a week among these sabbers, being treated as almost equals, and she'd started responding to adversity with talk of fairness or justice. When had anything ever been fair for her and Hellet?

'If you'd come here with a terminal disease would that have been so different? This is just what time has placed upon your shoulders. You can bear the cure or step out of time, as I did.'

'How are you going to make us do it, Yute?' Hellet asked. 'Lock us in a chamber until we agree?'

The assistant stiffened at the use of his name. His enamel forehead remained smooth but somehow Celcha could feel the frown. 'You mistake me. The library informs. It does not compel. We share information. It is for the recipients of that information to decide how to respond to it.'

'You already locked us in. That's not compelling us?' Celcha said.

Yute almost flinched. 'My apologies. I merely sought to delay you while I attended to another matter. I wanted to speak with you here, within sight of your ancestors' great works. A monument to possibilities that irresponsible actions on your part might ensure never come again.'

'Irresponsible?' Hellet fixed the assistant with his black stare. 'That sounds like judgement. Like opinion. Guidance is neighbour to instruction. Aren't you breaking your own rules, Yute?'

Yute shuddered. 'How do you know that name?' He sounded almost angry.

'*Even for assistants there was a before,*' Hellet quoted.

Yute bowed his head. 'I have overstepped myself.' All emotion gone from his voice. 'I've spent too long in the flow. Do what you will with the knowledge imparted. You will, in the end, come to understand it as I do, but the choice will be yours.'

Lies are a currency. The truth buys nothing save sorrow.

Real Economics, *by Mark Carnival*

CHAPTER 10

Evar

Evar followed the assistant's directions, or rather its single direction, as best as he could. Where doors failed to open to his touch, he had to lead his siblings on long detours, whilst remembering their route with sufficient accuracy to understand when they finally reached a chamber where the original direction had meaning.

For the whole course of the journey a constant anxiety kept him company – the worry that they might find they had simply enlarged their prison, swapping one chamber for a network of several dozen that still didn't connect with the outer world. Kerrol suggested that their escape had been promised from the moment they had reached a door that opened for them. Doors coded to canith must, he suggested, be part of a sequence that led to the canith door to the outside. Minutes later he undid any confidence he'd managed to instil by adding, 'Unless, of course, the library's design is intended to encourage cooperation between species, and we were in a part of the library that could only be reached by an accord between humans and canith. Or perhaps between humans, skeer, and canith.' A short while after that he even managed to sour the idea of escape by asking how one would know when the swapping of smaller prisons for larger ones had truly stopped and freedom had been found, or is freedom simply a sufficiently large prison? Clovis told him to shut up after that.

Their trek through the wonders of the library had most impact on Clovis and Kerrol since Evar had ghosted his way through many chambers on journeys through the Exchange. Still, it was hard to impress anyone who had lived their entire life amid a near infinity of books by using a larger near infinity held in chambers identical to the one they'd lived in. Both were, however, fans of shelving, being impressed by its height and the ease of obtaining a book without toppling an entire tower to get to it. They were less impressed by the constraints it imposed on getting places. Particularly when trying to follow a bearing. Fortunately, the only decision that ever needs to be made – bearing or not – was which of the other three doors to attempt to leave a chamber by.

Evar wasn't sure how long it took to reach the outermost chambers, but he was sure it was more than a day, and they slept twice. Despite the threat of the skeer, they saw no other living creature on their expedition. Clovis surmised that the skeer set guards only on the doors they couldn't open, in the hope that they would then capture the door when it did finally open. Once through a canith door there was no worry about skeer since the areas the siblings trekked through were presumably inaccessible to the insectoids.

'Well, we've reached the edge.' Kerrol stood looking back and forth across the expanse of wall.

'We have.' Evar frowned. The lack of a door meant that beyond the wall lay the outside world. Unless of course the architect – Irad as some legends called him – enjoyed cruel tricks. The lack of a door also meant that they had followed the assistant's bearing with insufficient accuracy.

'Left or right?' Clovis asked. It was the correct question. The more difficult one was how far left or right to go before turning back and going right or left.

Kerrol chose left and was outvoted, so they ended up going right, which was undoubtedly what Kerrol had intended. Evar considered reversing the decision and going left. But that would then turn out to be what Kerrol had intended. In the end he decided that it didn't matter.

They found the exit door two chambers later.

Evar stood back and looked at it. Just for once he was the expert.

He had experienced things that his siblings would soon face for the first time. 'There's a whole world out there.' He basked in the novelty of being the leader. 'Brace yourselves. It's not like anyth—'

Clovis cut his speech short by drawing her sword, walking up to the door and slapping at it. She was through before it had fully dissipated. Kerrol walked after her, giving Evar a pat on the shoulder as he passed. 'Sorry, brother, she's seen all kinds of worlds in the Mechanism. It's going to take quite a bit to impress her. Nice speech, though.'

Evar clenched his teeth against the grumbling he wanted to succumb to. The assistant had said there weren't any ghosts around, but there was a remote chance Livira had found them in the interim and was watching over him. If so, he was sure she'd be laughing at his pomposity, and he determined to create a better impression going forward.

'Evar!' Kerrol ducked back through the door. 'Come on!'

Beyond the door lay a sequence of natural caves adjoining artificial chambers. From the rubble heaped on all sides, and from the broken walls and cavitated ceilings, it was apparent that the place had been heavily damaged, collapsed even, then partially repaired at least once. Some passages were blocked, and the chambers had a deserted look, carrying the same cold, dampish aroma as caverns sculpted by nature.

'I'm going to say that the exit is very well hidden from the outside, and probably blocked too,' Kerrol said.

'Because there wasn't a skeer waiting behind the door,' Clovis said.

Evar understood why his sister had gone through the door ahead of them, blade in hand. She'd been expecting a skeer. More than one maybe.

They found no sign of the insectoids. In fact, they found very little. No bones, almost nothing organic, just rusted hinges and pieces of shattered planking in the occasional doorway. A chair leg here, a blackened pot there.

'I want something to eat.' Clovis sniffed at a cauldron whose base had corroded through long ago. 'We can starve out here.'

'We can starve in the library,' Evar said. 'Just not die from it.'

'Unless you can't reach a centre circle for some reason.' Kerrol rubbed his chin.

'I can't see that happening . . .'

As they approached what had to be the main entrance, the library light began to fade and the collapses became more of a problem, forcing them to squeeze through narrow gaps on several occasions.

'This is deliberate.' Clovis eyed up the wall of rubble in their way.

'The question is whether it's to stop canith coming in, or to stop something else,' Kerrol said.

'Either way' – Evar clambered up to the top and took hold of a large rock – 'we have some digging to do. Watch out!' With a heave he sent the chunk tumbling down the slope. He looked at his hands, wondering. He'd never touched broken rock before. He'd never touched anything that wasn't flesh, or books, or library, save for his food and the trees in the Exchange.

Clovis came up to join him, jumping between the larger rocks. Kerrol scrambled up after her. He stood, brushing rock dust from the book-leather skirt that covered his knees, then frowned at his dusty hands. 'This could take a while. Reckon we can do it before we die of thirst?'

In the end it took three retreats to the nearest centre circle and another period of sleep before they smelled any hint of an outside world. The rubble wall was backed against truly titanic slabs of rock that sealed the entrance tunnel. Rubble filled the narrow gaps between the slabs too. The siblings mined a path between giant rocks, wondering all the time if their efforts were simply going to reveal a path that narrowed to a crack and forced them to try another way until at last all their labour proved futile. As they dug further the library's light weakened rapidly, leaving them fumbling in the dark.

Evar coughed on dust, panted, coughed again, carried on panting as he hefted aside rocks from fist-sized to head-sized. His arms trembled with fatigue and his hands both ached and stung. Behind him, Kerrol and Clovis cleared rubble, waiting their turn at the digging front. A new scent was what first alerted Evar to a change ahead. The breeze came later, along with a whisper of sunlight. But at first there was only the smell of freedom, faint strains of life and the arid tang of desert.

The final squeeze proved rib-scraping and had Evar had a richer, more plentiful diet he wouldn't have made it through. He emerged in a small avalanche of pebbles and crawled from beneath a shelf of rock into dazzling sunlight. Rather than standing, he continued to crawl then sprawled exhausted on the nearest piece of mountainside flat enough to receive him.

Soon all three of them lay side by side, their manes dust-white as if they were true siblings from the same litter.

'It's not the same,' Kerrol said at last.

'No,' Clovis said, her face still covered with one arm.

'What isn't?' Evar asked.

'The Mechanism,' Kerrol said. 'It's close, but this is more real. I can feel every corner of this rock digging into me, and the wind is doing different things to the hairs on one arm than the other, and the sun . . . it's just . . . hotter, brighter. More real.'

'Oh.' Evar said no more but he was glad in a way, glad that he could have shown them both something new, and that reality had something to offer that the dreams of the Mechanism couldn't capture.

Some time passed as they lay, adjusting to the light, the temperature, and the wind. Evar had only ever left the library as a ghost and these things were all new to him too. Clovis was the first to sit up.

'We need water, then food, then shelter.' She shaded her eyes and gazed around. 'Is that this city of yours?'

Evar sat up. 'No.' The ruins she was looking at were too small for the city he'd seen, and surely too weathered. 'Maybe some sort of fort to keep the canith from using this entrance to the library.' He frowned. 'But why would the canith build their city outside the human entrance?'

Kerrol sat up, squinting and yawning. 'Because the humans built one there and it was easier to take it, then hike to this entrance from there? Or to use humans to open the closer door? I suppose it depends on what fraction of the citizens are going to want to come into the library on a regular basis. From what you've said about the humans it was almost none of them.'

'So, where's the city you were in?' Clovis asked.

Evar stood slowly and scanned the surrounding peaks. To his left the ground sloped away, trailing to a grey-brown plain whose distances lay beneath impenetrable haze. 'It's hard to say.' He had studied the mountains when he had first left the library, but out of fascination rather than a desire to locate himself at some future time. And he wasn't used to seeing huge objects from different angles. 'Maybe . . . over there?' He flapped a hand vaguely down the gorge to the right.

'We should find water down there at least?' Kerrol shaded his eyes and stared as if willing it into being. 'I mean, the stuff runs downhill. That's how rivers work.'

'Come on.' Clovis started to lead the way down towards the gorge, her usual poise deserting her on sloping ground after a life lived on the level. 'We can't just wait here.'

The sun swung through the sky, swirling their shadows around them as they laboured across the fractured landscape. Kerrol was the first to flag. Evar's siblings had been trained by the Mechanism and weren't literally jumping at their own shadows as he'd been in the Exchange, but Kerrol's interests had always been cerebral rather than physical and the unaccustomed exercise was taking its toll.

'Wait here.' Clovis pointed to the shadow of a large rock. 'Evar and I will go up to that ridge and see if he's right about where we are.'

Kerrol didn't bother to argue. He wasn't given to pride – perhaps a side effect of deconstructing personality to such a degree. Also, it didn't take his particular skillset to understand that Clovis wasn't in the mood for negotiating.

Evar knew he was needed as the one most able to ensure they weren't seen by hostile eyes. If Starval were there, then . . . but Starval wasn't there. As they climbed, Evar tried to keep his thoughts on his surroundings and what Starval had taught him about concealment in such places, rather than thinking about Starval himself.

His brother had vanished with Mayland, seemingly recruited to his plans for destroying the library. Mayland, who Evar had thought was dead, appeared to have simply found out how to escape before Evar did, and to have left all his siblings to carry on in their prison while he went exploring. Evar hadn't yet decided how he felt about any of that.

The sinking sun had stretched every shadow until one started to meet the next. Again, Evar couldn't help thinking of Starval. He'd have loved every bit of this. Evar, on the other hand, rather than loving it, was terrified that his education in such matters would prove inadequate and he'd let some enemy see them.

The last time Evar had seen his brother was with his knife at Mayland's neck. Mayland in turn had held the neck of an assistant who had abandoned immortality in favour of involving herself in humanity's affairs, and by extension those of the canith. Whether she counted as an innocent, Evar couldn't tell. But she had certainly been helpless, and it had hurt Evar to see Mayland kill her, especially with so little emotion. Starval, rapidly changing his approach, had killed a human to protect their brother, and then all hell had broken loose in the Exchange and Evar had fled, meaning to save Livira. He hoped Mayland and Starval had kept each other safe, and that Starval hadn't let their eldest brother lead him down a dark path.

'Down!' Evar grabbed at Clovis, but she found cover before he made contact.

'Where?'

'On the heights. Two skeer.' Evar slithered towards the ridge, keeping the folds of the rock between him and the skeer.

Clovis didn't ask if they'd been spotted. It was nice to be trusted. Evar crested the ridge first. He let the scene before him sink into his eyes, lit by the red embers of the setting sun, then slid back, book leather scraping rock.

'Well?' Clovis asked.

'Best take a look for yourself.' Evar wasn't sure he had the words for it.

Clovis advanced, following his path exactly. Moments later she came back without turning. 'Shit.'

What the skeer had built over the city was larger than the city had been and far taller than any of its towers. The structure climbed the slopes, encompassing the library entrance, clinging to the rock like a wasps' nest or strange organic growth. Its vast, segmented walls even looked like skeer armour, as if the whole thing might be one gigantic insect capable of biting the peak off a mountain. The entire structure, surely large enough to house a million skeer, was the curious, semi-translucent white of skeer plates, veined with deep blue that bled into lighter shades before rapidly succumbing to the white. Thick veins here, thin there, spreading into ever thinner traceries that escaped the eye.

'We need to leave,' Clovis hissed.

Evar was still marvelling at the size of the nest. 'What do they all eat?'

'Us, if we're not careful.' Her stomach rumbled as if to remind them that they needed to eat too.

It seemed impossible that her stomach had given them away, but the coincidence was hard to credit as a skeer chose that moment to send its alarm throbbing through the gorge whilst the shriek of its spiracle exhalation ricocheted off the cliff faces high above them.

'Run!' Evar shouted, and they ran.

*When planning a reunion with an old friend it is important
to choose a venue with many exits. Who knows what the
missing years will have wrought with the clay of memory?*

Hello, Darkness, *by Erasmus Young*

CHAPTER 11

Arpix

Livira had dropped into Arpix's life unexpectedly and, like a stone
hitting the surface of a pool, she had disturbed the order of things.
His order. Sending ripples to his farthest shores. She had been an
unwelcome intrusion, a small, dark child, awkward in clothes that
seemed to have been imposed upon her wildness much as she had
been imposed upon his serenity.

It hadn't taken long for Arpix to admit that, although many had
praised his intelligence and even whispered of genius, this girl from
the Dust with her bruised face and cut hands was of a different
order. A higher shelf. Livira hadn't so much disdained the library's
rules as wholly failed to acknowledge their existence. She had spied,
stolen, trespassed, and run wild. And, in the end, Arpix had come
to the conclusion that she was the breath that he hadn't understood
was required to keep him from suffocating.

All of them at that table had needed Livira, except perhaps
Carlotte, who was her own brand of chaos. All of them had agreed
on little concerning Livira save that you could never tell where she
would lead you. It had astonished them that such a creature could
have walked out of the Dust from a life spent within sight of a
single well and a few acres of jarra beans and dry wheat. None of
them, not Arpix, nor Meelan, nor Jella, could ever have predicted

that Livira's adventures would ultimately abandon them to a life lived within sight of a well out on the Dust and supported by a few acres of jarra beans.

A fiery death had been closing in on them from all sides. In Arpix's nightmares, which were many and often, the library still burned, and he burned with it. In reality, they had escaped at the last moment after two assistants reached them through the flames and smoke. What had provoked the assistants to such compassion Arpix still didn't know, but none of them had questioned it at the time. With the fire at their backs, they'd escaped the library and found themselves here, in the grip of another kind of heat, also pressing on all sides, and with the threat of a horrific but swift death replaced by that of starvation.

Arpix had expected to emerge in the Exchange, but perhaps the assistant who had used her blood to draw the portal had been tainted in some way – certainly she had been discoloured like her companion, but others had blamed that on their passage through the inferno. In any event, the portal had brought them directly to this place without the luxury of any of the Exchange's choices. The portal had smoked away within the hour, presumably as the assistant's blood was burned from the library floor.

'Someone's coming.' Meelan saw it now.

Arpix's considerable height advantage had enabled him to watch the dust trail for some moments already. It wasn't a good sign, but on the other hand there wasn't much they could do about it. It wasn't as if running was an option.

'More than one?' Meelan's habitual growl had become a rasp since living on the Dust. The dry air had put an edge on it. The sun had darkened him almost to Livira's hue and bleached the blackness from the top layers of his hair, leaving a deep reddish tinge. The mere notion that one of the city's richest families shared blood with the 'Dusters' would have given the king and Lord Algar apoplexy. Arpix was sad they would never be slapped in the face with that particular truth.

'Arpix?'

'Sorry. Just thinking.' Arpix adjusted his broad-brimmed hat. He'd woven it himself from dried bean leaves and was rather proud of it. 'Yes, more than one. Three or four maybe.'

The strangers – sabbers of one kind or another – were approaching at speed from the direction of the mountains. The crimson glow that had touched on their dust cloud had faded to nothing as the sun set. Soon dusk would erase them completely.

'Should we set a light?' Jella came up beside them, precious hoe in hand.

When they'd first arrived none of them had known where they were. Or when. None of the librarians, not even Master Jost, had ever left Crath City and they had no way of knowing if the mountains to the west were 'their' mountains or just . . . mountains. Fortunately, Salamonda had travelled in her youth and recognized, even from this angle, the peak that rose above their old home. With that information it fell to Jella, and her unsung fascination with maps, to deduce from memory that they had been deposited on a gods-forsaken plateau out in the Dust. Specifically, Arthran Plateau, the site of a ruined city of unknown age that had at several times in past millennia been excavated with varying degrees of success. Jella wasn't sure but suspected that the city might have been named Arthran. That 'might be' meant that they knew *where* they were with far more certainty than *when* they were.

'I say no to the light.' Meelan stepped into Arpix's silence with his own opinion. 'It's not like we've ever had any luck with strangers.'

That was certainly true. Over the four years they'd spent in the hollows of ancient excavations wanderers had called in on them several times. Stealing hadn't been the worst of it. Giles, one of the bookbinders, had been murdered in the night. Even the best of them had brought no food and had been an extra mouth to feed when they could hardly feed themselves. In fact, in the first year they had all nearly starved. Jella and Salamonda had fared best, and their labour had kept the rest alive, sowing a crop that came to harvest swiftly. Still, by the end of it, nourished by little but rats, Jella and Salamonda had been as slim as Meelan had been at the start, and Arpix a skeleton on the cusp of death. All of them had inhabited their clothes like strangers lost in billowing space. All except Radmelk, another of the bookbinders, who had been eaten by a horror that hid itself under the dust.

'They're running,' Arpix said. 'You don't raise that much dust walking.' He had never expected to be an expert on dust clouds. 'Coming from the mountains.'

'You don't run unless you're being chased.' Meelan rubbed his chin, staring at the shadowed mountains.

'And we know what's chasing them,' Jella said. 'I'll get the fire bowl.'

By the time Jella returned with the perforated clay fire bowl and a sack of bean husks to burn in it, Jost had caught wind of the situation. She circled Jella, hound to prey, peppering the air with her objections. The lethargy that normally wrapped her fell away. Arpix had long noticed that whenever she had something to complain about Jost found new energy from somewhere. The rest of the time she had a tendency to survive on the labour of others. The authority that came with being a senior librarian had all but eroded to nothing over the years they'd spent scraping a living from the Dust, but Arpix still sometimes found himself following her orders out of habit.

'Why in the world would you want to guide more vagrants here?' Jost raised both arms along with her voice. Her robes hung in tatters, played by the breeze. The material was dust-grey, the library's shade-coded hierarchy erased. All of Arthran's ten inhabitants had now been given equal rank by the pervasive dirt. 'You're inviting murderers and thieves over our doorstep! Again!'

Behind Jost, one of the younger bookbinders, Sheetra, rolled her eyes, but the four older ones looked worried. Meelan's brow had also furrowed, though perhaps for different reasons. He detested Jost and finding his opinion aligned with hers would weaken his conviction.

Arpix had never liked the leadership role that had first been thrust upon him by dint of age and height and cleverness at the trainee table. He'd accepted it because he liked sense and order, and the best way to maintain those things was from the top. But he hadn't enjoyed it and still didn't. Most of the time he let Jost think she was running the show. Looking out across the darkening plain though, he knew he had to win over unwilling hearts once again. He drew a deep breath and turned slowly to face them.

'I could appeal to your goodness, charity, and better nature,' he said. 'And I know you have those still, despite the dry grind our lives have become. But let me put it to you a different way.

'We've lived here four years. We scrape and water the ground. We grow beans, eat beans, return beans to the soil, grow more beans. This is our life. We haven't the strength to do more. We've seen the skeer nest. We've learned from our visitors that there's nothing better for us within a five-day march, and perhaps not beyond that either. If someone were going to open a magic door for us to escape through they would surely have done it by now.'

Arpix looked at his companions' downcast faces. Even Salamonda's habitual good humour had evaporated. They came to him for encouragement. To hear him call their one-tenth-full cup a good start. And here he was rubbing the varnish off the truth.

'If there is any hope to be had, any hope at all, how do you think it will reach us? Because I tell you it won't blow in on the wind or fall from the sky. It's going to be carried here by a stranger. Maybe not one of the ones running in our direction tonight, needing our help. But *maybe*. And if not with them, maybe with the next. All I can tell you is that if hope is to come our way it will be in a stranger's hands, and if we turn our backs on them, we will never know what we missed.'

Jella set the bowl on the blocks of a wall that the diggers had missed and the wind had found. 'I'll light it when they've had time to get a bit closer, so we know they'll see it.'

Meelan found his voice. 'Arpix is right, of course.' He leaned in close and muttered in a low voice. 'You're always right, dammit. Sorry.'

Arpix clapped a hand to his friend's shoulder. 'I'm often wrong, and you know it.'

They stood side by side, looking out into the dark, ignoring Jost's continuing objections. Meelan and Jost had lost the most when the library had burned and they'd been exiled to the wild. Meelan, his family's vast wealth and considerable influence; Jost her authority and the role she'd played for a lifetime. She'd been a librarian ten times longer than Arpix, who had only recently qualified when disaster struck. But where Jost seemed undone by the fire, clinging

to the remnants of her old station, Meelan had found the loss of
his money and responsibility as his family's heir to be a new kind
of freedom, though the options for exercising that freedom were
now very limited. He missed his family. Sometimes he called his
sister's name in the night. But the privilege and wealth had slipped
from his broad shoulders very easily.

Attamast rose first, from behind them, near full and casting its
faintly green light across the plain. Chenga, smaller and only half
full, crested the shoulder of a mountain an hour later, throwing its
whiter light in opposition to Attamast's. The dust cloud revealed
itself once more, much closer, illuminated by the two moons,
throwing one shadow towards them and a second back the way the
strangers had come. Jella lit the fire bowl and the light of twin
moons soon gilded its plume of smoke too while the orange glow
from within shone out through the earthenware's perforations.

'Damn, they're fast,' Meelan said.

'They're going to need to be.' Behind them, back where the roots
of the mountain range sank beneath the plain, a wall of dust glowed
in the moonlight. Scores in pursuit. Hundreds maybe. Nobody was
faster than a skeer runner. Maybe on a horse a man would be faster,
but even then Arpix had been told that a skeer runner could wear
a horse down. Their endurance was a thing of legend. Or so Arpix
had been told. Back in his old life nobody except a few academics
had even heard of the skeer until rumours had started to circulate
that they had been behind the canith migration, the thing from
which the canith had run and that had resulted in their armies
piling up against the walls of Crath.

The strangers got to within a mile of the plateau's edge before
Jella spotted the first flier. 'They're never going to make it.' She
pointed.

Within a short while they could make out five fliers in tight
formation, closing rapidly on their prey. Skeer fliers were less robust
than skeer runners, who in turn were less robust than skeer soldiers,
but even so Arpix had little doubt that a single one of the creatures
could slaughter him and all his companions without effort. They
were fast, armoured, all spikes and cutting edges, bigger than a man,
and of course they could descend upon you at great speed from any

angle. Meelan said they looked like winged spiders made of bone. It wasn't accurate but it did them some justice.

'They might make it . . .' Arpix had climbed the slopes from the plain to the plateau on two occasions and it had been a real struggle. The gap between the strangers' dust vanishing from view and their tiny figures reappearing as they crested the top of the tumbled cliffs was remarkably short. So short, in fact, that Arpix lost all confidence that the strangers were human.

'Canith?' Meelan muttered.

If it wasn't too late to douse the fire bowl Arpix might have done so. A cold hand closed around his heart as he realized that Jost might have been right all along. He could have invited their deaths among them. But, instead of taking action, he stood rooted to the spot watching the chase unfold.

The fliers were close too. Close enough to see the hanging clusters of their legs rather than just the flashing of their wings catching the light.

'Canith!' Jella's exclamation started as a yelp before she brought it under control. Years in the Dust had replaced her girth with a grim kind of fortitude.

There were three of them, running hard. Arpix would be stumbling after two hundred yards if he tried to run that fast, but this trio had been at it for ten miles and more. The one at the rear seemed to be hurting and the other two were holding back, not ready to abandon him.

'Come on!' Meelan shouted. 'Run!'

But with little more than a hundred yards to go before the canith reached the humans, the skeer dived upon them.

The smallest of the canith seemed to sense the attack and turned, drawing a sword that stole the colours of the moonlight and burned with it. The other two stopped running, one brandishing a weapon too small to see, the other picking up a rock.

'A rock?' Arpix snorted. He hadn't intended to speak but the contest seemed so unequal.

What followed happened too quickly for Arpix to follow the detail. It seemed that the first flier to attack the sword-wielder fell apart into pieces, as if it had hit a pane of very thick glass hard enough to shatter itself. The other two canith dived and rolled and twisted and ran. The sword-wielder appeared to slice entirely through the thickness of a flier's body, and a heartbeat later to swing up through the lattice of skeer legs seeking to skewer her and momentarily ride the largest of the fliers before decapitating it.

In the space of thirty heartbeats the fliers were reduced to a heap of twitching limbs and scintillating wings. The larger two canith took the lead, the shorter of these two supporting the tallest who appeared to have been injured. The sword-wielder followed, facing back the way they'd come, challenging the night.

'Damn . . .' Meelan shook his head in disbelief.

The friend of a friend can be the most complicated of beasts. Best approached with caution, and a net. Still less dangerous than a friend in need, however.

Navigating Social Seas, *by Captain Elias Root*

CHAPTER 12

Evar

The pursuit hadn't started immediately and for some miles Evar had thought that maybe the skeer alarm cry had been some general warning broadcast at the mountains. The direction they chose to head in was chosen mostly by the slopes. The valley aimed them at a dusty plain. Clovis refined the choice, aiming them at what looked to be a distant plateau. Always take the high ground, or at least, when you surrender the mountains, pick a hill.

They jogged down the last rocky inclines, dodging the occasional hardy bush, and followed Clovis onto the plain. At first the ground was a mixture of hard-packed, dry earth, grit, sharp stones, and serrated ridges of bedrock slicing up through everything else. After some miles it settled to a surface of baked mud riven by deep cracks and covered with half an inch of fine dust that recorded their trail in a drifting cloud at their heels.

When Evar first spotted the skeer tumbling from the mouths of half a dozen narrow gorges high on the southern slopes, he and his siblings had a lead of perhaps three miles.

'How many?' Kerrol asked, still having difficulty spotting the foe.

'Lots.' Evar couldn't make out individuals. He'd seen them only because the fact of their numbers made a white carpet, catching the last embers of sunset.

They began to run then. Evar was thankful that the terrain was at least level and even. On the mountain their unfamiliarity with slopes and rocks would have given a huge advantage to the skeer. Even so, before the darkness swallowed the dust wall raised behind their enemies, Evar was able to gain a sense of their swiftness, and the lead that had seemed substantial had already halved.

They ran on in the dark, the chase somehow more worrying now that they couldn't see the gap closing. Evar imagined the white horde suddenly clattering out of the blackness to engulf them with only a moment's warning.

The first of the moons rose to find Kerrol struggling with the pace. Evar and Clovis habitually ran the eight-mile circumference of the chamber. Kerrol disdained physical activity in the main and now had only his natural aptitude and long legs to rely on. Evar slowed to run beside his brother, trying to somehow pull him along by force of will.

Another dusty mile passed beneath their feet.

Clovis ran close to Evar. 'There's a light.'

Evar saw it, twinkling on the heights of the plateau. Without discussion, they both altered course. The light belonged either to someone strong or someone stupid. The skeer were going to catch them by daybreak and they wouldn't defeat them alone.

The light vanished as they approached the base of the slope to the plateau, hidden behind a series of tumbling cliffs. Evar led the way. He wasn't much of a climber, but he'd trained with Starval. Clovis helped him haul their exhausted brother up the steepest parts.

'Leave me,' Kerrol gasped.

'If you wanted us to leave you, you'd say something that made it happen.' Evar heaved him over a rough stone ledge with a grunt of effort, and Kerrol let himself be dragged, panting, up the slope.

The fire that had drawn them came back into view as Evar gained the plateau. Now less striking, bathed in the light of two moons, it was small and smoky. A handful of figures could be seen gathered around it, but it was still too far off to tell much else about them other than they weren't skeer.

'Nearly there! Come on!' Evar waited for the others then began to run.

He had to hope that there were more of the strangers ahead than just those glimpsed around their signal. A lot more. If not, then the skeer would roll over them in moments.

'Watch the skies!' A shout from Clovis.

Evar skidded to a halt and turned in time to see strangely skinny skeer plummeting towards them from the moonlit sky, iridescent wings trailing behind them, offering little resistance to their dive. White-armoured like those Evar had fought in the library, these creatures were clearly cousins to the ground-based skeer, but all legs and blades rather than bulk and strength.

At the last moment the skeer opened their wings to avoid smashing into the ground. The next moment was an explosion of action on all sides. Evar pushed Kerrol clear of a stabbing limb longer than a spear before being wholly occupied with dodging a forest of jabbing appendages. He lashed out with his knife but never had time to tell if he did any damage.

The frantic dodging and weaving continued. Kerrol cried out, pinned to the ground through one shoulder. Evar rolled, sliced, jumped to his feet and launched himself to deflect the killing blow. He ended up sprawled beside his brother, expecting to be slashed open. Instead, a spray of warm ichor splattered across his face and chest and the skeer's twitching body collapsed on him.

'We have to move.' Clovis grabbed his hand, yanking him to his feet. 'The runners are nearly here.'

Evar bent and pulled Kerrol's good arm over his shoulder. 'Coming.' He lifted Kerrol, straining to support him while he tried to hold his own weight.

Clovis muttered an oath and together they half walked, half carried their brother towards the signal fire.

The fire turned out to be smoking embers in a crude bowl balanced on a ruined wall. The figures were human. They weren't even armed.

Evar abandoned Kerrol to Clovis, mainly to encumber her, and strode towards the humans, arms raised in question. 'What the hell are you doing?' He snarled at them to set them going. 'Run!'

Amazingly, although they flinched like prey, they didn't flee before him. 'Run!' He clapped his hands.

'What's this?' Clovis asked in disgust. She had let Kerrol slide to the ground and had come to join Evar, sword drawn. The horde of skeer who had probably reached the base of the plateau by now were the biggest threat, but Clovis would leave the humans just as dead if they gave her any excuse.

'Leave them be,' Evar said. 'We need to keep going. Maybe they'll slow the skeer down, or fill their bellies, or something . . .'

Clovis shook her mane. 'We wouldn't get far even without Kerrol. And with him . . .' She shrugged and advanced on the humans. Some of them retreated but not far. They arrayed themselves behind the tallest of their number, a skinny male who barely reached Clovis's shoulder.

Livira might be dead, or she might be a million miles and a million years away, but either way Evar felt in that moment that she was standing before him, staring up at him with eyes that neither implored nor judged but very much wanted him to do better. 'Don't kill them, Clo.'

'I'm not leaving until I understand why they're still here and why they set that light.' She leaned in towards the leader and sniffed. 'Besides, I know this one.'

'You do not!'

'Yes, I do. I never forget an enemy. This one's the friend of your sabber. Probably her old mate.'

'He's not!' But as Evar came closer he could see that she was right. The human had hair on its face now, a dark bush of it around the mouth and chin, but it was the same male that had tended the wound Clovis had given Livira. 'Arpix,' Evar gasped, amazed. 'The lost friend!'

'I hate to break up the reunion.' Kerrol limped up beside Clovis, clutching his wounded shoulder. There was a lot of blood. 'But we have more company.'

Evar spun back towards the mountains and sure enough a dozen skeer had climbed into view, with many more clambering up behind them. These ones were somewhere between the fliers and the warriors in build. Long-legged, not as heavy as the warriors, not as fragile as the winged ones. He glanced back at Arpix. 'Why aren't you running?'

'Would there be any point?' Kerrol asked. 'By the looks of them I could probably outdistance the lot of them even now.'

Clovis readied her sword, glancing between the humans and the skeer. 'They're more scared of me than of the bugs. That doesn't make sense.'

The skeer, perhaps numbering forty or fifty now, came forward with more caution than three canith and ten humans warranted. Moreover, their advance slowed. Still almost a hundred yards off, they stopped and spread out in a straightish line, prowling, long limbs trembling, probing the ground with their white spikes.

'They can't, or won't, advance,' Kerrol said. 'Something's stopping them. I don't think they're happy about it. As far as skeer can be happy or sad about anything. Their emotions are said to manifest at a more collective level. I read once—'

'I don't care.' Clovis pushed past him, scowling at the insectoids. 'They can't come in. There's an invisible wall. That's why this Arpix and his pack are still here.'

Clovis shot out a hand and took Arpix by the neck, lifting him to his toes. 'What's going on here? I want whatever's doing this!'

'Clovis! Stop! It's why they lit their fire,' Evar shouted. He rounded on her, reaching for the human. 'They brought us here to save us.'

Clovis swung Arpix out of Evar's reach, setting her back to her brother. 'Whatever it is they've got, it's a weapon and I want it.'

'Madam,' Arpix choked out past her grip. 'Unhand me!'

And Clovis, probably shocked at being addressed in a passable version of her own language, released him.

'You can understand us?' Evar hadn't expected that. He hadn't thought many humans knew their tongue, but Arpix seemed to speak it better than Livira had.

Clovis shook off her own surprise. 'Good. Now I know that, I also know I can torture you until you tell me where the weapon is.'

'Ah.' Arpix released a long sigh. 'The dubious benefits of educating oneself.'

Often it is more important that someone leads than that they are a good leader or possess even a basic sense of direction.

The Immoral Compass, *by Marquee D. Sad*

CHAPTER 13

Livira

'You left without me!' Livira aimed her accusation at Malar's back. The soldier stood with one hand on the trunk of the nearest tree and the other on his sword hilt, staring down the row of portals.

'I did.' Malar didn't look her way. 'I was sick of being a ghost. At least now I can touch something.' He shrugged. 'Anyway, it was time to act. Too much talking just tangles everything up.'

'It's very dangerous if we don't go through the portals together. Holding on to each other. We could both end up here but in different times. Or be ghosts, but just to each other, or something . . . Anyway: don't do it.'

'I thought I saw something.' Malar didn't sound apologetic.

'An Escape?' Livira spun around. The Escapes scared her, even with Malar and his sword close at hand. They felt both horribly alien but at the same time tied to the library in some intimate manner. Her school master, Heeth Logaris, used to say that she was 60 per cent water by mass, 40 per cent minerals, and 100 per cent questions. But when it came to the Escapes her desire to avoid them trumped her desire for answers. 'What did it look like?'

'A woman.' Malar frowned. 'In a blue dress. I only caught a glimpse. Vanished way down there.'

Livira bit her lip, considering a host of possibilities. Gradually the living silence of the forest and the slow warmth of sunlight filtering down through the branches eroded her worries to the point at which her natural confidence could reassert itself. 'We should go find the book like the assistant said.'

'And be ghosts again.' Malar slapped the tree hard enough to leave the pattern of its bark across his palm.

'If we believe that assistant, we're going to be ghosts everywhere but here, forever, unless I bring this book back.' She understood his reluctance. She found it hard too, but Malar had defined himself, or been defined, by his physical talents, none of which he could exercise if he passed through everything, and everything passed through him.

Malar grunted. 'Which one? Which portal do we take?'

Livira took a few steps back, considering the problem. 'This one.'

Malar, still sulky, rolled his eyes, and then scowled as if angry at himself. 'We just fucking came out of this one.'

'This is a timeline.' Livira spread her arms, her pointing fingers sweeping across the portals that stepped away left and right to unknown distances. 'But it's discrete – each door is a step – back or forward in time. I'm not sure how much, maybe a decade, probably several. The point is that Evar found the book less than a year before the time we just left him at, the time when that assistant towed us away from him like we were naughty children.

'If we take the next portal that way' – she nodded to the right – 'well, we'll end up a decade or more too early. He'll be a little boy without the book, or won't even be there yet.'

Malar knuckled his forehead. 'If we go back . . . won't we just *go back*? We'll probably find that git of an assistant still waiting there.'

Livira held her hand out to him. 'I think I can find a way to the when and the where we want to go to.' When Malar hesitated, furrowing his brow, Livira stared at him and then looked pointedly at her outstretched palm.

'Fuck my life.' A growl. Malar folded his large, callused hand around her smaller, narrower one, and followed her back into the sparkling light.

Livira knew the place she wanted to go. She could picture it. The time, she had less of a feeling for, but the portals had brought her to the Exchange at just the right moment on basically every use. She felt that this was an integral part of their design and hoped that by simply opening herself up to the process, and wanting what she wanted, the library's magic – or technology as Arpix had dully insisted – would do its job.

The dazzle of the light faded to the image of hands in earth. Her hands. Her hands pulling her forward through green things growing. It reminded her for a moment of the bean rows at the settlement, in the first weeks when they were watered five times a day and the dust hadn't yet layered their leaves. A vivid, vulnerable green that it had always seemed cruel to coax out into her harsh world.

She stood up to find herself beside Evar's pool with Malar getting to his feet beside her. The three canith she'd left behind so recently were all in front of her, wholly ignorant of her presence.

Evar and Clovis were approaching from the book stacks. Livira had to admit that Clovis was a magnificent creature, with her flame-red mane and dark eyes flashing, the points of her canines aiming for her chin. Livira still bore the scar where Clovis had clawed her – a reminder, if she ever needed one, of just how terrifying it had been to have the warrior giving chase at her heels. Clovis seemed a far better match for Evar. Livira thought she herself must seem very frail to Evar in comparison. She'd been worrying about other things too, physical things, and seeing the pair of canith striding towards her suddenly brought those issues into sharp focus. After meeting Yute's cat, Wentworth, Livira had done some research on the animals. She'd read some very uncomfortable things about their mating habits. Things involving spines and tearing. Sometimes Livira wished her memory was less steel trap and more sieve.

The assistant in which Malar had been trapped – the Soldier – was walking through the greenery, careful to trample nothing, patrolling for rats perhaps, or weeds. He glanced Livira's way, registering her but saying nothing. Malar, drawn to his old prison and his old self, advanced on the Soldier, slowly, head tilted, studying him intensely. Livira left him to it and returned her attention to the approaching siblings.

The tall canith, Kerrol, rose from where he'd been sitting and put down a large scroll he'd been studying. 'What's the excitement?'

Clovis exchanged a glance with Evar before responding, 'There's no hiding anything from our brother, always so perceptive!'

Evar offered an uneasy grin and said nothing.

'The plan worked. I killed the Escape.' Clovis looked as if she'd enjoyed it.

'And the other thing?' Kerrol asked.

Evar answered this time. 'We found the tallest tower ever. A giant! I knocked it down with my face.'

'Remarkable.' Kerrol frowned. 'What's the book about?'

Livira hadn't seen the book until Kerrol mentioned it. But there, clutched tight at Evar's side, was her book, the book she'd made from repurposed covers and stolen flyleaves. The volume was a cuckoo that could sit within the library without being ejected by assistants as unchosen – the whole thing was merely books that were already chosen, but now redistributed and with added notes.

Livira wondered whether it had been her who had hidden it in the book tower. Her fabled memory didn't reach far into the period she'd spent trapped in that timeless space within the assistant's body. She hadn't been entirely imprisoned though – some aspects of her had leaked to the surface. Had she also completed her book? Written the final chapter with a white hand? Had she found some set of narrative and thematic threads to bind the disparate stories into some cohesive whole?

She advanced on Evar, the crop not so much as rustling as she passed through it.

Evar turned away from his brother without answering his question and walked off towards the Soldier who had found Malar in his path and stopped.

'Did you find it in this tower of yours?' Kerrol called after him, still talking about the book.

Livira took her chance, hurrying to walk alongside Evar. She glanced up at him, wondering what he would think now, knowing she was with him back before he had ever met her. The thought made her dizzy, turning wheels within wheels as she considered how many ghosts might have watched her through her life, might even be watching her now, and how all those moments were threaded through time.

The assistant was right – too much of this would cause problems – reality had indeed begun to feel very delicate. She reached for the book, hoping that bringing it forward, out of the loop that wrapped it around two centuries, might be as simple a matter as just taking hold of it. Her fingers brushed the cover and she felt a buzz in her fingertips, as if they might actually be able to touch something in this place. Hope swelled. She tried to take a grip of the book and, much like turning a page, she was gone.

A high-ceilinged drawing room painted itself into being around Livira. A room large enough to contain all the trainees' sleeping chambers but decorated with the detailed intricacy that a master craftsman might spend on a jewellery box. A table stretched nearly the length of the chamber, covered with white lace, painted porcelain, crystal goblets and flutes, with scrolled silver tureens and wide silver platters whose edges frilled and cavorted in the ecstasies of design. In the gaps, candlelight reflected from the depths of the darkest and most polished mahogany.

Ornamentation reached the rafters, or would have if they could be seen behind a flat plaster sky whose whiteness had been moulded into an upside-down landscape of raised patterns, a deep relief whose architecture radiated outwards from a central boss in ever more extravagantly complex circles. Livira's experience of interiors ranged from the mud-walled huts of her infancy to the rectilinear utilitarianism of the librarians' complex. None of the great and good had ever invited her into their homes. The closest she'd got to genteel living was the comfortable chaos of Yute's five-storey home. But she had, once, been beneath the roof of the king's lesser palace and this dining hall that she had written herself into must be, she surmised, based on that experience and on her imagination of what such places looked like – augmented by her own voracious reading.

The other diners, who had up to this point been blurs upon the scrolling excess of their high-backed chairs, began to solidify into real people who could have been plucked from the glittering crowd that had stood at the steps before the fifth door of the Allocation

Hall on the day Livira had so rudely pushed in among the darling children of Crath City's aristocracy. That act had been impulsive rather than considered. She'd had no specific goal in mind, simply the desire – or perhaps it had been closer to a need – to rebel against the judgements that had been placed upon her merely because of her appearance.

Ten years later, many of those same people had sat beneath the king's roof and watched as Yute presented Livira before the throne to mark her elevation to librarian. Now they sat at her right and at her left, reaching for dessert wine in sparkling crystal flutes.

With a shock Livira recognized Lord Algar, one seat down from the head of the table, a most honoured guest. He still wore his customary crimson eyepatch, but his diplomat's robes had been replaced with a dark velvet dinner jacket whose cuffs and lapels were edged with piping the colour of dried blood.

'Gods of death. I'm so bored.'

The mutter came from the seat beside hers and Livira glanced round to discover Meelan lowering an empty glass.

'Meelan!' For a moment all Livira could think about was the small group of her friends huddled at the centre circle as flames and smoke surrounded them. That frantic ever-changing mix of fear and bravery, hope, resignation, worry for each other, disbelief. At the time she had been armoured in the numbness of the assistant that had almost sealed her in, all her focus upon drawing that last circle to save them. The memory hadn't had the opportunity to resurface since, but it did now, a leviathan cruising from the darkness that lies beneath imagination towards a distant glimmering light, bursting through the mountainous tide of its own arrival, making every other wave no more than a ripple. 'Meelan!' A shout, a sob, a desperate gasp as she threw her arms around him and squeezed with a passion that was two hundred years in the making.

Genteel conversation stopped, sliced through and unsustainable in the face of such drama. Livira felt Meelan struggle for a moment, then stop, and finally return her squeeze in an embrace that while a pale shadow of her own was at least not a rejection.

'Sister?' Meelan extracted himself with gentle strength. 'Are you unwell?' Compassion softened his habitual growl.

'Sister?' And for a moment Livira was distracted by the discovery that she wore a gown that would put any of Carlotte's to shame, a confection of ivory silks, lace, silver wire and river pearls. 'Sister?' The hair that hung around her face in coils was the deep auburn of season's change, rather than her own black shock, which stood rather than hung. She grabbed a handful and pulled, wincing at the immediate pain in her scalp.

'Madam! Calm yourself!' An older man of considerable girth sat on the opposite side of the table, his own grey hair poked beneath the grey coils of his wig.

Livira set her hands to the polished wood of the table to steady herself. *Her hands?* Serra Leetar's hands. In this tale she'd taken Leetar's role, sister to Meelan Hosten. The chatter re-established itself like a fire returning to an insufficiently doused blaze, a wisp of smoke here, a glow there, a chuckle of flame igniting some far corner, kindling others to life. *The library is always burning.* Had Yute said that? It felt like a metaphor for . . . everything, really.

She'd fallen into a story that she didn't remember writing. How much of it was invention, how much based on her own truth, and how much might have flowed from the timeless knowing of the assistant, Livira couldn't say. But she felt the tale seeping into her, regardless of whether it was fact or fiction, filling her with understanding.

Livira looked up. The man opposite, the fat, greying man who'd called her madam, was Dantal Creyan, and it was to him that her father would marry her off in order to cement his long-sought alliances. Unless she took the only position offered to her following her showing at the Allocation Hall. She had wanted a position at the university and, having met Lord Algar and seen how his singular eye studied her with unhealthy appetite, she would even accept a place within the laboratory before taking up a commission among the diplomats. But no such offers had been forthcoming, and Leetar strongly suspected the long reach of Lord Algar had closed those doors to her.

Everyone had the right to be allocated even without the blessing of their family, but in this instance her father would accept the alternative to Dantal Creyan without raising a storm. Lord Algar lacked the man's wealth, and indeed had a fortune that paled in comparison to her own father's, but Algar's was old money. Lord Algar's aristocratic roots reached back at least as far as the king's and quite possibly further – though no one would ever say that out loud. If he put his long reach into her father's service, as he seemed to have intimated that he was willing to, that would compensate the loss of a marriage alliance.

Livira shot a scowl at Meelan and stood sharply from her chair. 'How could you have let them do this to your sister?'

Meelan, looking confused and worried, was saved from having to reply by a muffled commotion out in a nearby hallway that ended suddenly with the leftmost door bursting open. The newcomer, who strode in with a slight sway to his walk, as if on the deck of some modestly sized boat, was another grey-wigged man somewhat past his prime, red-faced and moustached. He seemed to be a guest, likely the owner of the empty place at the elbow of Leetar's prospective husband. The cut of his dinner jacket and the large gold-rayed medal pinned to his breast marked him out as a military man.

'What the fuck is going on?'

However many social niceties Leetar, under Livira's control, had trampled upon with her own outburst, the sudden appearance of a grey-whiskered general, apparently the worse for wear, was more worthy of attention.

Heflin Hosten stood up at the head of the table, shot a narrow glance in his daughter's direction then approached the general with outstretched arms. 'General Charant! Allow me—'

'You!' The general, who Livira suddenly understood to be the man who had organized the city's defences against the canith invasion, pointed at Leetar's father with outstretched arm and accusing finger.

'My dear Rodcar.' Heflin continued his approach, seemingly blind to the other man's anger. 'Let me show you this new weed I've got in from Tronath. Your pipe's going to thank you!' He reached a calming hand towards the general's shoulder.

For an older man the general's speed proved remarkable. Livira barely followed the fluid motion with which he seized the ornate hilt of the sword at his side and swung it with sufficient force to embed the blade in Heflin's neck.

Both of them looked surprised, but only one of them spoke. The general frowned in disgust and uttered a single word. 'Blunt!' He yanked the sword clear in a shower of crimson.

It was as if the blood had got into Livira's eyes. She screwed them up, and when she rubbed them clear found herself still standing but once more in a library chamber just on the edge of the crop circle. Malar stood facing her, looking as amazed as she felt. Evar was striding away from them, aimed at the Soldier out amongst the greenery.

'Blunt . . .' Malar muttered, and looked at his hands.

'You were there?' Livira looked at him sharply. 'In the dining hall?'

'That was real?' Malar's eyes widened still further, reminding her of the library guards and their owl-helms.

'Wait!' Livira tilted her head. 'That was you? You were the general? How did you even get into my story?'

His eyes narrowed. 'What? I'm not good enough to write about now?'

'That particular story. Killing people.'

Malar scowled. 'I glanced over just as you vanished. It looked like you touched the book and . . . bang . . . you were gone. Only without the bang. So, I came over and touched it too. I'm supposed to be guarding you, after all.'

Livira wasn't sure who had given him that job, but she let it slide. 'We were both in the story.'

'Not that I'm agreeing that makes even a jot of sense, but how are you supposed to grab the book and bring it back with us if you vanish inside it the moment you touch it?'

Livira thought about that for a moment. 'You know,' she said, 'I don't have the slightest idea.'

One of the worst things about humans is everything.
But I'll tell you what's ten times worse than a
human . . . two humans. And what's ten times worse
than two humans? You've guessed it: one child.

A Complete History of Humanity, *by Hubert Duck*

CHAPTER 14

Celcha

'Yute said you shouldn't talk to the ghosts,' Celcha said. 'I don't think he knew you already were. He said it like it was the worst thing you could do.'

'He's clearly not very imaginative then.' Hellet closed the door to their quarters behind them and began to tuck into the food on the tray he'd been carrying. He'd piled it with black bread and carrots. Celcha liked the bread, but carrots were a marvel and she'd eat nothing else if it didn't leave the tables bare.

The trainees had all made directly for the food hall on their return from the expedition to the first ganar chamber. Librarians Markeet and Sternus, however, had managed to delay satisfying their hunger a while longer, preferring instead to present themselves before the head librarian to devour her praise. Nobody expected a great work to be recovered on a training exercise, particularly from a location as close as the first ganar chamber, but the book – whose title Celcha had yet to learn – appeared to be the find of the week, if not the month or even the year.

'He thinks we're a problem.' Celcha hadn't liked being called a crack, or a rock in the stream. She'd been called far worse things, of course, but these things were said without malice by someone who had at his fingertips a repository of knowledge vaster than anyone who had not seen it could imagine. 'He said we're dangerous.'

'We are dangerous,' Hellet replied without concern.

'I don't think . . .' Celcha hesitated. It felt as if Hellet had spent more time speaking with his ghosts over the last few years than with her. As if she were the stranger, the outsider. 'I'm not sure you should talk to Maybe and the other one any more.'

Hellet peered at her through his fur in a way that strengthened the feeling she might no longer be his closest confidante, though she knew with certainty that she was the one who loved him most – the only one – and that whatever these ghosts wanted it wasn't all for Hellet. Perhaps none of it was.

Hellet chewed and swallowed. 'Didn't they bring us here?' he asked. 'Out from beneath Myles Carstar's heel? We're well fed, better treated. I know I prefer reading books and wandering shelves to hacking tunnels out with a pick, in the dark.' The air around him gleamed and glittered, stirred by turbulent phantoms.

'They did.' Celcha couldn't deny any of it. The good fortune that had befallen them was beyond her dreams and it hadn't truly fallen. It had been pushed.

Hellet shrugged. 'All right, I'll stop talking to them.' He bit off half a carrot and set the rest down. He wiped his hand and reached into his book satchel, pulling out the black book he'd retrieved from the ganar city within the library.

Celcha sat back, chewing on a heel of bread. She'd got what she wanted, but it had come too easily. All of this had come too easily, and she mistrusted every part of it. Hellet, however, she trusted. She had to. He'd never lied to her that she knew of. And if she didn't believe in him then what was there left for her to believe in? This was Hellet. All that remained of her mother and father. The same boy who had gone trembling to the whipping post and howled as the steel cane divided his flesh. Blows that had been meant for her.

So she said nothing and instead sat and watched as Hellet leafed through the black pages of his black book, frowning at the narrow silver script. The air continued to glimmer around him. Starve seemed particularly interested in the book, bending over or even through Hellet's shoulder to peer at a page from time to time.

'I don't think you should listen to them either,' Celcha said at last. 'That's probably as dangerous as talking.'

Hellet lifted his gaze from the pages before him. 'It's hard not to listen.'

'You could send them away.'

'Wouldn't that be talking to them?'

'Yes,' Celcha growled, 'but for a good reason.'

'My other reasons aren't good?' Before she could answer he carried on. 'I can send them away, but you can't?'

'I can't hear them, so maybe they can't hear me . . .' Celcha was unsure now.

'Oh, they can hear you.' Hellet showed his tombstone teeth. 'Starve likes you. Says you're well meaning.'

Celcha wasn't sure whether that was an insult in disguise and whether the fact Hellet proclaimed Starve's approval of her meant that Maybe had made no such statements, or even actively spoke against her. Suddenly the ghosts' presence, their secret conversations with her brother, felt so intolerable that she started the sentence that had so often waited on her tongue – the one that she had never spoken for fear of being unable to finish it.

'Send them away, Hellet. Either they go or . . .' And the words dried up in her mouth. It was both a hollow threat – she could never abandon him – and a foolish one, inviting him to choose against her. Such capital could not be spent without wounding all those party to the transaction. And still, she couldn't explain why it was so important to her, why she would set so much store by the words of an assistant who had done nothing for them but call them broken. Starve and Maybe had changed their lives for the better, shown them a new world and new opportunities. Yute offered only a dangerous cure for a condition that, for all they knew, he might be inventing. A cure or eternity serving the library in a white suit. All she knew was that it felt wrong. In the same way that she had known about the three collapses that might have buried her in the Arthran dig, she knew that something was wrong here too. Some instinct too deep to name or scrutinize had warned her of those cave-ins just in time, and that same feeling niggled at her now in a place where the ceiling was hand-cut bedrock that would never fall. 'Hellet . . .'

'All right, sister. All right.' He said it without heat and, rising from his chair, he pointed towards the doorway. 'Thank you, my friends. I will guide myself from here on.'

Hellet and Celcha had named them angels, Yute had called them ghosts, but whatever they were they seemed to know better than to outstay their welcome. A trail of glimmers flowed towards the doorway and vanished through the stout timbers.

Hellet proved as good as his word, and the ghosts upheld their side of things with the integrity of angels. All that day the air around Celcha and her brother remained free of any artifact of the light. The angels went unseen for a week. And another.

'Lutna's asked me to go with her into the city,' Celcha said as she settled into her bed.

'Good.'

Celcha closed her eyes. She wasn't sure if Hellet had been first to talk about wanting to see around the city or if it had been her. Probably it was Hellet. Both of them were plagued by curiosity but, although she had been the one to open the book that had got him caned, Hellet was less able to resist its call than she was. Even with an ocean of information and endless seas of stories at their doorstep, still the city, crammed with real life rather than the record of it trapped in ink, called to them.

Celcha would have asked for Hellet to come too, but Lutna had always seemed scared of her brother. All of the trainees seemed a little apprehensive of him, even those who were larger and stronger, as if the hairless tapestry of his scars told a story that unsettled them.

On the following morning, one of the trainees' rest days, Lutna and Celcha set off along the steep road leading from the wolf's head gate down to the city. The previous ganar had spent their whole tenure within the library and the librarians' complex, but Librarian Markeet was still basking in the glow of returning a book long alluded to in other important texts yet never found. In such a buoyant state of mind he signed off the permission for Celcha to visit the city in Lutna's care without protest. He did, however, assign a canith named Jhar to guard Lutna because of her royal connections.

The unspoken message was that Jhar would also ensure Celcha's prompt return.

Lutna led the way, chatting animatedly. Celcha had little experience on which to base a judgement, but it seemed to her that despite the girl's proximity to the queen, and the possibility that she might officially be allowed to demand that people refer to her as Princess Lutna, she was in most ways wholly unremarkable. She had gained the impression that Lutna was not thought of as pretty, clever, or entertaining among her fellow trainees. She was, however, kind, in an awkward, sometimes clumsy, sort of way. And Celcha, having lived among slaves beneath the threat of cruelties of many flavours, felt this to be an important attribute.

As they came down between the first houses that clung perilously to the cliffs, Celcha began to notice the looks that were thrown her way. The closer she came to walking abreast with Lutna, the more glances she got, the more raised eyebrows, the more sneers and muttering. The citizenry appeared much more relaxed when she followed a few paces behind the girl, though in her library blacks nobody would think Lutna a princess deserving of such obeisance.

For her part, Lutna kept urging Celcha to walk beside her, and chattered happily about various parts of the city as they came into view. Telling her what that spire was, which was the temple with the copper-green dome, whose grand house was being constructed so embarrassingly close to the outer wall. Lutna always had lots to say, though, unlike many of the trainees, little of it was about herself. She seemed to acknowledge herself as both surplus to requirement in the aristocracy and at the same time unlikely to measure up to the exacting intellectual demands of the library.

One topic that she had steered clear of, ever since her attempt to address Celcha in a ganar language that was not her own, was that of the ganar. Now, as they came down towards the grand square they'd seen from above, Lutna turned in the street and took hold of Celcha's left wrist – she had stopped taking Celcha's hands once she realized that the gnarled ridge along the back of each was the scar of an earlier mutilation where her claw-blades had been cut out as a child, and she had stopped taking the right wrist when her hand had closed around the iron of the manacle set there.

'Celcha. Will you come and see H'run and F'nort with me? I wouldn't ask but they were both so good to me when I was a child . . .'

Celcha resisted pointing out that Lutna was still a child, and that any ganar at the palace would be a slave who would suffer terrible punishments if they were anything other than nice to a princess.

Lutna, seeing her hesitation, pressed on. 'Honestly, they were more of a mother and father to me than my own parents were.' Her grip on Celcha's wrist grew tight and the pale green of her eyes glistened as if tears might be welling there. 'I just want them to see you. To see how well you've done and how clever you are. So they know there's more out there than what they've been born to. They're so . . . I don't know . . . accepting. I think it would make them glad to know that we're— that we work together at the library.'

Celcha tightened her jaw against a hot reply. She reminded herself that Lutna was still a child. That she didn't know what failing to accept their lot would mean for this H'run and this F'nort. In the end, she shrugged off her anger. It wasn't directed at this child who was merely trying to aim her kindness at a target too big for her to comprehend, something she was part of and that had grown about her so intimately she could hardly know where it ended and she began.

'I'll come.'

And so, with Jhar looming at their heels, the warrior so tall that neither of their heads reached above his hip, they came to the doors of the palace. Although, compared to the complex within the ganar chamber, the whole city was a small thing and the palace itself a drop in the ocean, it was an impressive structure. Being able to see it all at once from across the grand plaza, and then coming into its shadow, climbing its many steps and being swallowed between pillars so wide that it would take three Jhars to link hands around any one of them, made the building seem truly vast in a way that the ganar warrens had not.

Palace guards intercepted them at the doors, their initial respect almost certainly for the library guard rather than for the infant and the slave at his feet. In due course a functionary was summoned and came hurrying across the marbled doorstep to welcome the princess and her attendant.

With Jhar left in the shadows outside and a new escort in his place, Lutna led Celcha on a hurried tour through the areas of the palace not restricted to just the most senior royals. The interiors rapidly overwhelmed Celcha with their luxury in rather the same way that the library had overwhelmed her with its books. On its own any one of the marvels might have captured her attention for hours. Nothing so beautiful and delicate as that small sculpture she just passed had ever entered her world in the Arthran dig, or in the library, but the next plinth held another, different and just as wondrous – an elegant and vibrantly painted vase – and so on to the next until they became mere increments marked on the yardstick of this seemingly endless corridor.

Lutna led her through rooms carpeted with rugs of such softness and thickness yet intricately woven design that it seemed a crime to step upon them. They should hang on the walls, except that the walls were hung with paintings in which Lutna's ancestors were presented five yards high with such skill that they each seemed as if they might step through the doorway before them. They almost looked *more* real than real people.

Eventually Lutna had the guard – herself decorated like a work of art, every piece of armour and uniform worked to delight the eye – open a side door that gave on to bare stone steps leading down.

'What's this?' A cold drawl of a voice, arched with its own superiority. 'Lutna's got herself a new pet?'

Celcha turned from the doorway to see two human boys standing side by side, both somewhat older than Lutna and both considerably bigger. In fact, it seemed that anything that could be said about one could be said about the other. Many humans appeared quite similar to Celcha but these two were identical. Doubles from the same litter. One held the lead of a short-haired dog, too small to be a hunter.

'What's this one called, Lutna?' The boy without the dog strode up and grabbed a handful of Celcha's neck fur. A palace guard stood behind him, and the richness of the boy's garb, both in fabric and in colour and in ornament from buttons to buckles, left no doubt that he and his brother weren't strangers to being beneath the queen's roof.

'These are my cousins.' Lutna studied the floor. 'Acran and Bastan.'

'Prince Acran!' Acran announced with some measure of outrage. He twisted his hand in Celcha's fur and attempted to throw her to the ground. Celcha felt it sensible to let him and fell as far from the dog as she could. Even so, the beast flinched and barked.

'Your pet should say hello to our pet,' Bastan said, letting the lead slip.

Celcha narrowed her eyes at the dog and instead of advancing it retreated with a yelp and its tail tucked between its legs.

'Damn you, Mutters!' Bastan aimed a kick at it and the dog scampered back, barely avoiding the blow.

'She's not my pet.' Lutna kept her eyes on the ground.

'Not yours?' Acran's grin, which had been ugly to start with, turned uglier. 'Then she's mine. Can't have a slave without an owner running around Grandma's palace!' He stared down at Celcha out of deep-set little eyes that were as hard and bright as buttons. 'Come here.'

Celcha knew she should be scared. Scared was good. It kept you alive. Instead, a hot anger bubbled up through her. She made to stand, trying to keep the snarl from her mouth.

A foot in a slipper sewn with silver descended on her shoulder, keeping her on hands and knees. 'Come here like the animal you are, new pet.'

Celcha had suffered far worse humiliation before, but somehow it had been easier to take back at the dig. The fact that her guards shared some of the hardship of life on the plateau in no way excused them, but even so, the rage that trembled through her had to owe something to the luxury on every side and the fact that it was a child doing this. She pressed the anger into the cold ball of hate that sat deep in her chest, that had sat there year after year. The ganar were not warriors. They waited their moment.

On hands and knees, she crawled towards the young prince, wondering how long it would take this bored child to grow bored with torturing her.

Lutna, bound by very different chains to the ones that held Celcha captive, suddenly broke free of her paralysis with an anguished shriek. 'Stop it! Stop it! Stop it!' She flew at Acran, hands clawed. He shoved her back hard enough to slam her into the wall save for the quick reflexes of her guard.

'Acran, Bastan!' A tall dark figure down the corridor. 'Do stop that.' The individual, an exceptionally tall and very thin male human, wore a deep purple tunic with just the occasional silver button. A functionary of some sort, Celcha judged.

'Why should we?' Acran turned with a pout on his reddening face. 'It's just a ganar.'

'It is,' said the man, staring disapprovingly from beneath thin eyebrows. 'But it's one of the library's ganar, and the head librarian is very protective of her staff. So, unless you'd like a visit from your great-aunt, I would suggest finding another game to play, Prince Acran.'

Acran scowled, eyes glittering with the kind of hate that's hard to understand in one with a life so filled by privilege and plenty. He stepped forward and delivered a vicious kick to Celcha's ribs before striding down the hall, followed by his laughing brother.

Celcha got to her feet, hugging her side, and went quickly through the open door, into the bare stairwell that smelled faintly of stale bodies.

'Celcha,' Lutna called after her miserably.

'Come on.' Celcha went down the steps, leading though she didn't know the way. All she knew was that she'd seen enough of the queen's wealth and was more interested in what lay beneath it all.

*Kings in their castles, peasants bent within hovels, each
given cloth to fit the measure of their purse. But to exist
within a space is not to inhabit it. The king may rattle
through his halls, present only where and when he steps.
The serf might fill the day from dawn till dusk, from
horizon to horizon, from muddy toes to spangled sky.*

The Prince and the Purpose, *by L. J. Gray*

CHAPTER 15

Celcha

The many storeys and rooms of the royal palace that lay above
ground were supported and maintained upon a subterranean network
which might boast an even greater number of chambers, though
none of them as large or ornate as the meanest privy above. In these
rooms the servants laboured, most of them human, a few canith
working the heavier machinery like the iron mangles in the laundry
or hauling half a cow carcass from the cold room to the kitchens.

The lowest level housed the ganar, the slaves who served the
servants, carrying out the dirtiest and most dangerous jobs. Ganar
were sent to replace tiles on the highest tower roof, to unblock the
sewers, to tend the palace gas junction from where the multitude
of crystal lamps and open fires drew their breath. And some few
attended the royal children.

'It's mostly because of the queen's father. Back when he was king,
he had ganar attend his daughters. And when a king does something,
all the aristocracy do it too.' Lutna looked apologetic. 'It's because
of your fur. The little ones like to hug you. They say you're like little
bears, only you don't bite.' She bit her lip. 'Sorry.' She looked as if

she was perhaps regretting bringing Celcha here. As if her own memories of hugging her ganar nursemaids were turning sour even as she looked at Celcha's narrowed eyes and at the scars beneath her fur catching the lamplight where they reached around her shoulders.

Reflex and a measure of her own kindness had Celcha opening her mouth to tell Lutna that it wasn't her fault. But she clamped her lips closed against the words. A fault like this didn't have neat boundaries. You couldn't draw a line and say that those standing on this side were blameless and those on the other guilty. It was like the Dust. You might walk until you thought you'd left it far behind you, you might cross the badlands, climb the mountains, put it beyond your sight, build a new house and sleep easy. Only to wake and find that on neglected shelves the dust still gathered, and to know that however far you walked you would never be truly clean.

The ganar slept in small, unlit cells around a large square room where they socialized in the brief time between labours ceasing and sleep claiming them. Given that the ganar sleep cycle had been set by the rotation of another world, and that they were required to work at all hours, the central room always hosted some fraction of the population just in from their shifts. Lutna had timed the visit so that the pair she held in so much affection were sitting with three others at the table where a single lamp burned. All of them were slightly smaller than Celcha, their fur darker and a little longer.

'Princess!' A male with greying fur stood from his chair and opened his arms.

'F'nort!' Lutna threw herself into his embrace.

An elderly female, presumably H'run, stood with an exclamation that sounded like something in the language Lutna had learned from them.

Celcha waited in the doorway, the palace guard behind her, the woman's plume brushing the ceiling of the corridor and already thick with gathered cobwebs.

'I've brought someone to see you.' Lutna broke from F'nort's arms and looked towards Celcha.

With a measure of reluctance, Celcha stepped into the room, feeling like an animal on display.

H'run crossed the room towards her, bobbing her head in a curious way. Celcha could see that her blade claws had been trimmed rather than burned out, abraded to just a hard line across the back of her hands, parallel to her fingers.

'Hello.' H'run bobbed her head again. 'What clan are you, dearie?'

'I . . . I don't know.' Celcha knew the names of a few clans, but they had never been important at the dig.

'It's not important, I suppose.' H'run tutted. 'You look Rayan to me.'

'Maybe I am.' Celcha attempted to sound agreeable, not wanting to offend the old woman.

H'run patted Celcha's shoulder. 'Rayans aren't so bad. Too clever. Always getting themselves into trouble. But good-hearted.'

Celcha wasn't sure what to say to that. 'I'm pleased to hear it?'

H'run nodded. 'Come. Sit.' She turned and headed back towards the table. Lutna was already sitting beside F'nort, showing him a book she'd pulled from her satchel. Celcha's heart missed a beat just as it still did every time she looked up to see Hellet with a book in his lap. Cruelty's reach was as long as that of blame. She wouldn't ever forget how Hellet came to be broken.

She took one of the empty chairs and sat while Lutna regaled the ganar with tales of the library. She included Celcha in the stories and spent most of the time talking about the ganar chamber. Her audience nodded approvingly and asked questions – some even directed at Celcha, which she answered using as few words as politeness required.

Lutna seemed pleased with the whole business and got F'nort to speak some of the tongue that most of the palace ganar shared. The words meant nothing to Celcha, but she preferred the way it sounded in her ears to the harsh piping of humans or the slightly terrifying growls of the canith when speaking their main language.

At last, as it became obvious that the elderly ganar could keep away from their beds no longer, Celcha asked the question that Hellet had wanted her to put to them.

'Do you know anyone who works in the city gas room?'

Celcha wasn't sure what kind of answer she was expecting, but the knowing grins around the table weren't it.

'I didn't know they knew about that in the library.' F'nort showed his teeth. 'Never saw the other two down there.'

'I . . .' Celcha didn't know how to reply. Of course the librarians knew there was a central supply for the gas that lit the city's lamps, cooked their food, and warmed their homes.

H'run patted her shoulder again. 'Don't worry, dearie, everyone gets homesick even when they've never been there.'

'We go in the back,' F'nort said, yawning hugely. 'Green door. Ask for H'seen, she'll sort you out. Probably have to come back in a month, though. Always a queue.'

Lutna finally took the hint and stood up to go, releasing the ganar to their beds. Regular sleep was the only mercy Myles Carstar had granted the slaves at the dig, and that only because if you kept a ganar up too long past their bedtime you generally ended up with a dead ganar. The only reason that keeping them awake wasn't one of the official cruelties was that it was too hard to judge the line between discomfort and death.

Lutna led the way back through the palace. By the time they reached the shade of the pillared entrance and found Jhar waiting, Celcha still hadn't worked out a way to get the princess to take her to the gas room.

Hellet's request had come just as she was leaving the library. She was to ask the question if she met any ganar. There hadn't been time to quiz him about it, but Celcha's brother wasn't given to idle talk. Clearly it was important to him, so Celcha wanted to return with more than just a name. However, an industrial building where they piped flammable gas didn't seem like the place for even a distant heir to the throne to tour, and even if it was, Celcha didn't have a good reason for visiting or any idea why the other ganar had acted as they had.

'We should go to the gas room,' Lutna said as Jhar joined them.

'That doesn't sound very suitable, Princess Lutna,' Jhar growled.

Lutna craned her neck to look up at the canith. 'What did you just call me?'

'Princess Lutna.'

Lutna narrowed her eyes. 'And who gets to say no to princesses, library guard?'

Jhar growled in his throat.

'That's what I thought,' Lutna said. 'Now take us to the gas room, because I don't know where it is.'

Jhar's growl descended to his chest. He turned and led off down the steps. Lutna sagged with relief and shot an astonished glance at Celcha, as if to say: *Did that really happen?* She fell in alongside Celcha and said in a slightly apologetic tone, 'It just felt like you wanted to go there, and I feel so ashamed of my awful cousins . . .'

Celcha followed Jhar and Lutna through the streets. After all she'd seen since her walk up through the city on her way to the library many weeks earlier, she was able to take in more of it, appreciating more of the interactions carried out all around her. Even so, it still proved overwhelming and somewhat bewildering, and she was very glad to have a guide.

The gas room turned out to be on the far side of the city, down-wind of the prevailing gusts that rattled down the mountain valley, but far enough from the walls that an enemy couldn't easily attack the structure in the hope of creating an explosion. Jhar, appearing to have overcome any resentment at being told what to do by a princess, informed them that the gas wasn't particularly explosive in any case, though a naked flame in a closed room would be a bad mistake were there a leak.

The building had been constructed on the lines of a small fort, boasting thick walls and defensive positions on the roof. Apart from the crenellations on high, and its vault-like front door, the place was as brutally utilitarian as the buildings at Arthran. A host of pipes, each thick enough for Celcha's whole body to be needed to stopper it, emerged from one wall, brandished a valve wheel at the world, then plunged below ground.

A faint but tantalizing smell haunted the air around the gas fort – as Celcha now thought of it. She saw Jhar wrinkle his nose at it. Lutna didn't seem to notice it at all.

'Around the back, they said,' Lutna muttered. 'A green door?'

Jhar led the way. The three of them got stared at by every passer-by, all dressed in working clothes and seemingly bound on their own errands. The looks were mostly of surprise, some tempered with suspicion. Oddly, Celcha drew hardly any attention.

The green door was a small square of verdigrised copper to the left of another trio of enormous pipes emerging from the rear of the building.

'Go on.' Lutna nodded at the door. 'Who was it you had to ask for? H'sun? Make sure you tell me everything when you come back!'

'H'seen,' Celcha murmured. The scent of the gas was stronger here and tickled in her chest. She knocked on the metal plate. Three short knocks.

Nothing happened and continued to happen for long enough that Lutna began to say something, only to be cut off by the plate lurching forward half an inch then being hefted to the side. A black-furred ganar stuck its head out and stared aghast at Jhar.

'It's all right!' Lutna stepped forward spreading her hands. 'We're with her. We're not going to tell anyone.'

Celcha was too busy marvelling at the ganar's fur. She'd never seen black fur before. She'd seen it dark with dirt, but this was something different, fascinating her eyes. Embarrassingly, she found she was panting, hauling in one deep lungful after another, the scent of the air seemed to be doubling the size of her chest. 'H'seen,' she managed. 'Ask for' – another breath – 'H'seen.'

'No H'seen here.' The ganar started to wrestle the plate back into place.

'We're not going to tell anyone . . .' Lutna said, adopting the same tone that had brought Jhar into line. '. . . unless you don't take my friend Celcha where she wants to go. Otherwise, I'm going to tell everyone exactly what you're doing. And if you don't like that you can take it up with Library Guard Jhar Haccta here.' She raised and lowered her hand in the canith's direction as if the nearly three yards of his height might have escaped the ganar's notice.

Without waiting for an answer, Lutna bundled Celcha inside before retreating with a series of coughs. The doorway was so low that even Celcha had to duck. She straightened up to find the black-furred ganar blocking her path.

'Sorry about her . . .' Celcha dipped her shoulder in apology.

The ganar exposed his lower teeth in threat.

'I can go.' Celcha took a step back. 'F'nort sent me. He thought it would be all right.' She drew a deep breath. 'Why is the air so good here?'

The ganar shook his head as if wondering at her ignorance. 'I'm Redmak. Follow me. Don't touch anything.' With that he turned away and headed off into the growing darkness.

They passed through thirty yards of tunnel, turning left then right before emerging into a room lit only by tiny round windows in a high ceiling, each of the windows seemingly a tube cut up through yards of stone. 'No lamps in the gas house,' Redmak grunted. 'No flame. No sparks.'

The chamber housed several copper cylinders, like vast seedpods, all connected with pipes and punctuated with dials. Every pipe seemed to sport a handwheel so that its valve could be opened or closed. Another larger but similar chamber lay beyond the first one, filled with gloom and pipes in equal measure. Two ganar moved around checking dials; one of them paused to adjust a valve.

'I feel great,' Celcha muttered to nobody in particular. She felt wide awake, brimming with energy.

Redmak cracked a smile for the first time. As they walked, he began to point things out, parts of the gas system, each with its own function. He led her down a spiral stair fashioned entirely from wrought iron. The chamber below was lit only by what light filtered down from the already dim chamber above through glass-filled ports in the floor. Celcha waited at the foot of the stairs, breathing deeply, letting her eyes adjust. Her night vision had been trained in shades of grey over the course of thousands of days spent in the tunnels of the Arthran dig. It had, however, never been anything like as acute as it was now. Within a handful of heartbeats Celcha could see almost as clearly as if they were still outside. A score of ganar crowded the chamber around a single central steel hub, a great, dial-studded valve from which a single vast pipe led upwards through the ceiling.

Redmak explained that there were cylinders in which the gas was captured, compressed, compressed again, and held. Ganar worked great valves to bring one cylinder online when another became exhausted.

Although some of the ganar were inspecting the dials, and others operating lesser valves on the host of pipes snaking up the walls, it seemed that the bulk of them were simply socializing, talking in small groups. A distant bell sounded and a powerfully built ganar pushed a lever as tall as he was as they passed. Beneath their feet the faint hissing swelled to the roar of a thousand snakes.

'Cylinder change, on the hour, every third hour,' Redmak said. 'At least in high season. That's as fast as the cylinders recharge. The masters grumble and groan of course, and fight for the supply, but the ground gives us what the ground gives us, and if they keep breeding their children will have to find another way to light up the night.' He tapped a large pipe as he passed. 'This bounty won't last forever.'

Redmak led Celcha through the throng and presented her to the first fat ganar Celcha had ever seen. 'This one's Celcha. Came with a human child in library blacks, and a canith guard in the livery of the athenaeum.'

'H'seen.' H'seen was nearly as tall as Hellet. All of the workers were – some of them even taller and wider. She glanced at Redmak. 'This one doesn't know what's hit her. Look at her eyes.'

'It's the air,' Celcha murmured. 'The air's different.'

'It's closer to what we breathe at home, child.' H'seen put her arm around Celcha's shoulders, pressing the curve of her belly against Celcha's side, and steered her slowly around, letting her take in the scene. 'The gas they burn in their houses comes up from the decay of older cities beneath our feet. They call it methalayne. It gathers in voids, and we suck it up, compress it, push it through into the present city so our masters can see where they're going at night, cook their food, warm their rooms.

'There are always leaks, and humans don't like methalayne in their lungs. It's not a poison to them but it makes them cough and it takes the place of the air they need instead. They get weak, might even pass out. Canith are even worse with it. We ganar, however . . . Well, you've felt it yourself. We thrive. Because on Attamast methalayne's in the air everywhere. We need it. Without it we're half asleep.

'So, rather than constantly fight to keep this place gas-free, they have us work here instead. And because they can't come in without suits and breathing tubes, we have the place largely to ourselves. As long as the methalayne keeps flowing they leave us alone. Getting a job here is the highest reward. You might think you have it good in the library, or that the palace ganar live well on the scraps from the high table. But nobody here would swap. Once you've filled your lungs properly it's not something you're going to give up if you don't have to.'

The huge ganar stopped steering Celcha and stepped back to study her more closely. 'They've used you hard, Celcha. You're nothing but muscle and scars. Not long in the library then. Why are you here?'

'To breathe.' Celcha drew in another lungful, wondering if she could bear to walk away from this place or if they'd have to carry her out and bolt the doors on her.

Redmak shook his head. 'She didn't know about the air.'

'My brother sent me,' Celcha said. 'He wants to change the world.'

One fine day Truth met with Lies upon a mountainside with all of Hantalon spread beneath them: field, and town, and city stretching to the sparkle of the sea. With a disapproving frown, Truth asked of Lies how many she had slain. And true to her nature she answered with a lie. 'More than you, brother.'

The Basics of Deductive Logic, *by I. P. Franchise*

CHAPTER 16

Arpix

Arpix coughed several times, rubbing at his throat where the red-maned canith had previously grabbed him. He wanted to spit but it was a nasty habit that he discouraged in others and he managed not to.

'You threatened torture,' Arpix growled – you had to growl to speak canith. 'The irony . . .' Arpix had learned the language from a canith wanderer who had stayed at the camp for most of the second year. The canith's vocabulary in human tongues wasn't extensive and Arpix wasn't convinced he was particularly articulate in his own language either, so working out less common and more abstract words like 'ironic' had been a difficult task and even now Arpix wasn't sure he had the right term. 'The irony is that speaking your tongue is torture on my throat at the best of times, and after being half throttled . . .' He coughed again and this time couldn't avoid spitting.

'I'm sorry,' Evar said from behind them. 'My sister—'

'I can speak for myself,' Clovis snarled.

They were all walking towards the camp now, losing sight of the skeer runners behind the low stone wall and gentle undulation of the plateau. The camp sat at the centre of the invisible bubble that kept the insectoids from approaching. The protected area was a little over a quarter of a mile across, large enough for the crops that sustained them and to walk a dusty mile around their domain without coming too close to the edge for comfort.

'You're bleeding!' Arpix said it in his birth tongue then gathered himself to growl it through an increasingly sore throat. 'You're bleeding.' A bright notch had been scored over one of the metal plates sewn onto the leathers across Clovis's side and it continued past the edge, slicing into and through the tough hide. A couple of feet below the cut, blood was dripping slowly from the lower skirts of her armour.

'That's my business,' Clovis snarled. 'Where's this device?'

Arpix led them through the bean fields where he had spent so many months pulling strands of questing livira from the ground. The weed was as irrepressible as its namesake. He took them past the well that had been ropeless when they found it and had taunted them with the scent of unobtainable water. He lifted a heavy bucket from beside the guard wall they'd built around the hole. It was more of a goat-skin pouch than a bucket, and a third of the water had leaked out. Still, thirst doesn't critique. Clovis had the skin out of his hands in a flash. She didn't, however, thrust her face into it, instead taking it to her injured brother, Kerrol, who took a long slow drink.

As the canith passed the bucket around, Arpix took a moment to study them. Arpix had been tall from an early age and had continued to grow, upwards rather than outwards, after his classmates had stopped. He stood a good six feet five, like a weed hunting the light, Meelan said. Clovis, shorter than her brothers, overtopped him by more than a hand, and every inch of her lean, athletic form was packed with the kind of muscle that doesn't show itself until its owner demonstrates some remarkable feat of strength. She had a fierce vitality about her, an energy that unnerved him but which at the same time he found himself unable to look away from.

'What?' Clovis caught him staring and snarled a challenge.

'My apologies, madam,' Arpix growled through his sore throat. 'We get so few visitors.'

Clovis tossed aside the bucket and leaned over to stare down the well. She made a sharp yipping sound, trying to gauge the depth.

'It's nearly two hundred yards to the water,' Arpix said. 'Through the thickness of the plateau and into the aquifer below the plain.' "Aquifer" was another word he'd had to tease from their visitor at great length and, judging by the look Kerrol and Evar had just exchanged, he might have been taught something not only wrong but inappropriate. Flustered, he tried to rephrase. 'The buried lake.'

Clovis snorted. 'Ignore them. They're idiots.' She wiped her mouth and looked around at the small group with him. 'This is all of you?'

Arpix nodded. He led them on, over a low rise and down into the depression where they had made camp in the reconstructed shell of a building whose masonry had lain half covered by the dust. The canith wouldn't be looking at that, of course: they would be staring at the head, neck, and shoulder of the great queen, all slightly tilted such that it gave the impression the huge statue might be about to plunge back beneath the surface.

The stone head was a good ten feet tall when measured from the bottom of the slightly pointed chin to the top of the over-wide forehead.

'Look on my works, ye mighty, and despair,' Evar growled.

'What?' Arpix was often far from sure he wasn't putting his own interpretation on random snarling.

'A poem from antiquity,' Evar said. 'There was a city here once, I think.'

'Yes. There are old tunnels riddling the plateau. Most of them collapsed. If not for the things we found down there we would have died shortly after arriving.'

'Where's the weapon?' Clovis proved herself to be single-minded.

'I don't know.' Arpix raised a hand to forestall any more threats. 'It's somewhere below us, I assume. Buried with the city it protected. It might be as small as a pebble or larger than a city square. I have no idea. We discovered its existence in the same sort of way that you did – standing inside the zone, looking out at angry skeer, and thanking whatever gods were watching over us.' He turned away from Clovis to address Evar, who was larger yet somehow less intimidating than his sister. 'How did you get here? Do you know what happened to Livira and the others?'

Arpix had no experience of reading emotion on the face of canith but he felt sure that Evar's sudden stillness and the way he looked down at his hands, bringing them together to wrestle slowly with each other, was not a good sign. A coldness gripped him. 'Evar?'

The others had caught Livira's name. Meelan, who had been sitting on a nearby rock, stood up quickly and stared as if trying to squeeze the meaning out of their conversation. Salamonda's hand found Jella's and together they came to stand beside Arpix.

Evar met Arpix's gaze reluctantly. 'I met Livira in the Exchange. Her friend, Malar, was injured and we came through my portal, to my time . . . now . . . to heal him—'

'She's here?' A flicker of hope. Arpix couldn't help but look around, knowing himself to be a fool even as he did so.

'We went back to look for you. She insisted. We were all ghosts – you understand? We could see but not touch. She and Malar got bound up inside assistants.'

'Inside?' Arpix tried to imagine it.

'Inside.' A growl and a nod. 'I understood then that they had been trapped in the assistants that raised all of us.' He waved an arm at his siblings, both of whom rumbled in their throats. A noise that sounded like mourning. 'I came back to the now. But I was too slow. Both assistants had been destroyed.'

A short keening noise that was almost a howl escaped Clovis. 'The Soldier died hard. Many fell before him.'

'Destroyed?' Arpix understood the word; he just hadn't thought it was possible. 'An assistant?'

'By skeer warriors. Lots of them.'

'So where are Livira and Malar?' Arpix needed Livira to be somewhere. She couldn't have come to her end like that. Not broken by skeer. His voice had softened past the point at which he could get the raw edges of the canith words through his sore throat. But Evar seemed to understand anyway.

'I don't know.'

Meelan grabbed Arpix's arm. 'What's he saying? It's bad, isn't it?

I don't believe him.' Anger tried to hide another emotion and his voice shook with denial.

'How long ago?' Arpix asked Evar.

'Days. Days . . . I tried to save her. I ran . . . I was too slow.' And Evar, showing more and sharper teeth than Arpix had imagined he possessed, slowly tore his hand across his chest, leaving three deep, bleeding furrows.

Arpix turned away from the canith warrior, having no answer for Evar's pain or his own. 'Assistants,' he managed, reaching for Meelan's shoulder. 'Livira and the soldier, their spirits got trapped inside assistants . . .'

'No!' Meelan shook his head slowly, studying the ground. He looked up sharply, eyes bright. 'That was her? The assistants that saved us from the fire? That was her and Malar?'

Salamonda and Jella, understanding the emotions but not both sides of the conversation, closed in without questions, and for a long moment they stood, bound in a circle of each other's arms, voiceless in their grief.

For the next two days, Evar watched over Kerrol and treated his wounded shoulder with help from Salamonda. Clovis proved less nurturing than her brother and instead insisted that she be shown the abandoned workings cut into the plateau.

Arpix had explained that when they had first arrived they had survived only because of the limited equipment they were able to scavenge from the tunnels. Their first saviour had been rope. Not from some inhabitant of the buried city – rope would never survive that long, even in a desert – but from some more recent habitation, when perhaps some other travellers had discovered that skeer left the area alone and had stayed for a while. The rope enabled them to reach the well's water. Lengths of timber and a rusting hoe head had been other important finds.

What had really kept them from death that first winter, though, had been what they'd come to call 'Salamonda's little helper'. Nobody ever saw their hidden benefactor but the carcasses of rats, rabbits, even wild boar, and once a deer started to be discovered around the dig site, and it seemed that almost always Salamonda was the one to find them. To deepen what was already a deep mystery, it was very hard to believe that any boar or – even less likely – any deer dwelt within several days' march of their position. Yet the blood on the bodies was still fairly fresh, and some were even warm. The animals appeared to have met their death by way of a broken neck with some degree of laceration to the flesh around their throats or napes.

Arpix took advantage of his time alone with Clovis to practise his canith. The canith had many languages of course, but the one Clovis and her kin spoke was common on the western side of the continent.

Clovis proved taciturn to start with, offering a snarl or a snort by way of answer as often as a word or two. But her hostility did seem to mellow, a fact that Arpix attributed less to his charming personality and more to her discovery that the first human she'd seen, Livira – whom she had immediately tried to kill – had actually been present almost her whole life as part of the assistant who had raised her.

Clovis's exploration was aimed at uncovering the source of the city's protection, with the unspoken promise that she would steal it from them. In addition, the survey served to educate her regarding the terrain on which she might have to fight, a basic component on any military checklist. Unfortunately for her, because they had such limited reserves of fuel, all of it rather smoky, the survey had to be conducted mainly in the dark.

In the parts of the complex where some whisper of daylight reached in through fissures or reflection, it turned out that human night vision was better than that of the canith. Which left Clovis having to hold on to Arpix's arm, her head bent to his shoulder since most of the tunnels required even him to bend double.

Out of the wind and in such close quarters, Arpix became familiar with the scent of unwashed canith. It was a strong smell close up, but not, Arpix decided, particularly unpleasant. A musty scent that made him tingle.

He was under no illusions that standing in the rain, on the handful of occasions each year that there was rain, had left him in any way close to sweet-smelling, and he found himself hoping that his unwashed stench wasn't too foul in the famously sensitive nostrils of the canith. Clovis in particular, since she only had to dip her head a few inches more to bite him.

When Arpix and the others had first explored the passages, Meelan had joked that the digging seemed to have been done by dwarfs. Arpix found the place oppressive. The darkness always seemed to hide an enduring sadness, and despite the fact that he had never counted himself the sort to attribute emotions to places or things, Arpix was unable to shake the feeling.

'This is the end.' Arpix patted his hands across the rough wall in front of him. 'I think there's one more side tunnel back on the left. It leads to an intact chamber of the old city but anything it held was scavenged long ago, and the exits are blocked.'

'Take me there,' Clovis growled.

'Your mother never told you you get more flies with honey?'

'I don't want flies,' Clovis said.

'Oh, it's not about wanting—'

'And I don't remember much about my mother except that humans slaughtered her.' Clovis's growl grew softer but somehow more dangerous in the dark. The fine hairs covering her cheek tickled briefly against Arpix's ear.

'My mother and father, my grandparents, aunts, uncles and cousins were almost certainly killed when the canith invaded and the library burned.' Arpix had never truly taken their deaths onboard. He had left his family home to come to the library, and although he could walk there from the library door in half an hour, he had felt as apart from them as if he inhabited some distant island, isolated by overwork and by experiences they couldn't share. Even so, he had spent a slightly awkward evening with his parents once a month, all of them revisiting the same old topics for lack of overlap in their current lives. 'I haven't mourned them.' He admitted this for the first time to the darkness and a stranger who had nearly strangled him. 'I don't know how to.'

'You should cry their loss to the moons and vow revenge,' Clovis answered.

'Revenge on whom?'

Clovis made no answer.

'On the next canith I see?' Arpix asked. 'On the ones I see running from the skeer? Should I have doused the light and left you to it?'

'You should still howl for them, loud enough for the moons to hear.'

Arpix felt that perhaps he should, but could only offer, 'It's not our way.' He meant it wasn't *his* way. Salamonda had wailed for her lost ones, no room for shame in her grief. Arpix felt somehow lessened by the fact that his own mourning had been unable to step over such social constraints even in this forsaken wilderness. Instead, it ached inside him, along with the regret that he'd never been able to tell his quiet and reserved mother or his quiet and reserved father that their quiet and reserved son had loved them very much in his own strange way.

Clovis sniffed the air, or perhaps his neck, close enough to make Arpix shiver. 'You should howl for them.' Some gentleness in her tone made him imagine she might have intuited the depth of his emotion by scent alone.

She moved away.

'You're going?'

'I know the path back.'

'I'll come with you,' Arpix said.

'You should stay.' Clovis's growl became more distant. 'To not speak to the moons is to poison yourself from within. You should stay.'

'I . . .'

Almost beyond hearing she spoke again. 'Thank you for the light.'

. . . four grains of arsenic, two of alum, and three peppercorns.
Grind and mix with water gathered in an old shoe. The
resultant paste should be applied to the affected area.
For grief the only true cure is patience.
For patience there is no cure.

Assured Remedies, by *Tabetha Hawthorn*

CHAPTER 17

Evar

When not tending to Kerrol, who proved to be a very needy patient, Evar patrolled the perimeter, or at least where he judged it to be. He wasn't able to speak to the humans, though he did want to learn their language, and he didn't enjoy the way his presence seemed to unsettle them no matter how non-threatening he tried to be.

On perhaps his seventh circuit of the day, Evar heard what sounded like rockfall, the source of the noise hidden by the plateau's edge. He'd heard the odd stone rattle down from time to time, eased out of broken cliffs by the wind's persistence. But this sounded like something more substantial.

First, Evar made a thorough study of the skies. Clovis was still below ground with Arpix but he didn't need her present to hear her lecture him in his mind about the dangers from above. When he was convinced there were no fliers ready to swoop, Evar advanced quietly towards the meandering line where the flat ground fell away.

Poised to dash back towards the sanctuary, Evar peered over. The cliffs, formerly shaded in browns and rust, were clothed in white. More than a hundred skeer warriors were labouring to roll half a dozen or more big whitish-grey balls up the slopes and making hard work of it. They must have advanced to the plateau's base under cover of night.

A runner, secreted near the top, lunged at Evar and he fell back with a bark of surprise. His scrabbling feet found purchase before the monster dragged itself over the brink on long, sharp legs. Evar shot back to safer ground and turned just in time to see the runner bounce off the invisible wall and collapse into its own dust cloud in an untidy mess.

'Skeer! Skeer!' Evar sprinted back to the others.

'They can't get in, surely?' Kerrol, lying flat on his back, levered himself up to his elbows.

'Well, since they know that better than we do, let's assume they didn't come so far in such numbers just so we can laugh at them. They're bringing something with them.' Evar grabbed hold of one of the confused human males and pointed him at the plateau's edge. 'Skeer.' He said it in their tongue.

'Get Clovis!' Kerrol said, but Evar was already on his way to the tunnels.

Clovis answered his shouts almost immediately, emerging from the darkness covered in dust.

'Skeer! Over a hundred warriors, and they've brought something with them.'

'Show me.' Clovis hurried past him.

'Arpix?' For a moment Evar worried that Clovis had left him dead in the tunnels.

'He won't make a difference,' Clovis said. 'Let him howl.'

Evar followed her with a frown. 'Howl?'

But any answer was lost when the dozen or so skeer that had reached the top began to manoeuvre the first of the large spheres up onto level ground. The thing looked rather like a wind-weed ball but with far fewer gaps. It was woven from some sort of vitreous exudate of similar consistency to the skeer's own armour plates.

The ball jerked from side to side and it soon became apparent that it was less the weight of it that required so many skeer to propel it, and more the violent motion of whatever was trapped inside.

An awful scream rent the day, an inhuman cry, shuddering with rage. It seemed that whatever was in the ball had been unconscious for some while and was now waking. Another, weaker, scream rang out from somewhere down the cliffs. If these unknown captives had been awake the whole time then a stealthy approach would have been impossible.

Evar and the others watched as scores of skeer warriors slowly dragged seven of the spheres onto the plateau, lining them up close to the barrier that defied them.

Arpix, breathless and red-faced, came running up from the tunnels as the last sphere was rolled forward. All the humans were talking at once. Arpix pushed through them to stand between Clovis and Evar. 'Those are the screams of cratalacs. Very dangerous creatures, I've heard, though I've never seen one. They hunt only at night.'

'I think you're about to see seven of them.' Evar could see motion in all the spheres now, and the first to arrive was starting to crack in several places as the prisoner raged inside. All the skeer were drawing back, dozens already gone from sight as they retreated down the cliffs.

'The skeer must know your wall won't stop them.' Clovis turned to look at Arpix. 'We have brought a war to your doorstep.' She drew her sword, the blade brilliant in the sunlight. 'This is my fight, not yours.'

Arpix reached for her, showing a familiarity that astonished Evar. 'Livira always said you can't win a fight with a cratalac. We should retreat to the tunnels.'

Clovis shook him off without reprimand. 'Here I get to face one while the rest are trapped. It may still be sedated.'

'It doesn't sound sedated.' Kerrol was on his feet, rolling his shoulder and wincing.

'At least wait to see if it *can* get through the wall,' Arpix growled.

Grudgingly, Clovis halted before the line traced out with widely spaced marker stones. She stretched her neck from side to side with audible popping sounds. A claw like a black scythe broke from the first sphere, showering the ground with pieces of the container. A horrified shriek and several gasps went up from the humans. Arpix shouted orders at them.

The sphere fell apart, leaving the cratalac standing amid the remnants of its shell, shaking loose pieces off its carapace.

'Now that's ugly,' Clovis muttered.

The cratalac shared more in common with the skeer than with humans or canith, but where the skeer were white this thing was black shot through with a grey so close to that of the dust it seemed almost invisible in these places, as if it were a collection of black fragments in motion. Moreover, where the skeer had clean lines and simplicity, this beast was a nightmare of hooks and bristling hair and clawed limbs and jaws framing dripping mouthparts. It loosed another spine-shaking scream as two more of the spheres started to break.

Rather than focus its attention on the skeer who had captured it and rolled it unknown miles to a strange location, the cratalac aimed its fury at Clovis and those behind her. Those behind her currently being Evar and Arpix, as the others were retreating towards the tunnels, taking Kerrol with them.

Evar thought Arpix should go with them. In fact, looking at the cratalac, he was pretty sure he should go too. Not only was the thing larger than a skeer, it also evoked some primal horror in him that the skeer did not. It put him more in mind of a spider: its too-many legs and the alien way in which it moved them made his skin crawl. It reminded him strongly of several Escapes he'd encountered before but was somehow more loathsome in a deep, visceral way that sidestepped his intellect.

Clovis didn't share Evar's hesitation. As the cratalac scuttled forward, passing through the city's protection without hesitation, she charged to meet it. The creature moved with unnerving speed. Clovis threw herself into its clutches in a way that, whilst it must be calculated to increase her chances, was something Evar knew he would never be able to do. He would have danced at the margins of its reach, seeking to wear the thing down.

The savagery of what followed was unexpected even after seeing the thing fight its way out of the sphere. Clovis's white sword flashed; she turned and twisted amid a forest of limbs; black body parts flew in various directions, trailing arcs of ichor.

Evar found himself advancing despite his fear, but the suddenness of the instant in which Clovis was caught shocked him into a stumble. The cratalac raised her from the ground, pinned by the two curving horns of its jaws. Dripping mouthparts punched out and fastened on her chest, eliciting a cry of pain. Evar sprang forward, slashing with his knife at the nearest of the insectoid's limbs. For a few frantic moments the cratalac shook Clovis like a dog with a rabbit, the horror of it cut short by a flash of white that left her sailing through the air with ragdoll limbs. Half her armour stayed behind, hanging from the creature's remaining jaw-horn, the iron plates torn away or twisted.

'Clo!' Evar shot back, trying to reach her without exposing his spine to the enemy. The cratalac didn't give chase, but instead, thrashing and hissing, it stomped a half-circle with foreshortened limbs. Two of the other spheres were now in pieces, their occupants screaming at the sky, and the last four were breaking. 'Clovis!' Evar scooped up her sword before reaching her.

'Uh . . .' Clovis struggled to her knees. An ugly wound ran from her shoulder across her chest, blood pulsing bright crimson from torn flesh.

'C'mon!' Evar hauled her up, even as she reclaimed her blade, half carrying her towards the tunnels. In moments the cratalacs would shake off the last of their cages and sedation. In fact, the tattoo of footfalls behind them suggested at least one had already fixed its multiple eyes on their retreating forms.

Among all this, Evar realized with shock that he'd just passed Arpix, the frail human standing his ground though he seemed more bookish than even Kerrol and wasn't carrying so much as a sharpened stick to defend himself with. Evar slowed, his stride shortened both by the realization they weren't going to outrun the cratalac that had given chase, and by the thought of what Livira would say if he abandoned her friend.

He tugged Clovis's sword from her hand and turned with her. She would want to face her death head on, the same way she'd faced her life. Arpix stood a few yards closer to the advancing cratalac, one of the fresh ones, his arm raised to throw a rock at it. Evar roared at him to get back, but the human ignored him, instead throwing his missile. It missed the cratalac's head and impacted what might be loosely described as the shoulder. It should have been impossible to miss at that range but fear does unwelcome things to your muscles. In any event, hitting the cratalac square in the head with a rock five times the size and thrown three times as hard would probably have had little effect from what Evar had seen.

The beast came on without pause, a broken moment away from scooping Arpix up and shredding him. Arpix turned to run but he had no chance of escape. Amazingly, just before it reached him, the cratalac collapsed drunkenly, screeching worse than ever. The armour in a wide area around where Arpix had hit it was falling away, the flesh beneath smoking.

Arpix reached Evar and slung Clovis's other arm over his shoulders, taking some of her weight. A third cratalac was skirting the convulsions of the second, angling towards them but still shaking off its own sedation.

'Can you do that again?' Evar asked.

'No.'

'Get her to the tunnels.' Evar shrugged off Clovis's arm and readied himself in the cratalacs' path, white sword angled across his body.

More cratalacs freed themselves, two tearing apart the one that Clovis had maimed. Others approached Arpix's victim then backed off as if alarmed by its condition or the sharp, metallic stink rising from it.

Evar retreated slowly, giving Arpix and Clovis the time they needed.

At last, after what seemed an age, a shout came from behind him. Finding himself unexpectedly alive, Evar backed off rapidly, and when two cratalacs sighted him and began to charge, he ran like hell.

Evar reached the nearest tunnel mouth with his pursuers growing loud behind him, their scrabbling run accelerating in that final phase in which prey becomes food. He dived through the narrow gap in a hastily erected barrier of ancient timbers, dead thorn bushes, and rusting railings.

The whole lot exploded behind him as the first cratalac burst through. Ahead of him he could see flickers of flame and the motion of bodies, multiple humans and two canith retreating.

'Run!' They should have been deep in the mines by now, not wasting time on barricades. 'Run!'

The first cratalac filled the tunnel, its cries of fury deafening as it struggled to advance in the narrow confines while battling with the debris snared among its limbs. Evar opened a gap on it as he caught up with Arpix and Clovis.

'It gets . . . small,' Clovis managed.

'They won't fit in further on,' Arpix said, sharing with Evar the task of moving Clovis. 'We need to get deeper.'

They pushed on through an underground system Evar hadn't yet visited. Already he had to bend low and the sides were starting to close in. The human's torches were bundles of dry leaves and produced more smoke than light. With little visibility, little room, and the terrifying cratalac screams echoing around, Evar felt his grasp on the situation slipping. Panic began to fill him – panic at being trapped with cratalacs in the dark, panic at the state Clovis was in.

The attack came from an unexpected angle. A cratalac must have taken one of the half-dozen other entrances and flanked their retreat. Only the fact that it could barely squeeze through prevented a slaughter on top of the blind, rushing, screaming rout that followed. Evar jumped the thrust of a barbed limb, barely seen in the gloom as its owner lunged from a side passage. He dragged his sister with a roar of effort, careless of her wounds, only determined that she not end in the insectoid's filthy maw. After that it was all running and confusion.

'Kerrol?'

'I'm here.'

They were in a tunnel whose roof came so low Evar had been forced to crawl. The place hadn't been dug out by humans. 'Clovis?' He had her in his arms.

'. . . present . . .' A cough followed the weak response.

All the torches were out, though their smoke still stung his eyes. He could see nothing at all.

'Arpix?' He could hear Arpix calling the humans' names.

'I'm checking.' Arpix carried on. 'Henral?'

A human replied.

'Salamonda?'

Silence.

'Salamonda?' A pause before several humans started to talk at once.

Evar knew the woman who owned the name. An older human, solid and kind. She had been helping him look after Kerrol.

'Salamonda?' Kerrol surprised Evar with his concern.

'We must have lost her on the way,' Evar said. He felt guilty for not suggesting that they go back but there were at least five crat-alacs in the tunnels. The woman was surely dead already or in no worse a position than the rest of them, albeit in a different tunnel.

'. . . ask him . . .' Clovis managed.

'Ask who what?'

'Arpix. About the weapon.'

Arpix spoke, closer to them than he had been. 'It was mercury. That was all I had.'

'It poisons them that fast?' Evar knew from the education Starval had given him in such matters that mercury was a slow toxin that brought madness first, but only with long-term exposure.

'A catalyst,' Arpix said.

'A what?' Evar thought the human had the wrong word. It wasn't one he'd heard before.

'Maybe I have the wrong word. It allows a reaction that would not otherwise occur. It doesn't take part—'

'A poison to them.' Clovis cut across him, regaining a little strength.

'How did you get it?' Evar asked.

'The cliffs,' Arpix growled. 'Exposed ore. Cinnabar. Not hard to extract.'

'And a librarian knew all this because . . .'

'Livira told me. She got it from a book.'

Evar said nothing. Even here. Even here Livira reached out for him. Perhaps she was watching now, a ghost at his shoulder.

The other humans were still whispering about Salamonda.

'Make them be quiet,' Evar said.

To his credit Arpix didn't ask why. Silence fell.

'I don't hear anything,' Kerrol hissed.

'Me neither.' Evar wondered why the cratalacs had stopped their screaming. Trying to lure them out to somewhere accessible, he guessed. 'How long will they wait?'

'I don't know,' Arpix said. 'They're solitary hunters normally. Large territories. One of those things needs a lot of food to keep it going, and there's not much to eat out here.'

'I noticed.'

'So, by rights they'll start fighting each other, then separate. Maybe one will stay. Claim the tunnels, hunt the surroundings. But how long it will take . . . I don't know.'

'I'm going to check for Salamonda.'

'What?' Even Arpix sounded shocked.

'You are not.' Clovis found a grip on his arm and some measure of her old strength.

'Brother—'

'Say one more word, Kerrol, and I swear I will punch you in the mouth. I'm not having you mind-game me out of this.'

'Someone should,' Arpix said, his voice unsteady. 'And I love Salamonda.'

'So does Livira.' Evar could feel her at his shoulder. Whether she was standing there as ghost or not, she was with him. He had spent half his life in the book she wrote. Her kiss still tingled against his mouth. She wouldn't stop him. She'd go with him. 'I'll be careful.'

'Those things hunt at night so they're going to find you before you find them. And then they'll shred you,' Arpix answered.

Evar had spent too long as a helpless witness, unable to intervene. 'I can stick to the narrow ways they can't fit in. Salamonda might be lost in the tight tunnels. Or lying somewhere, hurt.'

'You need me with you.' Arpix didn't sound enthusiastic, but he did sound determined. 'You don't know the tunnels.'

'You can come,' Evar said. Though what Livira would think about him putting one friend in harm's way in the hope of finding another, he couldn't say. 'Stay close.'

Arpix, also forced to crawl, elbowed past him. 'You stay close. Grab my belt.'

Evar patted around and fastened a hand on the rope around Arpix's narrow waist. 'Done.' And they both started forward, in the direction they'd all come from.

'Bring that one back.' A curiously angry snarl from Clovis.

'She likes him.' Kerrol clarified from further back in the dark.

Clovis spat in outrage. 'I meant my sword!'

The hunt for Salamonda started slow and ended fast. At first Arpix and Evar patted their way silently, blind in the tunnels, listening hard. Evar kept sniffing the air, hunting the cratalacs' curious scent, a kind of dry rot that made him stretch his jaw in disgust.

They didn't have to go far to hear the noise.

'What is it?' Evar couldn't understand it. An arrhythmic banging and scuffing.

'Digging.'

'They're digging us out?' Evar didn't like the idea of that at all, but it would take a lot of effort, even with many cratalacs, since only one of them would be able to do useful work at any given time.

'Too far away,' Arpix growled. 'Digging something else out, maybe.'

'The protection?' It hadn't seemed that the skeer had exercised much control over their captives. The idea that they could locate and destroy whatever kept the skeer out hadn't occurred to him.

'Or Salamonda.'

'She's not calling for help . . .' Evar strained his ears.

'She wouldn't,' Arpix said. 'She wouldn't want anyone coming after her. Two idiots like us, for example. She'd know they'd just get eaten.'

'Let's see if we can get to her another way.' Evar started forward again, and Arpix, with a deep, trembling sigh, began to lead the way once more.

They'd covered another hundred yards or so before the screaming started. It began with the sound of earth and rocks falling. A ceiling collapse maybe, or a breakthrough. A cratalac scream followed, the first they'd heard since escaping the beasts. A cry like the earlier ones, full of rage and challenge. Then within moments the tunnels rang with multiple screams as if all five of the cratalacs to follow them into the dig were engaged in a furious battle. Evar couldn't say how long it lasted. Moments or minutes. The sheer volume and fury of the screams undid him, turning his muscles to water and shaking his bones.

'It's stopped?' Arpix's question ventured into the silence that followed.

'I—' Evar stopped. He heard something new. A human's voice?

'Salamonda!' And before Evar could react Arpix had pulled free and was running forward, presumably bent double.

'Arpix!' Evar gave chase, following the sound of retreating footsteps on his hands and knees.

At last a whisper of light from somewhere gave enough illumination for Evar to make out walls and tunnel roof. They'd left the safety of the smallest tunnels. Evar got to his feet and started to run with his head bowed, painfully aware that a cratalac could lunge from any of the dark openings he passed on either side. 'Arpix! Come back!'

'Salamonda!' Arpix ran on, easy prey for the monsters.

Evar caught up with Arpix not far from the entrance they'd come in by. Enough light reached in to show the slumped bodies of at least two cratalacs. So many pieces of them were scattered around that it was hard to know whether there were three in total, or one in several large chunks.

'Arpix?' Salamonda's voice, faint but not too distant.

'Stay!' Evar moved Arpix to the side and advanced with the white sword out before him, catching glimmers of daylight amid the gloom. Loose rock, dirt and debris crunched under his feet, the spoils from digging done to enlarge the entrance to the side passage just ahead.

Evar turned the corner. More cratalacs lay butchered amid the piles of earth they'd dug out. Some sort of collapse had happened, enough to open a dusty crack in the ceiling through which daylight had jammed its bright fingers, not enough to explain in any way the amount of destruction visited upon the insectoids.

'Evar?' Salamonda's voice emerged from the dust and gloom ahead.

Evar lifted his gaze from the carnage just in time to see something he didn't understand. An animal of some kind, smaller than a human . . . but it looked as if it had just walked into the wall and vanished. 'What . . . what was that?'

Arpix, who had not obeyed instructions, came to stand at his elbow. 'A cat,' he said in a voice full of wonder. 'I think it was a cat . . .'

Salamonda emerged, trembling and dusty, dirt in her hair. 'He's called Wentworth. He killed them all. I think Yute must have sent him to watch over me.'

*Reading is a dangerous sport, never more so than when we
turn the page and find ourselves there among the lines.*

Blunt Instruments, *by Morris Morris*

CHAPTER 18

Livira

Livira and Malar stood watching events that had happened perhaps
only weeks before the time they'd travelled from. Evar was by the
pool, talking to the Soldier among the crops. In one hand he held
the book that Livira had started writing hundreds of years before.
For a brief period after touching the book Livira, and then Malar,
were very surprised to find themselves participants in what seemed
to be one of the stories lying between its covers.

'Why did you kill him?' Livira asked.

'Who?'

Most people didn't have so many deaths on their hands that a
question like that would cause confusion. 'Leetar and Meelan's father.
In the story. You were the general and he was supposed to be your
friend, but you did your best to decapitate him.'

'If that means chop his head off, yes I did,' Malar replied with
some heat. 'I would have done it too if that sword hadn't been so
fucking blunt.'

'But why?'

'Because he deserved to die. Both of them did. Heflin Hosten
and General Rodcar Charant were scum of the worst kind. Hosten
pays Charant to take rich idiots on as colonels and majors.'

'Paid,' Livira corrected. 'They're all dead now, I expect. The canith
overran the walls.'

'Well, they might not have if Heflin fucking Hosten hadn't replaced good officers with morons. And that's not the half of it. Both of them were elbow deep in keeping the settlers outside the walls as a buffer zone, and squandering soldiers' lives in a dozen ways to line their own pockets.' Malar drew his lips back in a snarl, looking every bit as dangerous as the day Livira met him. 'There I was, in a place I'd never been before, with this human turd Hosten telling me I was his friend, and all this stuff – all the details about what he'd been doing to our soldiers – flooding into my head. So, I killed him. I'd do it again in a heartbeat.'

'Yes, but . . .' Livira squeezed the bridge of her nose between finger and thumb, trying to trap the understanding that was drifting through her brain like a cobweb. 'When you killed him, that's when the story kicked us out. You went too far . . . stepped away from what the story was doing. The general wouldn't have killed Heflin, at least not like that, not without there being something in it for him.'

'You're saying I should have played along?' Malar frowned. 'Why would I want to do that?'

'Because . . .' Livira screwed her eyes shut, visualizing the table scene. She had felt something – something other than confusion – when she sat there wearing Serra Leetar's finery. 'Because maybe that's how to take hold of the story. And taking hold of the story could mean we're taking hold of the book. And that's what we're here for – to take the book forward to when we came from.' She looked up, coming to a decision. 'I'm going to try again.'

'I'll come too.'

'You don't have—'

'I'm coming too,' Malar said.

Livira sidled up to Evar, watching him with fascination. She'd watched him unobserved back in the library of course, but that was when he'd been burdened with the grief of her 'death'. This was Evar before even their first meeting when she'd been a child, still with dust behind her ears.

'He can't see you, you know.' Malar strode up boldly and touched the book. The way he vanished wasn't something she could describe visually. It was closer to forgetting.

Livira darted after him and set her hand to the book.

A moment's confusion followed, a moment of lights and colours coalescing into the dining-room scene that had so amazed Livira the first time. She was surprised – both to see Serra Leetar sitting to her left, and to see that the look of astonishment on the girl's face matched her own. It was the looming presence on her right that commanded her attention though. The first thing she saw when she turned her head was that her neighbour wore a fine double-breasted jacket with a napkin strategically draped over the most vulnerable bits of the elaborate gold piping decorating it. She had to look up to see his face.

'Evar!' She set her hand to his shoulder, unable to resist seeing if she could touch him. Her hand was broader and larger knuckled than the ones she was used to owning, but none of that mattered once she discovered he was as solid as the chair she was sitting on. 'Evar!'

Evar turned his head, frowning. 'Sirrar Meelan?'

'I—'

'Oh, fuck no. I'm not having this shit.' This low-voiced, slightly horrified announcement from Leetar cut off Livira's reply to Evar.

Reluctantly, Livira turned around just in time to see Leetar take one of the sharper knives from beside her plate and hold it in her fist, base against the table, point upwards.

'What are you doing?'

'No, no, and fucking no!' Leetar slammed her face down onto the knife point and a moment later the dining room and everyone in it melted away.

'Ow! Ow! Ow!' Malar was bent double beside her in the crop circle, holding his eye and dancing from foot to foot.

'It wasn't real.' Livira put her hand on his shoulder.

'Bloody felt real . . .' Malar straightened slowly, taking his hand from his eye and examining it for blood. 'Damn, that was unpleasant.'

'You couldn't just have been Serra Leetar so we could get on with this?'

Malar scowled at her. 'Like you weren't just going to have Meelan drape himself all over your boyfriend?'

Livira bit her lip. 'I wouldn't have gone that far.' She studied the book stacks rather than witness Malar's reaction. 'Look, he's going.'

Evar had finished speaking with the Soldier and was already halfway to the corridor that led to the reading room and the Mechanism. Livira hurried after him.

'Look,' she said to Malar as he caught up, 'it's not dangerous in the story. You just killed yourself and you're fine. The worst that can happen is you get kicked out of the book. I should go in by myself. I'm better cut out for playing along than you are. You'll just end up drowning a guest in the soup tureen or something. And every time we veer too far out of character we're back here again.'

Malar scowled. 'I'll follow Evar. If you take too long, I'm coming in after you.'

'Too long?'

'Until I get bored.'

Livira stopped chasing Evar and gave Malar a hard, narrow-eyed stare. 'Just let me do my thing.'

Malar eyed her doubtfully but, after a long pause, nodded.

'Come on then!' And Livira flew down the corridor, not bothering with legs.

She caught up with Evar at the entrance to the reading room. A confusion of broken desks stretched out before them, heaped up into mounds in places, and at the centre of it all, the grey lump of the Mechanism.

'Stay out of trouble,' Livira instructed Malar as he came up to join them. With that, she touched the book and fell into a story.

'This isn't right!' Livira found herself near-blind, closely surrounded by clanking metal, and being jolted violently up and down by whatever large object she was suddenly astride. It wasn't right at all, but before she had an opportunity to expand on the subject she was falling: not in the way that she'd fallen into the story, more in the way you'd fall off a horse – which turned out to be exactly what she was doing.

Falling off a horse turned out to be really painful, and the armour she'd found herself encased in seemed to make things worse rather than better. She lay where the fall left her, flat on her back, with the air driven from her lungs. Livira listened to the diminishing hoofbeats of her treacherous steed. Her helmet offered only a thin bar of sky through its visor and, since the thing had twisted some way around her head, she wasn't even getting the full benefit of even that narrow view.

Eventually air began to leak painfully back into her chest, and she was able to sit up, accompanied by a sound like half a dozen pots and pans being rubbed across each other. She worked the helmet off her head – a tricky task involving straps and buckles which necessitated the removal of iron gauntlets, then leather gloves.

A rolling green landscape surrounded her, countryside of the sort she had read about only in books, and later been shown in the Mechanism. A rain-laced wind blew, and the tree branches danced to please it. In the fields sheep gathered in corners, seeking the shelter of dry-stone walls from the coming storm.

Wincing, and muttering curses that Malar would be proud of, Livira got unsteadily to her feet. Her armour was still shining where it wasn't mud-spattered. She looked at the crested helm in her hand.

'I'm a knight.'

Suspicion grabbed her and she turned, looking for the sea and finding it, a murky grey line beyond the slopes to the west. 'That means . . .' She steered her gaze and fixed on a short, dark, vertical line against the far side of the valley ahead. A lonely tower.

Livira knew this story. She even remembered writing it. It had been a shameless reworking of a very old tale that had bubbled around in the folklore of several civilizations that had become dust on the wind long ago. She was the knight in shining armour, riding a valiant – though apparently treacherous – steed. Her lover waited for her, imprisoned in the topmost room of the witch's tower. The story was the last one that she and Evar had explored together. The one that had tried to teach him that some things could not be saved – that the knight sometimes arrived too late. She had meant to add that a tragic ending didn't erase what had gone before. The shared kisses, the love beneath satin sheets, none of it was a waste, none of it was rendered meaningless, any more than a well-lived life was undone by the inevitable death waiting at the end. Little could remain of Livira's time within the Assistant. Timeless thoughts were quickly washed from minds caught in the flow once more. But she had kept within her the shadow of a glimpse at that perfect crystal

eternity in which all things are held in an omnipresent now.
Everything counted. No one thing eclipsed or deleted another.

Livira felt the knight's story invading her, his needs, wants,
and desires, images of the princess in the tower, the flood of her
hair, the heat of their passion. The knight had been Evar, and
now was her. Both of them in a single body. Evar's arms encircled her, strong, warm, encompassing, lifting her into his story.
She gasped, suddenly afloat on the overwhelming physicality of
him, half drowned in his mane and the animal scent of his
strangeness.

'I want you, need you, love you.' The growl of him in her ear,
shivering through her spine to clench her toes in mixed delight and
fright. 'Stay . . .' Gentle now. A prayer.

'I want to.' Fingers knotting his hair. Want to, need to, would
love to. 'But . . .' And slowly, painfully, reluctantly, she disentangled
herself, piece by piece by piece, then all at once.

It would be easy to surrender to the narrative, or she could refuse
it entirely and be ejected from the book once more. She chose a
third path. Setting her steel-plated back to the tower she tossed
aside her helmet and began to trudge towards the bleak horizon,
still with the memory of his arms wrapping her and with regret
aching in every step.

The storm broke. Icy torrents of rainwater poured past Livira's metal
collar and found every chink in her armour. The wind howled. The
sky darkened to the point at which it became hard to continue
believing that above the clouds the sun still burned. And in time
a grey mist swallowed everything so that Livira could no longer see
even the ground she walked upon.

In this grey void Livira closed her eyes and sought the story
she'd come for.

'Serra Leetar!' A servant ushered her inside while one of her father's
house guards lost the tug-of-war he'd been having with the wind
over the ownership of an inside-out umbrella. 'Whoever thought
we'd see such rain in Crath City?'

Livira glanced back over her shoulder to see Meelan following her in, and beyond him in the street, a gleaming carriage with the rain bouncing off its roof.

She thought she caught a glimpse of a child behind one of the carriage's large, spoked wheels, a curiously white child, not only pale as milk but wearing white too. The door closed too soon for her to be sure, taking the scene with it.

Leetar and Meelan allowed the servants to take their dripping coats. They'd been visiting cousins, but Helflin Hosten had summoned both his children back to the family home for tonight's grand dinner. Leetar's intended, or rather the old man her father intended for her – Dantal Creyan – would be an honoured guest, as would Lord Algar, who offered her only escape from matrimony, in the shape of a position among ranks of the king's diplomats. Such a position wouldn't by itself satisfy her father's ambition, but Lord Algar's offer came with promises of influence at court. The man's unhealthy interest in Leetar, an interest that lay behind the sweetened offer, was undisguised, as naked as the greed that her father allowed to blind him to it. Meelan had called it the choice between the frying pan and the fire. He'd offered to murder either or both of the men involved, though when Leetar had pointed out that there were three of them, he had balked at patricide.

Absorbing all this, Livira felt that there were more than three men involved, thousands more, in fact. Still shivering, even though she'd left the weather outside, Livira allowed herself, or more accurately Leetar, to be led into the drawing room and plied with hot chai. She sat and sipped, eyeing the first guests of the evening over her cup, resolving to play along. Malar had already demonstrated the consequences of sudden departures from the narrative. But perhaps it could be steered. Hopefully, since Livira had written it, the story was already aimed at a more satisfactory destination than currently implied. Either way, Livira resolved not to rock the boat just yet and to make it to the dining table.

An hour of small-talk passed, with the guests circulating like the slow swirl of leaves fastened to the surface of a millpond. A maiden aunt hovered behind Leetar and Meelan, an ever-present spectre both to guard their honour and to warn, by grim example, of the dangers inherent in holding onto it too long. In small-talk, Livira discovered, one probed for weaknesses, any useful kind of fault line was hunted out, whether it be social or financial, or simply a defect in one's look or sense of style. Small-talk resembled a battle of the open sort where combatants crossed blades in pairs or fours before carrying their wounds and their victories into some new fray.

Livira presented an elusive target by refusing to engage and instead answering each enquiry with obscure quotations she'd been forced to translate in Master Logaris's classroom. She felt the story ripple uneasily around these interactions, but at least she wasn't attempting to behead the host with a ceremonial sword, and she kept her place.

Evar Eventari arrived so fashionably late that he was the last through the doors and would have missed the entrées but for the fact that for so eligible a bachelor Heflin Hosten delayed proceedings with another round of aperitifs. Evar's main qualification for being the city's most eligible bachelor was his eye-wateringly large fortune. The fact that he was roguishly handsome added even more weight to this claim among the aristocrats' daughters. His apparent lack of interest in marriage made little impact on the river of invitations that flowed to the doors of his mansion.

The late arrival barely had time to stamp the rain from his boots before servants began to usher the guests into dinner with a series of gentle coughs and discreet nods, like the world's most polite beaters urging grouse into the sky for the hunters. Livira watched him go, not allowing herself too close for fear of forgetting his fictional status and seeking the reunion so long denied to her. She noted as he went that within the bounds of this particular story, the fact that he was a full-grown canith, dressed to the nines and in one of the richest drawing rooms in King Oanold's city, didn't raise a single eyebrow.

Livira's resolve lasted until the table, at which point she elbowed Meelan into the chair indicated for her, and took his place beside Evar. For now, proximity was enough. Livira focused on the flatware arrayed before her and forced herself to remember that she was here to claim not just this story but the whole book. She could discern the threads of the tale wrapping themselves around her and felt that if she allowed the process to continue long enough, bedding her throughout the story from first line to last, then possibly when she left, she and the book would have so tight a hold upon each other that she would be able to take it with her.

But as she took a firmer and firmer grip upon the story, the issue of who led who became less clear. It seemed that the story would no longer guide her to its proper destination, and that to claim ownership of it she would have to navigate to the same conclusion as she'd reached when writing it from within the strangeness of the assistant. An unknown and possibly unguessable conclusion.

Conversation flowed across the gleaming table; courses came, were devoured and removed. Livira kept her head down, picking at the meal, considering her options.

'Don't you like crab?' These were the first words Evar had addressed to her. He'd been far from silent before that, however, playing his part in the expected verbal fencing. Perhaps her silence had provoked him, since his conversations with the other young daughters around the table had all been initiated by the other party.

'I like this crab,' Livira said. 'And I'm sorry that he found his way to my plate after so many years scuttling beneath the waves.' She lifted one of the crab's large claws with her fork. The wrong fork for crabs. 'Did you know that they come from the Grey Sea? Three hundred miles overland. They can live to be fifty.'

'You don't approve of eating animals?' The idea seemed to interest Evar. He picked at the last of the meat from one of the claws he'd cracked earlier with a silver device that might have been modelled on something from the torturer's bench.

'I'm not sure anyone cares about my approval. Certainly not the crab.' She smiled. 'I have the luxury of being sentimental about animals and sometimes I choose to exercise it. If I were starving, the crabs would have to watch out just the same as any passing piglet, rat, or crow would have to.'

Evar showed his teeth and huffed his amusement in the way that so amused her. She eyed her right hand and threatened silently to stab it with a crab fork if it wandered towards the canith's.

'Need,' Evar said, 'makes many strange bedfellows. But it can also narrow one's view until bad choices are all there is to be seen.'

'You don't like your choices?' Livira swept her gaze across the young women adorning the table, each chafing against a chaperone.

'I wasn't talking about me.' Evar pushed his plate back.

They continued to talk as the courses marched on into dessert. The Evar that she'd written was more worldly than her own, and came with a sharper edge, but he preserved the original's other qualities that had so drawn her to him, and it pleased her to know that the attraction he held for her didn't rest on just the circumstances of his upbringing. She still wanted him as a rich lordling.

At last, the final silver platters were removed and Helflin Hosten stood up to announce that they should retire to the ballroom where a musical entertainment awaited. Later, once the meal had time to settle, there would be dancing.

Livira accepted the unnecessary offer of Evar's hand to help her rise from her chair. Several of the unmarried girls around the table stared daggers at her, but these were mild when compared to the looks thrown her way by Dantal Creyan, whose fleshy face had gone so red she wondered if he might be about to sweat blood. Lord Algar's singular stare was a cold thing and more chilling.

Slowly, amid rustling taffeta, the hiss of silk, and the soft silence of velvet, the guests flowed towards the ballroom. Evar's hand burned in Livira's. She knew he wasn't real, just memories brought to life and embroidered with fiction, but even so, the urge to wrap her arms around him and bury her face in his mane was overwhelming. Though to do so would require a chair to stand on.

Livira's grip on the story had been growing the whole time, spreading, though to take the book with her, as she hoped, would require the deepest bond. She needed to be woven into the tale, to know it as she had known it when the ink still glistened on the page. The path of the tale seemed obvious. She would, over the course of an evening's dance, win Evar's heart anew. He would divine her sadness, cut her suitors with harsh words, or perhaps the back of his hand whilst offering the chance to satisfy their honour on the duelling square like gentlemen. They would marry and in doing so he would save her from the trap of her birth and her father's wishes. It would be perfect.

Around them the story shivered.

Almost perfect. Livira brought Leetar to a halt before the ballroom doors. Evar walked another pace, their arms stretching between them, hands still holding.

'Serra Leetar?' Evar smiled enquiringly. 'Is something amiss?'

'Not perfect at all, really . . .' Livira frowned, and an echoing frown crossed Evar's brow.

'Can I help?' Evar stepped back towards her.

'I shouldn't need you to save me,' Livira said. 'She shouldn't either.'

The story shivered again, colour leaking from the vibrant gowns, the light of many candles growing thinner, somehow brittle.

'Your pardon?' Evar cocked his head. 'I don't follow you, Serra, but no, I don't think you need me to save you, much as I would be honoured by the opportunity.'

Tears prickled at the corners of Livira's eyes. She squeezed Evar's large, warm hand with Leetar's narrow, white one. 'Thank you.'

And, so saying, she let his fingers slide from hers, and turned to walk away against the flow of guests. As she let go of Evar's hand, Livira's grip on the story re-established itself.

A single servant pursued her: Twila, a young maid Leetar had known and liked since childhood. Twila caught up with her in the entrance hall.

'Ma'am! Ma'am, where are you going? It's dark out, and raining!'

The story thickened around them, everything crystal clear, every colour stolen from a rainbow. Livira felt her hold on the story deeper than at any point before. She could almost sense the smooth leather of the covers beneath her fingertips.

'I'm going my own way. I'd forgotten that I had other choices.'

Livira had thought that the servant might argue with her, but Twila simply turned on a heel. 'Wait there. I'll get your coat.'

Livira watched her go. The world waited for her outside and she'd have to negotiate it while balancing between her privilege and her ignorance. Perhaps she would call in at the library and see if they had any vacancies. And once she'd found her place, she might even invite the handsome canith to pay her a call.

A sudden flush of cold made Livira shiver and she turned, thinking that the doors had been thrown open. They remained closed. But in front of them, where there had been nobody, there now stood a white child. For a heartbeat Livira imagined it was Yute as she'd glimpsed him in the city back in the time when everyone in it had died in a day, victims of some unknown poison.

'You're not him . . .'

This child was a girl. Painfully thin, her white robes, thin as a nightdress, plastered to her by the freezing rain.

'Yamala?' But Yute's wife was dead, killed by Evar's brother, Mayland. And Yamala had never had the haunted look of this child: a stare that seemed to reach into Livira and start to freeze the marrow of her bones.

'No.' A small word from a small girl, but it sent a faint tremor through the foundations of the house. Every shadow stretched, reaching towards her.

'No what?' No, she wasn't Yamala? Livira desperately wanted to run as the child walked towards her but that would have been silly, and it wasn't in the story. The girl wasn't in the story either. With each step that brought the white child closer, Livira felt her grip on the story loosen. 'Wait, stop, don't—'

Don't touch me was what she'd been going to say, but the white child touched her and the world vanished.

Each alphabet is a marvel of evolution. No person, no committee, no nation can lay claim to the final product, and indeed there is no final product, just a twisting, tumbling beauty, barely able to hold its form from front cover to back. And yet these marks, without forming so much as a single sentence, spell out something greater than any book might contain.

Calligraphy and Other Martial Arts, *by Lee Chan*

CHAPTER 19

Celcha

'The beggar is more generous with his money than the lord.' Hellet eyed Celcha over the top of his current read. Already he spoke more like a librarian than a ganar just months out of the tunnels of Arthran. He practically inhaled books, and each left its mark upon him. 'Some rich men consider themselves philanthropists, but although they may give away a thousand times what any beggar will see in their lifetimes, it constitutes only a modest fraction of what they own. The beggar, on the other hand, will sometimes give his last penny to someone else on the street whose misfortune is still greater than theirs. Losing all their wealth at a single stroke and without hesitation.' Hellet put his book down. The scars curling around his shoulders and sides glistened in the library light. 'Those on the journey from beggar to lord, from famine to feast, are often the least generous. The lord who gives will still be rich. The beggar can mine his poverty no deeper and perhaps restore his penny at a stroke. For the rest . . . every act of generosity is a slip back down the ladder they've been climbing all their lives.'

'You're saying H'seen and the rest have too much to lose.' Celcha had returned from the gas house buoyed on her lungfuls of meth-alayne though carrying little by way of encouragement. H'seen had at least appeared thoughtful when Celcha spoke of her brother's aspirations for the ganar. Celcha had avoided specifics, but she'd repeated Hellet's recent oratory on the foul institution of slavery. She'd expounded on the criminal state of affairs wherein a proud people, who once descended from the moons themselves, now suffered beneath the heel of oppressors.

The sentiments were certainly ones that both she and Hellet had long harboured, holding them deeper than their bones, knowing that to speak them would be to ask for an ugly death. Since their arrival at the library, Hellet had found works that gave voice to these ideas. Books that were centuries old, so ancient that the language now spoken had twisted away from that on the page, and only by dint of shining the blaze of his intellect upon the lines before him could Hellet see to pursue the words.

The books recorded speeches in which humans and canith of great eloquence railed against similar treatment of their own kind. It was those words, in Celcha's mouth, that had fallen so flat in the dark halls of H'seen's de facto empire. H'seen had nodded wisely, said little, and sent her on her way with vague platitudes. Not a rejection, but certainly the hoped-for fire had not been lit. The silence from those who had stopped to listen had been stony. It had been the black-furred Redmak who led Celcha back through the gas house, far less talkative than he had been on the way in. He'd taken her to the square exit at the plant's rear and had said farewell with a firm 'don't come back' followed by a firmer slamming of the hatch.

H'seen and her workmates might still be slaves and endure what to their masters would be seen as intolerable, but from their own perspective, they had a long way to fall. Celcha understood. A similar cliff lay at her own heels where the plummet back to the Arthran dig awaited her.

'What now?' Celcha had asked her brother on her return.

Hellet had bowed his head and remained silent for so long that she'd worried he might have returned to his wordless ways. Eventually he had looked up from his thoughts. 'It would have been easier if they'd helped us. Safer. There were experiments I wanted to run. Tests that should be carried out. Now I'll have to trust the books, and my understanding of them. But we can still do this. By ourselves. We have to.'

Weeks passed and Hellet's resolve didn't appear to have many consequences. He had become more silent, more reserved, and busied himself with his reading. Celcha continued to spend time with Lutna and the other trainees and was allowed to visit the city several more times in Lutna's company. Hellet stayed behind, his only sight of the city the one he'd had on the journey to the library.

Month by month the library life seduced Celcha. She liked reading, loved books, even enjoyed the company of some of the trainees, especially Lutna, who managed to be kind and caring despite the dizzy heights of her upbringing. Winter came and icy winds howled around the mountain's flanks. With the passing seasons the idea of gambling all they'd gained at long odds in the cause of some ideal seemed more foolish. Most of Celcha was glad that Hellet seemed to have put his ambitions on hold. Some small part of her mourned the loss of that purity of purpose though, knowing that before long she would be finding excuses to further delay, or even undermine, her brother's plans.

A hand shook Celcha gently from dreams of flying above mountain peaks.

'W-what?' She opened bleary eyes. Library light lit the room as usual, but she knew it was late.

'It's time,' Hellet said.

'Time?'

'To show you what I've been doing.' Hellet handed her book satchel to her. 'Time to change the world.'

'But . . . I . . .' Celcha was suddenly afraid. The comfort of her bed, the safe haven of the library, these weren't things she wanted to give up in the name of a cause.

'But what?' Hellet studied her with wide, dark eyes. Would he give this up for her? He was her little brother and he loved her – they were each all the other had – and yet . . . would he? Should he?

Celcha ran her fingers through her fur, finding and touching the nootki tied there, each a silent witness to her deeds, a reminder of those who laboured in the dark even now, digging up a lost city to build another that they would never see. 'So, what are we going to do?'

'We're going to give the ganar something they haven't had in many lifetimes,' Hellet said. 'A choice.'

Celcha bowed her head. 'How?'

'Walk with me.'

Celcha and Hellet were allowed one 'day of ease' on the last day of each week, and even given a small stipend, though they had to convince a trainee to spend it for them since, in the city, a ganar with money would instantly be accused of theft. At best, they'd end up penniless and beaten.

This particular day of ease was all but over. The ganar, however, kept different hours. They not only needed more sleep than natives of this world but when their sleeping was combined with their waking, it totalled something rather longer than a day, leading to their sleeping periods shifting through the months so that sometimes, as on this particular day, they slept the whole time that the sun spent crossing the sky and woke in the evening.

Hellet had woken Celcha early rather than late. They wound their way unchallenged through the outer complex which lay empty but for a handful of guards and the occasional overly enthusiastic librarian. By the time they emerged into the large cavern that abutted the library wall Celcha had stopped yawning. For the brief period between first seeing this cave and seeing the chambers of the library, the cavern had been not only the largest by far she had ever seen after a lifetime underground, but substantially bigger than any she might have imagined.

'This way.' Hellet veered away from the well-travelled route between the complex and the library's white door. He led Celcha away from the bridges and rails of the official path and out into the uncharted chaos of the wider chamber. Somehow, the idea of leaving the path had never occurred to Celcha. She supposed it was because the library's door seemed a beacon, drawing her on towards its hidden mysteries. Even so, she couldn't help feeling mildly disappointed with herself.

Hellet navigated the way along a deep valley cutting across the cavern, all water-smoothed rock and sudden drops. He offered a belated, 'Be careful.'

They were soon out of sight of anyone crossing by the normal route, ten yards deep in an increasingly steep chasm. Celcha began to smell an acrid scent, as if something that shouldn't be burned had been cremated here. It grew stronger as they went.

'Here's our first stop.' Hellet worked his way around a narrow ledge. In the void to his left the library's light at last began to fail.

The ledge itself was blackened, and charred lumps crunched beneath Celcha's feet as she advanced, clinging to whatever handholds offered themselves. 'What's this?' Something shiny and silver caught the light and drew her eye with it.

Hellet bent and snagged a long-necked glass flask resting in the blackened hollow. In its rounded belly the flask held liquid silver – the thing that had snared Celcha's attention – brighter and more gleaming than even the most polished steel.

'It's called quicksilver,' Hellet said. 'But what it is exactly is less important than what it is in general.'

'Which is?' Celcha wasn't sure why her brother couldn't have explained this earlier, somewhere level.

'It's a catalyst. Something that allows a chemical reaction to take place but does not itself take part in the reaction.'

'Did Tutor Ablesan teach you a new language while I wasn't looking?'

'An agent of change,' Hellet said. 'We're going to need a lot of it.'

'Did . . . did you make it here?' Celcha looked at the burn marks. Here and there were rocks that hadn't come from the stone walls. Rocks that, whilst blackened on one side, were a strangely familiar reddish-orange on the other. They reminded Celcha of . . . 'These are from h—' She had been about to say 'home' but to call the dig site home felt like a kind of obscenity. 'From Arthran.'

Hellet nodded and showed his teeth. 'Cinnabar. It's the ore from which quicksilver comes. Smelting it is dirty work. The fumes are toxic and plentiful. I knew you'd try to stop me so I—'

'How did you get the rocks, the fuel, the glassware?' Celcha was too intrigued to be angry.

'They pay me too.' Hellet shrugged. 'I asked different trainees to get me different things. They don't say no to me. They're a little scared, I think.' He shrugged again, a deeper one this time. 'I told Benjon that the rocks reminded us of home, and we scatter them in our room.' Hellet turned away. 'Come on, let's get the rest.'

'There's more?'

'I've kept busy whilst you're out exploring with the princess.'

'Don't call her that.'

Hellet vanished from view around a shoulder of rock. When Celcha struggled past the obstruction she found him gathering more flasks into a sack.

'Be careful with this.' He handed a second sack to her. It proved surprisingly heavy. 'This took a lot of work and all the money they paid me plus some I stole from you and some I borrowed from Lutna to buy you a birthday present. Actually, that was most of it.'

'Hellet!'

'She seemed eager to give.' Hellet licked his teeth. 'Guilt, I expect. You can't buy your way out of what they've done to us, but she clearly wanted to try.

'Anyway, the quicksilver in those flasks is your present. So don't drop it.' He twitched, almost losing grip of his own sack. 'I spent all the money,' he repeated. 'Also, I may have poisoned myself a little. So, I don't want to have to do it again.'

Hellet led on, both of them burdened by their fragile loads of quicksilver. Celcha followed, feeling guilty that her brother had abused Lutna's trust, even while acknowledging that everything he'd said was true. Guilt was like that, sticking in places where it didn't belong, and rolling off others where it did just as easily as if it were quicksilver.

Counter to Celcha's expectations the way became easier rather than more difficult. Soon they were heading steeply down on stairs that had been carved into the rock.

'What is this? Where are we going?'

'These steps were made by the citizens of an earlier city that stood exactly where Krath stands now. The histories imply that the canith and the humans have been building and burning down each other's cities here for an unfathomable amount of time. This current one appears to be the first to host a lasting peace between them.'

'How do you know all this?' Celcha knew that her brother had become a voracious reader and had mastered the art even before reaching the library, but still, she too had been reading as fast as she could, and his books seemed to have divulged far more secrets.

'Yute told me. I think he wants to change my mind but can't quite bring himself to command me. So, instead he's settled on education and hope.'

'He could command you?' Celcha asked.

'Assistants can destroy matter with a wave of their hand. I'm sure that whatever constrains them it's not the laws of nature as we know them, but rather some code of ethics imposed by their creator.'

The fissure had become so narrow that if Celcha were to lean out too far to save herself from the drop, she could bridge it with her hands pressed to the far side. The illumination had faded to a gloom through which the occasional mote of library light still meandered like a lost firefly.

The door came as a surprise. A round door of corroded steel with a handwheel at its centre by which it might be unsealed. Someone had been digging through the rock around the door's perimeter and made considerable progress, though at no point had they reached past the metal rim.

'This would be a heap of rust, of course, if it were normal steel.' Hellet picked up a crowbar from a nearby ledge. 'It seized up long ago, so I'm having to dig it out. All that practice finally paid off.'

'You didn't need me at all,' Celcha said. 'Except to fetch and carry.'

'You played your part, sister. Lutna wouldn't have stamped her foot to get me into the gas house. I needed to know the basics of the system there.'

'But they won't even let us back in,' Celcha complained. 'Let alone fiddle with their machinery.'

'Don't need to.' Hellet jammed the end of his crowbar into the area he'd excavated around the edge of the hatch. 'It turns out we just needed to know their timings.'

Hellet exerted his strength, groaning. Celcha went to help him, lending her muscles to the effort just as she had so often back at the Arthran dig. For several long moments she was sure the door wasn't going to give. She'd reached the point of giving up when she realized that the hissing she could hear wasn't her own breath escaping clenched teeth or even the result of Hellet's explosive effort. Surprisingly, she gained a second wind, fresh energy filling her straining muscles.

The whole frame surrendered, and, rather than inching out, or toppling gently into the fall, it shot forward as if punched from inside, striking the opposite wall with force. Celcha's questions were drowned in the roar of methalayne blasting from the passage behind the door.

For some time, they clung to the rockface in the reflected swirl of the hurricane. The gas buffeted Celcha and filled her lungs. It made her feel lightheaded and left her unsure how much time passed before the hurricane died to a gale and then to a strong breeze.

'I don't understand,' Celcha called over quieting gusts. It wasn't just the confusion that too much methalayne had brought. Hellet had told her almost nothing of his plans. She wanted to believe his reticence to be because he feared being overheard or spied upon by the head librarian's agents even in their chamber. She feared his secrecy had other causes. She feared he thought her too weak for the task in hand. Yet here she was. Literally in the thick of the storm. 'How is all this here?'

'Krath isn't the first city to cook its meals on the grave gas of its predecessors.' Hellet spoke in a normal voice, audible over the rush of methalayne. 'Before Krath the humans built a city called Tanylarn at the library gates. This hatch and tunnel are their work. Ironically, their corpses, sewage, and waste are now rotting far below the Krath, making gas for those who came after them.' He held his hand in the flow and his fur streamed out. 'Maybe Maybe is a ghost, but this stuff is definitely full of them.'

'They'll find this place soon enough now.' Celcha looked up, half expecting to see a library guard peering over the edge of the chasm.

'So, we'd better get a move on.' Hellet handed her his sack and started to climb into the tunnel. 'This side of the mountain is lousy with caves. The methalayne has been gathering in them for aeons. By sealing known exits the city founders increase the pressure and the reserve escapes in the gas house where it's pressurized further and stored in cylinders ready for release into the city's pipes.' He turned around in the tight confines of the tunnel and reached back. 'Here, give me the sacks – *carefully* – and then come in.'

Celcha joined her brother, and together, like dust rats in a burrow, they followed the tunnel's slope.

'Let me tell you what we're doing,' Hellet said.

'That would be . . . helpful.' Celcha ground her teeth together and tried to remember that her brother did not think like other people did.

'This quicksilver – this catalyst – will change the methalayne into something that will put the humans and the canith to sleep. It doesn't join with the gas. It doesn't get used up. So, a vast supply is not required. It simply encourages the gas to change by itself through some miracle of alchemy. All I needed was enough to convert a sufficient portion of the gas at the rate at which it enters the storage chamber.'

'But they burn the gas!' Celcha's mind was reeling with the scale and insanity of Hellet's plan. She grasped at the idea that the burning would put an end to the madness. She didn't know a lot of alchemy, but things tended to stop working once you set fire to them.

'That's the beauty of it. The changed gas won't burn. When they connect the new cylinder, lights, hearths, and stoves all over the city will flicker into darkness and this new gas will hiss into their homes.'

'Whose—'

'Everyone's homes. Even the tenements have gas lighting. The streets have it. From pauper to palace.'

'How will this help the ganar?' To Celcha it sounded like a recipe for getting extravagantly tortured to death while at the same time casting a shadow of suspicion over all their kind.

'That's the genius of it. All from my little black book. The ganar' – Hellet paused and smiled one of the rare smiles that he'd kept from the days before the cruelty – 'are immune to its effects!'

The tunnel narrowed, forcing them to their knees. Celcha continued to follow, crawling on one hand and two knees while cradling her sack of liquid metal against her chest. It hardly seemed real that she was here, doing this. 'And what's the choice?' Hellet had said he was giving the ganar something they'd never had before: a choice.

'What to do, of course!' Hellet squeezed through a choke point with exquisite care. 'They will wake with their masters at their mercy.'

Celcha carried on. It was madness. It couldn't work. And if it did . . . what would they choose? What would she choose faced with a sleeping library? She and Hellet would get to decide how and if their colleagues . . . their enslavers . . . woke.

In the meantime, more practical problems faced them. Celcha's knuckles quickly became very sore. By the time they reached the first chamber large enough to stand in her hand was bleeding.

Physically she felt good: the methalayne revitalized her, making her feel she could run forever. It made her somewhat lightheaded too. At the back of her mind a small voice was saying disturbing things, finding all manner of problems, both practical and ethical, with Hellet's plan. It was telling her she should be utterly terrified. It was telling her that but for the gas she was breathing she would be running from all this. Probably screaming while she did it.

Celcha realized that despite the fact it should be pitch black, she could see. Whatever sight had served her ancestors on Attamast as it circled the heavens now revealed the underground world to her in shades of green and grey.

'Now the difficult part,' Hellet said.

'I thought that was the difficult part.' Celcha waved an uncertain hand at the round mouth of the tunnel she'd left stained with her blood. 'How did you even know the way? How did you even know it was possible? That we would fit?'

'Maybe and Starve told me,' Hellet said, frowning. 'But they didn't describe the route in great detail. The plan was they would guide us when the time came. But now we need to find where the gas house draws its breath from by ourselves. And give it something new to suck on!'

Mary understood the concept of momentum as it appeared in mechanics, both classical and quantum. She had, however, not known that it applied to her own life until she realized how fast she was going and stepped on the brakes as hard as she could.

Quite Contrary, *by Summer Young*

CHAPTER 20

Celcha

Celcha's life had changed quickly when Hellet discovered the book chamber back at the Arthran dig. It had changed dramatically when Librarian Sellna declared she was taking both of them back to serve at the library. Although her luxurious tenure at the library had only lasted a few months thus far, she had already grown comfortable in it. She was still a slave. Her chains might be golden, but they were still chains. Even so, without Hellet, who remained as unchanged as the story written in his scars, she might have fallen into routine and accepted her lot with the same gratitude that H'seen and her colleagues at the gas house seemed to show. She might even have reached the point when she would have fought to protect her gains rather than risk them in a larger cause.

With three words her brother had changed her life again. 'Walk with me,' he had said, and a short walk had shown her that his plans had been far more than idle dreams. With little more than a bucket of silver magic Hellet was going to introduce an agent of change. He would transmute the gas that warmed and lit the homes of Krath into a blanket of sleep to which the ganar were immune.

When they found themselves unguarded, with all of the city at their mercy, even faint hearts like those of H'seen and Redmak would beat with new resolve. The rest of the ganar would take still less encouragement to put down the tools of their labour, strike off their chains, and for the first time claim their own lives. Hellet's plans after that grew hazy. Clearly just marching out into the wider kingdom would be ill advised. The recovering canith and human soldiers would give chase to recapture them. Perhaps the ganar would claim the palace and hold the queen hostage while negotiating a peace. That was for others to decide. Hellet's self-imposed job was simply to place the choice in their hands.

Already though, Celcha's faith in the plan was faltering. Their venture through the cave systems beneath the city seemed hopeless. There were no maps of these hidden spaces. The ganar knew that links must exist between their current location and the place from which the gas house drank its fill. There were, however, no guarantees that the gaps through which the methalayne flowed were ones through which a ganar could squeeze. The ghosts had promised a path, but Hellet wasn't finding it.

The methalayne of Celcha's home world had invigorated her and woken her sight, but the concentration was higher than found on Attamast. She found herself both starved of other vital components of the air whilst being simultaneously intoxicated.

'We could lose ourselves down here and wander until we starve,' Celcha panted.

'It seems a distinct possibility,' Hellet agreed, also in difficulty. 'Though we'd suffocate long before that.'

'Then . . . what are we doing?' Celcha stopped in her tracks halfway across a small chamber the shape of a rotting squash. 'I thought you had a plan!'

'I did. I do. This is it.'

'A better one than this!' Celcha found herself wanting to shout but was too breathless for it. All her emotions bubbled closer to the surface. 'A better plan.'

'I had one of those too,' Hellet said. 'But you took it away from me.'

'Me?' Celcha put her sack down, retaining enough self-control to do it gently. 'How is any of this my fault?'

'You made me send Maybe and Starve away.'

Celcha couldn't deny that. Who better to guide them than ghosts who could fly through stone finding new ways, discovering connections? 'Well . . .' She tried to think of some defence and found none, other than her flimsy lack of trust. 'What's done is done. It's not like you can call them back.' She lifted her gaze from studying her feet to meet Hellet's eyes. 'Is it?'

Hellet leaned against the nearest wall, his chest heaving as his lungs hunted for what they needed. 'In the past, I've found that angels have a habit of turning up . . . at significant times. I don't know how they know or how they find us, but it seems they do. Perhaps it's what Yute said: that we're cracks in the world, in time itself, and that leads them. But if you want me to call them back, I'll try.'

Celcha slumped beside her brother and slid to the floor, struggling for breath. She had never wholly trusted Maybe and Starve, but the darkness of the dig had been hell and their golden light could paint them as nothing but angels. In the library light, and the comfort offered by the librarians, the angels had become ghosts. Since the only direction was no longer up, the ghosts also offered the danger of down, and Celcha's suspicions had hardened.

But here, in the dark once more, lost in endless caverns, her resolve faltered. Hellet wanted to find the gas house's intake. If the ghosts led them to it, where was the harm?

'Call them.' Her voice wheezed out of her.

Hellet nodded and opened his mouth to speak – and as he did so, the air between them began to sparkle.

The two ghosts led them through the tangle of caves where hidden waters must once have run in astonishing abandon among the roots of the dusty mountains above. Sometimes one ghost would vanish, scouting ahead for a route that the ganar could follow.

In time they came to a chamber which, although sculpted by a long-vanished river, showed the marks of chisel and hammer. The mouth of the gas house's intake was a wide horn of the same metal that the access hatch had been made from. It yawned from a low roof and sucked with a deep, constant moan. The gas flowed towards it at a speed that ruffled the fur across Celcha's back and sides as she stared up it.

Hellet lifted a flask from his sack and swirled its heavy contents. The absence of light stole the quicksilver's gleam, leaving it a curious deep purple colour in Celcha's augmented sight. A coughing fit seized him, and he almost dropped the glassware. He doubled over until it passed, then stood, wheezing.

'We could empty the flasks out here and hope that there's enough time for the reaction as the gas passes over.' Hellet looked up at the mouth.

'But?' Celcha heard the unvoiced qualifier.

'But the changed gas is heavier. It will sink rather than rise.'

'That tube leads to the concentration chamber.' Celcha followed Hellet's stare.

'There are other stages, purification stages, but yes.' Hellet nodded.

Celcha put her sack down. 'Get me up there.' She felt too weak for any climbing, but they'd come this far . . .

It took a few tries but at full stretch Hellet managed to provide a platform from which a similarly stretched Celcha could snag a seam inside the pipe. From there, with a degree of swearing and swinging, she managed to use what remained of her digging muscles to haul herself further up. She hung there breathlessly for a while, trying to recover from the effort.

The next part proved tricky. Celcha had to catch a heavy sack of precious, fragile objects whilst bracing herself against the walls of the pipe, all beneath the heavy burden of the knowledge that should she miss then the flasks would almost certainly shatter as Hellet caught them, rewarding him with a faceful of glass shards and toxic metal.

She caught the first one, just barely, and found herself slipping, her descent accompanied by the sound of tearing fabric. With a scream she jammed her elbows into the pipe walls and prayed to any god who might be listening, all of them in fact, in one wordless plea. Whether by divine intervention or basic physics, Celcha didn't fall. She repositioned herself, sure that only the upwards rush of gas inhaled by the gas room far above had kept her from a disastrous plunge.

The torn sackcloth exposed a flask but had released none of

them so far. She took the neck of the bag in her teeth, put her trust in her footholds, and reached for new handholds. In this manner, with her back to the pipe's wall and the sack almost scraping the opposite side, she inched upwards.

The nightmare struggle that followed felt as if it took hours. At several points she thought she'd passed out for a few moments but had managed to jam herself in the pipe too tightly to fall.

In the end, long after she felt she'd exceeded the limit of her endurance, she reached a level section and was able to painstakingly manoeuvre the sack past her into the relative safety ahead. With all her muscles trembling, and her lungs aching with the effort to find what she needed, Celcha began to descend for the second sack.

It felt unreasonable that their success should hinge on feats of athleticism and dexterity that Celcha would have bet on herself to fail ten times in a row. She found herself angry that Hellet and his damned ghosts had put her in such a ridiculous position: saviour of a plan that had no right to succeed. But somehow, against all odds, Celcha caught the second sack and managed to position it beside the first.

The climb felt as if it was at the very least a hundred yards. Celcha knew that without the regular rims where one section was fixed to the next, she would never have made it. Without the upwards rush of gas trying to lift the snug ganar-sized blockage she constituted, she would never have made it. And without the iron in her arms from a lifetime of digging, she would never have made it.

Celcha lay in the horizontal section gasping for breath and trembling with fatigue. She could hear the machinery of the gas room up ahead. She was within striking distance. She had in the sacks before her the alchemical magic needed to put an entire city to sleep.

At last, she crawled on, pushing the sacks ahead of her as gently as she could, glass squeaking against glass. A crunching sound told her that at least one flask had already broken, but whatever effect its contents might be having on the methalayne were swept ahead of her.

After ten yards the tunnel began to dip slightly and to narrow, speeding the flow of gas. Celcha's journey was over; a dog might manage the remaining distance but not a library-fed ganar. She took the first of the flasks from the sack in a shaky hand. Everything they'd done so far could be undone or walked away from. This act, this unstoppering of the flask, this pouring of the liquid silver . . . this was what would either get them killed, or change history, or both.

Celcha tried to imagine it. A whole city drugged to sleep. Several thousand ganar suddenly handed the power of life or death over the humans and canith who had subjugated them. For a moment visions of the ganar slaughtering their former masters ran through her head. Surely it wouldn't come to that? Surely having been shown the ganar's power and having been shown mercy the city of Krath would change its ways? Their queen would sign a new accord. A three-way peace. An equality.

'. . . eeeelcha . . .' Hellet's distant voice carried on the gas flow, a note of query in it, she thought, rather than panic.

Doubts still assailed her. She wasn't intended for decisions this big. She had never wanted anything but a chance at comfort, the right to earn respect, a life not overshadowed by constant fear. And in that moment of reflection the decision was made for her. The ganar had none of those things.

She opened the flask, poured it out, watched the quicksilver trickle away down the pipe, driven by gravity and the force of the gas that smoked as it passed over the scurrying droplets. She opened another and another and another, tipped one after the next until they were all gone, then shook the sacks to free the trickling contents of the broken flasks. And finally, wearily, she shuffled back to the drop, then began to inch down it for the last time to join her brother.

'Where?' Celcha struggled to see. 'Where am I?'

'You fell. I caught you,' Hellet wheezed. He lifted her to her feet. Above her the mouth of the pipe gaped, still inhaling its endless breath.

Celcha patted herself down. She had cuts on her elbows and her ankle felt as if hot skewers had been driven into the bones.

'If they catch us, you'll have to kill me.' The pain from her ankle, although a pale shadow of the cruelty done to her in Arthran, reminded her of the punishments for even small infractions. She didn't want to find out what the city kept in store for her latest crime.

'Of course.' Hellet showed her the knife he had in his book satchel. 'Their power over us is finished. One way or the other.' He took her hand and pulled her towards the crack they'd entered the chamber by.

'What now?' Celcha hobbled after him, wheezing.

Hellet answered in short bursts of words punctuated by ragged breaths. 'They'll switch cylinders in about two hours. Hopefully the quicksilver will follow the gas into the cylinder. At the least it will sit somewhere in the compressor. When the new cylinder goes online the altered gas will flow everywhere in the city. It will be dark outside, cold; the city will still be awake. The gas won't burn, so the lights and fires will go out and it will spread. The ganar will inherit the city come morning. We'll need to go out there and tell them what's happened. After that they need to decide their own fate.'

Celcha frowned. 'We're a bit like the library then.'

'How so, sister?'

'The library puts knowledge in your hands and it's up to you to understand it, judge it, use it. It gives you opportunity and leaves you to take it or ignore it. We've done the same. Only a bit more forcefully.'

'I suppose we have.' Hellet nodded then broke off to cough for a score of paces before finally controlling himself. 'We should hurry. Methalayne's the proof that you can have too much of a good thing.'

Hellet remembered the way out, which was fortunate, since both ghosts had vanished soon after leading them to the intake. Celcha followed her brother in a daze, her mind wandering. Her thoughts fractured and diffused into the gas. She managed to worry that Hellet might become as disoriented as her and lose the way. It was her last coherent worry for a while.

Celcha woke with a yawn. She luxuriated in the moment of comfort, as complete as any experienced in her library bed. The rocks digging into her side, the small stones embedded in her cheek, the ache of her ankle, the rawness of her lungs, and the knife twisting in her brain, all introduced themselves one by one, forming an orderly queue. Memory arrived last, prompting her into an ill-advised scramble that, instead of putting her on her feet, simply rearranged her across the rocks and very nearly pitched her into the chasm on whose side she had collapsed.

Hellet lay on the narrow path ahead of her, snoring loudly. Just below them, the gorge into which she had almost thrown herself appeared to be filled with a yellowish fog that lapped at the path just a few yards from Celcha's feet.

'Hellet!' She hobbled over to him and started to shake him. 'Wake up!'

Her brother woke with a comfortable yawn that mimicked her own so closely that she immediately took a firmer hold and warned him to stay still, in case he also completed his return to consciousness with a startled lunge.

'How long did we sleep?' Celcha knew it was a foolish question as she asked it. 'And what's that stuff!' She aimed Hellet's attention at the fog.

'Oh . . .' Hellet struggled to his feet. 'We were unconscious long enough for someone at the gas house to shut off the supply and for the changed gas to back up to . . . here.'

Celcha looked at the undulating surface of the fog, a strange yellow sea. It seemed closer to them than it had been. 'It's still rising.' A faint acrid scent reached her nostrils and clawed at her eyes. 'We should go. Now!'

'Yellow?' Hellet retreated ahead of her, muttering to himself. 'It shouldn't look like that.'

By the time they reached the top, the rising gas had swallowed the place where they'd been lying.

Hellet stared down at it. 'It's heavier than air but it will mix as soon as it finds a breeze. It's going to spread over the cavern floor and then follow us down the stairwell. So, it will put all the librarians to sleep too.'

Celcha had been wondering about them. They didn't need gas for light and in consequence the supply ended further down the mountain, leaving the library kitchens to cook the meals on charcoal-burning stoves.

'We should hurry.' Hellet set off towards the stairs at quite a stride.

'Wait.' Celcha, limping on her sore ankle, felt unsteady on the treacherous cavern floor.

'Hurry!' Hellet snapped the word, sounding more worried than at any time during their wildly dangerous adventure so far, and apparently with less reason.

Celcha gritted her teeth and hurried. The fog had stung her eyes even when she wasn't in it, so she shared some of her brother's urgency. She'd rather not be wandering blind inside it, waiting for it to clear before her streaming eyes could show her the world again.

Together they wound their way down the stairs and through the complex. They saw nobody in the complex's corridors save a lone guard who sniffed as they passed, as if their fur still carried the reek of methalayne, and a few kitchen staff who lived on site. The librarians and apprentices had yet to rise for the day.

Hellet stumbled through the passageways, head down, looking the opposite of someone celebrating a triumph. His muttering accompanied them through the complex, a repetition of alchemical formulas, a litany of science that meant nothing to Celcha but sounded curiously like a mourning song.

At the wolf's head entrance two armoured guards watched them leave as the sun started to rise over the sleeping city.

'You two shouldn't be going out alone,' one man called after them.

Celcha turned back to address them. You didn't ignore a master, especially not a guard. 'Librarian Sellna sent us to get—'

'Not together she didn't.' The other guard stepped towards them. 'One of you stays here. You know the rules.'

Celcha hadn't heard this rule before, but then again, until last night's activities, Hellet hadn't left the library since his arrival. It made sense though: two of them leaving together was much more likely to be an escape attempt.

'I'll stay.' Hellet stumbled past her. 'I'll stay. It's my fault.'

'What's your fault?'

'The mercury. I think it poisoned me. Did something to my mind.'

'Mercury?' Celcha wasn't following him.

'The quicksilver. It should have worked. I was so sure. I did the calculations. I did them so many—'

'I'm not leaving without you.' Celcha started back towards the guards with him.

'Celcha!' Hellet grabbed hold of both her wrists and steered her towards him, staring into her eyes. 'I need you to go down and tell the ganar what we've done.' He glanced away at the approaching guard. 'I'll be fine here. They'll all be asleep in a short while. I'll join you at the gas house. Now go!' He released her roughly, pushing her away, down the slope.

Celcha couldn't argue with the logic, but something felt badly wrong. Yet Hellet was right: the ganar had to know. There wasn't much time and they needed to understand that. To seize the opportunity. She was scared of what they might do, scared of the consequences, scared of everything, but Hellet had been right, things couldn't be left the way they were.

'I won't be long!' And with that she was off, jogging down the slope on tired legs, wincing each time she put weight on the ankle she'd hurt.

An unrooted sense of disaster chased her, nipping at her heels. And down below, the silent city waited beneath a rising sun.

There's always a bigger fish. And sometimes it's not a fish.

Competitive Angling, *by Posey Idon*

CHAPTER 21

Arpix

Between them Kerrol and Arpix helped Clovis back out of the mine workings. The cratalacs were all dead, torn apart in some inexplicable way by Wentworth, who although huge for a house cat, seemed no more dangerous than a biggish dog. Salamonda had not yet given an account of how Yute's pet had managed to defend her to such devastating effect.

Arpix explained this to Clovis as she slumped against him, one arm around his shoulders, the other around her brother's. He told her that Evar was scouting the perimeter. That brought her first, pained response.

'At least someone's doing something sensible.'

'Kerrol and I are not?' Arpix felt rather aggrieved.

'You should not have gone after Evar,' Clovis grunted. 'You are frail and have no sense of self-preservation.'

'I suppose I should have left you to bleed in the dark too?' Arpix counted himself as slow to anger. Glacial, Carlotte had been fond of saying. But something about this warrior canith was getting under his skin even as her hot breath puffed across his neck.

'Yes,' Clovis snarled. 'There's an order to these things. Secure what can be saved first. Recover the wounded later if they are still a problem.'

Arpix hefted Clovis up higher, trying to compensate for the height difference with Kerrol as they entered the taller tunnels near the entrance. His own snarl was half from the effort of lifting her and half anger. 'You are *not* a problem. And the wounded will always be at the top of any list I write!'

'Well, you shouldn't be writing any lists, human—'

'Awww, your first fight!' Kerrol snorted and helped his sister towards the daylight.

'We're not fighting!' Both of them said it together.

Kerrol shrugged and they advanced a few paces before he added, 'It seems as if I'm to be the last one to get a pet human. I have my eye on the Meelan, or perhaps the Salamonda. She seems capable and comes with an able guardian.'

As soon as they got Clovis outside, Arpix set to checking her injuries.

'This needs to come off.' He indicated the torn leather armour that seemed, on closer inspection, to be made of book covers meticulously sewn together and reinforced with metal bands that turned out to be book hinges.

Clovis snarled. Causing him to snatch his hand back. 'If more enemies come—'

'If more enemies come, you'll be no more use against them in armour than out of it,' Arpix said sternly. 'From the amount of bleeding I'd say that you've got at least one wound that needs stitching. And if it's not cleaned it will probably sour and poison your blood.' He frowned at the armour. 'It would be better if we could cut this off. I don't want to move your shoulder.'

The growl in Clovis's throat was blood-curdling, her eyes narrow and aimed squarely at him. Kerrol leaned over and pulled Clovis's knife from the sheath on her hip. 'Here, use this.'

Arpix glanced from the proffered blade to Clovis's terrifying scowl. 'Are you sure you don't want to . . .'

Kerrol shook his head. 'I'm good, thanks. She bit me last time I tried to help her.'

Arpix looked around at the others. Normally Salamonda would pitch in to help with something like this, but it seemed that being cornered by half a dozen enraged cratalacs and then watching as Wentworth turned them into a collection of cratalac pieces had been as much gore as the woman could cope with in one day. Jella was looking after her, both of them huddled out of the wind against a tumbledown wall.

'Meelan, could you get me some water? A lot. And some cloth.' Arpix knew the last request would mean trimming some from someone's clothing. They really had next to nothing, even after the years they'd spent trying to build up their supplies.

Next, Arpix met the challenge of Clovis's fierce, grey-eyed stare. 'Don't bite me.' He knelt beside her with the knife. 'It's not sanitary.'

He worked methodically, unpicking the armour's stitching and setting it in the sun for later when he would take their bone needle and try to repair the damage done by cratalac claws. He tried to avoid Clovis's eyes though he could feel her stare burning on his neck as he worked.

Cover by cover, he exposed her shoulder and followed the wound down towards her ribs. Some of the thick, leather rectangles still bore traces of the original decoration and titles. 'Observations on the mating rituals of the apterygiformes,' Arpix translated from Wegian.

'The what?' Clovis panted through her teeth, wincing as he pulled the cover away. The flesh below was torn and sticking to her armour.

'Apterygiformes,' Arpix repeated. 'A genus of flightless birds, I believe.'

'You know too much.' She put her head back.

Arpix studied Clovis's injuries. The cratalac had done a lot of damage. Without the armour it would have torn through her ribs and pierced her lung. Ripped the entire thing out, probably.

Meelan set down a bucket of water and handed Arpix a square of grey cloth. Arpix did his best to clean the cloth then turned to consider the jagged, black-crusted tear that ran from high on Clovis's shoulder to past her ribcage. She really was magnificently muscled, lithe rather than bulked up like some of the library guards had been. The basic canith body structure didn't seem that different from his own: proportionately narrower in the chest, a higher and longer ribcage, a barely visible covering of short fur, in Clovis's case shading from the almost crimson of her mane to something between golden and tan. The lower legs were the main structural difference, the feet elongated and only the toes making contact with the ground. There was a word for that . . .

'Digitigrade!' He only knew it in his own tongue and then only from an obscure book on anatomy.

'What?' Clovis growled.

Arpix shook his head. 'This is going to hurt a bit.' He reached forward with the damp cloth.

'You don't scare me, human boy.' Clovis showed her teeth.

He bent to the task, starting around the edges, setting the cloth to the bloody fur over the hard muscle of her abdomen.

An hour later the wound was clean and the bucket full of reddish water.

'It's getting a bit dim for stitching.' Arpix felt as if he was making excuses. He'd never sewn up such a large wound and the prospect daunted him. 'Better to wait for dark and do it with the fire-pot close by.'

He stood, stretching the ache out of his back. Evar, who had passed by the mine entrance to check on Clovis a few times during his scouting, was standing about thirty yards off. He beckoned Arpix over. Wearily, Arpix went to him.

'You should be careful.'

It wasn't the greeting Arpix had been expecting. 'I should?'

'With Clovis.'

'I . . . I'm doing the best I can. I'm not a doctor. I got all this from books. This place . . . everything's dirty, I've got no equip-ment . . . if she gets sick it won't be because I didn't try.'

'That's not what I meant.'

Arpix frowned. 'I don't understand then . . .'

Evar snorted. 'My sister is . . . She's had a hard life. Her family was taken from her, violently, at a young age, and she never forgets it. It makes it difficult for her to trust others. And. Well. Let's just say, these things have ended poorly in the past.'

Arpix looked back at the hollow and the small group gathered there, then back at Evar. He felt as if he'd started a book on page two hundred in the middle of a complex plot twist that stood on a long story to which he was not privy. 'Honestly, Evar.' He struggled for the right words in canith and growled them through an increasingly sore throat. 'I have no idea what you're talking about.'

It was Evar's turn to frown. 'She likes you. You know that?'

'Me?' Arpix took a step back in surprise.

Evar rolled his eyes. 'You didn't notice her sniffing you?'

'Sniffing?'

Evar shook his head. 'Or the fact you've had your hands all over her and still own the same number of fingers?'

'I'm *saving her life*!' Arpix protested. 'If the wound's not cleaned, she'll die!'

'And you're the only one who can clean a wound, are you?' Evar showed his teeth in amusement.

'Oh,' Arpix said.

'*Oh* indeed.'

Arpix felt his face colouring. All of him was suddenly too hot despite the reaching shadows and the wind's chill.

'And you?' Evar asked. 'What do you think of my sister?'

'W-well . . .' Arpix stuttered, his throat dry. This was territory he'd never trodden. Rarely even thought about. 'I mean . . . she's magnificent, of course. But . . .' He couldn't really think of a 'but'. He waved his hands about a bit, hoping some explanation might drop into them. Perhaps Wentworth would appear out of nowhere again and drag him off, saving him from his current mortification.

'Just be careful.' Evar turned and walked off. 'And don't hurt her, because Livira will be cross with me if I have to beat you.'

The sun had slipped low to the horizon by the time that everyone was gathered in the hollow before the mine opening. The shadow of the forgotten queen stretched across them, and the sky became a bruise.

Evar finally returned from his scouting to report that the skeer had retreated to three camps that were evenly spaced around the plateau.

'Perhaps they think the cratalacs have us trapped underground,' Meelan said.

'They'll want to see them leave before they'll believe we're dead,' Jella speculated.

'They probably want to capture them again. The creatures seem like a formidable asset,' Kerrol said.

Translating for both parties kept Arpix too busy to add his own thoughts to the mix.

'Can you eat a cratalac?' Salamonda asked. 'I feel like you should be able to. You are what you eat, after all, and they were going to eat us.'

That was enough for Arpix to interject, 'I'm as tired of beans as any of you, but those things looked like a spider's nightmare and smelled worse on the inside than they did on the outside. I wouldn't want to risk it. I mean if we poison ourselves out here—'

'Too salty,' Evar said.

'You tried some?' Arpix looked at the canith in faint horror. 'Raw . . .?'

Jost, sitting opposite him in the circle, gagged.

Evar shrugged. 'I've never tasted anything that wasn't grown around our pool. I was curious.'

Meelan shook his head. 'The real question is what are we going to do now?'

'Do? What is there to do?' Librarian Jost had been uncharacteristically quiet since the attack, muted by the horror of it all no doubt. 'We need our visitors to leave. They've clearly angered the skeer. We never had any of this before. What's next? More monsters? Rocks catapulted at us? Spears dropped from the sky? These sabbers can take themselves elsewhere and the skeer will follow.' She ran her fingers through her long hair, thinner and paler than it used to be, then nodded as if agreeing with herself in the absence of other support.

Meelan scowled at her. 'I meant that this all has to mean something. The canith that Livira found centuries in our future have found us, out here, in all this nothing.'

'Well, we did shine a light for them,' Jella said. 'And they made a dust cloud . . .'

Meelan turned his hard stare her way, but she just gave him a weary smile. 'It's not just the canith. There's Wentworth too. Yute sent him.' Jost snorted and started a retort, but Meelan carried on, talking over her dismissal. 'Yute knows where and when we are.

He's watching over us. He expects something from us. All of us, canith and humans. Something more than huddling here in the dust and eating beans until we die. We didn't just drop here at random. The library sent us. We thought it was so the skeer couldn't eat us. But maybe there's more to it. Maybe there's something important here. Something we need to do.'

'He's right.' Arpix wasn't sure that he was, but he understood that what they needed more than the truth was a purpose. Yute had said something about that years ago. The deputy head librarian and former assistant had extolled the virtues of the gift of purpose. They needed a direction, even if it pointed to exactly where they were. Direction would draw them together. With direction there would be no talk of the canith being sent away – not that they could be sent away, and not that Arpix would send Clovis wounded into the wilds even if he could. 'He's right. We've been missing something this whole time. Clovis was right when she wanted to search the mine for whatever it was holding back the skeer. That might not be what we need to find, but we need to find something, and we won't if we don't look.'

Evar had been squatting beside Kerrol, not slumped like the rest of them but poised for action. For some while now he'd been gazing up at the queen's head as the last rays of the sun played across the timeworn stone, throwing the features into a sharp relief of crimson and shadow. Arpix wasn't sure the canith had heard a word of what was probably the most impassioned speech he'd ever given.

'She . . .' Evar got slowly to his feet, frowning deeply. He raised a hand to shade his eyes. '. . . looks . . . familiar . . .' He turned to look down at the others. 'No?'

'What are you talking about? Who looks familiar?' Arpix stood too, trying to see if out past the giant head and shoulders emerging at a slant from the plateau's surface there was someone approaching.

'Oh dear gods . . .' Jella's voice shook with barely checked emotion. 'The nose . . . It's the nose.'

'What's the nose?' Arpix wondered if everyone had gone mad. Or perhaps it was him. He'd read that quicksilver caused insanity when it poisoned you.

'The statue,' Meelan said faintly. He was catching it too, whatever the madness was.

'There's never been a nose,' Arpix said crossly. The nose, or at least the end of it, had been knocked off the statue. 'What? You think we're supposed to be looking for the nose?' It was ridiculous. 'A magic nose? You think that's what holds the skeer back?'

'I think you're right.' Jost had stopped tugging her hair and was peering at the statue with her head to one side. 'How did a sabber see it when we didn't?'

'What are they all staring at?' Clovis snarled, sounding as impatient as Arpix felt. 'Who's familiar, Evar? How can you even tell? They all look the same to me, at least until I've had a good sniff of one.'

Then Arpix saw it too. It struck him in one sudden moment, like a fist that ghosted through all his ribs and struck him square in the heart. It really *was* the nose. It was big, but not *that* big, yet somehow it had been the key to recognizing her.

'Damn . . .' Arpix didn't even chide himself for swearing. 'Is that . . . it's Carlotte, isn't it?'

*The evil that men do lives after them; the
good is oft interred with their bones.*

Julius Caesar, *by William Shakespeare*

CHAPTER 22

Evar

'How did you recognize her when we didn't?' Arpix asked, amazed.

Evar didn't know. 'Maybe because canith faces are different and
we look for different features to hang our recognition from? Or
because you had more on your minds when you first came here? I
think it might be something you see early on or never.'

Arpix translated for the others. Some nodded, thoughtfully, while
others debated in their swift bird-like chatter. 'How do you even
know Carlotte?'

'I was with Livira when she found her.' The young woman was
perhaps the last human Evar had taken a close look at before arriving
at the plateau. He hadn't been sure she was a friend to Arpix or
the other humans, but either way he hadn't been keen to repeat the
story of their encounter because it had seemed inevitable that it led
to a grisly end. 'The library was on fire, and she was running from
the flames.' The last part he didn't want to say, even now. 'A band
of canith had her captive.'

Arpix's brows raised at that. He pressed his lips into a thin line
then took a deep breath. 'She must have escaped them.'

Kerrol loomed over them both. 'How is a human girl, that Evar
saw days ago, immortalized in stone, here, in an ancient statue? The
thing has to be a thousand years old if it's a day.'

'She must have escaped the canith,' Evar echoed Arpix, thinking hard. 'And made it to the Exchange. From there she could go to any time.'

Kerrol shook his dark mane. 'But, if I've understood you, you can only visit the past as a ghost that nobody can see or touch, and you can't touch anything yourself?'

'Yes . . .' Evar drew the word out through his teeth.

'It appears,' Arpix growled, 'that Carlotte managed pretty well for a ghost.' He went over to translate to the other humans before returning with the clay pot and a supply of bean husks to burn. Just lighting the thing took an age of striking stones together to catch and kindle the sparks. It was full dark by the time he succeeded.

Evar had to force himself not to flinch as the flames began to lick up. He'd been fascinated by his first encounter with fire but since then its destructive side had dominated, culminating in the library inferno. He doubted he would ever be comfortable near an open flame again.

Arpix roused Clovis from her half-doze and began to stitch. Evar started a new conversation, more to distract Clovis from the pain than through any urgency.

'So, brother, sister, what are we going to do?'

'Well, we can't just hide on this hill for the rest of our lives.' Clovis snarled as the needle went too deep.

'I'm all for hiding,' Kerrol said. 'My shoulder hurts. And besides, I like watching these humans. It could take me years to learn all—'

'We're not spending years here!' Clovis shook her head. Arpix tutted and told her to be still.

'Agreed.' Evar didn't plan to copy the humans. He hadn't escaped the chamber he'd lived in all his life to be trapped on a dusty plateau for the rest of it. 'But where do we go? What do we do? And why?'

'We find our kind,' Clovis said. 'We raise an army and we come back here to end the skeer.'

'Why?' Evar shook his head. 'Why spend the lives of canith who value them to end the lives of skeer who seem indifferent to their individual fate? War is the means to an end. It can't be an end in itself.'

'Because—' Clovis winced as the needle tugged. 'Because they control the library, and it's technology that wins wars. People keep building cities at the foot of the mountain, and burning them down, for a reason. The library is the ultimate weapon.'

Kerrol leaned forward, the light of Arpix's fire-pot casting him in warm angles and invisibly black shadow. 'Now we come back to the war that matters. The one our brothers have chosen sides in.'

'Mayland?' Clovis scowled at him. 'What was he even talking about? And why did Starval go with him?'

Kerrol grinned. 'You're too busy with the small picture to see the big one, sister.'

'Not watching what's in front of you was what got you stabbed,' Clovis growled.

Kerrol shrugged. 'I'm not the one being stitched up by a human.'

'Enough!' Evar overrode Clovis's hot reply. 'Kerrol's talking about Mayland's pet mythology.'

Kerrol took over. 'I am. The idea that there's a struggle between the library's creator and his brother. An ideological war between those who believe the library should serve as a kind of universal memory. A memory we can easily access after we obliterate ourselves, which is something we appear to do on a regular basis as soon as we discover the means to do it efficiently. And, on the other side, those who believe we should start from scratch each time. Those who think that the handful of ignorant children who survive the periodic calamities should start again in a place like this. Banging the rocks together.' He shot a glance at Arpix, who ignored him.

'There are more sides to it than that,' Evar protested. 'There's whatever it is we have now. It's certainly not easy access. Easy access would be an assistant bringing you the book that answers the questions you have, and finding the relevant section for you, and translating it too. And there's a host of other options.'

'People don't like a host of options.' Kerrol held up two fingers. 'No matter how nuanced debate might be at the start, if lots of people are involved then it ultimately condenses around two poles deemed to be irreconcilable. And then you have your war. Which in and of itself is an argument against the library. When evolution has shaped us to tribalism, how can we be trusted with the means to reduce tribes to dust?'

'That sounds insane,' Evar said.

'Not really. If you pick the solution you think is best out of a host of possibilities then everyone is going to have a slightly different answer to the problem. You need support, so you accept a few small changes and move to someone else's solution. Now there are two of you behind one idea. You need more. The process repeats and repeats. You see people coalescing behind an idea you hate, and it becomes more important to be lined up behind something vaguely palatable that has the numbers to oppose them than it does to get exactly the solution you wanted. In the end there are two solutions, aligned against each other. And in the library's case, two ideologies and an uneasy truce.

'Mayland would call it a lesson learned from history. I'd call it a natural consequence of allowing crowds to decide how some complex problem is to be tackled.' Kerrol licked his teeth. 'In any event, neither of you is going to pick a side based on the issues. Almost nobody ever does.' Evar opened his mouth to challenge Kerrol to tell him what he would decide when his brother hadn't even made up his own mind. Kerrol pre-empted him. 'It's obvious what you two are going to do. Evar's going to take whatever side his human girl picks. And Clovis is going to choose the opposite.'

Arpix looked up from his stitching. 'Rather than jumping into somebody else's war, perhaps we could work out what we're here for and what we're going to do about it.'

'He's not wrong,' Clovis growled. She put her hand over the hand in which Arpix held the needle. 'Tell us about this Wentworth. It seems a formidable weapon.'

Arpix absently removed her hand from his and continued to stitch. 'Wentworth is Yute's cat. But Livira once stole a book that described the library's greatest guide to be a creature red in tooth and claw, and whose name began with "V" or possibly "W". At the time we thought it was the head librarian's dog, Volente. It seems we were wrong and that it was Wentworth.'

Evar tried to imagine the creature that could destroy five crata-lacs at once. 'If Yute sent it to you then why hasn't it helped? I mean, apart from today. If you were dispatched here for a reason, shouldn't this Wentworth be telling you what it is?'

Arpix looked over to the other humans and asked a question. Salamonda replied.

'She says he was always lazy. More interested in sleeping in the sun than anything else.' Arpix shrugged. 'To be honest, I never saw him move. He'd just lie there like he was dead. Volente never spoke either. I think they're more like guides. You ask for something and they take you to it. Wentworth must have built up some affection for Salamonda over the decades she fed him and let him sleep in her kitchen. Even then, the most he's done over the past four years is stop her dying.' Arpix leaned down to bite off the thread he'd been using. 'Done. Don't tear them.' He stood and looked around at the night, at the stars shining frosty in the black vaults of heaven, at the walls of the hollow they sat in, catching glimmers of the fire-pot's glow as they curved away.

'Wentworth!' He called to the night, following the name with human chatter. 'Wentworth!' He looked around, shrugged, and sat back down beside Clovis.

'What did you say?' Evar asked.

'I told him I had something for him,' Arpix growled. 'Or more accurately I asked, "What's this?" Cats seem to like a mystery more than a straightforward offer.'

Clovis sat up slowly, wincing. 'What's that?'

'No, *what's this?* You've got to make it sound tempting.' Arpix held out his hand as if concealing some tempting morsel.

Clovis shoved his arm aside. 'I said, what's that?' And she pointed.

Sitting in the shadows behind Evar was a cat. It didn't seem particularly big to him but it was the first one he'd seen, and he hadn't much idea how large they should be. It was certainly quite fat.

'Wentworth!' Salamonda was on her feet, crossing the hollow with surprising speed. The cat allowed himself to be fussed while giving the impression that this was a special one-time favour to the old woman.

Arpix slumped and muttered something to the night.

Evar didn't speak the language, but he knew what the man had said. 'All we had to do was call him . . .'

A story is how you tell yourself truths
you're not brave enough to hear.

Carved into a desk by Livira Page

CHAPTER 23

Livira

Livira found herself once more encased in iron, jolting along on the back of a white stallion. She narrowly avoided a tumble into the heather this time by dint of leaning forward and embracing the horse's neck. Fortunately, it seemed a patient animal, quite unlike the skittish warhorses she'd read about in other stories. In her version of the tale the knight's steed was named Amble, and was fond of apples, sunshine, and standing still.

In the end Livira did fall off, but during the act of dismounting, and it was a less violent affair than toppling from the saddle of a moving horse. She fell backwards into the springy arms of a gorse bush, one spur caught in the left-hand stirrup. After untangling herself and stretching out the kinks in her back, Livira struggled to remove her helm. She tossed it aside, wondering what Malar would have made of all this armour. She could imagine him as a particularly foulmouthed knight in battered old mail, leaving a trail of shiny-armoured corpses behind him.

On a nearby ridge Livira sat down and watched the tower, still half a mile off. This was her take on the princess in the tower, a story that rattled through the millennia, told in a near infinity of tongues, told by species that you wouldn't mistake for human on even the darkest and foggiest of nights. Livira had wanted to explore what it really meant to be trapped and what it really meant to be rescued. The prison could be anything: a library chamber, a well in the Dust from which you couldn't stray, or just a life that – however luxurious – had made you its captive, struck away the legs of your independence one after the other. She had wanted to examine the role of the rescuer and the rescuee. Neither was easy. Sometimes one was hard to tell from the other. Sometimes the knight's armour was their own iron tower from which a rescue was also required.

In the end she had just written a story and hoped that it would prompt the reader to do the hard work. She'd spent most of her time on the witch, truth be told. The witch tended to get overlooked in these tales.

Livira sat with her iron-clad knees drawn up to support her iron-clad arms. The tower stood like a dark finger of stone raised against a slate sky. She watched the white-capped waves applaud the cliffs to the west. To the east, the green patchwork of agriculture began to assert itself over the wilds.

Livira ignored the tug of the wind, sinking her roots into the story, claiming it page by page without so much as taking a step towards the tower. She thought about going down and knocking on the door. Asking the witch what she thought about the whole business. But it seemed that wouldn't be necessary. She'd come to claim her book and as the author she didn't need to follow the plotline down the hill. She already knew where it led. The assistant had said she just needed to take hold of the book, and that was what she was doing, as surely as a tree took hold of the earth whilst a seed became a sapling, and the sapling stretched up to reach for the heavens.

The white child came as Livira had known she must if she were to foil this attempt as she had foiled the five before that. Whatever story Livira had tried to follow, the white child had appeared when she got close to her goal, emerging unexpectedly from a shadowed doorway, or from behind a mask, or rising from an ancient lake, or clambering over a high wall. Every time she had broken Livira's grasp just as success threatened. Fear wasn't her only weapon. The story thinned around her, tore like a dream when the light of waking shines out through all the holes in its logic.

This time Livira wouldn't move. She wouldn't be surprised. Not even if the white child clawed her way out of the peaty soil or tumbled from the horse's belly in a gory tide of blood, bile, and half-digested grass.

As it happened, this time the white child approached out in the open. Livira saw her coming up the valley. Where she walked, the countryside paled before her, and in her wake she left only bedrock, bleached to the whiteness of paper, as if her mere presence had erased the story, exposing the blank page beneath.

Livira set aside her sword and sent Amble ambling away with an iron-gloved slap to his haunches. She focused on her guest's advance, setting her mind to the task of resisting the attack she constituted. Where the story thinned, Livira shored it up with detail, explanations, and justifications. Whatever the challenge, she met it. This was her world. She could marshal the forces of history and of magic to her cause. Chance itself would dance to her tune. Coincidence was her messenger boy.

The white child's progress slowed. For the first time she seemed to feel the slope and to have to fight the tug of the heather, and the soft sucking of the peaty ground. The bleached area around her shrank and shrank again. Her wake narrowed from broad swathe to thin trail.

When the child was no more than twenty yards away, leaning into the brisk wind that now plucked at her white wrappings, Livira hailed her unwanted visitor.

'Who are you? Why are you doing this?'

'For the library.' The girl's voice reached her through the wind's complaints, thin but clear.

'You're wrong,' Livira protested. 'Taking the book back will save the library. The assistant said so.'

'The . . . assistant . . . lied.' The girl struggled closer.

'They don't lie,' Livira called out, though even as she said it she realized that she had no proof either way. She wanted the book so she could exist in the same time and space as Evar once more. The rest was conjecture. She didn't even know where she stood in the library's great war. She loved the library, or at least she loved books. She valued the knowledge and the passion they held. The memory of races and species beyond knowing. The culture and achievements of untold millennia. And yet she had seen how access to such riches could accelerate the seemingly never-ending cycle of destruction, the race from pointed rocks to nuclear fires in which worlds burned. Yute championed the current compromise, and even that carried a sharp edge with which one civilization after the next seemed determined to slice its own throat. Yamala had wanted freer access. Perhaps something like Yute's ring that held within it every book ever written and would not only translate the contents for you but find, within that endless forest of pages, the information you sought. If Yute's compromise was handing toddlers a sharp knife, then Yamala wanted to place a brimming cauldron of burning oil into their arms and advise them to run downstairs. These were the solutions offered by the children of Irad, the founder. And his brother Jaspeth? He seemed to want the library erased and for the survivors of each apocalypse to start from scratch without even history to remind them of their ancestors' mistakes.

Whoever was lying, the child or the assistant, it made little difference. Livira couldn't choose between the options. She just wanted her life back, or, failing that, some new life where she could speak to Evar and be heard. Take his hand and be held.

'I just want to go home,' Livira said. The girl was close now, mere yards off, pulling herself forward using the gorse bushes, her hands bloody.

'You don't know me?' The girl looked up, pink eyes pinning Livira with the coldness of their regard. 'They say to know a person you need only walk a mile in their shoes . . .'

'They do say that,' Livira agreed through clenched teeth.

'And still you don't know me? I'd heard that you were clever.'

'I don't understand.' Livira's head ached from trying to keep everything together. The child's influence was undermining everything, chewing away at it, sucking out the colour. Livira's grasp on the story had almost been sufficient, but now it was as if, one by one, her fingers were being peeled back from the prize that she had so nearly wrestled into her possession.

Something tickled at the back of her mind even as everything she wanted was being taken from her control. Another story. A fable like this one. A tale that wormed through the foundations of an unexpectedly large and diverse collection of literary traditions.

'Rumpelstiltskin!'

'That's not me.' The white child's smile revealed white teeth in pale gums, the smear of blood across them shockingly crimson. She was closer now, almost close enough to touch.

Her shoes? The blood's crimson flowed briefly into a vision of ruby slippers. No, not those. The answer came in a moment of epiphany just as the small white hand reached for her. Two ordinary-looking leather shoes. The middle pair of three. Arranged in a neat row at the bottom of a cupboard in an attic room where the dust lay like sorrow.

'Those shoes felt so strange on my feet.' Livira's paralysis released her, and she took a step backwards, avoiding the girl's clutching fingers. 'You're Yute's lost daughter.'

The child stopped as if she'd walked into an invisible wall.

'Your name is . . .' Livira hunted the vaults of her memory. Yute must have mentioned it once, surely. Or if not him it must have tumbled past Salamonda's lips on the ceaseless flow of chatter, even if just once over all the years.

The girl narrowed her eyes and pressed on through whatever barrier had stopped her.

'Yolanda,' Livira said. 'Your name is Yolanda.'

And Livira was back in the reading room – holding the book – watching as a huge insectoid Escape scattered reading desks in its hunt for Evar and Starval. Livira didn't remember the scene, but she knew both brothers survived it. She turned and saw herself, or rather the assistant she'd been trapped within for so long. The assistant watched her, its expression neutral, eyes glowing a soft blue. For some reason Livira's shoulder ached.

'You got it!' Malar stepped in between the assistant and Livira. 'We should go.'

Behind him the Escape swept the assistant up in its huge beetle jaws and began to pound her into the ground. Livira looked away and saw Evar emerging from his hiding place, his brother Starval trying to stop him. Even here when Livira was buried inside the assistant he couldn't abandon her, or perhaps he just couldn't abandon anyone.

'Come on!' Malar grabbed her arm and pulled her roughly away. 'This has all happened. He's fine. We need to go.'

Livira didn't fight him. She let herself be drawn away. Her last glimpse of Evar was as the Escape abandoned its prize and began to chase him instead.

Malar brought her back to the pool. The book seemed to burn in her hands, radiating some fraction of the heat of the fire that had failed to consume it.

'Time to jump.' Malar stepped to the edge.

Livira looked back the way they'd come, wondering. Yute and his family had wrapped her into a war she'd never asked to be part of. Something too big for her. Even the sides were unclear, the choices too large to be grappled with. 'I don't know what I should do, Malar. I don't know which side I'm on.'

Malar turned and frowned at her. 'People don't choose sides up here.' He tapped his head. 'That's where they think up the reasons for the choice after they've made it. The reasons they're going to tell everyone. But the truth is that they made the choice here.' He slapped his chest. 'We fight for the people we love. We fight for the ideas we want to be true, whether they are or not. It's a bit like this fucking pond. You just jump in with both feet.' And so, saying, he slapped her between the shoulder blades, hard enough to topple her into the pool.

A hermetic seal will defeat nearly every invasion, be it virus, gas, or merely an unwanted draught. It will not stop an unwanted idea. To prevent the spread of any idea, true, false, or untestable, one simply needs a more compelling narrative to occupy the minds of those you wish to keep ignorant.

Tyranny Without the Stick, *by Vlad Putative*

CHAPTER 24

Celcha

Celcha got no more than a hundred yards down the steep slope, not even halfway to the most intrepid of the houses that scaled the mountain, before some sixth sense brought her stumbling to a halt. The tingling hairs on the back of her neck turned her around.

The mouth of the howling wolf's head was belching a yellowish fog, all of it stripped away by the wind before it could reach Hellet on the platform in front of the library's entrance. The altered gas that had backed up in the chambers behind the gas room's intake had reached the library complex and poured through its corridors. The librarians, trainees, and staff would all be slumbering now. Celcha wondered how long it would take for the pressures to equalize and the flow to stop.

As she watched, two assistants walked out of the entrance, emerging from the fog that spilled around stone canines taller than a ganar. They approached the platform and Hellet backed away before them. The pair stopped close to the lip of the platform, looking down past Celcha at the city.

Another assistant emerged from the fog. Then two more. Then five together. And in the space of sixty breaths several hundred walked out, more assistants than the whole staff of the library complex. Celcha wondered if the gas had driven them out but that made no sense. It probably hadn't even reached the library, and you would have to search many of the vast chambers to find a single assistant. How they had all reached the entrance so swiftly, and more importantly, why, Celcha had no idea.

The crowd of assistants formed a rough semi-circle behind the first pair, who stood alone, front and centre. Celcha watched, hypnotized. Lutna and the rest would be furious to have slept through such a spectacle.

The pair of assistants were a male and a female. The male had started to talk, striding up and down the platform's edge, gesticulating at the city in a most un-assistant-like manner. The wind took most of his words but not the edge of anger or despair they carried. Celcha's uneasiness grew, crawling around the roots of her fur, fingering its way up her spine. Assistants were characterized by their detachment, their endless calm. This looked more like mania.

The assistant pointed at Celcha's brother, and although none of the audience looked his way, Hellet stumbled back as if struck. He sank to the ground and set his hands to his face.

Without warning, the assistant dug his fingers into his own chest and tore loose a ragged slab of white flesh, dripping with opalescent blood. He let it fall and the horror continued as he tore at himself with both hands, wrenching off his flesh and tossing it aside. The blood ran from him, not spurting like an artery but flowing as if he were melting in the morning sun. The female assistant beside him started to do the same thing, though more methodically and with less passion. Tearing herself apart.

As Celcha watched, it seemed – impossibly – that a new creature was being revealed within the ruin of each of the two assistants. Smaller, slighter beings. The process wasn't entirely physical, but almost as if the new beings stepped through the portal of the assistants' falling blood. Two white children. Not fleshed in shiny enamel like the assistants but in skin over muscle, only every bit of it the same matt white as a new page.

At the end of it all the two white children stood in what must be two pools of their own blood and dissolving flesh. The male one jumped lightly down onto the path and began to descend. The other followed. Celcha stood, rooted to the spot, expecting them to confront her, but they passed by without comment, without their pink eyes once flickering her way.

She looked to where her brother was sitting. Already the audience of assistants was beginning to disperse, the first of them starting to walk back towards the library while most still watched the departing children. Celcha followed their gaze, studying the pair of retreating backs. The children were heading for the city.

Part of Celcha wanted to go to her brother. To learn what the assistant had said when he had pointed at him. Part of her almost knew and was too afraid to have that fear confirmed. Trapped by indecision, she looked down at the departing children and the city, then up at her brother and the assistants.

In the end, with a small cry of hurt, she turned and hastened after the children.

Celcha had to divide her attention between not falling on the steep path down from the library entrance and not losing sight of her quarry. The children might be new to their bodies, but they covered the ground swiftly and Celcha was built for endurance rather than speed.

She passed between the first houses with barely a glance. Soon she was following the pair of white figures past the succession of houses that lined the road down towards the rear of the grand plaza. Narrow homes towered, jammed up against the cliffs to one side or teetering on the drop to the other. The street lay quiet: there was nobody to remark on the passage of two strange not-quite human children or the unescorted ganar struggling to catch up with them.

Celcha had barely dented the children's lead by the time they disappeared into the maze of streets behind the plaza. There were no narrow homes nestling elbow to elbow here, just high walls surrounding the gardens and properties to the rear of the great buildings that fronted onto the plaza itself. Celcha ran on, her breath short and panting. Behind one of these tall, spike-topped walls lay the gardens of the palace. She had glimpsed them from the windows when Lutna had given her the tour. Sparkling pools glimmering beneath verdant treetops. Strange birds with vivid plumage pecking in the shadows around the feet of marble statues.

The roads were deserted, but unless you had business with the city's great and good you had no business here. Still, Celcha would have expected to see a gardener coming or going, a nightsoil cart, a delivery for the kitchens . . . something.

She lost sight of the children and reached a turn where both choices seemed equally likely. Puffing, she took the direction that would lead her to the plaza. At least there she would have a clear view and might find them again.

Celcha stumbled breathlessly into the grand plaza, its sunlit stone-paved acres stretching before her. Astonishingly, even here there was nobody. Hellet's plan had worked. The gas from the tainted cylinder had run through the city's pipes, and then, for whatever reason, H'seen had not changed cylinders. Her decision had let the wind clear the gas from the city and caused the stuff to back up through the newly opened passage to the library complex. Celcha worried that, without the next cylinder and the one after that, the humans and the canith would wake up before the ganar had organized and decided on a course of action.

She felt suddenly guilty at the size of the unasked-for responsibility she was about to thrust upon the ganar who had expected to wake to another ordinary day. Perhaps Hellet had found himself overburdened by the same sense of guilt back at the library entrance when the assistant who became the child had accused him with a pointing finger. She wondered if that had been Yute – somehow so enraged by this disruption to whatever plans he'd had for the city that he'd literally torn himself apart in protest.

A glimmer of motion caught Celcha's eye. There, between the pillars of the great temple to the Mother God. At the top of the steps. At first it seemed just a trick of the light, but it was enough to set her moving once more, angling across the plaza towards it, thinking that she might have found the children again.

The ghosts. She saw them with more clarity than ever before, as if they were limned by golden light. Hellet's ghosts. Maybe and Starve. One tall, one small. The difference between them was accentuated by this newly sharpened view. As she drew closer, she saw with amazement that while the tall one was indeed the canith she had always taken him for, the smaller one was a human female. The pair of them stood at the top of the steps, holding each other's hands, with eyes locked, both oblivious to her presence as she sought the cover of the temple's side wall.

As she watched in amazement the pair began to dance. They left the steps and spun in the air, laughing. The dance devolved into a carefree game of chase. A dance of joy at the success of their plan? Celcha allowed herself to breathe. Perhaps it *had* worked after all.

She slid into the shadowed alley between the temple and the Hall of Records. She knew that the temple owned many ganar, housed in the basement and set to the preparation of the dead, a series of grisly procedures that for reasons beyond her understanding the followers of the Mother God liked to subject their corpses to.

In the alley she saw her first actual people. Two of them, almost lost in the shadow of the high wall that they'd rolled up against. Whatever sleep the gas had wrought in them did not look to have been a particularly gentle one. They lay at awkward angles, their faces hidden, and a stench hung about them. Celcha gave the pair a wide berth, half afraid they would wake. The reality of it struck home. She hoped none of them had been tending a fire or climbing a ladder when the gas struck. Still, she reminded herself, these were people who would see her crucified for disobeying their commands.

At the back of the temple, she found the ganar entrance that she'd seen slaves slipping in and out of on one of her previous visits to the city. Lutna had said the temple ganar were better treated than the palace ganar, though they had dirtier jobs to do. A canith guard slumped in an observation box nearby. It smelled as if she'd vomited before passing out.

Celcha tugged on the door, then knocked timidly. All the while she thought of the two ghosts dancing in the air. Why were a human and a canith so pleased by the usurping of their kinds' power? Why had they coached Hellet along this path? Seeing them clearly for once had resolved her doubts into solid questions that burned for answers.

Unable to open the door, Celcha went over to the guard box and lifted the key from the curiously still canith. She'd never seen a canith sleep before, so she accepted that they slept like the dead and moved on.

The passages under the temple held an acrid scent that needled Celcha's eyes and throat. She wondered if this was the gas they'd released or just the chemicals used to preserve and prepare the dead in the catacombs. Even without gas lighting down in the ganar areas, the gas, being heavier than air, would have wound its way down the stairs and collected in their workspaces.

The basement corridors were low-ceilinged and lit only dimly by intermittent lanterns. Many of these had gone out and the few that still burned were guttering as if at the end of their oil. The place held a silence different to that of the library. A haunted silence, trembling with threat. Celcha gritted her teeth and reminded herself that neither darkness nor death were inherently scary, and that the ganar who worked here would need a confident, fearless herald to bring them the news, not some timid girl jumping at every shadow.

As she progressed, a charnel stink began to compete with the chemical taint still haunting the corridors. 'Hello?' Her voice sounded thin, lost among the shadows. 'Hello?'

She turned through an archway and descended a short flight of stairs. An age-stained oak door stood ajar at the bottom. When Celcha pushed on it the door resisted her in much the same manner as if someone were pushing back against her. 'Hello? Is there someone there?' The darkness on the other side lay unbroken.

Celcha gave another tentative push, and then, realizing that this was foolish and that she had to find someone quickly, she put her shoulder into it. The realization that she was battling against a body didn't come at once but in the same way that rain will wet fur, soaking steadily in until it reaches the skin. She guessed it must be a canith to be so hard to shove aside.

With an effort she forced a gap large enough for her to squeeze through. Barely a whisper of light followed her, but it seemed that some of her massive dose of methalayne still haunted her veins, enabling her to see better than she should, better than she wanted to. Three ganar lay in the corridor beyond the door, two having collapsed against it.

'No!' Celcha's heart began to pound, and her stomach became

an icy hole through the middle of her. If the ganar had been put to sleep, what was this all for? She needed to get back and warn Hellet so they could escape before the city woke. 'No, this is all wrong!'

Celcha knelt beside the nearest ganar. Perhaps the gas had a lesser effect on them, and their sleep would be lighter. If she could wake some of them . . . The arm around which her fingers curled was not warm. The muscles weren't relaxed in sleep but stiff and unyielding. In a rising panic she grabbed the second ganar and shook him. This one proved just as stiff, and when Celcha hauled him over she found herself staring at open, bloodshot eyes bulging in a contorted face above a bloody mouth. The fur on the ganar's chin and chest bore traces of dried foam, a papery residue now.

Celcha released the corpse with a shudder of disgust and jumped to her feet. A wordless cry broke from her and she ran on into the darkness, weaving unsteadily. She passed the third ganar and tripped over a fourth that sprawled just beyond. On her hands and knees, she stared in horror at the bodies filling the corridor beyond. Some were locked together as if they'd died tearing at each other. They'd all been trying to get out, but none had made it further than the door.

'Hellet . . .' Celcha retched, spitting stomach acid onto the floor. 'What have we done?'

She ran then, as if the gas was still here, and it was her choking and dying. She tore at the part-open door in the same blind panic that must have gripped the ganar who had expired against it, her nails scoring additional grooves before she finally tore herself through the gap. She ran without thought, upwards, always upwards, seeking the light, seeking air, lost within the structure.

Rather than escape the building she ended up stumbling into the vast, vaulted hall of the main temple. She fell to her knees beside one of the great pillars that bore the ceiling aloft. The peace of the Mother God's house was a lie. The bright colours that streamed through stained glass to paint the stone-flagged floor were a cruel parody of the vitality snatched from so many just hours before. The god had done nothing to protect her children . . . or their slaves. Ganar, human, and canith had found a final equality. They had died the same horrible death. And Celcha had delivered it to them. It hadn't been Hellet who crawled through that last pipe and poured the quicksilver into the underground heart of the gas room.

Celcha looked up uncomprehendingly from empty hands that were so full of guilt. A golden sparkle had drawn her eye. There, just inside the closed iron doors of the temple, were the two ghosts, the canith and the human. The ones who had delivered the black book of poisons into Hellet's hands. The ones who had steered Celcha and her brother to just this place and time. The ones who had danced and cavorted above the dead city.

She watched in total disbelief as the pair bent their heads together and kissed. *Kissed!* The shock and terror that had crippled Celcha burned away, replaced by an anger so great it left her breathless, unable to speak. 'You!' She wanted to boom her accusation. To fill the great hall with it from flagstone to cornice. But nothing emerged from the lips that framed the word.

She started to run, to charge at her enemy. But they had already turned away. As her pounding feet closed the gap, the last glimmer of the pair slipped through the fabric of the closed door. She arrived too late, hurled herself after them, and was thrown back by the unyielding iron.

She found her voice then, trapped within the temple while the ghosts ran free, and howled after them, venting her rage, her hurt, her betrayal. 'I will find you!' She beat the doors until her fists bled. 'I *will* find you . . .'

When the flesh has rotted from them there is little difference
between a city and a skull. Both watch you with empty
eyes and the kind of grin that will follow you home.

The Last Empress of Charn, *by Heinrich Slylieman*

CHAPTER 25

Celcha

Celcha toured the dead city, still unable to believe that the calamity had fallen with such completeness across every house and hall. She thought that she would find someone, anyone, a lost child, a rare individual whose lungs were somehow immune, a princess in a draughty tower . . . She remembered her own princess, little Lutna, who had been only good. She would be lying twisted in her bedding in her room on the trainee corridor, choked by the yellow fog. There would be no family to mourn her, nobody to perform her funeral rites. She would rot there. Alone. Celcha found herself on all fours, crying as if she were the source of a river. She reached for her only defence: her anger, and let it lift her to her feet.

Humans would come. Canith would come. Krath was not the only city that paid fealty to the queen. People would come and in time they would understand that no god of death had swung their scythe through the population. They would understand the cause and even without firm proof their suspicions would fall upon the ganar. Even with ganar dead piled in the bowels of the palace, the temples, and the gas room itself they would not believe any other capable of such a crime.

The lives of those ganar Celcha hadn't already killed would become still more miserable if they were not immediately executed. The people who had worked alongside her in the Arthran dark would suffer. The same people who had entrusted their nootki to her keeping would feel new cruelties from Myles Carstar's hands, and he would enjoy bestowing them.

Celcha turned back towards the mountain. It thrust above the city, too huge to notice the small encrustation of life and death around its feet, yet somehow still too small to encompass the enormity of the library. The library had been the co-author of this destruction. It had put too much knowledge into her brother's hands, too fast for even his genius to keep pace. It had given him power without the wisdom to know how little he understood it. It had made murderers of them both, twisted good intentions into genocide.

Celcha started back the way she'd come. What she'd done could not be put right. That left only vengeance.

She reached the wolf's head entrance still fuelled by anger, hot with the rage that kept the aches and exhaustion of the day from claiming her. The platform where the assistants had gathered was deserted. Hellet had vanished. The yellow fog trickled from the stone jaws now, reaching no higher than her knees, and swirled away along the cliff faces to the west.

She climbed the steps and stood between the two puddles of blood that the assistants had left behind during their transformation. Celcha could only guess that one of them had been Yute, and that in the face of the slaughter below, the end of the first peace between human and canith, neither could keep to whatever vows had bound them to their service. The emotion that she'd sensed running through Yute, his talk of timeliness and influence, must have driven him to regain a mortal form and step back into the flow of time to see if he could do a better job of guiding the species from inside it than he had from the outside. His partner must have shared the sentiment.

The shimmer of light across the blood's surface hypnotized Celcha's eyes. Despite her resolve to search the poisoned halls for her brother, something kept her there on the windy platform. Surely Hellet wouldn't have waded through the toxic gas. If he'd wanted to make an end of himself there were plenty of cliffs offering a cleaner exit.

She turned, meaning to go and look over the nearest one. She might stand there a while, considering her choices with a view of the city before her and a precipice at her toes. She took one step before something seized hold of her ankle and pulled her back. A moment later she tumbled into a fall that felt further than anything the local cliffs had to offer.

Celcha hit the ground hard, face forward, and lay there, winded.

Grass tickled her cheek. A warm sun pressed against her back, the light dappled around her, lacking the sharpness that had illuminated the mountainside. She knew she wasn't there any more. She had never touched grass. She knew it only from glimpses of the palace grounds. The earth beneath her fingers was soft, alive, dependable.

Slowly, she raised her head. Trees surrounded her. Ancient, gnarled trees, the relief of their bark a hundred times craggier than the oldest human. She'd yet to see a truly old ganar. Trees and more trees, marching away in vaguely ordered lines, interspersed by pools of light, just like the one she'd fallen into, only smooth-edged circles rather than the puddled gore of a slaughter.

She sat with a groan, aware that the memory of recent horrors wanted to press its way back into her mind. To hold them off, she tried to keep as still as possible and continue to soak up the strangeness of the place, not the least of which was that she had reached it just by falling over. No, she hadn't fallen. Someone had pulled her. She turned sharply and standing just to her left was an assistant.

'Where are we?'

'This is the Exchange.'

Celcha looked around again, checking that it was all still there, still real. 'You pulled me through this . . .' She waved her hand at the pool. 'Door? Are they all doors?'

The assistant nodded.

'Why?' The question felt too big to expect an answer to. She narrowed it. 'Why did you pull me through?'

Instead of answering, the assistant opened his hand to reveal a small black circle against the whiteness of his palm. A hole almost, though one that revealed only darkness. Celcha moved closer and as she did so she saw that it was a black ball, not a circle, just so black that it offered only two dimensions to the eye.

'What is it?'

'Something that escaped,' the assistant said. As he spoke the sphere moulded its shape into that of a miniature black stallion which galloped around the perimeter of his hand, then to a black fire which raged in his palm before changing again, into a butterfly, like a piece of the night sky. It fluttered away among the trees. 'Like this place, it is built of expectation and imagination. If you had had more fear in you, it would have reflected your nightmare back at you. But you are not scared any more. You have lost too much for that.'

Celcha's loss settled onto her, sinking into her bones. The day's events couldn't be held back any longer. If the blackness had still been in the assistant's palm it would have become a scattering of corpses. 'I'm looking for two ghosts.'

'They have already gone.'

'Where?'

The assistant indicated half the forest and its pools with a single sweep of his arm. 'Into the future. They will be hard to find, Celcha, but there is no better place to start than right here. You should not chase them, though. It will hurt you.'

Celcha looked up sharply at his use of her name. She stared at the blank white eyes regarding her. 'Who are you?'

'I . . . I am starting to forget that already. Yute was right. In the end I recognized myself as more than broken. I saw that I was a fracture in the world itself and, as he predicted, I asked for the cure.'

'Hellet . . .' Celcha's voice broke around her brother's name.

Hellet inclined his white head. His voice continued without inflection, though it faltered as if he were struggling to speak. 'It is hard to follow . . . this conversation . . . to follow your life. Time is a river to you. A pond to me.'

'Why, Hellet? Why didn't you wait for me?' Celcha took his hands in hers. They felt hard, smooth, cool, as if carved from the stuff of the library itself. 'Those ghosts did this to you. We could have found them together. We could have—'

'Leave them be. The library did this.' Hellet fell silent and still; then he spoke again. 'The library. And it is a thing that cannot be broken from the outside. That is why.'

The rules of the ballroom may be unwritten and the laws of physics deeply graven, but a library book demanding to be read would cause less scandal than the lady who took a man's hand unasked.

Debutante or Bust, *by Lady Ellinoor FitzGerald*

CHAPTER 26

Arpix

Arpix didn't know what to do with Clovis's attention, so he did what he'd done in the past when flustered by Carlotte's teasing and ignored it. He did not, however, cede the job of tending to her injuries to one of her brothers, or to Salamonda who would probably have done it better now the stitching part was over. It was something he'd started, and he liked to be thorough. The library had taught him that. Master Logaris had taught him. Though the huge teacher had always said that Arpix had been born with the lesson stamped across his bones.

Clovis hissed. She lay on her back, propped against an earth bank, while he knelt beside her with cloth and bucket.

'Sorry.' Arpix moved the cloth away from the wound. 'I was thinking about something else.'

'One of your human girls?' Clovis asked, artlessly.

'A teacher of mine. He died—' Arpix stopped himself. Both of them could reel off a litany of crimes that the other's kind had perpetrated against those they'd cared for. Arpix wrung the cloth onto the thirsty ground. Perhaps the kind of healing they were both part of now was exactly what they needed if the larger, unseen wounds were ever to close. They would still be scars on their memory, but scars were meant to be lived with.

'Tell me about this weapon.' Clovis watched him, drawing a deep breath in through her nose. She licked one long canine tooth.

'You think there's more to tell?' It had been three days since the cratalacs. Three days since the discovery that they could call Wentworth. Three days since Evar had recognized the great statue as a woman he had seen once, and they had known half their lives. 'We've looked for it. You and I have looked for it. Or felt for it in the dark, at least. You've seen the boundary stones that mark how far the forbidding reaches.' Arpix had been thinking for four years now about whatever it was that kept the skeer from the plateau. He had no answer. Clovis repeating the question wouldn't change that.

'I've seen that you're the clever one.' Clovis continued to watch him, her grey eyes capturing some of the sky's merciless blue. 'The other humans listen to you even though you speak the quietest of any of them.'

'Because my throat's sore with all this growling to you.'

'Cleverness is the key.' Clovis carried on as if he hadn't spoken. 'You just need me to turn you.' Her hand came to rest on his thigh. He frowned at it.

'Are you sure you haven't started a fever?' Her hand felt hot against his leg. Burning, almost.

'It's like Evar with this Carlotte of yours. He saw what you couldn't because he looked from a new angle. You've looked at this too long from the same place. The Assistant – your Livira – she taught us about science. I didn't listen. But your teacher, he gave you both the same lessons. I think you listened. Very hard.'

Arpix covered her hand with his own. He'd meant just to move it politely, but somehow his hand stayed on hers a heartbeat longer than it needed to. Two, three, four heartbeats. He lifted hers and set it on the ground. Her smile was small but victorious.

'Science prompts me to ask a series of structured questions. Investigations that will allow the formation of theories that can be tested. I have some of the questions, but the answers would be too difficult to come by.'

'What sort of questions?' The sun had edged their patch of

shadow aside and found them. Clovis continued to study him from hooded eyes.

'Can the skeer cross the boundary? I know they don't want to, but is it a wall to them, or if a giant picked one up could it be carried through? Once they're in does the effect vanish, like climbing a wall and getting into a garden? Or does the resistance or compulsion grow stronger? Then there's—'

'That's a lot,' Clovis sat up a little more, wincing and pulling the remnants of her armour around her. 'You're going to need a skeer.'

'You've spotted the problem.' Arpix nodded. 'And even if we were able to overcome one of the things, they come in packs and take their dead with them.'

Clovis shrugged then looked as if she regretted stretching her wound. 'So, send your tiny monster.'

'Wentworth?' Arpix hadn't even considered it. The cat *had* slaughtered five cratalacs to save Salamonda, and he'd brought them a deer and a boar in the past. Who knew what the limits of his abilities were or how likely he was to do requests . . . The cratalacs had certainly been a deadly foe, but they had come in single file at very close quarters. To retrieve a single skeer, something far too big for the cat in any event, Wentworth would have to kill every other skeer in its pack and every skeer that answered any cry for reinforcements. That seemed like a tall order.

'You said this Yute of yours sent him for a reason. Why not this reason?'

Arpix looked across the hollow to where Salamonda was weaving bean leaves into storage baskets. He wasn't entirely sure that Yute really had sent Wentworth. The cat might just have had a soft spot for the woman who'd fed him for so many years.

It was a good time to approach Salamonda. Jost was still down at the mine entrance poking pieces of cratalac around with a stick. The creatures horrified her, but she seemed unable to leave their remains alone. Jost would object to what he was about to do, and perhaps she would be right to, though her objection would not be moral or scientific, just born from fear and from fearing to make any change. The same fear that had paralysed all of them for too long.

He hung his cloth on the side of the bucket and went across to sit beside Salamonda.

'You'll be wanting *Wentworth*.' She growled his name the way the canith said it.

'I might,' Arpix agreed. 'I only met him a couple of times. I didn't really pay him much attention, if truth be told. But it's hard to imagine him as something made rather than something born.'

'The world's a strange place, right enough.' Salamonda kept up with her deft weaving, the dry leaves threatening to crack and break at every opportunity. She looked up at Arpix, her eyes seeming much brighter now that the sun had burned her face to a nut brown. 'What do you need from him?'

Arpix pressed his lips into a narrow line. 'When he saved you from the cratalacs, what happened? How did he . . . do that?'

Salamonda hadn't spoken about it yet, not even to Jella, that Arpix knew of. She'd hidden behind the trauma of it all, which was fair enough in Arpix's estimation. He would have soiled himself, stuck in that tunnel with those nightmares advancing on him. The screams alone were enough to loosen anyone's bladder . . . But now he needed to know.

Salamonda nodded, as if he'd explained himself in words rather than written it out in his expression. 'It was dark. And those things . . . they're complicated . . . I didn't know what I was looking at really. All legs and jaws. So, I didn't see it clearly. But it seemed as if he . . . got bigger. As if he filled the corridor. Though he was still the same size, which makes no sense, I know, but that's how it was. He hooked the first one forward like he'd caught a mouse. His back feet started tearing at it and . . . it just got torn to pieces. I can't say it clearer than that. He was as big as he needed to be.'

'I think we need him to be pretty big,' Arpix said. 'I need a skeer brought inside the circle.'

'We should wait until Clovis is better.' Evar seemed as nervous about the whole plan as Arpix was, which wasn't encouraging since he was their best warrior by a very large margin.

They stood at the perimeter, facing west towards the mountain where the skeer hive clung at the library entrance. Evar, Arpix,

Meelan, Salamonda, Jella, and Sheetra, the youngest and most daring of the bookbinders.

'She might not get better.' Arpix hadn't said it so clearly before, but Evar needed to understand. He'd left Clovis in Kerrol's care. Despite his efforts, poison had got into the wounds, or stayed there. He'd picked two dozen of the short black cratalac hairs out of the cuts, but others might have evaded him. 'She needs someone with more skill at healing than I have.'

A blood-curdling growl rumbled deep in Evar's throat, and he showed all his teeth, but Arpix didn't feel as if he were the target, simply the witness to canith distress. Evar gave a curt nod and drew Clovis's white sword from his belt. 'Do it.'

Arpix turned to Salamonda. 'Do your best.'

Salamonda called Wentworth. She could have been in her kitchen five years ago calling with a bowl of fish heads in hand. As before, it seemed as if he would ignore the summons, only for him to be found sitting behind them as they turned away, disappointed.

'I've nothing to give you, fat lad.' Salamonda ruffled the cat's head apologetically. 'Just beans.'

Wentworth eyed her dubiously, as if expecting some juicy treat to be dangled before him momentarily.

'What we need, Wentworth, what we really need, is a skeer. A whole one. Brought right here. Do you think you can do that? Safely, mind. I don't want you getting hurt.'

Wentworth stalked around her as if she hadn't spoken, headbutting her legs in the same way he would in her kitchen to coax a meal out of her.

'Maybe you should—' But somehow on his third pass around Salamonda's legs the cat didn't reappear, and Arpix swallowed his suggestion. 'I guess we'll wait and see.'

Wentworth didn't reappear until the following afternoon. Evar spotted a large dust cloud in the direction of the mountain. Arpix came to the perimeter and estimated it to be a band at least as big as the one that had chased the canith to the plateau. 'It has to be skeer.' There weren't enough of anything else in the area to raise such a cloud.

Within a quarter of an hour, all the plateau's residents were out on the western edge, ten yards or so behind the perimeter. Kerrol remarked that a clever skeer would use a long stick to move the perimeter stones out an extra twenty yards and tempt the incautious into their clutches. Arpix didn't translate that, but he did thank a broad swathe of gods that the skeer didn't appear to have Kerrol's initiative.

Clovis had to be carried out. Arpix hadn't wanted her to be moved, but she insisted, saying she demanded to meet the enemy at the gates. Arpix had pressed her back onto her bed of dry leaves when she'd tried to rise. 'You're not well enough.'

Clovis had grabbed his arm, but her grip lacked the strength that she'd nearly strangled him with on her arrival. 'You're just worried about your stitching, human boy. You can always do it again. It's not as if you have much else to do other than farm beans.'

'You should lie dow—'

'I should have died in battle. I've no intention of rotting here. I'll walk out to meet them before I die lying down.'

In the end they'd settled for carrying her out to watch.

Jost had been among the last to arrive and had stared in horror at the approaching dust cloud. 'You did this!' She advanced on Arpix. Starvation and the sun had aged her over the last four years, streaking grey into once lustrous red hair, setting wrinkles around the corners of eyes that had a bright, unhealthy glitter to them. She raised hands that seemed more like claws, both darkly stained with the life juice of cratalacs. 'You!'

Arpix refused to defend himself. He had done it and he wasn't sure it had been right. Jost came on, but even from what might be her deathbed, Clovis's growl proved enough to make the woman stumble to a halt, a puppet with cut strings.

'Definitely skeer. Can't see what they're chasing.' Meelan had the best eyes but even he didn't spot the insectoid's quarry until they were so close that the edge of the plateau nearly stole them from sight.

Several score of skeer runners were hot on Wentworth's trail. He showed a surprising turn of speed as he bounded ahead of their thundering advance, but it seemed impossible that he could outpace them. Unlike the warriors, the runners were all legs and built for speed. Of the various skeer castes, the runners were closer to the cratalacs, their arachnid-like knees higher off the ground than Arpix's head.

As the runners closed on Wentworth, he vanished through a small portal very similar to the ones that the assistants used. It opened just before him and closed immediately after his tail vanished through it. Two hundred yards on he reappeared out of a second portal and paused to lick his paw. The infuriated skeer charged on, relentless.

The chase vanished below the plateau's edge, and a short while later Wentworth appeared at the top of the steep climb, peering down to torment his pursuers. He arrived at the perimeter with the leaders of the pack just moments behind him. The foremost one proved so intent on its quarry that it ploughed headlong into the boundary . . . and recoiled as if it had met a physical barrier.

Three other skeer made slower impacts, the chitin spikes of their feet tearing gouges in the baked mud as they tried to stop in time.

Wentworth turned and, with a casual swipe of his paw, hauled one of the fallen runners through the barrier. Arpix couldn't describe it any better than Salamonda had. The cat was somehow huge, so that the skeer was a mouse in his grasp, but also . . . just a cat. The two competing realities coexisted in Arpix's mind long enough for the skeer to be pulled through.

The insectoid disintegrated in the process. Rather as if it had been pulled, or pushed, through the bars of a prison cell. The mess of armour fragments and ichor, along with pale, flopping internal organs that resembled fish guts, fell in a noxious heap, with pieces spreading a few yards into the forbidden zone.

Jella dry-heaved, and the sound, combined with the sight that had prompted it, caused Arpix to do the same.

'Another!' Clovis called weakly. 'Again.'

Evar came to stand beside Arpix. 'What did we learn?'

Arpix straightened up. He wasn't sure they'd learned anything of use. They knew for certain now that it wasn't just a compulsion, and that breaching the perimeter had almost immediately fatal physical consequences. Which was good, since otherwise the skeer could simply have catapulted unwilling members of their hive into the encampment. Though whether any of it was any use . . .

Jella came to stand beside them, hugging herself. 'Did that skeer die for a reason? We shouldn't just be killing them for nothing.'

'Sometimes you just have to ask questions,' Arpix said, 'and hope that the answers reveal something unexpected.'

'What answers are you going to find in that lot?' Salamonda came across, both arms full of dusty, purring cat. She looked disapprovingly at the scattered remains.

'I'm not sure.' Arpix forced himself to look at the mess he'd made.

'It will make them hate us even more.' Jost's voice carried a cracked note of hysteria, but that didn't mean she was wrong. 'They'll bring more horrors to hunt us out of our tunnels. Like men use ferrets to core a rabbit warren.'

Arpix didn't think the skeer hated, but Jost could well be right about the result, hate or no hate.

'Is it me?' Evar loomed over the humans, his growls silencing anything else Jost had to say. 'Or does that skeer look different now?'

'Of course it looks different, brother.' Kerrol corralled the humans from the other side. 'It's been turned inside out.'

'I mean the heap, idiot.'

Arpix narrowed his stare. For a terrifying moment he saw what Evar meant and thought that somehow the skeer was piecing itself back together. But it wasn't that. Though something *had* changed.

It was the oldest of the bookbinders, a hunched and grey-haired man called Nortbu, who seldom made any comment, that saw it. 'It's drifting,' he said.

He meant drifting like sand was said to, out where the dust grains put on weight and got to be called something else. And, unlikely as it seemed, it appeared that Nortbu was right. It was as if the remains were being very slowly swept up by an invisible broom or powerful unfelt wind.

'It's being pushed back towards the boundary,' Arpix whispered.

'Good.' Meelan gave a small shudder of revulsion and turned away.

'Don't you see?' Arpix looked around at the others.

'I do see.' Sheetra turned away too with a shrug. 'It's ugly.'

'Get me the bowl!' Arpix barked it as a command. The others, unaccustomed to his tone, all moved to obey, though it was Jella who hurried all the way to the hollow and returned breathlessly with the largest of the precious bowls they'd recovered from the workings.

Arpix went forwards, holding the fragile dish of fired clay in both hands. He felt painfully aware of the shifting ranks of skeer only yards ahead of him, a multitude of emotionless black eyes focused on him, all of them coldly wanting his destruction. He found himself trembling, and at the same time glad that the skeer, despite their collective cleverness, never seemed to have adopted missile weapons, since any of them should have been able to crack his skull with a thrown rock.

Arpix knelt and, trying not to retch, scooped the most juicy-looking chunk of the pallid internal organs into his bowl. The skeer had a dry, unhealthy reek to them under normal circumstances; when torn to shreds they had an acrid pungency that kept trying to turn his stomach inside out.

'Arpix!' Salamonda called out. 'Not the food bowl!'

'Sorry . . .' Arpix backed nervously away from the thronging skeer. With ten yards between them he turned and hurried back to kneel at Clovis's side. 'I've got it!'

Clovis eyed his gift dubiously. 'A bowl of offal? Is this a traditional love token among humans? A canith would at least have brought something he killed himself. But you are small and—'

'It's not a love token. It's a key.'

'A key to good health?' Clovis showed her teeth. 'Because if I have to eat this shit to get better . . . I'll do it.' She reached for the bowl.

'A key to a weapon.'

Kerrol came up behind them, Evar at his side. 'So, it *is* a love token then.'

'It's like he's known her for years.' Evar nodded.

'I don't understand.' Clovis struggled to sit up and managed it.

Arpix pointed to the pale beads of skeer ichor already crossing the bottom of the bowl and starting up the gentle curve of the side. It was as if he were blowing on them with all his strength. 'Just on this side. Away from the centre. Away from whatever's doing this.'

'It's like a compass!' Evar exclaimed.

'Exactly.' Arpix said. 'This will find the source for us.'

*There are few enterprises where the discrepancy between
the hopeful party's assessment of their chances and the
truth yawns so widely as in the matter of digging for that
which was lost. The owner of any ticket in any lottery
may count themselves on to a sure thing by comparison.*

The Treasure Seekers, *by Nes Ebit*

CHAPTER 27

Evar

Even with Arpix's compass there were no guarantees of finding
what they needed. They needed the source of the protection against
the skeer to be both portable and accessible. Arpix had pointed out
that although they should now be able to triangulate its position,
it was entirely possible that the device was buried too deep to reach,
or was too large to move, or wasn't even a device but some kind of
aura rooted in the soil and rocks themselves.

The work was hard, and even though Kerrol and Evar were
physically stronger than the humans, the tunnels were cramped for
the smallest of the human females, so the canith could offer little
help. Kerrol stayed with Clovis while Arpix made his calculations,
wandering the tunnels with his bowl of gore and a feeble, smoking
light to see which way the skeer blood ran. Evar had to admit it
was a stroke of genius that would likely have never occurred to him
even if they'd grown old on the plateau.

Evar had walked the larger tunnels, holding the leaf lamp and
choking on the smoke while Arpix studied the contents of his bowl.
Wherever he went, the ichor in the bowl would try to crawl away
from the source of the forbidding. Having something that always

points away from the object you're looking for is, it turned out, exactly as useful as having something that always points at it. The hunt moved to the narrower tunnels, and Evar had to leave the humans to the task. He'd returned to help Kerrol nurse Clovis.

'Drink, Clo. You need to drink.' His sister was getting weaker. Evar had never seen sickness before, and although he'd seen injuries dealt there had always been the centre circle to quickly reverse any damage. The idea that Clovis, the peerless warrior, would die on her back, slowly poisoned by a wound that should have healed . . . It wasn't one he was ready for. As badly as it would have hurt him, it might have been better if the cratalac had torn her heart out, giving her the quick, bloody death of a soldier. Though, even as the thought crossed his mind, he realized that, outside the pages of some tale of heroes, most soldiers died slow, ugly deaths from their wounds, days after the terror and thrill of the battles in which they had received them.

Clovis guided the bucket's edge to her mouth with trembling hands and choked as she tried to swallow. Evar would rather dig in the dark than sit there watching her die. But at the same time nothing but the chance to save her would take him from her side.

'Easy.' He let her get her breath.

Kerrol sat close by, watching them both, knees drawn up beneath his chin. He understood. He'd studied them for more than half their lives. He understood exactly, and that was why he had nothing to say, no words of comfort, just silence. There was nothing to say.

The humans came and went, all of them streaked with dirt. Salamonda brought a steaming bowl of bean stew and set it beside Clovis. Pieces of earth fell from the old human's hair – even she'd been digging. Evar got to his feet in frustration. He struggled with the few human words at his disposal. 'I dig! Not sit. Do nothing.'

Salamonda gave him a tired smile and measured a small gap between finger and thumb.

'Either she's insulting your manhood,' Kerrol said, 'or saying that the tunnels are just as small as they were yesterday.'

Evar slumped down with a growl. The mountains burned red in the distance, hurling their shadows towards the plateau. The need to do something ate at Evar. He drew the Soldier's sword and set it across his knees.

The night came, and with it a thin wind that ruffled every hair Evar owned and stole his warmth. The wind was one of the hardest things to get used to after a life lived in the still air of the library. It felt as if unseen hands were constantly touching him, invading his privacy, overly familiar.

If he considered the wind to be a price paid for freedom, then the sky was part of the prize. Evar sat beside his sister and watched the stars. The night sky rewarded attention. Like most things, it revealed new depths the longer it was studied. Parts of the sky that Evar had thought empty would slowly offer up fainter stars buried in the blackness. Here and there lengthier observation would pull faint veils of light from the depths, wisps of coloured mist that might in themselves be made of yet more stars, innumerable, hauntingly distant. Evar felt himself at once both infinitesimal and yet woven into the vastness promised by the sky. A peace so great and enfolding that even the distant hunting call of a cratalac couldn't shake him from it.

At last, Attamast, the greater moon, rose to pale the skies with its reflected glory and break the spell. Evar lowered his gaze, eyes finding Clovis sleeping beside him, her breathing fast and shallow. She looked frail, as if the warrior who had led them to the plateau had been replaced with a version of herself from fifty years in the future, skin tight across her bones, cheeks sunken.

In the moonlight, the skeer out beyond the perimeter took on a ghostly glow, their pale bodies seemingly lit from within. They had returned with the evening while the humans still laboured underground. Scores of them milled around the border stones, endlessly circling, as if the latest tactic was to keep their prey totally contained while some new horror was summoned to deal with them. Perhaps it would be more cratalacs, or something worse.

'Don't.' Kerrol spoke even before Evar knew he was getting to his feet. Ignoring his brother, Evar strode towards the perimeter, white sword in hand, blazing with the light of Attamast. 'How is that going to help?' Kerrol continued at his back. 'You could kill them all and they'd replace each one with a hundred more. It's not going to make Clovis better.'

'It might make me feel better,' Evar growled, but already Kerrol's words were undoing his anger, making it seem childish.

Even so, unwilling to dance so helplessly to his brother's tune, Evar advanced three more steps, aiming the Soldier's blade squarely at the face of the nearest skeer who had stopped to watch him. Just a yard separated them now. The dry stink of the creatures filled his nose, shot through with the sharp metallic scent of their communications.

Evar had threats and promises he wanted to challenge them with, but under the black-eyed stare of their incomprehension he knew the gulf between them could not be bridged. They didn't hate him. They didn't understand him. The cratalacs might have been utterly inhuman but at least their rage seemed like common ground. The skeer didn't care one way or the other. This was simply their nature.

Evar wondered at their efforts to claim the library. It was hard to imagine the creatures reading a book, much less writing one. And yet there were doors in the library only they could open. Chambers given over to their records.

The nearest skeer took a sudden step forward, startling Evar from his contemplations. Its fellows to either side did the same, over-stepping the stones laid out to mark the boundary. Evar scrambled back in panic. 'The barrier's down!'

The creatures came on, a yard past the stones, two yards, three. Not charging, but making a steady advance as if they were somehow pushing the invisible wall before them. 'Get her back!' Evar yelled at his brother. He swung his sword at the nearest skeer, hoping to warn them off, but none of them so much as flinched. He backed away quickly, ceding ten yards to the insectoids.

'Clovis!' Kerrol's voice behind him.

Evar whirled around fearing to see Kerrol hunched over their sister, hunting for signs of life. Instead, she was right there, barging against him, cursing in pain, and somehow reclaiming her sword from his hand.

'Clovis! Don't!' He reached for her injured shoulder but hesitated, knowing the agony it would cause.

Clovis stumbled on, the white blade cutting an arc through the night before her. Evar, refusing to let her end herself in such a

manner, lunged, meaning to drag her away. But even with her back
to him and her blood running poisoned in her veins, Clovis was
better than him. She lurched away at the last instant and set him
on the ground with a kick to the side of his knee.

'Come on, you whoresons,' Clovis snarled, stumbling at her foe,
cleaving another arc through the darkness.

Evar fully expected her to be torn apart before he could gain his
feet. But against all odds the skeer came to a halt before her. She
aimed a thrust at the nearest one, but it had started to retreat and
already it was beyond her reach. It wasn't just the one she'd singled
out: dozens of them were withdrawing before the threat of a single
sick canith.

'Clovis! No!' Evar threw himself forward as he rose. This time
she couldn't escape him, and he managed to get both his arms under
hers, struggling not to hurt her whilst at the same time holding
her back.

The skeer retreated more swiftly than ever, the darkness swallowing them until even their moonglow was little more than
suggestion. 'What's going on?' Evar didn't understand.

Kerrol reached them and took Clovis's sword arm, steering her
gently back towards the settlement. 'Ask them.'

The humans were emerging from the hollow before the mine
opening, still just moon-edged silhouettes before Queen Carlotte's
illuminated face. Arpix headed the group, his face as dirty as the
rest of him. In both hands he carried a dull ball of what looked
like rust-flaked iron, dented and scarred as if it had been kicked
about by iron feet for years.

'We found it,' he said. 'Dug it out of the wall three levels down.'

Kerrol released Clovis's arm and went across to lay a hand on
the iron ball. 'With hindsight it would have been sensible for us to
stay nearer the centre. If you'd moved a little more to the east when
bringing it up, you would have been missing three canith.'

Evar sagged a little, understanding that the skeer had not retreated
from Clovis but had been pushed back as the sphere had been
moved and with it its repulsion field.

'The weapon . . .' Clovis shrugged him off, managing to support
herself again.

Evar went to join Kerrol, looming over Arpix. The human hefted the ball into his hands. The thing proved surprisingly heavy. Evar lifted it to eye level. 'So, what do we do now?'

'Take . . . take the war to the enemy,' Clovis said.

Arpix frowned and went to help Clovis back to her bed. 'Hopefully it won't come to that.' He nodded at Salamonda, who stood with Meelan at the front of the dirty band of humans. 'You could call him now.'

Evar impressed himself by understanding the last part even though it was in human tongue. Clearly the Exchange had tutored his mind in the language over the time he'd spoken with Livira.

Salamonda faced the night. 'Wentworth! Wentworth!' She clucked and called out something in human. Evar felt she'd said that it was time to find Yute.

The cat came nosing its way through the forest of the humans' legs. It didn't pause to hunt for treats this time, simply pressing on out across the plateau. They could all see where its path was heading. Back towards the mountain.

'Damn,' Arpix muttered.

Clovis leaned against him heavily, a grim smile on her face. 'Told you so, human boy.'

Over-dependence on epigraphs reveals not only the pretensions of the text but a fundamental character flaw in the author. The only writing crime worse than this is when the epigraphs doesn't come to

The Seventeen Critical Elements of the
Modern Novel, *by Edna Average*

CHAPTER 28

Livira

Livira, still clutching her newly reclaimed book, staggered out of the portal and immediately turned to berate Malar who followed her.

'Stop pushing me!'

'Everyone needs a little push now and then.' Malar drew his sword with the same fluid motion he always used to greet trouble.

Livira backed away, hands raised. 'We don't all need a little stabbing too.'

'Get behind me,' Malar snapped, advancing past her.

Two canith were watching them, a tall one leaning against a tree not far from their portal, and one that looked to be considerably shorter crouching close by. This second one looked up from whatever he'd been poking with his knife on the ground and showed his teeth in a grin. The tall one had a golden mane, the short one a mane so dark black that in places it looked a midnight shade of blue.

'Mayland. Starval.' Livira knew them both. As an assistant memory had no meaning. A timeless being has no memory. But now she remembered them, though in the wisps of a waking dream.

Starval hid from everyone, himself most of all. He studied endings, and how to bring them about. Mayland studied change and had never believed in either endings or beginnings. Both were, in their own ways, more dangerous than Clovis with all her razored edges.

'Correct.' Mayland pushed himself off the tree trunk and bowed politely. 'What has Evar been telling you about us?' Neither he nor his brother paid Malar any regard at all.

Livira found the question a little strange. 'Well, for one thing, he told me you were dead, Mayland.'

'Not dead. Gone.'

'And you left the others behind? Evar always wanted to escape that chamber. How could you leave him there?'

Mayland shrugged. 'You know how it is with the Exchange. Time gets away from you.'

Seeing Malar still bristling in the corner of her eye, Livira reached out and set her hand on his sword arm. 'These are Evar's brothers. They won't hurt us.'

'His fucking sister put a hole right through me,' Malar snarled, keeping his blade ready.

Starval stood, his grin a little wider. 'Clovis has quite the temper. We're both more reasonable. No stabbing.' He held up an open hand as he returned his knife to his belt with the other. 'Promise.'

'They weren't with Evar and the tall one when we met them here that first time.' Malar kept his sword raised, eyes flitting from one canith to the other.

'I was there,' Starval said. 'I just tend to keep to the edges of things.'

'I came along a bit later,' Mayland said. He watched both Livira and Malar closely, as if calculating something. 'I see you have the book that Hellet asked for.'

'Hellet?' Livira shook her head, holding the book tightly to her chest. 'An assistant sent us.'

'They have names, you know.' Mayland came to stand at his brother's shoulder. He looked to be nearly as tall as Kerrol, while Starval was more like Arpix's height. Very tall for a man, very short for a canith. 'Just because they forget them doesn't mean that we should. Sometimes they reclaim them, like your friend Yute did.'

'And Yamala,' Starval said, no longer grinning.

A flicker of annoyance crossed Mayland's brow. He glanced left and right along the world's timeline, the row of portals stretching into the past and future. The portal he'd been standing closest to was off the worldline. Livira wondered where it might lead and remembered her own brief venture onto another world. The air had savaged her lungs and driven her back in moments. But Evar, who as a ghost had been able to stay, reported short, broad humanoids covered in golden fur, gathered at the entrance to a library of their own.

'Time is always short in this place,' Mayland said. 'Which is odd, since in another very real sense there's no time at all here. But the fact is that people, both welcome and unwelcome, are apt to turn up if you linger. So, forgive my forwardness, but have you decided which side you're on?'

'My own,' Malar growled, sounding angrier at being ignored than he would have been at insults or even an attack.

'He means in the library's war,' Livira said.

'And I meant what I said.'

Livira added herself to the list of people ignoring Malar. Mayland's question was a big one, very big, and he seemed curiously invested in the answer. Livira had assumed that her association with Evar would ensure their safety where the brothers were concerned, but the glint in Mayland's eye had started to fray that certainty. As the Assistant, Livira had known that, while personable enough, Mayland had committed himself to learning the lessons of the past, and to applying them without fear or favour. The present, he said, was the gateway to the future and what was learned from history had to be carved upon it, even if that meant it bled.

'I've yet to pin my colours to the mast.' Livira chose a nautical reference, thinking of the tome she'd taken the first page of her own book from: *Great Sailing Ships of History*. She hoped Captain Elias would approve. 'Yute says compromise—'

Starval moved so fast that it didn't seem real. In the space of a fingersnap he'd twisted in past Malar's extended sword, drawn his knife, and set it to Malar's throat, while holding the wrist of the soldier's sword arm with his other hand.

'You got me!' Starval looked down with amazed delight at the thin cut across his ribs where Malar's blade had caught him as he twisted out of its way.

'My weapon's nearly three feet longer than yours,' Malar muttered with Starval's iron at his neck. 'I should have run you through.'

'I'm fast.' Starval grinned, then frowned. 'But not as fast as I thought.' He shook Malar's sword arm gently. 'Anyway, I've made my point. Put the sword down. We're not here to kill Evar's girl. You're her friend, so we're not here to kill you either, unless you make us.'

Malar probably retained vague memories of training Starval to use knives in the first place, adding practical knowledge to what the book had given the young canith. Livira doubted he intended the young assassin any harm either. Even so, both of them held the other's gaze for a few heartbeats more before Malar returned his sword to its sheath and Starval rehomed his knife.

'I know all about Yute and his compromises.' Mayland came in closer now the naked blades had been clothed. 'This is where they've brought us all. Each city built on the dust and ruin of the last. A world that's little more than a cinder, subjected to repeated flashfires as one species burns itself down to make room for the next to have a try.'

'But you're a historian; Evar said so. You're really telling us that what we need is to burn the history books?'

'It turns out that the most important lesson that history teaches us is that history should not teach us. Lessons should be learned, not taught. Wisdom has to be earned, and no number of words can wrap the gift of knowledge sufficiently to keep it safe from misuse. The definition of madness is repeating the same action and expecting a different result.'

'Tell that to the man digging for water.' Livira knuckled her forehead, trying to muster a less glib reply. She couldn't argue against the facts. Yute had been the one to bring to her attention the burn layers that stratified their geology. The histories recorded the reasons for them, but the fact of them was written in char in the sides of any hole you dug, and before you reached any water you would have cut yourself a path through millennia of rise and fall, rise and fall.

'I understand what you're saying, Mayland, but didn't the first people to raise a city here also fail, only without the benefit of a library of past learning to blame for the disaster? Can burning the books really be the right answer?' Burning books felt as if it could never be the right answer, any more than throwing children off a cliff could be. But the words to turn that emotion-based answer into a logical truth evaded her tongue.

Mayland shook his head. 'We tried once without the library and a thousand times with it. I'm not talking about burning books – books burn all the time: you still have the stink of their smoke on you, and I was raised beside the char wall. I'm talking about the library. Close its doors. Hide them. Bury it. Collapse the chambers if you must, but that's mere drama. Simply put it beyond use and the job is done. The curse of memory is lifted from our peoples, and they can live in the freedom that brings. Maybe they will find new paths. Maybe they will walk the same ones, though without the burden of knowing it.'

'Ignorance is bliss?' Livira looked at him doubtfully. Her own mind's refusal to release any iota of the past had defined her, made her, elevated her over others. And yet its blade cut in more than one direction. Yute had spoken of nostalgia as a poison, a knife that, as they grew old, men applied to their own flesh with increasing vigour. Memory should perhaps be an art, not the blunt refusal to surrender a single moment of experience, but a curation in which consideration is given to what has space on the shelves and what is consigned to the midden.

'Did you ever meet someone clever who was truly happy?' Mayland looked out across the exchange, something leonine in the angles of his face where the dappled sunlight slid over his skin. 'I don't say this place is easy to let go of. I don't say the library isn't precious. It's all we have of a countless multitude of cultures, vanished people, dead languages, all their works, their dreams, their faith.' He swung his amber gaze back to Livira – he had Evar's eyes. 'Imagine a path across a desert. Halfway along its length a brick of gold rests. You watch as one traveller after another reaches the spot and with great delight sees the gold. They pick it up and labour on under its weight. They die among the dunes, unable to leave their treasure behind,

unable to walk the distance with such a load to carry. Their skel-
etons punctuate the road. Whatever it might be that they can
purchase with this wealth, should we not bury the brick before the
next traveller happens along?'

Livira felt as if the canith were drowning her in words. She
considered herself a talker, but Mayland spoke like a prophet,
somehow weighting his pronouncements with a gravitas that drew
the listener on almost regardless of the content. 'I . . .'

Starval moved swiftly to his brother's side. 'We should go.'

Mayland showed his teeth, running a long tongue across their
serrated length. A sigh left him. 'We should. Thank you, brother.
My enthusiasm carried me away.' He made a short bow towards
Livira and Malar. 'Another time.' And with that he strode briskly
to the next nearest portal and was gone, Starval following in his
wake.

Livira blinked. 'What was that about?'

'Someone they want to avoid is about to arrive.' Malar shrugged.
'He'd said enough in any case. Always had a mouth on him, that
one.'

Livira frowned, still staring at the off-world portal Mayland had
taken. 'What did you think about what he said?'

'Doesn't matter.'

'What?'

'I already told you: we choose sides with our gut. The words are
to make us feel better afterwards.'

'And which side are you—' Livira remembered what he'd said.
Malar was on his own side.

'Yours.' The soldier didn't look particularly pleased about it. 'I'm
always on your side, Livira. Even if you can be pretty stupid for
someone so clever. We're family. I don't know how that happened.
I certainly didn't want it to happen. But you don't choose family.
So, all his words don't matter shit. I'll take the side you take.'

'And which side am I going to take?' Livira had no idea. Mayland's
arguments still wrapped her.

'It would be easier if they were strangers, not boys we raised,'
Malar said. 'It would be easier if the black was bad, and the white
was good. If the Escapes were demons and the assistants were

angels. Then you could persuade yourself there wasn't any choice. But you never had a choice, Livira Page. That's what Yute called you, wasn't it? Page.'

'I never had a choice?'

'You brought one thing out of the Dust. Just one thing that didn't wash off or get burned with the rest of your rags. The corner of a page of a book. You're not going to destroy the library or let it be destroyed. Right or wrong – and fuck knows which it is – it's not going to happen. So, best just admit it, and start working out how to sell the decision to your brain.'

Livira opened her mouth to say something about two centuries in a library chamber having made quite the philosopher of Malar, but an assistant stepped from the portal beside her and put the words out of her mind.

'You have the book. Please give it to me.' He held out a white hand.

There are few journeys more painful than going back to a place you haven't seen in many years. If you are lucky, it will have changed beyond recognition and, by having done so, will allow you to ignore the still larger changes in yourself.

No Returns: A Librarian's Tale, *by Ook Longarm*

CHAPTER 29

Arpix

They started their trek as a group and soon became a straggle, limping their way across the margins of what had once been the Dust but currently was something considerably more habitable and perhaps even more difficult to walk across. Arpix, like most of the others, had worn his shoes out years before. The scraps of leather around his feet were held together with dry sinews and optimism.

Arpix took what Clovis called 'point', leading the way, or at least following Wentworth. He had their hoe with him and poked at any suspicious patch of ground, wary of the creatures Livira had called dust-bears. He'd never seen one, but they were things that you tended only to see while they were eating your legs. The few travellers to reach the plateau had all spoken of the ambush predators in fearful tones. Wentworth seemed oblivious to the danger, and Arpix wasn't sure whether that meant the cat was skilfully navigating around their pits or was simply unaware of the threat.

Every now and then Arpix asked Wentworth to pause while the stragglers caught up. There were no skeer in evidence but that didn't mean anyone should leave the orb's protection zone. At any time, a skeer flier might drop from the sky without warning.

For the first few miles the skeer who had followed them from the plateau had attempted attacks from almost every angle. Arpix was pleased to discover that when they blocked the way it took no effort to drive them aside with the orb's aura. If the skeer had been able to hem them in it would have been an unequal pushing match. At Meelan's insistence, Arpix had tried the obvious experiment, advancing at speed without warning to see if the skeer would be engulfed and killed, but each time they moved aside without any apparent injury.

Jost, who had been loath to move in the first place, had finally been motivated by the idea of a return to the library, the source of her authority. Also by the fact that she stood no chance if they left her alone. Even if the plateau's protection had remained, the woman was clearly unequal to the labour required to feed herself.

It was Jost who demanded that Arpix give her the orb so she could trap the skeer somewhere they couldn't escape from and thus reduce them to piles of offal like the one Wentworth had pulled too close. Arpix politely declined and pointed out that no such topology lay within many miles of their position.

Eventually, the skeer divided into two groups and went on ahead, both seemingly aimed at the closest mountain where their hive hugged the library entrance. They had no problem outpacing the humans and injured canith. Arpix listened to the muttered specu-lation about what kind of reception would be waiting for them in the valleys and gorges ahead.

Kerrol and Evar essentially carried Clovis between them, though pride kept her legs moving for most of the way. An uncomfortable memory plagued Arpix every time he looked back at the canith trio. Livira had escaped the Dust with three soldiers, including one who had died of his wounds on the journey. The other one had had a broken arm or something similar, which echoed Kerrol's injured shoulder. Only Malar had escaped without serious injury, though he still bore the scars of the battle on his face.

It took all day to reach the valley that once led to Crath City. The scar of the old road still marked the ground, even after two centuries. Arpix guessed that his hometown had suffered a gentler doom than most of its predecessors. His people hadn't reached the fire limit that Yute had spoken of, a common or garden war had burned their city down to the foundations before they'd had the opportunity to recreate the fire of the ancients and burn themselves down to the bedrock. And the canith who had done it clearly hadn't lasted too long before the skeer they'd been retreating from had found and obliterated them in turn.

Arpix walked on, his feet sore from the unaccustomed miles. Unexpectedly, Jella had kept him company at the front. He should have expected it. The library had shaped the girl, playing on her timid nature and desire to please everyone. But the harshness of the plateau had carved most of that away and revealed a young woman with greater reserves of stamina and courage than the rest of them. She might still flinch from a scorpion or the rawness of an open wound but faced with the far greater challenge of survival against the odds, Jella had demonstrated a fearlessness that put his own worries to shame. She had taken on the environment with both hands and made a better job of the fight than Arpix and Meelan.

'Penny for your thoughts.' An old saying Jella had found in a book and was fond of using.

'You're overvaluing what goes on in my head.'

'I'm sorry about the canith. Clovis, I mean. I know you like her.'

'I don't—' Arpix swallowed the denial. He did.

'I always said it would take a warrior to batter down your walls.'

'She's a fighter, that's for sure. Don't count her out yet.' Arpix pressed his lips together and held his face stiff against the unfamiliar emotion threatening to twist it.

'Salamonda says we're going from the frying pan into the fire.'

'She likes her kitchen analogies.'

Jella snorted. 'The plateau was a lot like a frying pan. Flat. Hot.'

'And the fire?'

'You know.' Jella gave him a sideways look. 'Yute's bringing us back into his war.'

'Well, to be fair, it's not really his war. He spent hundreds of years just watching over the city and shelving books. And the canith rolling over Crath's walls . . . that had nothing to do with Irad and Jaspeth or whatever you want to call them. I mean, if it hadn't been for Livira we wouldn't even know there was a war . . .'

'You know I'm right.'

Arpix wondered if Jella was channelling Carlotte; there was definitely something of her old friend in the forthrightness on display. And she was right, probably. Yute wasn't calling them back to be librarians again. Arpix wondered what the mysterious deputy and his equally strange wife were planning, now that the uneasy compromises they had supported had ended in disaster and fire. He trudged on for a long dusty while before surprising Jella with an answer to her first question.

'I'm thinking that this would be so much easier if there were a dark lord who hated the world and wanted to tear it down. We'd all line up against that one.' He reached for a favourite saying of his own that he'd dug up from a tome probably every bit as old as the one Jella found hers in. '*Honourable men may differ.* That's our curse here.'

As the arms of the mountain started to reach around them, they saw their first skeer since the warriors had abandoned them out on the plains. Small bands of skeer runners flanked them, high on the slopes. Overhead, fliers flitted across the paling sky like errant dragonflies. Ahead the hive loomed ever larger. It was easy, from a distance, to consider it an oversized wasp nest. Closer in, though still miles off, and the mind began to strain to encompass quite how oversized it was. The architects and builders of Crath City had for decades stretched their imagination and their skills ever higher, piling their rocks more artfully until golden spires seemed to threaten the very sky itself. But the organic mass the skeer had adhered to the mountainside overtopped any of the fallen towers from Arpix's time. Quite how such a thing could have been built, apparently without tools, Arpix had no idea.

Wentworth idled his way relentlessly up the valley, often saving his legs by passing through a brief-lived portal to gain a few hundred yards. He waited for them, half asleep atop a stray boulder that winter had prised from the heights and left for spring to find in the valley. 'He's taking us right to the nest, isn't he?' Meelan asked.

'Looks that way.' Arpix said unenthusiastically. His arms hurt from carrying the iron ball. The thing weighed about the same as a plump baby, no challenge at first, but after fifteen miles his arms felt as if they were twice their normal length. He eyed the blue-veined walls of the nest, not at all keen to put the orb to the test against the near infinity of skeer the thing must house.

'You think they have Yute in there?' Evar called the question from back down the road.

'He's in the library, more likely. This is the way Wentworth wants to take us in.' Arpix waited for the canith to catch up.

'We could try the way we came out,' Evar said. 'No need to make a fight of it if we don't have to.'

'I think we should.' Jella added her opinion into the mix. 'My mother didn't teach me much that stuck, but she did tell me not to kick a nest of . . . well, anything. And the first time I did, I really wished I'd listened to her.'

'Another vote for Jella's mother.' Salamonda came huffing and puffing up behind the canith.

Arpix nodded, still staring at the vast nest. 'There's got to be a brain in there somewhere, and we really don't want to attract its attention. If it starts thinking about how to deal with us . . . well, I could think of several ways to make this orb useless.' He called to the cat. 'Wentworth, we're going this way!'

Despite all he knew about the canith, Arpix found himself face to face with his prejudices when, with Clovis between them, Evar and his brother led the way through the ruins of the city before the canith entrance to the library. Time had taken the elements in both hands and used them to scrub the crumbled remains to almost nothing. Even so, Arpix could see the remnants of an architecture to match any of the works of man he was aware of.

In what Arpix still thought of as 'now' but was really 'his time' lost centuries in the past, there had been an army outpost in this valley. If any trace of canith ruins had been visible at that time, nobody remarked upon them. The intent of the outpost had clearly been to deny the canith access to the library, even if the system of doors within meant that there would always be chambers that only men could enter, containing more books than all the king's subjects could ever read even if they did nothing else.

Not only had the wild 'dog soldiers' that King Oanold had so derided stormed over his royal walls, but they'd built palaces to beggar his own. And yet that narrative, which the king's lies had written on Arpix's soul, still stained his thinking despite the facts washing over it countless times. He shook his head and promised himself he would do better.

'Let me.' Arpix went to support Clovis as Evar started up the slope, hunting for the crack through which he'd escaped the library less than a week before.

The first rock landed two yards in front of Arpix, and he stared at it stupidly, unable to explain it to himself. Three more smashed down. Then thirty. Then it was raining.

The skeer fliers could have come in closer to drop their missiles but they sacrificed accuracy for deadliness, releasing the rocks they carried from a much greater height. Little aiming was possible, but the extra distance ensured that, when they did hit, the rocks would do more than sting.

Amid a deafening thunder of rock hammering into rock, Arpix struggled up the slope, supporting Clovis on one side as her brother did most of the work. Evar's shouts were lost in the din, but his waving needed no explanation. He'd found the fissure and was beckoning them forward.

A terrible scream pierced the cacophony. It came from behind Arpix and if he'd turned to identify the source, the slope would have tripped him. He lurched on, ignoring Clovis's curses as he dragged her onward. Visions of injured friends threatened to swamp his sight, but he needed to get Clovis into cover.

Sharp fragments peppered Arpix's face as a chunk of stone exploded against a boulder to his left. Rock dust filled the air, adding to the confusion. Clovis's burden left him suddenly and a moment later, as he turned to go back for Jella and the others, he was grabbed from behind and dragged down.

The rain of falling stones stopped just moments after Evar pulled Arpix into the cover of the fissure. It cut off almost completely from one beat of his heart to the next, just a scatter of late impacts and then nothing. Meelan and Salamonda stumbled up to him, grey with dust. Blood coated Meelan's forehead, running into his eyes.

Arpix shook off the hand on his robe and scrambled back out to his friend's side.

'Where are you hit?' He grabbed Meelan's shoulders. 'Meelan?'

'I'm hit?' Meelan wiped his face and stared at his crimson fingers in astonishment.

Arpix held Meelan's head still. 'It's a cut.' Sharp fragments must have sliced his scalp. He handed Meelan into Salamonda's care. The eldest and youngest of the bookbinders staggered into view, Nortbu and Sheetra, the girl clutching her shoulder, one arm hanging limp.

'Jella?' Arpix scanned the slope as the dust settled. 'JELLA!'

A grey figure approached.

'Jella?' His eyes said no but he refused their evidence.

Jost walked past, expressionless, her mouth half open.

'Arpix!' Evar called from back inside the fissure. 'They'll come back!'

It was true. The skeer wouldn't have to hunt for ammunition: suitable rocks were within arms' reach practically anywhere they might choose to land. The hive's brain had at last given Arpix and his friends serious consideration – they had elevated themselves from 'distant annoyance' to 'approaching threat', and this was the result.

'Jella!' Arpix refused to leave her. He could see four bodies on the slope, all clothed in dust and broken stone. Logic dictated that they were Jella and her bookbinder colleagues, Kleeson, Henral, and Brigha, but he recognized none of them.

'Jella!' Two of the bodies stirred and a low groaning reached him.

'Arpix!' A heavy hand closed on his shoulder. Evar had emerged from the crack. Kerrol had shuffled the others below ground. 'Arpix!' Evar's hand pointed to a cloud of fliers rising from the rocky slope to the west. A literal cloud, perhaps a thousand of the insectoids. 'We have to go.'

'You do.' Arpix nodded. 'Look after them for me.' He shook free and ran back down to the nearest body, skipping across the rocks in his disintegrating shoes.

The closest of the fallen was Kleeson, a quiet, studious man who had nearly earned his librarian's robes but never complained about falling at the last hurdle. The groans had come from him. Blood bubbled from his mouth, and as Arpix rolled him to his side the scale of his injury became apparent, his chest cratered by an impact not even a skeer warrior could survive. Kleeson watched the sky, wide grey eyes filled with innocence and vague surprise.

'I'm so sorry . . .' Arpix felt ridiculous, apologizing as if he'd spilled the man's chai at dinner. 'I'm so sorry.' He moved on, passing the second figure for the most distant who had managed to lift themselves a little from the ground.

'Arpix!' Evar's despairing shout. The whirr of skeer wings filled the air like the promise of a coming storm.

Arpix reached the moving figure. It was Jella. 'Up!' He wrenched her to her feet, not even questioning where the strength came from. 'Are you hurt?'

'I . . .' Jella set a hand to her bleeding nose. 'I just fell.'

'Come on!' Arpix dragged her forward, only to have the woman collapse with a cry of pain.

'My ankle!' Jella sobbed with the agony.

A shadow swallowed the slope.

'Leave me!' Jella tried to pull free of his hands. 'Run!'

'Never going to happen.'

'Arpix.' Jella looked at him, horrified, her eyes flitting to the mosaicked sky above them, skeer-dark and sun-bright. 'Damn you, Arpix! Run!'

Arpix bent and tried to pick Jella up. Privation had stripped her to a shadow of her former self, but it was still all he could do to lift her now that the terror had left him. He was still scared of course, but he wasn't terrified. He'd been terrified of leaving her alone to die. He wasn't terrified of dying with her. Just scared. 'We're going to make it.' He managed a couple of staggering steps up the slope. 'Nothing to it.'

The first stones of the new rain hit close by.

Suddenly Evar was there. The canith slung Jella over his shoulder with a grunt and began to run back up the slope so fast that Arpix could barely keep pace. Rocks hammered all around them, exploding with breathtaking fury.

Arpix didn't expect to reach the fissure. But he did, and waiting hands hauled him down in Evar's wake.

The majority of each breath we take is gas of types that will not sustain us. The truth, like oxygen, is necessary if we are to live. And, like oxygen, if it is all we get, it will kill us.

The Good Lie, *by Emily Mendicant*

CHAPTER 30

Evar

'The orb!' Arpix started back towards the daylight in a moment of panic. 'I dropped it.'

'You did.' Evar revealed the iron ball. It filled his hand and seemed to shiver with a distant excitement. 'I picked it up.' He offered it to the man.

'Keep it,' Arpix said. 'Maybe you'll hold on to it better than I did.'

Evar shrugged and stowed the ball in his book satchel.

The humans had lost two of their number but at least they were out of the rock storm now. Within the fissure the outer edges of the pervasive library glow replaced the slanting shadows of late afternoon. The small band of survivors navigated the chaos of the ruined pre-library complex and reached the large cavern separating the living quarters from the library proper. Here Evar ceded his place supporting Clovis to Arpix and led the way, although he had only crossed the cave once before. The humans strung out behind him, bloodied and battered, negotiating the convolutions of the cavern floor as best they could. Ahead the white rectangle of the canith door into the library shone like a beacon.

Wentworth had been waiting for them at the entrance to the main cavern. Now he was content to follow at Salamonda's heels, occasionally straying to investigate an interesting-looking hollow or some forgotten fragment of an old page.

Evar approached the door and reached for it slowly, only half believing it would respond. Having library doors open for him was still a moment of great significance. He'd spent his whole life beating against their obdurate refusal and only seeing them open in his dreams. He still struggled with the reality. He had never imagined that they would melt away before his touch like mist. Even now, it felt as if they had lied to him with their permanence and with their white surfaces so hard that even iron couldn't make a scratch.

'Come on.' He beckoned the humans through. It was strange to think that without him they would be trapped in the chamber just as his people had been trapped in a different chamber until Livira set her hand to their door and freed them.

The room beyond already looked too big to easily fit within the mountain, and that was without considering the others beyond it, hundreds of them at the least, possibly thousands. Evar hadn't paid it much attention during their escape but now he stood in the entrance, drinking it in. The first canith chamber. The gateway to the knowledge that his species had accumulated over untold generations and to which they returned time and again after each cataclysm visited upon them, be it by their own hands or those of some other.

From the top of the steps, he could see across the whole span of the chamber, across a patchwork landscape of shelving from different eras, much as Livira had described in the first human room. He knew that out past other doors there were books written not just in ink on paper but in knots in string, notches on sticks, collections of different shells threaded on cords, bumps and holes set onto thin sheets of leather, stories and wisdom recorded on whatever medium presented itself to the people of the time. Perhaps the skeer wrote theirs on sheets of the same exudate that made their armour and their city, forming the letters from scent rather than ink. The urge to record was nearly as old as memory itself. What was life if not a song sung to the music of the past for the future to hear?

'We need to find the centre circle,' Arpix said, coming up behind him with Kerrol and Clovis.

'The healing only works for recent injuries,' Evar said.

'And we have recently injured among us.'

Evar felt immediately ashamed. He'd been too focused on Clovis. From the top of the stairs that led down the wall to the chamber floor Evar could see the whole four square miles of it. It took a moment to spot the clear circle in the midst of thousands of acres of shelving. 'Come on. I'll lead you from the shelf tops.'

Evar was far from comfortable walking along the narrow planking atop shelves that reached many times his height, but he'd sprinted across them when the automaton had given chase, and he'd leapt every gap that presented itself, so he had no excuse not to repeat the feat at a more leisurely pace without the pressure of imminent death. The others followed along in the book canyons below while he steered the straightest path he could towards the spot that memory marked as the centre circle.

It took them the best part of an hour but at last the humans stumbled into the circle. Immediately the one called Sheetra gasped in relief as the circle's healing effect started to repair the shoulder a skeer's rock had smashed.

Evar felt his thirst ease and the tiredness drain from his limbs. Their leaky bucket of water had not lasted long on the crossing from the plateau, and the waterskins that Jost and Arpix retained didn't go far when shared between almost a dozen. The only water he knew of in the library was the pool in his home chamber. The circle's impact on his thirst was welcome but not sufficient to erase it entirely and he sucked his tongue speculatively, imagining a life sustained only by the circles' illusion of water.

Kerrol and Arpix came in last. Clovis hung between them, seemingly lifeless. Her impression of a corpse was sufficient to set Evar running to check her for a pulse. He reached her as the other two laid her on the floor. Salamonda fashioned a pillow of books. Arpix drew out a small, dried gourd and held it to Clovis's lips, giving her the last of the water he'd somehow hoarded since departing the plateau.

She coughed and opened her eyes. 'I dreamt . . . that we escaped . . .' A whisper, her gaze unfocused.

'We did escape.' Kerrol's voice cracked slightly, the first time that

Evar had ever heard any emotion other than gentle amusement from his brother.

'Humans!' Clovis grabbed Arpix's arm, coughing and spluttering on the water, spilling some. 'We found humans.'

'You did.' He stroked her mane absently, eyes bright. 'You found humans.'

'I . . . I wanted to . . .' Clovis closed her eyes, drifting off.

'She's too hot,' Kerrol said. 'Her breathing's not right. This place can't help her. The damage was done days ago.'

Arpix spoke without looking up from Clovis. 'It might help. It can undo the damage that's been done in the last few hours. It can undo the new poisons being made in her blood hour by hour. It can keep her here.'

'She would want more than that.' Evar knew that Clovis would never agree to being held on the threshold of death, helpless but forbidden release.

'It's a chance to rest,' Arpix said. 'Marshal her forces. Regroup and counter-attack.' It sounded as if he were trying to get orders to Clovis past her unconsciousness.

'So, we just stay here and wait?' Kerrol asked.

The distant sound of crashing shelves forestalled any answer. Evar exchanged looks with his brother. 'It can't be?'

'It might be,' Kerrol said.

'What?' Arpix growled. The other humans were looking around as if expecting something to burst into the circle any moment.

'I don't know,' Evar said. 'Watch her.' And with that he was scaling the nearest shelves, aiming for the heights.

Gaining the shelf top, Evar couldn't see the automaton bearing down on them. The shelves in this canith chamber were higher than those in the one they'd first escaped into though. It might be that they were tall enough to hide even something as large as the metal beast that had pursued them for so many miles.

The distant sound of more wood splintering brought Evar's gaze to the western door. With a sigh he set off towards the destruction's source. He made steady progress and found himself almost welcoming the distraction. Without it he would still be responsible for around half a dozen fragile humans while watching his sister die a slow death. He made a leap of three yards and pinwheeled his arms with a cry of alarm as sixty feet of age-weakened shelving undulated beneath his feet, spilling books onto the floor far below.

Evar fell to his knees and then to his belly, clutching the shelf top, waiting for it to fall or stop trying to fall. In the end it decided to stay standing, and Evar edged away, promising to be more conservative in his future leaps.

The crashing that drew him on was not the continuous thunder that the automaton had made as it barrelled through shelf after shelf. Rather it was an intermittent thing, with gaps that might stretch minutes between short periods of splintering and crashing.

Evar closed in cautiously. In the boredom of his days on the plateau he'd had plenty of time to consider why some huge mechanical monster had given chase with such dedication. He'd come up with nothing. His best guess for why it had arrowed after him, ignoring his siblings, was either that it had seen him first, or that its random choices had just panned out that way. Nothing else made sense.

When at last Evar got his first sight of the source of the din, he was amazed to find himself looking at a smaller, though still much larger than him, version of the original automaton. It was working its broad-shouldered, almost round body along one of the wider aisles, its elbows stripping books from the shelves about eight feet off the ground, spilling them onto the floor behind it in untidy mounds with loose pages fluttering.

This one was perhaps twice Evar's height and if it had been made of flesh and bone rather than copper and brass it might have weighed twenty times what he did. A relief of fur picked out in gold covered its body and arms, and on the backs of both hands a single blade jutted forwards, looking large and sharp enough to slice a skeer in two.

Evar's elevated perspective offered a new viewing angle that tickled his memory. 'I've seen you before . . .' He tried to remember where. It wasn't as if he had done much travelling in his life or met many strangers. So how did he know this creature, or at least the creature on which the metal creation below him had been modelled? The most likely answer was that he had seen a picture in a book

– but that wasn't what his memory was telling him. The recollection was fresher and more vivid than that of something flipped past in some ancient bestiary years ago. 'Livira . . .' It hit him as the automaton below twisted its short, thick neck to look up at him. He'd been with Livira in the Exchange. They'd chosen an off-world pool and he'd found himself among these creatures, yellow-furred, barely half his height, within a library not dissimilar to this one. Only Livira hadn't been there when he turned around, and he'd returned to find her still choking out the noxious air of the creatures' home.

The shelf shook beneath Evar's feet. The automaton pounded on the wall of books and planks and once more everything began to fall. Evar saved himself with a twisting leap across the aisle behind him, hitting the next set of shelves high enough for the shelf top to fold him around it, knocking the air from his lungs. He clung on, straining for breath, while black spots swarmed his vision, and behind him the ruins of the opposite shelves surrendered to the automaton's advance.

Evar hauled himself up and lay gasping, hoping he was hidden from below. The thing should never have spotted him on his high perch and yet it had somehow felt his eyes upon its back and looked up. Evar's hope didn't last longer than it took the automaton to shake off the avalanche of books and broken timber then crash into the base of the shelves supporting him.

He tried to rise and leap for the next shelf top, but the surface beneath his feet fell away and he fell with it. Had he dropped the distance through clear air he would have broken both legs and quite possibly the rest of his bones too. As it was, repeated impacts with shelves in the act of breaking, combined with what might be called a cushion of books if books were in any way soft, left him groaning on a mound of literature with a shard of shattered shelving impaling his upper left thigh.

The mechanoid came at him, gears groaning, eyes burning with a hot red light. It looked to be in far less good repair than the giant one he'd encountered before, but still, it was in much better shape than he was.

Evar tried to roll to his feet but the length of timber sticking through his leg brought the effort to an agonized halt. It hurt worse than any injury he'd had before, but the real hurting would come later. For now, shock wrapped him in a numbing blanket and the pain was a kind of nausea, flaring at every twist.

The automaton came on, wading through book drifts over a yard deep, piling volumes before it in an ever-shifting bow wave. It was the thought of Clovis bellowing instructions at him that finally got Evar moving. His sister would be disgusted at him. He hadn't even drawn the sword he'd taken from her. He shuffled away on his backside, propelling himself with his one good leg.

The automaton started to run, filling the air with flying books. Clovis would have wanted Evar to meet his end on his feet, even if it was just one foot, but Clovis wasn't there to watch. Evar drew the white sword and levelled it at the onrushing metal bulk. Either one of the automaton's great feet could stamp the life out of him, and even if his weapon could pierce its hide, he doubted he would be able to do enough damage to stop the thing before it reached him. His last thoughts weren't of the automaton or of Clovis. They were of Livira and how much he regretted being too late to save her or even to say goodbye.

He thrust his sword at the brass belly that threatened to crush him as the mechanoid lunged for his head. The point of the thing's hand-blade struck the library floor where his head had been and skittered across the stone. Fingers as fat as his wrist followed, reaching to close around his face. The crushing embrace never quite happened. The hand obscuring his vision shuddered to a halt; the fingers trembled as if wrestling with some invisible helm around his head. And at his side Evar's forgotten book satchel jumped and rattled and buzzed with such vigour that it threatened to pop every seam at once.

A complicated, rasping crack tore the air. The sound of something important breaking. The noise stopped abruptly and so did every other noise. The library's silence swept in like a wave, swallowing everything. No books fell, no timbers creaked, and until Evar inhaled implosively, he wondered if perhaps he had gone deaf.

It took him several minutes to extricate himself from beneath the metal hand. He had to surrender Clovis's sword, a foot of which was bedded in the frozen automaton's stomach, and to take great care to avoid snagging the bloody shard of wood emerging from his thigh. Terrifyingly, while trying to wriggle clear, Evar caught a whiff of something burning. The fear stirred him to greater efforts and proved to be something of an anaesthetic, allowing him to effect the last half of his escape in a quarter of the time. All the while the stink of burning grew stronger, so that Evar expected to see flames curling up around his head at any moment.

Finally, he was clear, dragging his satchel with him. He looked around wildly, too spooked by the threat of fire to let his gaze rest on anything long enough to understand it. Nothing . . . just the hulking automaton towering over him, frozen in place, stooped with one hand still clawed around the space where he had been.

Evar drew in several deep breaths and let his nose lead him. Gingerly, he opened his book satchel and a faint smoke wafted out. The iron ball warned back inquisitive fingers with waves of heat. It did seem to be cooling though, for which Evar was very thankful. Quite what had happened he wasn't sure, but it seemed clear that in some manner the orb had stopped the automaton, and that the action might have broken the device along with the internal workings of Evar's assailant.

'Shit.' He sat back with a snarl. He was certain of very little, but one thing he did know for sure was that it was going to be a very long hobble back to the centre circle.

Some things are built to thwart those that try to break them. The better they are at that job, the more vulnerable they may be to being broken accidentally.

A Century of Main Battle Tanks, *by* Commander Ian Wrigglesworth

CHAPTER 31

Livira

The assistant that Mayland had called Hellet held his hand out for the book. He'd sent Livira back for it and had called it a danger. His exact words echoed in Livira's memory though she would like to have forgotten them:

You have written a wound into the world, broken laws whose age it would be meaningless to describe. There is a book that is also a loop. A book that has swallowed its own tale. It is a ring, a cycle, burning through the years, spreading cracks through time, fissures that reach into its past and future. And through those cracks things that have no business in the world of flesh can escape.

More importantly, at least in Livira's estimation, Hellet had said that without bringing the book forward she would remain a ghost in any time that Evar was flesh, and he would be unable to be anything but a ghost where she had form. Hellet had said nothing, however, about giving the book to him when she returned with it.

'I never agreed to give you my book.' Livira held it to her chest.

'It's not safe,' Hellet said without expression. 'Neither now nor then, neither here nor there. You should let me destroy it.'

'Destroy it?' Livira echoed. She might have guessed that something like this was coming but she hadn't allowed herself to, heading off each stray thought that wandered in that direction. Malar had said that she wouldn't take the side of the book-burners, no matter what the larger argument might be. And now this assistant expected her to let not just any old book be destroyed, but the one and only one that she had written herself. If she had bled upon the pages and written every word in crimson the bundle she held to her breastbone could not be more part of her. To erase her stories, the thoughts and passions, the tears that had fallen, and take them utterly from the world . . . She tried to loosen her grip on the covers. She felt foolish, but also unable to let it go. Despite the vastness of the library and its unmissable message that books were as common and as numerous as grains of sand on a beach, still she had always felt that the combination of ink, quill, and hand had given her thoughts a kind of immortality, that they would outlast her flesh and wait out the millennia on library shelves, occasionally being discovered and rediscovered by intrepid explorers. Maybe her ideas would even find another mind in which they echoed and took on weight as the reader wrapped pieces of his own soul around the pieces of hers that rested on the page, as they had with Evar.

Livira snorted with bitter laughter at her own ego, her hubris, her arrogance. And still she couldn't force her arms to set her little book in that white hand.

'You don't have to.' It was Malar. 'Fuck him. It's your book. It's not even that bad. I liked the bit . . .' He frowned. '. . . the bit with the thing. That was pretty good.' He turned his pale glower towards the assistant. 'She's keeping it.'

The assistant looked at his outstretched hand and lowered his arm. Livira had been tensed for coercion of some sort, or perhaps just argument. Having been on the other side of a pair of white eyes like those watching her, she should perhaps have known better. Coercion and argument were not the tools of the timeless.

The assistant indicated the portal through which they'd emerged.

'That's it?' Malar seemed disappointed that there was to be no fight. 'You dragged us behind you like a child's toy before, and now you're just letting us walk off?'

'You were time-echoes,' the assistant answered. 'It's our duty to correct anomalies that won't correct themselves. The Exchange is not your place. You should leave and not return.'

'Where will this portal take us?' Livira didn't want to return to the pool in Evar's chamber and find herself having to dodge skeer whilst following Evar's trail that might lead through doors that wouldn't open for her. In the past she'd felt that her exits from the Exchange had been portals of opportunity. Now she just wanted a portal to open for her and Malar, exactly where and when she needed it.

'She said: Where will it take us?' Malar still sounded ready for a fight.

'To the library.' The assistant answered as if 'the library' was all the detail anyone could ever want. As if it were a single thing, one point, not endlessly spread out across time and space.

'We'll work it out.' Livira took Malar's arm. 'Come on.' She was sure of one truth where assistants were concerned. Persistence would not wear them down. Even the geological persistence that would eventually wear down the mountain ranges where the library pretended to conceal itself would not change an assistant's mind. 'Hold onto my arm. If my aim's off, I might well need you to kill something.'

Livira thought it more likely that they would end up lost in the library a thousand chambers deep than face to face with a skeer, but talking about the danger was a good way to get Malar's attention. She led the way into the portal, focusing her thoughts on Evar, but not just Evar. She had lost others too: Arpix, Jella, Meelan, and Carlotte, and others. Yute had taken her childhood friends from the Dust into the Exchange; Neera and Katrin would be rubbing elbows with the head librarian and Lord Algar. If the portal could deliver her to them all, without splitting her into separate chunks or arriving decades late, she'd be very grateful. She tried to beam that gratitude into the mix of images that she followed through the spinning chaos within the portal.

'Where the hell are we?' Malar looked around, startled and suspicious.

A warm room, dimly lit, low rafters hung with garlic, onions, bags of spices, a pot bubbling on the stove. 'It's . . .' Livira wanted to say it was Salamonda's kitchen but, before she could finish speaking, a portal smaller than the one at her back opened just above the main table and sprouted a grey-sleeved arm. A white hand patted around, fastening on half a loaf of bread.

'Yute?' Livira crossed rapidly to the table and caught the disembodied arm around the wrist. Instantly she was jerked forward by something far stronger than the arm she had hold of. 'Malar!' She shouted the soldier's name and reached for him with her spare hand. Their fingers locked together as the kitchen spun away, tumbling into the distant recesses of whatever grey void it was that had swallowed them.

For a moment Livira could see Yute, standing startled before a towering shelf of emerald-green books. She felt her grip on both the hands she held slipping. Yute filled her vision for a heartbeat, and in the next her grip broke, and she fell, rolling head over heels, flipping through space, hitting the floor, bouncing, hitting it again, and each time with an awful cracking sound as if her bones were breaking.

She staggered from a portal almost too dizzy to stand, feeling sick and bruised, though other parts of her brain were telling her with great certainty that she had simply lifted her foot in the Exchange and set it down in this new place.

Livira found herself facing a curving, book-lined aisle in what could be one of ten thousand parts of the library. Two things struck her immediately. The first was the awful stink of the place, a mix of sewage and decay. The second was that many of the books had been torn from the shelves and that a few yards ahead of her a half-naked old man appeared to be sleeping on an irregular bed of them. He lifted his head, bleary-eyed as the twists and turns of Livira's journey suddenly caught up with her and set her reaching for the nearest shelves to keep herself upright.

'Who the hell are you?' The old man struggled into a sitting position, pulling a stained purple robe over his sagging belly. He peered at her with deep-set eyes that were black and hard with suspicion. Comical wisps of grey hair formed a border for the bald dome of his head. 'Guards! Guards!' He looked around. 'Damn their eyes. Where are they?'

Despite the terrifying completeness with which Livira's memory imprisoned the past, it wasn't until the man started calling for guards that she recognized him. 'Recognized' was too strong a word. She deduced his identity with considerable certainty from a collection of scattered visual clues.

'You're him,' she said. And felt instantly foolish. 'You're the king.'

Hate and Love run a race in which Love is both the tortoise and the hare. Hate shoots the hare with the starting pistol and reloads without undue haste before setting off after the tortoise.

Cabbages and Kings, *by Wally Russ*

CHAPTER 32

Arpix

'He's taking too long.' Clovis, who had seemed to be knocking on death's door only a few hours earlier, made it to her feet against all expectations and all of Arpix's advice.

'Do I have to push you over to get you to rest?' Arpix had run out of sensible threats.

'I'd like to see you try,' she growled, licking her teeth with a long tongue. Despite the challenge in her voice, her eyes held an invitation that made him look away.

'Kerrol. You're supposed to be good at persuasion. Can't you get her to be sensible?'

The tall canith shrugged and leaned back against the stack of books he'd fashioned into a chair. 'I'm not a medical expert but I feel that my sister is at her best in a fight. Lying down might work for most patients but Clovis is—'

'Shut up and help me look for him.' Clovis aimed a kick at Kerrol.

'I have to draw the line there.' Arpix put himself in Clovis's way. 'If you leave this circle, you lose all of its support.' He reached for some military analogy. 'It would be like sending your reserves away at the height of a battle.'

'Sometimes you have to toss the strategy book aside.' Clovis advanced.

'Kerrol! Help me!' Arpix found himself grappling with Clovis, both his hands locked in hers.

Kerrol lay back. 'No, this is good bonding. It's all very healthy.'

'What are you talking about, you idiot?' Arpix realized he'd said it in his own tongue and growled his next words in canith as he struggled to hold Clovis back. 'You can see how sick you are. I'd never be able to stop you otherwise.' Even fresh from her deathbed the canith was ridiculously strong. Arpix had never been athletic, but you couldn't help but build some muscle when you spent so much of your day carrying stacks of books about, hiking across library chambers, and climbing endless ladders. Years on the plateau had worn much of that fitness away but had replaced it with the products of a different kind of labour.

Clovis leaned into him, confusingly close, her hot breath on his neck. She seemed to be enjoying the contest far too much. She sniffed at his ear.

'I thought you were sick!' Arpix found his arms being pressed down to his sides. Clovis might be only a hand taller than him but close up that made a world of difference and made him wonder how his friends must see him as he towered above them. Meelan didn't even reach his shoulder.

'Maybe it was you who gave me a fever.' Clovis grinned and licked the side of his face. A heartbeat later he was falling, legs swept from under him. 'But my brother needs me.' She walked on towards the opening of the nearest aisle. 'He's an idiot. They're all idiots. But he's the one most likely to get himself killed without my help.'

By the time Arpix got to his feet, Clovis had reached the edge of the centre circle. Her step faltered as she left the rejuvenating aura and entered the aisle. She shook herself, snarled, and pressed on. Kerrol walked past Arpix, following his sister.

'Where are you going?' Arpix understood Kerrol to be of little use in a fight even when his shoulder wasn't injured.

'Ours is what the textbooks call a highly dysfunctional family, but someone has to keep it together.' Kerrol shrugged, muttered a pained curse at having flexed his shoulder, and followed his sister.

Arpix turned towards his friends, who'd all been watching the canith with fascination. 'None of you leave this circle. For any reason. I'll be back!' And before any of them could offer to come with him or try to keep him there, he hurried after Kerrol.

He caught up with them fairly swiftly. Clovis walked as if she were fifty years older, leaving Arpix to wonder how she'd put him on the ground quite so easily.

'We're never going to find him, you understand that?' Arpix asked. He didn't like to nag but nobody could find anyone else in a library chamber unless they'd agreed on a meeting place they both knew.

'You understand that he was carrying the weapon?' Clovis replied.

'Oh.' That particular fact had escaped Arpix's attention. It didn't help in finding him, and it didn't make finding him more urgent, but it did mean that his loss would have even larger consequences if they didn't locate him.

'We'll have a bit of a walk around and by the time we go back, hopefully Evar will be there.' Kerrol nodded to himself.

'It's fine,' Clovis said. 'I have a plan.'

'Which is?' Arpix asked.

Clovis took his hand and pulled him closer, before slinging her arm over his shoulders and using him as a crutch. 'I brought my favourite human with me, and he's very clever.'

Arpix sighed. He considered sliding out from under her arm and leaving her to it, but worried that she might genuinely need him in order to stand. He furrowed his brow, thinking furiously. It just wasn't possible to find one person amid thousands of acres of shelving.

'There was a *lot* of crashing.'

'Yes.' Clovis leaned on him and nodded.

'So, whatever was doing this was leaving a trail of destruction. It might be too large for the aisles.'

'That's what I was thinking,' Clovis said.

Arpix ignored her. 'And it came from the west. But we didn't see any damage when we came to the centre circle from the main door. So, it seems unlikely whatever it was has been crashing around in here for weeks or longer. Plus, we didn't hear it at all until after we were settled. All of which tells us . . .'

'Something good.' Clovis sagged against him.

'That we should go to the west door and follow the trail of the thing that Evar went to investigate.'

Clovis straightened up, took her arm off Arpix, and slapped him on the back. 'Told you I had a plan!'

Clovis proceeded to lead the way, first to the wall and then to the door, setting a pace that whilst no challenge for Arpix must have taken a toll on anyone as sick as she'd been and still was.

At the west door the trail they were looking for was one a blind man could follow. Even in the wider aisles books had been knocked from shelves with abandon, often splintering the wood on which they rested. Where the gap narrowed, something wider than three canith together, and stronger than ten, had pushed over whole units of shelving, some fifty yards long. In three places whatever they were following had battered its way through the shelves and into another aisle, pulverizing books by the score and bringing down others in sufficient number to bury the floor a yard deep.

When they finally rounded a corner to discover the author of all the destruction it was the canith who gave gasps of recognition, but it was Arpix who was finally able to name what they were looking at.

'It's the same damn thing that chased us before. Only a lot smaller!' Clovis started a wary advance but Arpix grabbed her arm.

'First: Stop! It might start moving again. Second: Smaller? This thing is a *lot* smaller than something else?' The metal guardian was larger than anything Arpix had seen in the library. Larger than the winged man in Chamber 2 whose hand the trainees would shake for luck. Larger than Volente. Certainly larger than Wentworth or the Raven.

'The other one could barely get through chamber doors,' Kerrol said.

Clovis put her hand on Arpix's where it held her arm. 'Do I have to knock you down again?'

Arpix released her with a frown. 'At least let's try to approach it from the other side. It will be easier to escape along a narrow aisle than down one it's already widened.'

'Tactical thinking.' Clovis nodded. 'You know the way to a girl's heart.'

Arpix deepened his frown, drawing out a barking laugh from his tormentor. 'Come on.' He led away in search of an alternate route. 'Why would a giant mechanical ganar be chasing you anyway?'

'A g-what-now?'

'Ganar. They're small herbivores, about this big.' Arpix held his hand about four feet off the ground. 'I've never seen one, but they used to be quite common. The histories say they were brought down from one of the moons. Attamast, if I remember correctly. That seems unlikely but—'

'That small?' Clovis bared her teeth. 'I look forward to meeting some in person. I have some questions for them about why these metal bastards keep coming after us.'

'I read that the ganar are clever. Cunning too. They won't come at you from the front.' Arpix glanced back at the giant metal ball of the automaton's body. 'Unless, I guess, they're big enough to punch through shelving.' Another memory niggled at him, just out of reach. Not a good memory. A record he'd read of . . . some kind of bad treatment meted out to the ganar? He shook his head, but the memory remained stuck somewhere back behind his conscious thoughts. Livira would know. She never forgot anything.

They found the blood trail before regaining sight of the automaton from the other side. Clovis smelled it first then Arpix caught sight of a lone crimson spot darkening on the library floor.

'Still wet.' Kerrol straightened back up and pointed to another further along the aisle.

It took only a few minutes to catch up with Evar. They found him hobbling along, lost in his own small world of hurt, gasping each time he put any weight on his injured leg.

'Little brother!' Clovis got his attention.

Kerrol caught one of Evar's arms while Arpix pushed Clovis out of the way to take the other side. 'We'll be carrying you too by the time we get back if I let you take his weight.'

This time Clovis let him have his way.

The slowly increasing application of pressure
can move mountains. Hunger is such a pressure.
Most of our morals are molehills.

Eat Prey Eat, *by Gilbert Sullivan*

CHAPTER 33

Livira

Livira had come face to face with King Oanold on one other, very different occasion and she had never expected to see the man again, even from a distance, especially not two centuries after his city was burned down.

'You!' The king's face convulsed with disgust. 'You're that damnable Duster girl Yute gave a librarianship to.'

Livira hadn't expected to be recognized, but she was wearing a librarian's robe, and the day of her appointment had clearly left a deep impression on the king. Not a good one. 'Where is Yute?'

'Questioning me? Me!' King Oanold looked around in outrage. 'Guards! Guards! Where the hell are you?'

Two soldiers came hurrying around the aisle's curve, both clutching arrow-sticks. They were unshaven and the larger of the two barely fitted into his bloodstained jacket, leaving Livira with the distinct impression that he'd stolen it off a corpse.

'Arrest that woman!' Oanold pointed at her unnecessarily.

Livira knew the 'sticks could throw their projectiles hundreds of yards, but the aisle's curve offered the hope that she could take herself out of their line of sight before they could aim and fire. She turned to run.

A man behind her captured her arms as she rotated towards him.

Bony fingers encircled her wrists. Livira looked up and met her captor's one-eyed stare. An ugly smile twisted thin lips.

'Algar.' She spat the name and broke free of his grip. Why an idle, skinny lord thought he could overpower a hard-working young librarian she had no idea. She didn't have to plant her knee in his groin to escape, but she did it anyway.

Unfortunately, the man behind Algar was bigger, stronger, and more accomplished in the arts of capture. Livira found her left wrist seized with merciless strength, then twisted so painfully that she had to drop to her knees to escape the agonizing angle.

While Algar leaned against the nearest shelves, moaning, the king set a soiled grey wig on his baldness and, flanked by his two soldiers, approached her with a smirk.

'See there, gentlemen? The Duster shows her true nature, a creature of violence, lashing out at her betters.'

Livira glared at him but decided to give the soldier holding her wrist no further excuse to see whether he could break it. 'Where are we? How are you here?'

The king nodded at her captor. 'If she speaks again without being spoken to, break her arm.' He came close, but not close enough to kick, and ran his eyes up and down the length of her before turning away. 'Follow me.' He leaned towards the larger of his guards. 'Jakmo, help Lord Algar. He seems to be indisposed.'

The soldier holding Livira twisted her arm up behind her and pushed her on. She walked awkwardly across the fallen books, unable to adjust her path. Even fractional movements filled her shoulder joint with pain. Whoever the man holding her was, he seemed to know a lot about hurting people.

For those first few steps, bowed over to relieve the pressure on her arm, Livira's head was too full of pain, fear, and confusion for any speculation. Even so, despite all these distractions she somehow noticed something that seemed to escape the notice of everyone around her. Right in front of her, seemingly in the place where she had come to rest on the library floor, a web of thin cracks ran out in all directions like those on a pane of glass where a stone had struck. They became lost beneath the shelves and fallen books, and Livira was propelled onward before she could focus on them.

Even so, it amazed her. A lifetime in the library had schooled her in its impervious nature. In all that time she had seen one possible scorch mark and no cracks or damage whatsoever. And yet, just behind her, dozens of black cracks ran through the stuff of the library where part of her felt she'd merely stepped out from a portal, and part of her felt she'd hit the floor with considerable force, but not sufficient to break herself, let alone the ground beneath her.

The stink of the place still managed to register through Livira's discomfort. It was as if these people had never discovered that the chamber corners slowly made organic matter vanish and had instead been befouling the area in which they'd chosen to live. Her stomach threatened rebellion and she was saved from vomiting over herself perhaps only by the fact that technically she hadn't eaten anything for over two hundred years.

The king led on, passing a couple of junctions at which a single soldier had been positioned. Another corner and without warning they were in the centre circle. Livira felt the healing aura flowing through her.

The smell here proved worse, if anything. The floor space had been divided into dozens of areas by book walls, most of them chest high, some taller. Livira could see at least two dozen people, though many scores more could be hidden from sight. All were men and women from Crath, mostly soldiers, one woman in torn finery. Another man Livira felt she recognized from those gathered outside Yute's house on the day the canith came, but even her memory had limits and she was less good with faces than with facts.

'Where's Yute?'

The crack of her arm being brutally broken reminded Livira of the king's instruction. She fell to the ground screaming, all control swept away by the tide of pain. She lay on the grimy stone for what seemed an age, breathless and hurting, before lifting her eyes to the circle of men around her. The king wore a broad smile and a chain of office that some attendant must have put around his shoulders. The soldiers looked bored. Lord Algar seemed much recovered and regarded her with cold interest. She noted that the front of his expensively lace-frilled white shirt was bloodstained, mostly around the chest. She didn't think he'd looked like that when he escaped into the Exchange.

'Get up.' King Oanold's smile vanished.

Livira was about to protest when she realized that her arm, though still painful, was no longer agonizing. The centre circle was in the process of healing her, just as it had unwound her insult to Lord Algar's nether regions. Awkwardly, she got to her feet and straightened up, half expecting a blow at any moment. She wondered where Malar was and whether he'd be able to save her without killing anyone. It seemed unlikely.

'How the hell did you get past my guards?' The king was about her height and despite the pervasive stench of sewage and rot she could smell both his lavender perfume and the stale sweat it sought to hide. Oanold moved his head from side to side as he studied her, as if trying to peer through her eyes at some truth lying behind them. 'You were going to kill me in my sleep, weren't you? You're Yute's assassin.'

Livira realized that Oanold hadn't seen her arrival. He'd been sleeping. It must seem to him that she had leapt the shelf tops, evaded his guards, and climbed down to where he lay.

'Answer me!'

The soldier behind her sank his fist into the region of her left kidney. The rule of law appeared to be one of the things they'd left behind when abandoning the city.

Livira groaned. 'I'm a librarian. I answer to the head librarian.' Technically Oanold had no authority over her. They were in the library, after all.

It was Algar who answered. 'Since your canith friends killed the head librarian it's Acconite who now holds that position.' He raised a hand and snapped his fingers. 'Acconite!'

Deputy Acconite had always kept a low profile in the library. He'd specialized in recovering technical books, primarily on warfare, from the far reaches of catalogued library space. He had been the driving force behind the rapid development of the 'sticks the king's soldiers now held. Without Yute working to thwart him, Acconite might have armed the military with beams of fire that would have turned the canith army to ash. Livira wasn't sure where she stood on that issue. She had rather liked her old life . . .

The man who shambled into view, answering Lord Algar's summons, bore little resemblance to the Deputy Acconite that Livira knew. The man had voted in favour of her dismissal, more than once, but even so her heart went out to him. His dark robe hid the grime but not well enough, the neat black triangle of his beard had become a greying straggle, but it was his eyes that spoke most eloquently of unknown horrors, all his old surety and arrogance gone, replaced by an unfocused emptiness that even the hardships of the Dust had never written on the faces of Livira's people.

'Yute—' Livira remembered the crack as her arm had broken and bit off her objection, though it sickened her to be trained by such crude tactics and so swiftly.

'Yute is a traitor, and we shall have him soon,' the king snapped. 'He and his rabble can't hide forever. It's just one room!' He beckoned the husk that had once been Deputy Acconite closer. 'So, tell your head librarian who sent you and where he's hiding!'

'Nobody sent me. I came by myself.'

The slap came from her left, as violent as it was unexpected, rattling her teeth, setting half her face ablaze and filling her ear with a sharp ringing tone.

'Yute sent you,' the king said, his good humour seemingly restored by the blood dripping from her nose.

Lord Algar's brow furrowed. 'I wonder about that, your highness. The girl is Yute's special project. It seems odd that he would send her rather than one of the other Dusters or someone among the no-accounts he brought up from the city. This one's always been headstrong. She may have come of her own accord.'

The king echoed Algar's frown. 'So, she's a lone wolf assassin?'

'I didn't even know you were there,' Livira protested, ducking her head against an anticipated slap. 'What was I going to kill you with? I don't have a weapon.'

'Check her.' Algar nodded to one of the guards.

The man rummaged in her book satchel. Other members of the group were beginning to gather, emerging from their book huts. 'One book, string, ink. It's just junk.' He tossed the satchel aside. Livira's eyes followed it despite her trying to feign disinterest.

'No food?' A new light entered the king's eyes.

The soldier patted down her robes. 'Another book.' He moved on down her legs. 'No food.'

A sigh went through the onlookers. Most of the men and women joining Livira's audience were thin, hollow-cheeked, but not skin and bone. They were like Livira's people in the settlement after a hard season, but not like they'd been that one time when there had been two hard seasons in a row; they were hungry rather than brought to the brink of death by starvation.

'And how,' said Lord Algar in a coldly measured tone, 'would you climb down thirty feet of shelving within sight of the centre circle, and not see his majesty sleeping below you?'

'How would she?' King Oanold asked. 'Why would she? Without so much as a knife?' The king and his lord might both be hollow men with ugly appetites and no concern for others, but Algar was known as an intellectual and the king for possessing a shrewd intelligence that had sustained his rule for three decades. Oanold knuckled his forehead with both hands. 'There was a light. I thought I dreamed it. But there was a light.' He lowered his arms and narrowed his gaze. 'A light like the ones in that bewitched forest!'

'There's never much meat on a Duster,' Algar said, provoking a puzzling bark of laughter from the soldier who'd slapped her. 'But she looks decently fed, wouldn't you say?'

The king came forward, reaching for Livira. She backed away but the man behind her grabbed her elbows. Oanold pinched her upper arm through her robe, as if she were livestock. 'You're right . . .'

'Where did you come from, girl?' Lord Algar seemed to have taken over as the inquisitor. 'Clean, well fed, magical lights . . .' His single eye flicked to hers. 'You can open those doors of light!'

King Oanold stepped back. 'I'll give you a count of ten to open a magic door for us. Defy me and I'll have Jons cut your legs off.'

'Jons!' Livira swung around to find that the grizzled soldier behind her, the man who had broken her arm without a moment's hesitation, was indeed the Jons who had brought her out of the Dust with Malar.

'Hello, Livira.' Grim-faced, no kindness in his eyes.

'What are you doing?'

'Obeying my king.' Jons shrugged. 'Surviving. I was always a survivor.'

'One!' King Oanold brought Livira's attention back to the matter in hand. 'Two!'

'I can't open doors. It doesn't work like that.'

'Three!'

'You'd be mad to kill me.'

'Four!'

'I know the library better than Acconite. I can guide—'

'Five!'

'—you out of here!'

'Six!' Something in the wet quiver of Oanold's lips said that this was no more a bluff than the broken arm had been. The circle's healing might stop her bleeding to death if they chopped off her legs, but it wouldn't grow them back.

'Seven.' Oanold counted on into the pause her shock had made. These maniacs were actually going to do it. From the blood spatters most of them wore they'd already done something similar since arriving in the chamber.

'All right, all right! I'll do it.' Livira slid a hand into her robes. 'I need my book.' She pulled the small black book from her inner pocket and thumbed it open with one hand. Instantly, darkness swallowed the light.

Livira had a choice to make and no time to weigh her options. She dropped the book, ducked, and ran. She could have chosen to run with it, but then she would have become a fleeing bubble of darkness, something easy to chase. This way the worst of her antagonists might stumble around for some while in the static darkness she left behind.

Livira emerged from the dark and immediately ran into a chest-high book-wall. Winded and hurt, she straddled it even as the top sections began to fall, and rolled over into the enclosure beyond, which was empty save for a pile of dirty cloth and a spare boot.

Driven by the animating effects of terror, Livira vaulted the next wall into another small enclosure. She stomped her way over a much-deflated formerly fat man who had managed to sleep through her earlier screams but not through her booted foot's arrival on his belly. The encounter left Livira sprawling forward, her feet tangled in the man on the floor. She hit the next wall hard enough to topple the central section. As she crawled forward over the tumble of books, the merciless light showed her a nightmare she'd been wholly unprepared for.

A glistening skeleton lay partly covered by fallen books, the bones picked clean but still fresh enough to gleam, save where the flensing knife had scored them. Keeping close company with fresh bones was never going to be pleasant but two things tore the scream from Livira's lips. The first was that the right forearm and hand were still covered in flesh, the skin not even bloody. The second was the shock of black hair still attached to the scalp of the grinning skull. Very black hair with a reddish tint brought out by the light. The kind of hair the people from her settlement had, and that was common all across the Dust.

Livira ploughed on into the next wall, no longer sure of her direction or whether she'd stopped screaming or not. It shook but resisted her. She threw her whole weight against it and again it shook, and then wobbled and came down, spilling most of its books on top of her.

She emerged from the heavy rain of paper and leather into a reeking enclosure with no exit. A figure lay there, hunched in a corner, naked and smeared with grime. A black-haired young man with both his legs absent at the knee, the amputations healed over. Livira didn't want to recognize the face peering at her through those filthy locks. She wanted her memory for faces – already the weakest part of her memory cage – to let go of everything it had hold of. Then she wouldn't have to understand that this was Gevin. Gevin who had been a small child when Acmar had carried him from the Dust as they followed Malar.

Glancing back through the walls she'd crashed through, Livira could see the man she'd woken scrabbling as if worried she'd stolen something precious from him. He grabbed an object from the floor and held it jealously to his chest. A legbone, scraps of flesh still adhering to it here and there.

'Run, Livira,' Gevin said behind her in a hollow voice. 'Run. This is hell.'

Any doctor soon comes to understand the burden of hope.
While suspicion might be inconvenient when it comes to
the business of dispensing medicine, it's the chains with
which trust binds a physician that make escape so hard.

Life and Other Sexually Transmitted
Diseases, *by Chris Barnard*

CHAPTER 34

Evar

After the shard of wood was pulled from his leg Evar began to
heal rapidly. The removal and, worse, the digging about for splin-
ters, had to be done outside the circle so that no foreign bodies
would be sealed in to cause problems later. None of it was less
than awful, and for once Evar was glad that Livira was not there
to see him howl and writhe and try to fight off the ones trying to
help him.

He'd been in worse shape than Clovis when they finally hobbled
into the centre circle. They both let themselves fall in untidy heaps,
not prepared to move again until the library's magic had done its
work. It was surprising, then, to have the humans, none of whom
even spoke their language, come across and show their concern, not
just for Arpix, but for all of them, even Clovis who had treated
them more or less like scenery. Scenery she didn't approve of.

Lying there with Jella and Salamonda fussing over him, Evar
felt that perhaps there might be hope for both their kind, separately
and together. He remembered the city he and Livira had visited
where it had seemed that humans and canith had lived peacefully
together, and that whatever had slain them could have been an

outside act, the work of some cowardly poisoner who wanted to tear down what they'd built.

Within a couple of hours Evar was back on his feet with nothing but the odd twinge to remind him that his upper thigh had been run through. Clovis still looked rough, but a lot better than she had before. Arpix argued that they stay longer, but Clovis said he'd told them that every chamber had a centre circle, so they were never going to be much more than a mile from one if they needed it.

Grudgingly, Arpix agreed and the whole group moved off. Evar wasn't sure of the point at which Arpix's agreement had become a necessary part of their plans, but he had no great objection to the idea, just surprise.

Their first task was to revisit the automaton, since neither Evar nor Clovis were willing to leave the white sword embedded in its metal belly. Clovis was especially adamant on the point.

It wasn't hard to find their way back. The main group remained a few aisles away while Evar and Kerrol went to retrieve the blade. Arpix came with them, saying he wanted a closer look at the mechanism that had nearly killed one of their number.

The three of them stood, surveying the destruction surrounding the bulk of Evar's assailant. None of them proved eager to approach it, all sharing the idea that the thing might at any time spring back into action.

'And you say that the huge one that chased you was much the same?'

'Yes,' Kerrol answered.

'Giant mechanical ganar . . .' Arpix mused. 'One of them a vast mechanical ganar that had remained motionless for decades, centuries maybe, even as skeer passed by. And then you three turn up and it hounds you across three chambers until an assistant scolds it.'

'Yes,' said Evar. He'd not really thought about how long the thing had waited, doing nothing, before they'd emerged. But the chamber's shelves had been built around it. It seemed ridiculous to say, but it was almost as if it had been waiting for them to come out.

'Did the canith and ganar not get along?' Arpix asked, frowning.

'You'd have to ask Mayland,' Evar said. 'There's nothing my brother doesn't know about history. At least not if it got written down. I do remember the ganar now, though I never really thought about what they looked like. I was never really interested in their history on our world. I was fascinated by the fact they lived on Attamast. I could tell you about some of their wars up there. It's said that after one war the whole moon burned for a year and the night went back to twilight once Attamast rose.'

'Well, whoever made this one did not appear to like canith.'

'It probably would have attacked you too,' Evar said, though Arpix was closer to being right than he knew. It did feel as if there were something personal about all this.

Wentworth led them through six more chambers before they met their first skeer. Evar had given the Soldier's sword back to Clovis after recovering it from the automaton's body. She was far from fighting fit, but even at half strength she was five times more dangerous with a sword than he was.

They were fortunate that the skeer's presence was advertised well in advance by the fact that the door to which they were heading was open and could be seen to be open above the shelf tops when the aisles ran their way. Evar imagined that to hold the doors open it must take a creature of at least sufficient intellect to be able to read if taught to do so. Otherwise, the skeer could simply anchor a goat in place rather than occupy one of their number with the task.

He thought again of the ganar automaton waiting outside the chamber door. There had been another creature waiting in much the same way. A skeer. Only it had been closer, and primarily intent on keeping the door from closing again rather than on doing them harm. It had called for others to do the harm part.

Much as expected, a stealthy reconnaissance involving the use of a ladder and peering over shelves confirmed the presence of a single skeer warrior in the doorway. Evar, who had left the orb behind with Kerrol, returned to report.

Arpix translated his companions' thoughts. 'They're saying we should push it out of the way with the orb.'

'If it still works.' Evar still thought it might have broken when it broke the automaton. It couldn't have been intended to grow so hot, surely?

'The problem,' Arpix said, 'is that we don't know for sure that door will open for canith or humans. If we push the skeer out of the way and the door closes, we can't go the way Wentworth is leading us.'

'I'll go kill it.' Clovis drew her blade and started forward.

'That didn't go well with the cratalac.' Arpix got in her way.

Evar expected her to flatten him but possibly she thought him too fragile to risk violence with. 'This is not a cratalac.'

'And you are not well!'

'This is great.' Kerrol loomed over both of them, setting a hand on Clovis's left shoulder and Arpix's right. 'A domestic dispute, and you're using your words. I really should be taking notes.'

'Don't listen to him,' Clovis said. 'He's manipulating us.'

'Give me the sword,' Kerrol said, 'And I'll go slice this bug up.'

'You?' Clovis snorted then spat. 'You'd end up tripping and falling on the sharp end. You wouldn't last half a minute against a skeer, and even Evar could take a skeer down if it's just one on one.'

Kerrol stepped aside. 'You heard the lady.' He waved Evar forward.

'He's got you there, Clo.' Evar held his hand out for the sword. Against another swordsman there was no argument that Clovis's skills would prove far more useful than Evar's. But to fight a skeer involved running and jumping and dodging and skidding and turning, a lot of it. The strength and bulk of the things meant sword skills were far less important than athletics, gymnastics, and waiting for your moment. Clovis's illness had made little impact on the lessons her wrist had learned over the years, but her strength was still a shadow of its normal self.

'Don't die.' She handed him the sword with a snarl. 'I want that sword back.' She rounded on Kerrol as Evar took the hilt. 'And you! Don't think I didn't see what you did there. You got exactly what you wanted. Again.' She narrowed her eyes at him. 'That's only going to work up until the point it doesn't.'

Kerrol ignored her and spoke to Evar instead. 'You need to be in the doorway when the skeer dies, otherwise you might as well have just pushed it back with the orb.'

For all the confidence he'd shown in rising to Kerrol's challenge and taking Clovis's sword, Evar felt far from sure he knew how to defeat a skeer warrior. His first attempt had not gone well, though he had only been armed with a crude, homemade knife.

As he left the cover of the shelves and closed on the skeer, his sword began to look progressively smaller, while the skeer's bulk seemed more daunting by the yard.

The insectoid was facing away from him, standing its duty statue-still. Evar set his feet carefully, making no noise, but maintained a good pace, knowing that his scent would likely give him away and the slower he went, the more warning he'd give his foe.

'It's asleep,' Evar breathed to himself. Part hope, part growing certainty. The skeer outside his home chamber had presumably waited anything from weeks to decades for the door to open. It had been in some sort of hibernation from which it took several long moments to emerge.

Evar increased his speed. 'It's asleep.'

He could be very wrong. Foolishly, embarrassingly, fatally wrong. An incautious attack could find the skeer snapping around to impale him on its arm spike. But similarly, if its hibernation were of a shallower sort, he would need to be quick to take advantage of it.

Evar gambled with his life. He started to sprint. At the last moment he used one of the skeer's hindmost legs to vault onto the segmented whiteness of its back. With the armour slick beneath his feet and the first tremor of waking running through the warri-or's body, Evar thrust his blade at the back of the creature's head.

Common steel might easily have failed to pierce the thick, blue-veined armour plate that served as an external skull. The Soldier's weapon, however, was of a different order, and its point emerged amid the skeer's eye cluster.

Taking a leaf from Clovis's book, Evar used his whole body weight to twist the blade, cracking the armour and amplifying the damage inside the skeer's head. The insectoid bucked, writhed – throwing Evar clear – then sagged to the floor, twitching.

Evar made sure to keep position so that the door couldn't re-form.

Kerrol would be watching from the ladder top. He'd bring the others.

Evar felt no sense of victory, and it was shame rather than pride that filled his chest as the others came up. He was far from sure that he would feel any different had he defeated the creature in face-to-face combat rather than assassinating it while it slept. He was discovering that killing didn't sit well with him. Escapes felt different, as if they were neither properly alive in the first place, nor truly dead when he put a weapon through them. The skeer, though the nature of its intelligence remained mysterious, was clearly alive and recognized by the library.

Evar left it to Clovis to recover her sword. She gave him a grim nod.

'The orb's working.' Arpix pointed at the ichor that had run down the corridor as if there were a gradient. It pointed away from the direction of their approach.

'Good to know.' Kerrol sighed out his relief.

'I should stay.' Evar watched the last human, Sheetra, pass through. 'If I don't stay here, we could all be trapped forever . . .'

'That logic's going to leave a trail of us standing like idiots every two miles,' Clovis growled.

'Yute might be in the next chamber,' Arpix suggested, though he didn't look particularly confident. 'We need to make a choice.' One option left individuals isolated and at the mercy of any skeer patrol that might happen by. The other option could see them trapped, potentially for another two centuries, only this time without seeds to grow food from and without a pool to water them.

Evar, who had spent his whole life trying to escape one chamber, felt the decision crushing him as if a real, physical door were trying to slide back into the space he occupied.

Kerrol returned to where Evar stood in the doorway.

'I don't think I can do it. I just can't let it close.' Evar looked up at the area the door would fill if he were to step forward.

Kerrol shrugged. 'It's a scary thing.' He held his hand out.

'You're going to try psychology on me.' Evar could feel it coming.

'No, you've already decided you're staying. I just wanted to shake your hand in case we don't get to come back to you.' He looked at his open palm.

Evar nodded grimly and took his brother's hand in the warrior's grip. Kerrol yanked him forward, hard enough that they both fell over.

'What have you done?' Evar gazed up at the white wall where he'd been standing. 'You idiot!'

Sheetra turned and hurried back to the door, setting both hands against it. 'It won't open.' Evar didn't need that translated even if he hadn't caught the gist of it anyhow.

Evar untangled himself from Kerrol and, not even bothering to stand, lunged at the door. The sight of it melting away before his outstretched fingers was more beautiful than any of the dawns he'd seen since his escape.

'Bastard!' He got to his feet and rounded on Kerrol.

Kerrol was already walking away. 'I think you mean, lucky bastard.'

Advancing from finger paints to the quill pen enabled writers to whisper more prettily. The printing press allowed them to shout.

The Empty Page, *by Tess Eliot*

CHAPTER 35

Arpix

Arpix had always counted himself as a cautious man. He admitted to being studious, and acknowledged that he lacked Livira's chaotic genius, Jella's fortitude, Carlotte's vivaciousness, or Meelan's determination. War had come and set him running through a burning library. A strange escape had dumped him on an island of relative safety, and there he'd stayed, seeing no direction to take and lacking the courage or foolhardiness to strike out into the unknown.

Once again it had taken outside pressure to make him move, and now here he was, following a magical cat through the library, looking for a new direction. His horizons had been broadened to such a degree that his old life looked small and blinkered. Still, he wanted it back. He wanted his quiet, ordered days back, growing old among the towering shelves, exploring the space between two covers while sitting in a comfortable chair, with a hot cup of chai within arm's reach.

Doors closed behind him one after the next. Doors that could be opened only by the touch of a willing canith. And still Wentworth led them on, stepping from shelf top to shelf top via some distant intermediate space, never needing to jump.

Clovis walked at Arpix's side, further complicating his life. He'd sometimes felt that women were a different species – a stupid conceit, he acknowledged, but one that stood as effective shorthand

for his awkwardness and inability to move any conversation or
relationship away from the comfortable ground of academia into
spaces that seemed dark and uncertain. Spaces where the floor itself
might vanish beneath you and injury seemed a certainty. Even with
a friend as bold and salacious as Carlotte he'd always felt happier,
calmer, steering back towards safe ground, telling himself there
would always be another day, better timing, more auspicious omens
– any excuse would do. Women weren't a different species, but
Clovis definitely was. Textbook fact. And she was female on top of
that. Carlotte had been forthright and as suggestive as it was possible
to be without actually unbuttoning his clothes. But there had always
been escape routes, and Arpix had taken them, while all the time
part of his mind was screaming at him that he was an idiot, and
another part that he was a coward.

Meelan had even asked him one day if he liked boys. To which
Arpix had sighed and said that he wished it were anything so simple
and reasonable as that. 'I think I just hate myself, Mee,' he'd said.
'I can't see any other logical explanation for constantly getting in
my own way, for pushing aside things that would be good for me.
But' – and he had held up a hand to forestall his friend's inevitable
repetition of old offers to help – 'it is in my nature, mine to bear,
and I think if I were to change . . . it might break me. So, please,
let's not speak of it again.' And, with his eyes prickling and his
hands trembling, he had walked away from Meelan, and still to this
day his imagination could not tell him what might have been on
the boy's face as he watched him go.

All of which had made Clovis both a revelation and an existential crisis. She was a force of nature, like a flood, or a forest fire.
Social niceties were nothing to her. The body language with which
he'd so often deflected that sort of attention was as meaningless to
her as his own tongue. It was one thing when Carlotte had suddenly
started to find his slightest attempt at humour to be hilarious, or
his library tales fascinating. He'd been able to ignore her playful
touches. But when a seven-foot canith puts her face an inch from
your neck and breathes you in, it's hard to pretend there's nothing
going on.

Even so, if Clovis's attentions had sparked nothing in him he would have been able to answer her in kind, even if it meant simply turning his back. But they hadn't. Something about her lit a fire under his skin, and it turned out that there was no lying to a canith about such things. Whatever his mouth told her, her nose told her something else.

And even then, if it had just been his traitor body walking away from the script he'd played his life by, he could have, with difficulty, reined it in using the power of his will. Probably. But it wasn't just his body, or her body. Something in her directness, her lack of concern for almost everything that concerned him, her total honesty, something in that mix called to him. The strangest thing of all was that although she was clearly capable of taking on an army of Arpixes and had thrown herself at an enraged cratalac armed only with a sword . . . the strange thing was that he worried for her and wanted to protect her.

'What are you thinking about, human boy?' Clovis growled at his side.

'What we'll find when we reach Yute.'

'Liar.' She gave a lazy smile. 'You were thinking of me.'

The next door Wentworth led them to was closed, but Evar went ahead to scout it and came back to report that three skeer warriors were waiting before it, facing the door. Possibly in the same sort of hibernation that the previous one had been.

'Use the orb to squash them against the door,' Clovis said.

It was the sensible suggestion, and not dissimilar to Evar going forward and stabbing his blade through the last one's head. Even so, the idea of casually murdering three skeer didn't sit well with Arpix and he said so.

'What would you suggest instead?' Clovis asked.

Arpix had already remarked that while she was ready for any fight, she wasn't ready to make a fight out of anything. A good general listens first, when there is time to listen, and Clovis would make a good general.

'We could come from the side and just move them out of the way. It wouldn't put us in any danger.'

'They would bring more of their kind here,' Clovis countered.

'And after the lesson with the rock, perhaps the next one they'll learn will involve spears . . .'

Arpix frowned. 'The door we came through is closed. They can't get out to call for reinforcements.'

'Perhaps the other two doors are open or open for them,' Clovis said.

'We could check.' Arpix met her gaze.

'That seems a lot of effort to save the lives of three enemies who don't seem to care whether they live or die anyway.'

'We could send a human and a canith to both doors,' Evar said. 'If they open for either one then we know the skeer can't get in or out that way.'

'We'd all need to go to both doors.' Arpix shaped the imagined iron ball between his hands. 'It's the only way to keep safe from any skeer that might be wandering out here.'

'A journey of over four miles.' Clovis grimaced. 'To maybe keep three skeer alive. Skeer that might cause us problems later.'

'We should vote on—' Arpix broke off as Kerrol, who he hadn't seen leave, reappeared around the end of the aisle.

'Squashed the bugs.' Kerrol tossed the orb to his sister.

Arpix found his mouth hanging open and closed it. Evar seemed similarly amazed. Clovis took it more in her stride though still looked a little puzzled as she turned the orb over in her hands.

Kerrol explained himself. 'You were going to argue over it. It's a fault line in the group dynamics. Couldn't be allowed to widen. Better that I take the hit. You don't trust me anyway.'

The group advanced to find the pulverized remains of three skeer decorating the foot of the door. Their gore rippled across the white surface, seeking to get away from the orb even in death.

Clovis advanced unperturbed. 'Let's see what they were guarding.' Her hand came to rest against the door. She frowned and turned back to the others. 'Arpix?'

Arpix wondered if it was the first time she'd spoken his name. It seemed impossible but he couldn't remember another. He liked how it sounded in her mouth, growled out but still not a threat – more of a promise. He went forward to stand beside her. 'Let's hope it's not a ganar door, or a larnix door, or something even—'

'Just try it.' She laughed.

So, he did. And it melted before him, the ichor spraying out down the corridor under the orb's pressure.

Clovis stood for a while, sniffing. 'I can smell something.'

'Me too, and I wish I couldn't.' The reek of skeer guts was over-powering to the point where Arpix's eyes were starting to water.

'Humans.' Clovis nodded. 'Not close, but lots of them.'

'Define lots.'

Clovis licked her teeth. 'My nose is clever. But it can't count.'

Cautiously, the group moved into the chamber, with Evar and Arpix at the front. Evar in case of problems; Arpix in case those problems were caused by Evar being a canith.

The room, or at least the tiny fraction of it that Arpix could see, appeared similar to the typical library room. It always amazed him that people had had the energy and industry to erect such a vast amount of shelving so far from the known entrances, and fill them with the books that the assistants would otherwise leave stacked on the floor. It certainly lent credence to the slow migration of the chambers – or perhaps it should more accurately be described as the quick but highly infrequent exchange of chambers.

Livira had spoken of written accounts from travellers who had ventured deep into the interior. They spoke of seemingly endless rooms lying beyond the range of any but the most intrepid explorer, where books lay in drifts, taller than a man, untended, unknown, unloved. It had always amazed and saddened him that such a wealth of knowledge and culture, speculation and imagination sat out there, beyond the capacity of mankind to make use of, just waiting for the next fire to sweep through.

The shelves in Arpix's small patch of the current chamber were in good condition, fashioned from dark oak and topped by carved animal heads that looked down upon the travellers in the style of cathedral grotesques, as large as a human head and set every few yards. Each had been picked out in great detail by a master of the craft, some indistinguishable from the true animal, others given human expressions ranging from contemplation to amusement, some wise, some leering, some comically bored.

The group carried on, trailing Wentworth through the lefts and rights, broadly following the wall for a few hundred yards into the chamber. Evar sniffed the air from time to time. 'Definitely humans.' He confirmed Clovis's earlier judgement.

The attack, when it came, wasn't well organized or executed with precision. A handful of figures clambered up onto the shelf top forming a T-junction with the aisle down which Wentworth was leading Arpix. The animal heads peering from the heights of this particular unit turned out to be no longer connected to the plank supporting them, and the people above snatched them up, throwing them down as missiles.

It was hard to miss when your target was confined within an aisle two yards wide, but at least half of the six heads thrown their way would not have hit anyone. A stag's head, complete with antlers, came spinning towards Arpix, and Evar pulled him out of its way. A second, more compact head, shot towards Evar with more force than the rest. He caught it in one hand. The slap of wood against flesh was loud enough to make Arpix wince, but the canith seemed unconcerned.

The last missile went over Arpix's head, and when he turned, he saw that Clovis had impaled it on her sword.

'Wait!' Arpix called up to the humans above them. 'Wait! We're not here to fight. We're looking for Yute!'

The people, on the point of retreating down the ladders that must rest against the far side, hesitated.

'Those are canith!' One of them spat. He bent to reach for another wooden head.

'Yes!' Arpix called back. 'But good ones. We're librarians. Friends of Yute.'

The people on the shelf top exchanged glances. Arpix could see that some of them were Livira's kin, thick black hair, fawn skin. But canith were always going to be a hard sell whether to city dwellers or those from the Dust. Death and destruction had been what the canith brought to the doors of both.

After a few muttered words the group started to descend their ladders. Canith had a history of taking prisoners and exploiting them. Arpix understood the mistrust.

'Wait! I'm not lying!' Arpix was embarrassed by how unconvincing he sounded.

Half of them had vanished from view already. One of the remaining women, possibly the one whose shot would have brained Evar but for his preternatural reactions, sparked a moment of recognition. She had a thick rope of black hair reaching past the small of her back, and even from this angle there was something familiar about her.

Arpix opened his mouth to shout again, but Jella beat him to it. 'Neera?'

The girl coughed in surprise. 'Who . . . Do I know you?'

'It's me, Jella.' Jella elbowed past the canith.

'Gods!' Neera gestured to one of her companions. 'Pull a ladder up.' She sat on the shelf top, legs dangling, peering over short-sightedly. 'We nearly killed you.' She sounded horrified, though Evar snorted his amusement. 'I'm so sorry!' She leaned further over, looking to be a hair's breadth from toppling into the fall. 'Is that really you, Jella? You're so thin!'

The ambush point had been chosen well, and a ladder was needed to avoid a long detour to reach the spot where Neera and her crew had waited below their single spotter. Arpix clambered up first, followed by Jella and the rest of the humans.

Jella and Neera staged a dangerous reunion twenty yards above the ground, hugging each other and weeping and remarking on how skinny the other was.

'How did you get like this?' Neera stepped back, astonished, and it was all Arpix could do to keep from grabbing her as she backed towards the edge. But she seemed at home on the shelf top, well aware of its dimensions and unbothered by the drops despite having been raised in the flattest place in the kingdom. 'How are you so thin? So dark!'

'We can discuss it,' Arpix said. 'On the ground.' The drop to either side had put a tremble in his legs and dizziness threatened.

'Are they really safe?' Neera frowned doubtfully at the canith below.

'They are.' Arpix knew that, like Livira, Neera had been taken captive by the canith who raided her settlement. 'That one with the dark mane. That's Livira's . . . special friend.'

He had to reach out to catch Neera then as her amazement set her back another step. Dizziness took him and both of them might have fallen if not for Jella. 'We really should get back on the floor,' she said, releasing them both from her grip. 'The slow way.'

Wentworth, who had vanished at the first sign of trouble, reappeared once everyone was at the same level and on the same side. Neera and her companions greeted him like another old friend and made a fuss of him.

'He brings us food,' Neera explained, looking up from stroking the cat. Wentworth for his part made a show of disdain, as if he were suffering their attentions out of kindness, though when the man scratching his neck stopped doing it, Wentworth butted his hand with his head. 'He brings rats mainly, but also chickens, and once . . . a horse. That's how we've survived. Also Master Yute's pockets. He can reach in and bring out bread, sausages, onions, sometimes a hot pie.' She looked wistful at the memory. 'But he can't do it too often and it takes a lot of rummaging.'

Salamonda, who had been the last one over before the canith, frowned at this particular revelation. 'Pies?'

'Yes.' Neera nodded. 'It's true. It sounds crazy but it's real magic.'

Salamonda pursed her lips. 'It might be true, but it's not magic. Someone made those pies that Yute's been stealing!'

Arpix interjected himself into the conversation. 'How long have you been here?'

'Weeks!' one of Neera's companions said.

'It's been terrible,' said another.

'Even with Yute and Wentworth there's not nearly enough to eat. And then—'

'And before that?' Arpix pressed on with his line of questioning.

'Before that was the fire and the running,' Neera said. 'The canith took the city . . .' She looked nervously up at Evar and his siblings.

Meelan laughed behind Arpix. 'Weeks?'

Jella took Neera's hand. 'We've been outside, on the Dust. For years.'

'Years?' Neera's confusion furrowed her brow. 'How can that be?'

Arpix sighed. 'We all stepped forward in time to be here. The portals we used can do that – move us through the years as well as to other places. Yes?'

Neera nodded. 'Yute told us we were hundreds of years in the future of our old lives.' She said it with the tone of someone who had yet to truly believe it.

'Well, the door we came through didn't bring us as far forward as the route you took,' Arpix said. 'We've had to wait four years for you to appear. I guess we're just lucky it wasn't four hundred.'

Neera looked at him with wide, round eyes, wrestling with the concept.

'We need to find Yute,' Arpix said. 'Is it far to go?'

Yute, and his small band of mainly Livira's former neighbours from the settlement, had set up temporary camp in the north-west corner. He greeted their arrival with a disturbing degree of relief. Arpix would have preferred the unperturbed confidence of a man playing the long game and in charge of all the variables.

'Well done, Wentworth!' Yute went to one knee to fuss the cat. 'Well done!'

The joyous reunions among library employees in Arpix's party and Yute's were put on hold by the towering presence of the three canith. All eyes, save Yute's, were turned their way along with the 'stick held by one ageing library guard whose name escaped Arpix.

Yute stood up from greeting his furry companion to look at the newcomers. He opened his arms and Salamonda barrelled into him, nearly knocking him over. Arpix took the opportunity to introduce the canith to Yute's group of perhaps a dozen.

'Some of you know me. I'm Arpix. Formerly a librarian. My friends and I have spent four years living on the edge of the Dust, eating beans we grew and whatever Wentworth dropped for us. These three canith are Evar, Kerrol, and Clovis.' He indicated each in turn. 'Without them we would still be on the Arthran Plateau and might well be dead. They have spent all of their lives, saving the last week or so, trapped in a single chamber of the library. They have not raided settlements in the Dust, or attacked cities, and are no more responsible for the activities of other canith than you are for those of other humans that you've never met or heard of. Please treat them with respect.'

Yute disentangled himself from Salamonda and added his own recommendation. 'This is where war with the canith has led us and left us. Out there' – he waved his arm towards the centre of the chamber – 'our own kind are refusing change, turning inward on their hunger. Let us embrace a different path. One I have seen trodden before.'

Arpix frowned at the mention of others. 'There are more survivors?'

'Can you tell us who?' Meelan asked, and the others chimed in with too many questions for any one of them to receive an answer.

'What are they eating?' Arpix spoke into the pause. 'What are you eating, for that matter?'

Yute brightened. 'Let me see if I can show you. You look as if you could use a meal. A drink at the least.' He held up a white hand to forestall their excitement. 'It won't be much, I'm afraid.' He reached into the pocket of his robe and kept on reaching as if his pocket had a hole in it and his arm were sliding down his leg, though Arpix couldn't see the shape of it under the deputy's robe.

'Just . . . a . . . moment.' Yute's face took on a look of concentration, his eyes not seeing what lay before him. 'Here!' And to Arpix's astonishment he brought out eighteen inches of blood-dark smoke-cured sausage mottled beneath the skin with lumps of pork fat. He handed it to Salamonda. Arpix's mouth immediately filled with saliva and his stomach growled as if it were independently attempting to speak canith.

Salamonda looked from the sausage to Yute and back at the sausage. 'This is mine.'

'Yes, it is,' Yute said. Which seemed obvious. He'd just given it to her. What surprised Arpix almost as much as the mysterious appearance of the food was that Salamonda should lay claim to it so firmly. The word 'selfish' was not one that Arpix would ever have associated with the woman.

'No,' Salamonda said. 'I mean . . . it's mine. I made this.'

Yute shrugged somewhat guiltily. 'I've been thieving from your kitchen.'

'How?' Salamonda sniffed the sausage while two score eyes watched the item's every move. 'I mean . . . it burned down, didn't it? Or the canith took it. It's certainly not hiding in your pocket . . .'

Yute looked down. Arpix could almost imagine the man's feet shuffling beneath his robe. 'A little here. A little there. I mean, legally it's actually my kitchen.'

'You're making no sense.' Salamonda said what Arpix had been thinking.

'I reach back across the years.'

'Through your pocket?' Salamonda handed the sausage absently to Jella who stood closest to her.

'Yes.'

'Back in time?'

'Yes.'

'Stealing from my kitchen?'

'Yes.'

'Damn you, Yute!' Salamonda raised both her voice and her hand. 'I thought I was going mad. I told you about it. Things going missing all the time. I blamed the delivery boy, I blamed Wentworth, I blamed poor Martha who came to clean. I . . .'

'I'm sorry, Salamonda.' Yute stepped in range of the hand that had been raised to strike him. He set his own hand to her upper arm. 'Back then I didn't know it was me either.' He glanced at Jella who was staring at the bounty in her grasp, trembling with restraint. All three canith were sniffing too, despite their pride. 'Eat, Jella, eat. Have a bite and pass it on. I'll see if I can reach in again and find the water pump.' And, so saying, Yute began a second slightly comical dive into his unfeasibly deep pockets.

He had to reach deeper this second time and Arpix could see the effort vibrating through the man's narrow frame. Without warning, Yute jolted, his face twisting in sudden panic. A yelp of surprise escaped him, and he pulled – or tried to pull – his arm clear. For a moment Arpix wondered if he were going to see a man vanish into his own pocket in some sort of surreal accident, but before anyone could get to him to offer help, Yute managed to yank his arm free.

'That was . . . so . . .' A cracking sound split the air. Neither loud nor quiet, but a definite sound that Arpix felt from the top of his head to the soles of his feet. 'Someone caught hold of me.'

For a moment the sausage was forgotten. The sound had admitted no direction, but it felt significant in the same way that the noise might had they been standing on ice above a deep lake or in front of a dam wall. Yute saw it first, something astonishing to all of those who had spent years within the vastness of the library. A crack running through the ground beneath their feet. Almost too thin to notice but commanding the eye with its wrongness even so. A black crack. And from it, almost imperceptibly, a black mist began to seep.

No one treads lightly enough to leave no tracks in this world. Others might see our trail as bruised hearts and broken promises, or perhaps saved souls and conjured smiles. But not one of us looks back at our own path without seeing disappointment in every step.

Great Expectations, *by Charles Dickensian*

CHAPTER 36

Livira

Livira almost escaped. That she didn't even consider staying to try to help Gevin was a decision she felt would haunt her her whole life. But, given her current circumstances, her whole life might not take her much further forward. She had vaulted the enclosure's wall and, animated by terror, had threaded a path around the handful of hunger-weakened refugees standing between her and the nearest aisle leading from the centre circle.

Something had punched her in the back of the shoulder, knocking her from her feet. The bark of a 'stick arrived at the same time, and she started to fall. They'd shot her!

Being shot had felt like the blow of a fist. The pain didn't have time to kick in until they were on her, and by that point the agony of the metal projectile being dug out of her flesh with the point of a knife eclipsed the original injury. She howled and fought, but the weight of several men pinned her down, releasing her only as the thing they called a bullet dropped to the ground beside her.

She rolled over with a groan as soon as they released her. The circle's healing was already at work, soothing her pain, knitting flesh together. King Oanold stood flanked by two guards, a delighted smile on his face. Lord Algar regarded her with cold curiosity, the black book in his hand, firmly closed.

'We're going to have to take her foot if she doesn't promise not to run away again,' the king said, sounding thrilled by the idea. 'We can start with toes.' He looked down at her. 'Unless you just want to open a magic door for us now and avoid all that?'

'Why can't you just walk out of here?' Livira hated the fear in her voice, but it was real and she couldn't hide it. The king and his followers had turned cannibal and didn't even seem ashamed of it. They'd perverted the library's gift of healing into an abomination that kept their victims alive as they were devoured, maintaining the freshness of the meat. And they'd ignored the sustenance it offered, which although a misery in the long term was still a world better than killing and eating people. And as outraged as Livira was at all this, her voice told the true story. She was utterly undone with terror that they would do the same thing to her. Eat her alive.

'Just where have you been hiding these last few weeks?' Algar drawled.

'Two of the doors won't open, and there are monsters behind the other two.' King Oanold proved more forthcoming. 'Which is why we'll be using the door you open for us instead. A door that takes us back to Crath.'

'Crath City?' Livira sat looking up at Oanold in astonishment, still hugging herself against the fear and the pain in her shoulder. 'Even if you could go back . . . it was full of canith.'

The king gave her a pitying look and shook his head, grinning around at his subjects as if Livira were a deluded child. 'My armies crushed those dogs the same day they jumped our gates. Rodcar Charant is too good a general for any pack of sabbers to pull down.'

'But the fire . . .' Livira shook her head. 'You ran away. That's why you're h—'

A solid kick to the ribs shut her up.

'A tactical retreat to draw the enemy away from the palace and expose their flanks to Charant's arrow-sticks. The general had cannons too, thicker than a man. Fresh from the laboratory forges.'

'You lost,' Livira wheezed, unable to deny the truth despite the likelihood of another kick.

The king shook his head, laughing. 'Lost?' His laugh became a theatrical booming. 'Lost to dog soldiers? No, child, we're going back. My throne's secure. You've fallen for the big lie. People like Yute will say anything to get the crown off my head. Sabbers over-running Crath City, who can believe that? I've soldiers here who saw what was happening. The canith were just in the low town, and that's always been full of traitors.

'My kingdom will rise to the call. We'll harry these hounds out into the Dust and drag their bodies back to decorate the walls. If it hadn't been for them setting that damn fire . . . blind luck they separated us, and we ended up here. Those white monsters could eat ten canith each for breakfast. Even my troopers have difficulty putting them down.'

'White monsters?' Livira tried standing up, wincing in pain and expecting to be thrown down again any moment. 'You mean skeer? Six legs, more eyes?'

'Demons.' Lord Algar's eyes slid to the side to measure the king's approval. 'Unholy creatures from the deepest hells, loosed by the foolish experiments of librarians like Yute.' It seemed he wasn't going to include Livira among the librarians' ranks even when levelling allegations of atrocities against them. 'Dark magics like this.' He held out the little black book with which Livira had summoned a bubble of night.

'It's not magic,' Livira said, 'just something you don't understand. You think the light here is magic too?' She regretted the words as soon as they left her lips, but the man's stupidity had pulled them out of her. A guard stepped forward and slapped her across the face, a stinging blow. For a moment it put an image of Malar in her mind. He'd slapped her on the steps of the Allocation Hall, and it had been wrong despite the good intentions buried beneath it. Right now, though, she would welcome some of his violent shortcuts to good goals, like freeing her from the hell she'd dropped herself into.

At a nod from Algar, Jons took hold of Livira's arm once more and twisted it behind her.

'I believe you were counting to ten, your majesty,' Algar said, his single eye boring into Livira.

'So I was.' King Oanold nodded with practised gravitas. 'And despite your treacherous attempt to flee, girl, I will show you how decent humans behave, and begin at one rather than carry on from where we left off. I believe you were going to open a magic door for us.' He coughed importantly and swelled his chest. 'One!'

'Wait!' Livira's panic rose through her, threatening to overwhelm her intelligence. 'I can open a door for you but—'

'Two!'

'—it takes a lot longer than you're giving me.'

'Three!'

'Maybe it does, maybe it doesn't,' the king interrupted his own count. 'But you can still do it without your feet, certainly without your toes. And losing them will be both an incentive for your efforts, and a punishment for your escape attempt. Four!'

'I can't! I just can't. Please!' Livira hated herself for begging. She hated how this crude, stupid man had reduced her to a blubbering mess simply with his boundless cruelty. His methods took no cleverness, no wit, no skill, and yet were as effective as a hammer to the head. 'Please don't!'

'Seven!'

Livira had missed five and six in her distress.

Dozens were watching her now, expressions ranging from stony to empty to hungry. Only a handful bore traces of sympathy and none of those showed any signs of objecting. The alleged head librarian, Acconite, studied his hands with dedicated intensity.

Livira had imagined Malar coming to her rescue. She wanted it so badly that the images her imagination painted of his bloody arrival were sufficiently vivid to fool the eye – nearly. But however much she demanded that he step into the circle from one of the nearest aisles, he remained sealed away behind distance or time or both.

When something did emerge from one of the aisles Livira had been staring at wildly over the shoulders of the king and his guards, only she saw it, and when the others finally noticed the thing, Livira was the only one to understand what it was.

Oanold had decreed that the skeer were demons, but alien as they were, the creation that emerged behind him was closer to a product of the hells described in Crath City's many temples. A pitch-black skeleton, taller than any man, bleeding drops of smoking tar from its bones, the only deviation from the remains of a regular human, apart from the colour and the fact they moved without the need for flesh, were the talons at the end of each finger, and the distended jaw full of shearing teeth and dagger fangs.

'Nine!' Oanold's count held everyone's attention. The man beside him only turned as the skeleton dipped its head to chomp into his neck. The black skull lifted sharply, tearing large chunks of meat free in a crimson shower. And the screaming started.

Livira knew an Escape when she saw one. She found it less terrifying than being mutilated in cold blood by people who hated her and would eat what they cut from her. But it was still terrifying, and she ran just like everyone else did.

Livira sidestepped a pale-eyed soldier, twisted from the clutching grasp of an old woman in soiled finery, and sped down the nearest aisle that led away from the Escape. She ran like a wild thing for a hundred yards, taking one turn after another, putting distance and barriers between herself and all horrors, both alien and human.

She began to slow, gasping for breath, trying to tame her panting so she could hear any pursuit. Her thoughts caught up with her soon enough. She'd seen Escapes in all manner of scary forms before, but they'd always looked as if somewhere in the world, or on some other, there might be real creatures built along the same lines. The skeleton however, with its devouring maw and fleshless frame, seemed built of fear, a creature out of the pages of some horror novel. Moreover, it seemed curiously suited to its victims, a group of starving cannibals, of whom many – surely most – would have had misgivings about the nature of their meals.

Over her still-pounding heart and the scattered screams – none as distant as she would have liked – Livira could hear no sign of any chase. The boom of several 'sticks brought an end to the screaming and prompted Livira to carry on. She walked as quietly as she could, avoiding the books which even this far from Oanold's camp had been scattered from the lower shelves in large numbers. She wondered if it was an act of vandalism or if they'd been looking for something . . .

Livira thought that with the chaos of the Escape's attack, the distance she'd run, and the convolutions of the shelving, she'd done enough to win clear. So, it came as a terrible shock then when thirty yards further on she turned a corner and found herself face to face with two of Oanold's men.

'Would you look at that, Bertat! It's a Duster.'

Livira could tell that under the human grime both were palace guards, with golden tassels still attempting to gleam on their epaulettes. Both had untidy growths of hair on what would previously have been shaven scalps. One greying, the other a drab brown. The pair had little else to set them apart. They could be brothers. The older man had a seam of scar across his forehead. The younger man had the same amused cruelty in his eyes that the king had. The other just looked hungry. Both appeared to be intent on recapturing the king's prisoner and largely unconcerned about any nightmares stalking the aisles.

Livira turned to run but one of them got a hand on her shoulder and yanked her back.

'Hello, boys.' Malar had missed a dozen opportunities to arrive with perfect timing, but Livira forgave them all for his appearance now, walking unhurriedly along the aisle she'd just come down, his sword in hand. 'I wouldn't advise reaching for those 'sticks. You don't have enough time.' He continued to approach, neither slowing nor speeding his pace, his arm at his side, blade lifted only enough to keep it from skimming the floor. 'Draw steel if you like.'

The younger guard wrapped a thick arm around Livira's neck. 'Watch me snap her like a twig.'

'Snap who? The librarian?' Malar shrugged. 'You'd think she might be useful in a library, but do as you feel best.'

'You don't want her?' The older guard sounded puzzled.

'A bit young for me.' Malar sucked his teeth, eyes narrow. 'Besides, I'm more the killing sort.' He brought up his blade. 'I mean, I'll stab you through her if you like, but it seems poor sport. You'd have more of a chance with a weapon in your hand.'

The younger guard, apparently feeling outraged at the challenge to his manhood or whatever it was that made people ready to gamble their lives on a sharp edge, threw Livira roughly aside and drew his blade, a shiny length of steel with a richly enamelled hilt, in keeping with his station.

'You too?' Malar tilted his head towards the older man in query.

'Do I know you?' the man asked.

'I doubt it.' Malar limbered up his wrist. 'You may have heard of me, though. They call me—' Mid-sentence Malar lunged, skewering the younger man through the throat. A side swing half decapitated the older man with his sword partway drawn from the scabbard. 'Malar.'

Malar held a hand out to Livira and pulled her to her feet.

'Not so fast.' A steady voice some way behind Livira.

She turned to see Jons about thirty yards back along the aisle, staring at them both down the gleaming barrel of a heavy 'stick. Sweat slicked his short dark hair to his forehead, and he stood with his feet apart, broad shoulders hunched around his aim, face red, eyes calm.

Close to his head a strand of smoke coiled upwards, the smoulder of the fuse that would ignite the chemicals whose swift combustion would drive the projectile forward. Fire amid the aisles!

'Fucksake.' Malar spat on the ground. 'You can lose yourself in the library, they told me. Never see a fucking soul for days, they told me. And here we are with every Harry, Tom' – he yanked his sword from the second guard's neck, aiming his gaze at Jons – 'and fucking Dick, showing up like they're taking stage cues.'

'You should run along, Malar,' Jons said, his aim unwavering. 'King wants the girl. Didn't say nothing about you.'

'I'm a bit old for running, Jons.'

'Just let us go.' Livira tore her gaze from the bleeding bodies at her feet. 'He's your friend. You helped save me as a child. Nobody knows we even met out here.'

Jons shook his head almost imperceptibly. 'You're the girl who opens magic doors. The king said so himself. I need a door even more than a square meal right about now. Got black devils in with us now, as well as the white ones outside.'

'I don't know how to open doors,' Livira protested. 'The Exchange is—'

'You won't change Jons's mind with words, Livira. Words hang on trust, and trust is hard to come by, especially when you're pointing a 'stick at someone. Soldiers're always getting fucked over with fancy words.'

'Ain't that the truth,' Jons said.

'But you're forgetting who I am, old friend.' Malar started to walk towards the man.

'Next step's the one I blow your head off. I'm wise to your tricks, *friend.*'

Malar lowered his voice. 'When he shoots, you have to run.'

'I'm not leaving you!' Livira was outraged.

'Then I'll have got shot for nothing.' Malar kept on walking towards Jons. He raised his voice, addressing the man again. 'You should wait until I'm closer. You won't have time to reload.'

'Hard to miss at this range.'

'Even so.' Malar gestured with his head, indicating the corpses behind him. 'You're remembering who I am, Jons. Palms starting to sweat. Aim wavering. It's not so easy when—'

The 'stick boomed, a thunderous sound, much louder than Livira had imagined it might be. Malar jerked around and stumbled back against the shelves. Smoke bloomed around Jons and a ringing silence filled the emptiness behind the shot. For a moment it looked as if nothing but the books were holding Malar up – his graceless slide to the floor inevitable. In the next heartbeat he shrugged himself away from the shelves, leaving crimson-spattered spines behind him.

'That could have gone better,' Malar croaked, and began to shamble towards Jons. 'You should run. You think you've got time to reload, but you don't.'

Jons glanced behind him, considering escape, then with a curse he broke open his arrow-stick along an unseen hinge and began fumbling in the powders that would propel his next projectile.

Malar staggered on, making slow progress, a scarlet trail behind him. The bullet appeared to have gone through his chest and Livira couldn't understand how he wasn't dead. A terrifyingly slow race ensued, Malar consuming the space between him and Jons one agonized step at a time, Jons going through the many intricate stages required to fire his weapon again. It almost seemed that he had to perform his own little miracle of alchemy right there before them.

With barely six feet between them Jons began to raise his 'stick while the point of Malar's blade trailed lazily behind him as he closed the last few steps.

It had taken Livira far longer than she'd hoped to find a suitable book. She knew, from experimentation that would appal any librarian, that books make terrible missiles. Aside from having aerodynamics only slightly less chaotic than that of a playing card, they opened in flight and after that any attempt to instil aim into the initial throw was lost. The book Livira required was bound shut, slim but not floppy, small but not too small.

Her throw arced in the air, slicing a curved path that at first would have had it strike Malar between his shoulders, but ended up skimming past his sword arm and following an ever-sharpening turn that brought it crashing into the side of Jons's head.

The 'stick boomed again and another cloud of smoke billowed. Jons turned to run, somehow evading the rising swing of Malar's sword, though the blow took the weapon from his hands and threw it against the shelves.

Livira, who had been sprinting after her thrown book, passed Malar and threw herself at the back of Jons's legs, making no attempt at a grapple. The man came down with a clatter and an oath, joining Livira in a tangle on the floor.

Jons was rising before Livira could, one hand pulling an ugly knife from his belt. Livira, unable to twist free, screamed and tensed for the thrust. It never came. Jons's arm stiffened and then went slack. He'd risen onto Malar's blade and unlike when his bullet had passed through Malar's chest, Malar's sword found something immediately fatal on its journey through Jons.

As Livira disentangled herself, Malar sat down heavily, his back to the shelving. He coughed and bright red blood peppered the air. His voice came faint and wheezing. 'One of those healing circles would be good about now.'

Livira came to kneel at his side. She felt calm. She knew she should be weeping, begging Malar to stay, telling him she loved him. But this was Malar. He wasn't going to die, not here in the library shot by an idiot, not anywhere. 'It's going to be fine.' She believed it.

Malar put his head back, blood dribbling from his chin. He raised an eyebrow. 'Fine?'

That look put a crack in Livira's armour and a scared, tragic, empty feeling tried to leak in through it. 'We can fix this.' She put both hands over the hole in Malar's chest, as if hiding the problem was halfway to solving it. 'Pressure on the wound!'

Malar coughed again and blood bubbled between Livira's fingers. 'Fuck . . .' He wasn't looking at her. 'You'd think this couldn't . . . get worse.'

The smoke from Jons's second shot wasn't dissipating as it had after the first shot. If anything, it seemed to be getting thicker. Livira followed Malar's gaze to where, some yards away, a thin column of smoke was rising amid the loose pages that Jons's 'stick had fallen onto. Books that had been tumbled from the shelves scattered the whole area. As her eyes fixed upon the exact spot, an orange tongue of flame woke and licked upwards.

'No!'

For a moment Livira was trapped, unable to take her hands from Malar's wound. Perhaps too far away to stop the flames spreading in any case.

White smoke swirled, hinting at a ghostly figure. 'Not today.' A white foot came down to snuff the flame. And Yute's pale child stood before them, her pink-eyed stare impossible to read.

Livira was never sure when it was that Malar died, only that her hands were on him and that he was not alone.

*Bravery doesn't enter into it. The reason you face your
fears is to stop them jumping you from behind.*

The Lives of Lestal Crow, *by Lestal Erris Crow*

CHAPTER 37

Evar

'Escapes!' Evar sank into his fighting stance, knife in hand. At his
side Clovis readied her sword.

A ripple of panic ran through the humans, and disturbing shapes
appeared fleetingly in the black mist steaming from the crack.

Frowning, Yute walked slowly towards the shadows.

'Master!' Meelan hurried after the man, though whether to wrestle
him back or just stand by his side Evar couldn't tell. Either way it
was brave if he didn't understand the threat and foolhardy if he did.

Yute raised one hand to warn Meelan back. The other he reached
out towards the mist. 'I never thought to see the library's blood.
This place was not built to crack, and yet something has cracked it.'

Evar realized that he was understanding Yute. More than that,
he couldn't tell what tongue the man was speaking. His meaning
was simply given up, as if he could whistle and achieve the same
effect. 'It makes enemies,' Evar warned. 'It hunts your fears and
becomes them.'

'Oh, I doubt that.' Yute glanced back at him. 'I'm terrified of
cocktail parties, awkward silences, and catching leprosy. I doubt it
will become any of those.' He moved his hand as if trying to conduct
the black haze before him. 'More realistically I would say that the
blood would take whatever strong emotions you have and knit them
around any other ideas that happen to be close at hand.' He circled

his fingers and the mist directly before him swirled, condensing into a black sphere. A click of his fingers and the ball flowed into a bunch of black flowers on black stems. 'Colours are more difficult . . . apparently.' He pressed his lips into a thin line, concentrating. Another click and the flowers became an odd-looking weapon. 'My old umbrella,' Yute explained. 'It was black anyway.'

Arpix joined the deputy and peered at the mist. Although physically all he shared with Yute was a narrow frame, both held such a similar bookishness about them that in that moment Evar could imagine them father and son.

Evar lowered his knife and straightened up. 'I've been running from my own fears my whole life?'

Yute looked back, raising white eyebrows. The umbrella dissolved into mist.

'Didn't you just tell me as much?'

'Yes . . . but I didn't know the Escapes could be other things. Good things.'

The librarian bent to examine the crack, his frown returning. 'Most fears could have been good things before we let them harden into what they are.'

'Leprosy?' Kerrol came up behind Evar.

'*Most.* Cocktail parties I might have embraced and become a people person and led a happier life. If I'd turned more enemies into friends, perhaps I could have persuaded our king to find a peace with the canith. But this' – he reached towards the mist again – 'this is a tool, and like any tool it can be both a weapon and a danger to those who wield it if they don't properly understand its use.' The mist seemed to have reached its limit, extending about five feet above the crack before dissipating into nothing. Narrow at the point where the ground released it, blooming wider as it climbed. It held no odour and put no taste into the air.

'It's a weapon.' Clovis approached, the humans parting before her.

'It's dangerous,' Yute acknowledged. 'It shouldn't be here. There have been intermittent leaks from some of the mechanisms for a while, but the structure of the library itself has never cracked. Until now.'

'Do you know where Livira is?' Evar felt ashamed that it had taken him this long to ask. 'Is she alive?' A thought struck him, but Arpix beat him to asking:

'Can Wentworth find her?'

'So many questions.' Yute counted them off on white fingers. 'No. I hope so. And yes.' He looked for the cat. 'Wentworth has never not been able to find something I wanted. The main question is whether you're able to follow him to it or not. Or if he can bring it back.'

A commotion at the rear of the gathered humans drew Evar's attention from the conversation. A small group was approaching the chamber corner along one of the many aisles that opened onto it, a patrol of some sort perhaps. Meelan gave a shout of recognition and ran towards them. For a moment Evar thought that Livira had returned, summoned by her name and the fact of his need for her. He started forward too. But Meelan's run ended in the embrace of one of the two young females in the group of humans.

Evar watched the pair embrace. They had their arms around each other, hugging very tightly. The woman was of a similar height to Meelan, hair long, brown, and curling, where his was short and black, clothes more colourful than any of the other humans'.

'Brother and sister,' Kerrol said. 'Not a mating couple.'

Arpix, overhearing them, snorted. 'Yes. She's his sister, Leetar.'

Yute came up behind them, calling his people away from the crack which ran across the aisle, appearing from beneath one set of shelves and vanishing beneath those on the other side. 'Let's keep our distance. We will need to relocate as I believe it would be inadvisable to sleep near to such a crack. Specifically, to dream near it.'

He set a hand to Arpix's shoulder. 'We could try following Wentworth to Livira but first I need to know how you evaded the skeer.'

'Oh.' Arpix went across to Clovis and with a boldness that made Evar and Kerrol suck in their breath, anticipating at the very least a slap that would put him on the floor, he reached into her weapons bag and drew out the orb. 'This pushes them away. We found it under the Arthran Plateau.' He looked slightly embarrassed. 'After being trapped there for four years.'

Yute nodded absently as if four years were a trifle. He took the iron ball into his hands and turned it over and over, as if looking for some maker's mark. 'Ganar work, I think.'

'That's . . . a strange coincidence,' Arpix said, and he spoke briefly about the automaton several chambers back and the much larger one that had also chased the canith. He finished by taking back the orb when Yute handed it to him, saying, 'I didn't know the ganar had this sort of technology. I thought they were quite a simple species?'

Yute raised a single eyebrow at that, seeming surprised and perhaps a little disappointed in his protégé. 'They came from the moons, Arpix!'

Arpix nodded, chastened. 'I suppose that *would* take more than a long ladder.'

'The ganar are part of our unfortunate cycle. They have been masters of ships that sailed from Attamast and landed on our shores. They have been slaves. And they have been all things between.

'The automata are a curious phenomenon. Unlike most such constructs in the library they have never served as guides or aided in the curation of books in any way. Whilst functioning they defend their existence. They're actively aggressive to humans or canith that go near them, but I've never heard of one giving chase before. And all the ones close to Crath City were destroyed in the early years of the establishment of that cycle's library complex. The large one Evar and his siblings encountered may have moved in after the fire. Generally, they stay where they are.'

Arpix handed the orb back to Clovis before turning to face Yute again. 'But what are they for? What are they doing?'

'I always believed they were hunting someone,' Yute said.

'Hunting?' Arpix looked puzzled. 'But you said they just stop where they are. For decades at a time from what Evar described. Longer maybe.'

'A hunt in the library is a hunt through time. You're no more likely to find the person you're looking for in one chamber than the next. So, the best policy might be just to stay where you are and wait for them to come to you.'

'But they chased us,' Evar said. 'They chased *me*. Why would steel monsters in the shape of ganar have been hunting me for centuries? That makes no sense!'

Yute shrugged. 'That I couldn't tell you. But you used the Exchange and there are many, many dangers associated with that. It sounds as if you've made an enemy who has also had access to the Exchange and has seeded hunters across the years, all looking for some manner of revenge.'

Evar shook his head. 'I went to Attamast. That's the only time I've even seen ganar. But I was a ghost. I couldn't have been there for more than a minute. I couldn't touch anything and none of them saw me.'

'You would be surprised who can see who.' Yute's pink eyes seemed focused on the space between Arpix and Evar, the angle suggesting a child might be standing there. 'The most important thing if you ever see a ghost is never to speak to them. That can lead to a world of pain.' He made a dismissive motion with his fingers and turned away.

'Why would a ganar orb stop a ganar automaton?' Evar asked, remembering how hot the thing had got, how close – it felt – to breaking.

Yute shook his head. 'That's like saying why would a human defence stop a human attack? They're not one people. Even if you consider a particular time, their kind will divide into nations, religions, races. And if there's nothing else to fight, and sometimes even if there is, they will fight each other.'

Evar had to accept that. His study of various canith histories with Mayland had shown him that his own kind had fought endless bloody wars between different factions, often when the only real point of dispute was which leader should prevail over which.

'Livira, then! Wentworth can guide us. We don't have to worry about skeer.' He looked around. 'Is this all of you? I remember more . . .'

'There are more.' Yute became grave. 'Several more patrols. But they're out there to help us evade the larger group. I just spoke about how ganar will fall to fighting among themselves as humans will. The group I led from the fire has split into two factions. It turned out that King Oanold was among those who escaped the city into the library. When he first came to the Exchange he was disguised as a duchess. He unveiled his true identity later in my absence. There was . . . bloodshed.' The librarian shook his head in sorrow.

The red-haired older human who always seemed to be barking complaints looked up sharply at the mention of Oanold and moved in closer, but it was Neera, Livira's friend from the Dust with the long, lustrous hair, who spoke up. Although she seemed to be following Yute's side of the conversation, her words made little sense to Evar. He picked out a few here and there amid the flow. Yute supplied the young woman's meaning.

'She's saying that King Oanold refused to believe either the limits of my and Wentworth's ability to supply food, or the facts of the defeat we had left behind us. Even the fire appeared to be something he'd minimized in his mind. He considered our departure precipitous. He demanded more food and a return to his city at the time he left it. Both those things were and are not possible. I showed him to the centre circle and explained how it could sustain us all, but he believed that to be a lie and declared himself ready to torture me and anyone he thought I might care about until what he wished to happen happened. It was only due to luck, and the sacrifice of several good people, that we escaped him.'

'And Wentworth,' Neera said. Evar understood that bit. He was sure the cat had played a role in Yute's people being able to win free.

'We have been avoiding them for several weeks now,' Yute concluded. 'They send out patrols and sadly several of our people have been captured, but they mainly stick to the centre. Morally, it would be right to offer them the chance to leave with us. Also, I can't leave behind the people he took prisoner.'

Clovis huffed. 'This king would demand the orb.' She slapped the bag holding it. 'I might have to kill a lot of them to change his mind.'

'Is it so important which of us holds it?' Yute asked gently.

Clovis opened her mouth wide, displaying the full serrated array of her teeth. 'Yes.'

'We can come back for them,' Evar said, anxious not to delay the search for Livira. 'We can move faster with a smaller group. Scout the way for those who might be too weak for anything but the shortest route. We can't leave the library by the canith door or the human door. If we go out into the world the skeer can beat the orb. At least the fliers can. We need to find an exit far from here.'

Arpix finished translating him for the others. Some of those from Livira's settlement spoke of a friend called Gevin and another named Katrin. One city man was very animated when talking about Katrin. None of them were happy about leaving them behind. It seemed they didn't trust their king to treat his prisoners well.

Yute nodded and listened. 'I understand, my friends. But if we go to the centre with the canith there will be a battle. We've seen what happens when the king's soldiers meet canith. Many will die. Katrin and Gevin might well be casualties too. And if we go without the canith, Oanold will take us into his custody. If we don't have the orb to give him he will likely just repeat his original, impossible demands. Though it's possible that these weeks spent surviving on the centre circle's gift will have softened their resolve. In any event, I do not think Mistress Clovis will hand us the orb to take to him by ourselves. Something I cannot fault her for.'

The decision required some toing and froing, with Arpix working to smooth fears and deal with complaints. However, within the hour, the group was ready to leave. They were to search for an exit from the library. One that lay sufficiently distant from any skeer nests. Also, they were to look for Livira.

Yute knew of an exit that humans could open, but it lay more than two hundred miles away. Arpix and several others seemed surprised by the existence of any such door, though most were just daunted by the length of the journey. Since Yute could navigate to this remote entrance it was agreed that they start by asking Wentworth to find Livira. If the route the cat led them on diverged too much from Yute's path they would have to choose between them, and an exit seemed the most popular choice – though Evar already knew that if Wentworth continued to lead, he would continue to follow.

'Of course,' said Yute, 'if Livira is in the future, Wentworth will lead us to the nearest door into the Exchange. And even if one has been left unattended by an assistant, it would be highly inadvisable to go through it.'

'You led hundreds of people through the Exchange,' Evar countered.

'The alternative was that they suffocate or burn alive,' Yute said. 'It was not a wise decision. It was a . . . human one.' He went to one knee and held out a hand as if it might contain some morsel of food. 'Wentworth!'

The cat did not appear.

Yute looked up. 'Volente is much more obliging.' He called again, 'Wentworth!'

Salamonda came forward. She had around her waist a torn sheet as a kind of apron. Evar had noticed it before and always wondered if it was an example of fashion. The older woman made a clucking noise and stamped her foot. 'Wentworth, you come here right now if you know what's good for you!'

The cat strolled into view as if he just happened to be passing.

Yute shook his head and stood up. 'I've fed that cat for well over six hundred years.'

Salamonda bent to scratch the cat's neck. 'We need to find Livira.'

Wentworth sat down, extended a hind leg across his body, reaching for the ceiling, toes splayed, and began to lick his furry thigh.

Evar exchanged a glance with Arpix. Jella opened her mouth and said nothing. Meelan asked the question: 'Does this mean she's—'

Wentworth abandoned his grooming without warning and started to amble off towards the shelves.

'He's found her.' Yute looked more confused than relieved.

'That's good, no?' Evar looked between Yute and the cat's retreating rear end, ready to follow.

'It . . . is.' Yute nodded. 'But look where he's headed.'

'In Livira's direction?'

'He leads where you can follow. If he was heading to one of the doors he would go this way, that way, that way, or this way.' With each option Yute indicted the direction of the chamber's four exits. None of those directions was Wentworth's. The cat was heading directly towards the middle of the chamber.

'Livira's in the same room as us?' Evar started to follow the cat, disbelieving, while at the same time willing him to go faster.

Clovis took his arm. Not in her normal way – as if it were a wrestling match and she needed a lever to throw him – but in a manner she had rarely used. 'This could be bad, brother.'

'Bad?'

'You can't smell it?' She lifted her head and sniffed deeply. 'I've been smelling it ever since we arrived.'

And Evar could smell it. Even without drawing another breath. The scent that had hung in the air, faint but persistent. He'd just been too focused on everything else to acknowledge it.

Blood. Old blood. Fresh blood. Blood and excrement. Lots of both.

Just as a person can be divided into component elements,
3.2% nitrogen by mass, 0.1% magnesium, etc., each of
us can be viewed as a mix of cat and dog, yin and yang
replaced with miaow and woof. Ironically, too much of either
makes for a fine feline or hound but a terrible human.

The Pigeon-Fancier's Guide, *by Omega Prime*

CHAPTER 38

Arpix

Wentworth led the way towards the chamber's centre, and everyone followed. Yute's band dragged their heels, exchanging nervous mutters. Had the library allowed any shadows Arpix felt Yute's people would be jumping at each one. These were not warriors. A mother held a baby to her breast; a boy of perhaps twelve followed his father.

Arpix noted, though, that none of them suggested leaving Livira to her fate. He wasn't sure they would have gone for anyone other than Livira. All through the good fortune that had taken her from a hut on the Dust to the quarters of a full librarian, she had remembered her roots and supported those who had fared far less well. It was the story of that care which bound them to her.

Such was the fear written across the faces of Yute's group, however, that without additional help perhaps even Livira's need couldn't have moved them forward. It seemed that whilst their journey to this place from the Exchange had been far shorter than Arpix's, they had seen plenty of horror along the way.

The addition of three canith to their side, and the orb to protect them from the skeer, allowing an escape from the chamber, appeared to have tipped the balance in Livira's favour. Normally, no descendant of the Dust would ally themselves with sabbers, but the nature of the opposition made them acceptable if not trustworthy. Oanold's implacable hatred for sabber kind gave Yute's followers faith in Evar, Kerrol, and Clovis's intentions, at least as far as the king was concerned.

Arpix walked with Clovis and Kerrol just behind Meelan and his sister. Leetar carried on a whispered conversation with her brother as they walked, both of them exchanging their experiences. At first there seemed to be an argument about which of them was now the older sibling. Later, from the snatches Arpix caught, he learned that the door they had first taken from the Exchange was not the same one that had brought the group here. There had been some misadventure and a retreat.

On both occasions that Yute had ushered the survivors of the fire through portals from the Exchange he had made sure they all left before following on through himself. He came last to ensure nobody was left unattended amid the door-filled forest. Unsupervised use of the doors could lead to disaster, he'd said. Later he'd admitted that even he was not qualified to use the Exchange safely. At that, a shiver had run the length of Arpix's spine, thinking of the many journeys Evar and Livira had taken through those same portals.

Leetar confessed to Meelan that following the soldiers' passage through the first door King Oanold had revealed his presence among them, shedding the disguise in which he'd fled the fall of his city. He had taken command and some sort of bloody conflict had ensued in which quite a number of soldiers were killed.

Leetar glanced back at this point and her voice fell below hearing. The next audible parts of the conversation indicated that after his arrival Yute had managed to get the king and his soldiers to return to the Exchange to try a second portal. That door was the one which had led them to this part of the library. Leetar did not yet appear wholly convinced that she was separated from her old life by more than a distance that could be measured in miles, and by the fact that the city had been on fire and full of canith. The idea that hundreds of years had also passed was, for now, a step too far for her imagination.

Despite their evident worry, Arpix found it hard to share the apprehensions of Livira's countrymen. He knew the library as a place of peace, more familiar than the home he'd been raised in. Whatever King Oanold's failings, and they were many, the man was hardly a monster. Arpix had read of rulers who impaled thousands in their streets or hunted out witches for burning on the thinnest of pretexts.

Next to these historical figures Oanold's corruption, fragile ego, and bigotry were unpleasant realities, but things that could and should be fought rather than run from. Even if they hadn't discovered that Livira was in the chamber, Arpix imagined he might vote for an attempt to make peaceful contact with the king's faction in the hopes of reaching an agreement. A sizeable part of Arpix looked forward to the normality of seeing scores of his fellow citizens and some of the central elements of his old life. Four years of isolation on the margins of the Dust had taken a toll on more than just his body.

Arpix felt safe enough with the two canith flanking him. He enjoyed being the shortest of a trio. For most of his life he'd towered over nearly everyone. Especially Meelan, his closest friend.

Arpix had always felt a distance between himself and the world, and although he knew that it was his innate reserve that had created the gap rather than his height, his stature still felt like the embodiment of that disconnect. Eye contact required an extra step, which took away spontaneity. Everyone had to look up first.

Clovis walked beside him, easy in her skin. Magnificent in it, truth be told. He shook his head. He used that word about her too often, albeit only within the confines of his skull. *Magnificent.* The closeness of her, the sheer physical presence, affected him in ways he was unused to, ways that left him unsettled and from which he had always steered away on the rare occasions he'd encountered them in the past. This time, however, he was neither sure that he could absent himself from her company, nor that he even wanted to despite the excess of nervous energy she filled him with.

Part of him wished that they weren't always in such extremes both of danger and of circumstance. Though, when he tried to picture them talking in a quiet, stress-free library, or strolling the streets of

Crath, his imagination failed him. And there were no streets to go back to now, no peace, no part of his old life to return to.

Arpix couldn't picture Clovis in his previous existence – taking her to tea with his parents, for example, totally defeated him – but he could easily imagine her growing bored of him in such a context, dismissive of his interests. And that would hurt. It was, almost certainly, best if he let go of this thing, whatever it was, and instead trod a more prudent path.

Although – if Wentworth was correct – they were walking towards her, Livira was, in a very real sense, already walking beside Arpix. He could hear her voice in his mind, asking him why he was still waiting for his life to begin. All his years of caution, all those years when she had asked him seemingly every day what he thought he was getting ready for. Those days when she'd told him that the race had already started, and he needed to join in or be left behind. Livira's advice would be, and always had been, to grab what was before him with both hands. And now she would be saying that if he really had for so long been saving himself for something better, something extraordinary . . . *how was this not it?* How was Clovis not it?

A tap on his shoulder made Arpix look around to see that Kerrol had stopped walking and was letting others go on ahead. Arpix fell back too. 'What is it?'

'You looked troubled.'

'We're in troubling times.' Arpix enjoyed the privacy offered by the canith's language. The settlers from Yute's group, who were passing them by, probably thought that the two of them were gearing up for a fight, judging by the growls and snarls. Certainly, there was mild alarm in the looks thrown their way.

Kerrol started walking again once the back of the party caught up with them. 'You looked as if your troubles might be of the oldest boy-meets-girl kind.'

'How could you—' Arpix broke off, remembering that people were Kerrol's study, whatever species they might come from, and that relationships were as much a part of people as water was a part of blood. Without water, blood was just a red dust. In his library life, Arpix had come close to cutting himself off to a dangerous level, to becoming dust, moved only by the wind rather than by the pulsing of a heart.

He sighed and, after a long pause, admitted, 'I worry.'

'You seem to have summed up your existence in two words, Arpix. Clovis worries too little, because she has suffered too great a hurt and has armoured herself against cares of all kinds. Somehow you have sidestepped that armour. She might liken it to a stiletto slid through a joint.'

'And your advice is?'

'It's more of a warning. Though a different kind from my brother's one.' He paused, rumbling in his throat, a deep sound that seemed to travel the length of him. 'My family will not all take the same side in the library's great war. And it seems that we will all become embroiled in this conflict. I want you to consider that the library, though it has been home to you both, has shown a very different face to Clovis than it has to you and your friends. There will come a time of choosing, and it might well be that this time will be easier for you if you don't choose my sister first.'

Arpix sighed. 'It's never easy, is it?'

Kerrol set a hand to Arpix's shoulder. 'And we didn't even get to the biting part yet.'

'Biting?' Arpix glanced uncomfortably at the large hand beside his neck.

'The females of our kind, when in the throes of . . .'

'They bite?' Arpix said, horrified.

'Famed for it.' Kerrol nodded. 'A good thick mane offers some protection to the largest arteries, but I'm not sure yours is . . . big enough.'

Arpix was still fumbling for an answer when he walked into Clovis. She warded him off, gently enough, while staring daggers at Kerrol. 'My brother's filling your head with nonsense.'

Kerrol strolled on past her. 'I saw you were waiting for us, and I felt he needed to know.'

Arpix rubbed his arm where Clovis had grabbed it to steer him clear of a collision. 'Was . . . was any of that true?' He felt his face turning crimson and was mortified.

Clovis turned away and followed her brother. 'No,' she said over her shoulder. 'Manes are no protection at all.'

Arpix had more questions. Whether or not he had the courage to ask them was not something that was put to the test since at that moment scattered shots rang out in the distance and, in the following silence, distant screams rose.

Immediately Evar picked up speed, urging Wentworth on. The group jogged behind him, a pace that started to tire the smaller children quickly. More turns, more aisles, another 'stick blast, isolated this time. They hurried on, running now to keep up with Evar's barely restrained jog. Clovis, despite her weakness, forged a path to take her place behind Evar. Arpix kept his place just behind her and Kerrol, his view blocked by canith backs.

A turn left, right, two more lefts. Without warning, a terrified cry rang out at the front of the group. Clovis readied her blow before Arpix could blink. Then Evar's voice came, raw with emotion.

'Livira!'

You need not look for sorrow, it will always find you.

Zen and the Art of Skateboarding, *by Tommy Hanks*

CHAPTER 39

Livira

'I can't leave him here.' Livira knelt beside Malar's body. His blood pooled around her knees. 'They'll eat his body.'

'Won't they kill someone else to eat if they don't get this?' The white child – Yolanda – gazed down at Malar with dispassion.

Livira didn't answer. She was too numb, too lost to find a counter-argument. Dragging Malar away, saving him from the indignity of being devoured by filth like the king and Lord Algar, would condemn another to death. Maybe Katrin or Neera or Leetar had been hidden in one of those cells, waiting to have parts of their bodies carved off.

She nodded and stumbled away, blinded by tears, her chest emptied of air by a long-hissed-out breath of anguish and yet too paralysed by hurt to draw in any replacement. Yolanda passed her and led on. Livira followed, hitching in her breath at last. She had had three fathers – one out on the Dust that she barely remembered, and two from the city. A good one and a bad one, though they were both good to her. Yute had been the voice of reason, and Malar had been her lesson in heart.

Shouts and the sound of pounding feet came from behind. Yolanda started to sprint, her bare feet making no sound. Livira stumbled after her then broke into her own run and found that running was all she wanted to do. With her librarian robes fluttering in protest Livira overtook Yolanda and tried to outpace her own grief, tried to leave the sorrow and the nightmare behind her, veering this way and that, ricocheting from the shelves on one side then the other.

A figure loomed in her path, strong arms caught her, lifting her from her feet. She screamed and fought, ready to die rather than be taken by Oanold's men once more.

'Livira!' The arms held her without violence. Her kicks and punches were not returned. 'Livira!'

And there he was. Evar. Holding her close. His mane in her face. He squeezed her hard enough to make her ribs creak, and pressed his mouth to her neck, breathing her in. He had thought her dead and his relief trembled through him. The sheer physical reality of him overwhelmed her. They had parted hundreds of years ago, though it only felt like days. And from within the prison of the Assistant she had watched him grow, watched his whole life from behind the bars of her timeless cage. That had seemed like an eyeblink until he wrapped his arms about her, and now it felt like the lifetime it was.

Others surged around them, and Evar was setting her to her feet. She held him a moment longer. 'I missed you.'

She was standing once more and old friends surrounded her, joy and tears on lean, dirty faces. Meelan, Jella, Salamonda!

'Arpix!' Livira released the others to throw herself at the over-tall librarian. She clung to him as if he were a tree and a flood raged around them. Amazingly, she felt his arms enclose her and return the embrace with a fierceness she'd never thought he had in him.

'It's good to see you.' Arpix sounded un-Arpix-like too, his voice choked by emotion.

She looked up at him, blinking away tears. The face that peered down at her across the length of his chest was gaunt, and somehow older than the one she remembered. Even so, it was him: her unwilling partner in crime, her moral compass. Her Arpix.

Two more canith approached. Dark-maned Kerrol, who made Arpix look short, and Clovis with dust taming the redness of her mane. Livira saw them with a kind of double vision: through her own eyes as Evar's siblings – the enigmatic brother, the fierce and dangerous sister; and more dimly, through timeless eyes, she saw the children who had grown in her care and felt an echo of the love for them that had taken root even past the impervious skin of an assistant.

'The Soldier saved me,' she said. 'Malar died fighting. Twice.'

And even though she didn't explain herself, and despite the foolishness of it when the enemy might be close at hand, all three canith put back their heads and howled to the unseen moons.

Livira added her own cry of sorrow to the canith's howls, her heartache lost in the resonant depths of their howl, then carried on its rising note. Others in the party exchanged worried glances, fearing the sound might draw the king's soldiers. Arpix and Meelan, who among Livira's friends had known Malar best, both looked stricken.

As the howl fell to silence Livira saw Yute, though he must have been there all the time, his whiteness hard to miss. The grief on his face was underwritten by older lines of sorrow that had not been there when Livira had last seen him. Malar had never spoken of it directly, but Livira had come to know that he did other jobs for Yute, not just shepherding trainees across the city. There were prob- ably senior librarians who had spent less time in Yute's company than the soldier had. The nature of their relationship remained a mystery to Livira, but she thought that they were each, perhaps, the closest thing that the other had to a friend.

Yute set a hand to Salamonda's shoulder. The woman had not known Malar well, but she knew him as one of Livira's protectors and had tears in her eyes for him.

'The Soldier died well.' Clovis raised her sword. 'But those who killed him will not. They will fall before me like wheat before the scythe.'

'The man who killed him is dead. By Malar's hand,' Livira said.

'And the others?' Clovis's gaze snapped around to fix on Livira.

'There were no others.'

'One?' Clovis asked, disbelieving. 'Only one?'

'He had a 'stick. A projectile weapon. The Soldier refused to run. He stayed to save me.'

Clovis spat. And the fury on her face was something terrible to behold. All the worse for Livira understanding the grief it was trying to keep at bay. The Soldier had cared for all the children in his way. He had trained them. Tolerated them. Taught them more than they knew he was teaching them. But it had been Clovis with whom that bond ran deepest. They shared warrior souls, and like reaches to like.

'I will see his body and say my farewells.' Clovis slammed her sword back through the loop on her belt.

Evar, who had stood back to let Livira's friends crowd about her, came closer now and she took his hand, a lifeline to keep her from drowning in misery. She had fought so hard to reach him, but Malar's life had never been some coin that she was willing to pay for passage.

Yute stepped into Clovis's path, dwarfed by the canith. As one, the humans sucked in a sharp breath. Livira had seen Malar nearly killed when doing something similar, but surely Clovis was more trusted now, though she still had her hand on the hilt of her sword. She and her siblings seemed to be travelling with Yute and his party. Suddenly Algar's words played through her mind: *Since your canith friends killed the head librarian.* That couldn't be true? The words escaped her mouth: 'Where's Yamala?'

The question seemed to undercut Clovis's rapidly building anger. Unexpectedly, Arpix reached the canith's side and set his hand to her sword arm. The fierceness left Clovis's eyes, and she lowered her gaze.

'Mayland killed Yamala.' The words came from beside her. Evar's voice.

'No!' She looked up at him, astonished. And then, 'I met him just recently. In the Exchange.'

Livira left Evar's side and went to stand before Yute. She wasn't sure if it had been days since she last saw him or centuries. It felt like a lifetime, and although theirs had never been a relationship that hugs or touching was a part of, she took both his hands in hers, finding them strangely cool. 'I'm sorry about your wife.'

Yute met her gaze, the old kindness in his eyes along with an older sorrow. 'I'm sorry we've lost Malar.'

It was enough to start Livira's tears flowing again. She tried to choke them off with anger. She looked over Yute's shoulder to

Clovis, who stood conflicted, twitching as instinct vied with unfamiliar emotions, pulling her this way and that. Evar must have told his sister that Livira had lain trapped at the heart of the Assistant. It was written in her eyes and the way they could no longer meet Livira's.

Livira opened her mouth to say that Yute should stand aside, that he should clear Clovis's path and unleash her on King Oanold's soldiers. But the words wouldn't leave her tongue. She had seen Clovis as a small girl, fierce around her hurts, seen her grow, seen her show Evar the first flesh-and-blood affection of his new life. 'There are too many of them, Clovis. You can't dodge bullets.' Part of her desperately wanted to loose the warrior on the king, Algar, and the monsters who served them. The soldiers might be battle-hardened and carrying the most advanced arrow-sticks, but even so Livira thought Clovis would put a large hole in their ranks. Perhaps even win. But 'perhaps' was not enough. And Evar would not stay back while his sister fought.

Livira looked away from Clovis and Yute, studying the familiar faces all around her. People she had known most or all of her life. Neera coughed, and for the first time Livira noticed her among those crowded into the aisle. All of them so precious to her and so vulnerable. She wanted to tell them that they had to attack, that what Oanold's people were doing was so heinous it couldn't be allowed to stand. She wanted to tell her people from the settlement that little Gevin was being eaten alive. To tell Clovis that the body she wanted to honour was being dragged away to be feasted on. But there were children here, a baby, friends. All her mind would show her was the aftermath: Neera, Yute, Arpix, Evar, all of them shot through like Malar had been, gasping out their final breaths in a welter of their own blood, more meat for Oanold's kitchen.

Livira fell to her knees beneath the weight of it. Evar and others crowded forward with cries of alarm. She felt their presence pushing on her from all sides, adding to the pressure. A scream built inside her in the space where the two halves of her were being torn one from the other by opposing forces, by impossible choice.

The scream, which felt as though it might physically tear her apart so her body could match her mind, never came. Yolanda came instead, stepping quietly around the corner.

At first only Livira saw the girl, past the legs of those surrounding her as she remained on her knees. Yolanda stood, watching, so white, so lacking colour that she seemed not to be a part of the world. Then Yute turned, drawn by an invisible thread, and saw his daughter. With the muted gasp of a gut-shot man, he joined Livira on his knees.

'You should not be here.' Yolanda's voice felt like a chill wind, as if she really were the ghost her paleness painted her to be. 'Have you not heard the summons, Father? The cracks are spreading. We need to go.'

'My child . . . Yolanda . . . We thought you were—'

Yolanda silenced the aching rasp of Yute's voice with a raised hand. 'Can you not hear it?'

'I hear something.' Yute got slowly to his feet, struggling, as if the weight of all his centuries had suddenly fallen upon him. 'But I didn't understand what I heard. I've forgotten so much. Made so many mistakes.' Yute winced as if stung by a memory. 'Your mother—'

'My mother might have taken my side, but the others have slain her, and still you won't commit, Father.' She turned and walked away. 'Hurry. They're nearly here.'

A heartbeat after she disappeared from view into another aisle the percussive explosion of a 'stick being fired rent the air. Muffled shouts rang out. Not close, but not far either.

'Come on!' Livira set off after Yolanda, breaking the indecision that had paralysed the group.

Any experienced librarian will tell you that much of what is found among their shelves defies classification. Most often by virtue of being many things at once. Sometimes those categories show only minimal overlap, and sometimes, as with 'hero' and 'villain', they are almost entirely the same thing.

Who Indexes the Indexers? *by M. L. K. Dewey*

CHAPTER 40

Evar

'Livira!' Evar intercepted the racing girl, sweeping her into his arms, lifting her from the ground, and spinning to absorb her momentum. For several heartbeats she fought him in her panic, and Evar took the blows until with a sudden stillness she understood who had hold of her. In that moment she collapsed against him, burying her face in his mane as he pressed his own to her neck, inhaling her. He hadn't truly believed it until that moment when her scent filled him. He squeezed her, trying to tame his strength in case she might break. He had thought her dead. He had hoped against hope that she wasn't. That the spirit which had entered the Assistant had escaped her white prison when the skeer destroyed it. But he hadn't known, he hadn't believed, and he had lived with the ache of her absence for what might only be days but felt like a thousand years, all the time trying to deny the hurt and the loss and the hope.

'Livira.' A whisper now as her friends erupted all around them with cries of joy. Feeling the others start to tug at her, Evar reluctantly set her down. Before he released her though, Livira tightened her arms about his neck and her lips found his ear.

'I missed you.'

Evar stepped back as Livira's friends surged around. Her unexpected arrival had been the sudden intake of a breath he'd been short of ever since he found the Assistant's broken body. For the long, glorious moments during which they had been alone in each other's arms, held in the privacy of a fictional forever, Evar had felt himself mended.

For Evar, who had so seldom been hugged, it was a state he could happily have drawn out for an age, but the world had too quickly reimposed itself. Livira's fear and grief demanded an accounting, and the friends who crowded around were people she had known far longer than she had known Evar, and from whom she had been parted for far longer – at least on their side of the equation.

Evar found the human's speech easier to understand when Livira spoke it, and the effect also cast a new light of understanding on what the others were saying. The news that Malar had been killed hit Evar like a blow to the chest, taking the air from his lungs just as effectively as seeing the Soldier's body lying broken amid the drifts of skeer corpses. The Soldier was truly gone now. The human that Evar had carried to the healing circle and watched being returned from the brink of death had been the Soldier's inner spirit. That spirit was now extinguished.

Clovis made to advance on those that had killed Malar, and Evar was ready to go with her. She hid her full anger, but it still found an echo in his chest. Yute's intervention took the wind from both their sails. Evar's brother had killed the man's wife, and it seemed that Yute had known Malar better than any of the siblings.

Though it wasn't until Livira addressed Clovis that Evar realized what he might lose if they went seeking vengeance. He needed to stop thinking of the humans as weak just because they were smaller and slower than him. Arpix had taken down a cratalac. This king's soldiers apparently had weapons that compensated for their lack of martial skills. Clovis could die. Evar could die, with just a brief hug as the totality of his reunion with Livira.

The white child had arrived with the enemy at her heels, and Evar had been happy to follow her path away from the advancing foe. However cryptic her talk of being summoned, Evar would choose it every time over the alternative, which seemed to be at worst the chance to be killed by an exotic weapon, and at best to show how well he could slaughter humans, all the while with his human girl and her human friends watching him become the gore-soaked animal he feared they might secretly already believe him to be.

The girl, Yolanda, led them to the chamber's north door and the sounds of pursuit faded behind them. She walked as if she knew where she was going. Livira pulled Evar down to her level and whispered to him that Yute was the girl's father and had not seen her in nearly twenty years after she had become lost in the library.

This seemed unlikely: the child didn't look much older than ten years, and surely wouldn't have been allowed to wander the aisles as an infant. He kept the observation to himself, however, not being confident about the human lifespan or the time taken for them to grow. He had assumed they were similar to canith, but some of the things Yute had said made it seem as if he was extremely long-lived. Evar found himself worrying about whether his whole life would seem like a season to Livira, and he would grow old and fail while she was still green in her youth. He caught himself in the midst of his anxiety and snorted at his own foolishness. There were enemies behind him, skeer ahead, and likely more horrors beyond them. They might all be killed in the next hour or day, and here he was worrying about a future decades away.

Clovis gave him a sharp look. 'Stay focused.'

He looked towards Livira. She was back in the midst of her friends, catching up with the missing years. Evar found himself eyeing the males and wondering if any of them had designs on her, or had shared past intimacies. He pushed the thoughts away, ashamed of himself. He showed his teeth and looked ahead, focused. Clovis was right. She normally was when danger threatened.

The door required the touch of a human. It melted before Arpix's hand. The skeer warrior that had been guarding the way now watched them from a distance, having been driven back by the orb in Clovis's keeping. It stood some way off, almost lost among a forest of what at first seemed to be book stacks of unprecedented height.

As Yolanda led them into the forest, Evar understood that each stack was in fact a metal pole reaching from the floor to the distant ceiling. Each pole braced against its neighbours with struts about ten yards above the ground and again at the very top. The poles supported circular shelves every couple of feet, from which tomes of various sizes offered their spines to all points of the compass. Clearly, the chamber had been fashioned for those with the power of flight. So, unless canith had sported wings in their past, whoever built and stocked the shelves had been of no race Evar knew.

The lone skeer shadowed the group for a while at the limits of the orb's protection before retreating from sight, presumably to summon reinforcements.

The forest of shelf-towers reminded Evar of the Exchange and he wondered if the architect had known of that place. The ordered array of towers meant that every few paces brought into view a new set of seemingly endless corridors between them, narrowing to invisibility as they reached for the distant walls. Evar had read that the effect was seen in orchards, though he had yet to taste the fruit of any tree and the trees in the Exchange remained the only ones he had seen in the flesh. And even those had proved to be a kind of illusion.

Yute walked just behind his daughter, hunched around some unknowable pain. He made no attempt to speak to her. Evar guessed that he had somehow understood on first seeing Yolanda that, whilst she might have been lost at some point, she had found herself and could have returned to him – even if only as a ghost. But she had not.

The Soldier had very rarely been the one to offer comfort during Evar's early years. What little of that had come his way had been from the Assistant. But Evar did remember one thing the Soldier had told him not long after he and the other children had stumbled out of the Mechanism that first time. Evar had been asking about his parents, distressed as much by the loss of his memories of them as by their physical loss. The Soldier had looked away into the chamber and said, as if to nobody in particular, that Evar would never meet two people more capable of wounding him, or people he was more capable of wounding. The bonds between parent and child were, he said, as dangerous as they were wonderful, as full of darkness and terror as they were of joy and light. Evar had never spoken of it again, but he felt now that if he had repeated the Soldier's words to Kerrol, his brother might know the whole cloth of Malar's story.

Yolanda's path through the chamber did not seem to be angled at any of the doors, a fact that intrigued Evar. Livira didn't appear to have noticed, engaged as she was with her fellow survivors from the fall of her city. She did, however, seem distracted even from them, often glancing back towards the door they'd entered by. Evar wondered if thoughts of Malar might be turning her head in that direction, but the look he saw on her face held more fear in it than grief, and there was an anger there too, struggling to assert itself.

If they had been alone, Evar would have asked her why. But the presence of the others around him was a pressure, an audience that sealed his mouth rather than prompting a performance. Evar had been in the company of just three people for so very long that being part of what seemed a throng weighed on him in ways he didn't properly understand. What he did understand was what a blessing the time he had spent alone with Livira in the Exchange had been. Without that privacy, and the solitude they'd found in being ghosts, nothing could have grown between them. He was sure of that.

'We're going to a reading room!' Evar said it out loud as he realized.

That caught Livira's interest. She hurried to join him near the front of the column and called to Yolanda, 'You're taking us to a Mechanism?'

Evar missed a step. The greyness of the Mechanism filled his mind. The stuff it was built from felt like a physical representation of what it had done to his memories. It had taken Livira's presence to slowly restore to him the time he'd spent lost inside her stories. Those memories of shared adventure, discovery, and heartache, although not shared directly with Livira, had made it feel as though they'd spent a lifetime together. They had put flesh on the bones of a relationship built on brief encounters and hectic escapes. But he had come to realize, perhaps only truly since releasing her from his arms and into those of her friends, that although he had clothed himself in part of her soul, Livira had not been there with him. She had only the bones of that experience. And what frightened him more than anything that might lie in the chamber behind them, or in the place to which the white child was leading them, was that Livira's affection for him might be just that, affection rather than love, a mixture of pity and curiosity, founded on little more than a shared kiss. A puddle beside his ocean.

'Are you all right?' Livira reached for Evar's hand. 'You don't have to come in.' She looked worried herself and he remembered that her first experience in the Mechanism had been in the blindness of a subterranean world on the battlefield of species that shared more in common with skeer and cratalacs than with humans.

'There are two people I would go into the Mechanism for,' Evar said. 'And both are you.'

The group had nearly reached the reading room when Evar caught the ominous sound of distant crashing.

'It's another of those fucking metal monsters!' Clovis snarled, gazing to the east. The construct would have to fight its way through the forest of shelf-towers and would in theory be visible from the correct angle, but the distance would probably swallow too much detail to be sure of much, other than that something big was coming.

'We were chased by this enormous—'

'I know,' Livira said. 'Malar and I watched you. We were ghosts after the skeer destroyed our assistant bodies. We followed you until that assistant you met dragged us away.'

'You were there? Watching?' Evar was amazed, horrified, and comforted in equal measures.

'I thought maybe that thing was chasing me.' Livira shivered. 'It felt as though it was. It could touch us. It kicked Malar across the corridor.'

'It was a ganar.' Arpix joined the conversation. 'I mean, shaped like one. There was another smaller one that nearly killed Evar.'

The white child stopped and rounded on them. 'It was made in the likeness of a particular ganar. Both of them were. All of them were. The same ganar. Though all ganar may all look the same to you . . .'

'What?' Evar looked at the child in astonishment. 'How many of these monsters are there? And which ganar? And why? And how?'

Yute answered the first question. 'There are many, though the vastness of the library makes them seem few. The first kings of Crath City spent many lives and resources aiding the librarians to clear those few found close to the entrance. They were all hostile to humans, though not given to lengthy pursuits.'

Yolanda answered the second question. 'They are made in the likeness of Celcha. A ganar who mastered many of the mysteries of the Exchange, all while causing far less harm than you two have.' Her pink eyes took in Evar and Livira with disdain.

Livira, perhaps stung by the accusation, pointed at Yolanda. 'You tried to stop me taking my own book, so don't talk to me about doing damage! I was sent there by an assistant to prevent it harming the library, and you tried to stop me. Many times.'

Yolanda ignored her. 'Your last question, Evar Eventari, was "how?". The how of it is that this ganar, Celcha, applied the power and the influence she gained from her use of the Exchange to have these automata built as agents of her revenge. They were built to hunt and kill you and Livira Page.'

Evar shook his head. 'That's nonsense. I've never even met a ganar. None of them is going to devote themselves to killing me.' Though as he said it a cold tingle ran the length of his spine. What the child had said made no sense, but it also had a strange kind of truth to it.

'I've never seen a ganar either,' Livira protested. In the distance the crashing came again as more shelf-towers surrendered to overwhelming force.

'Well, a ganar has seen you and she was not well pleased.' Yolanda turned and led on towards the corridor to the reading room, now just a hundred yards or so away. 'Using the Exchange comes with a price. Any assistant worth their keep should have prevented you from doing so. As to your book – it should have stayed in the past where its damage was limited. The assistant who sent you to retrieve it has been corrupted and intended only harm.'

'You found your book?' Evar asked Livira. He nearly called it his book. He felt that he had lived among the pages as long as she had, maybe longer.

The worry lines scoring Livira's face deepened, the carefree nature that defined her banished. Evar found himself hating whoever had done that to her.

'I found it. But they took it.' She looked in the direction they'd come. 'Back there . . .' She paused. 'Those cracks . . . I think they all spread from where I hit the ground when the Exchange spat me out.'

Evar reached out a hand and set it on her far shoulder, guiding her closer to him. 'Can one book really cause that much trouble?' Whether it could or not, the fact seemed to be that metal monsters created solely for the purpose of hunting and killing Livira were on the march, and Evar, while having no idea how to stop them, had no intention of letting it happen.

Livira shrugged his hand away and advanced on Yolanda. 'You couldn't have told me any of this while you were trying to stop me?' Anger in her voice.

'Would you have believed me? Do you believe me now?'

'I don't know . . . maybe. But it would have been nice to have had the chance to decide.'

'There are rules.' Yolanda glanced at Yute. 'Though my father seems to have forgotten them. Rules about what can be said and done in given places and given times. Which lines can cross, which must stay apart. And you ran headlong through all of them. I tried not to repeat your crime.'

They walked on without speaking.

They reached the passage to the reading room well ahead of the automaton, and entered it, leaving the distant sounds of rending metal and crashing books behind them. Evar noticed that Yolanda had picked up a fairly big tome along the way. A volume whose cover displayed a large circle in which a black half swirled symmetrically into a white half.

The chamber Yute's daughter led them to contained nothing but the Mechanism at its centre. If there had ever been reading desks here, not even their dust remained. An assistant waited in front of the Mechanism's door.

'Is that . . .?' Livira squinted as if there might be some detail that would tell one assistant from the next. 'Is he the one who—'

'He who was Hellet,' Yolanda said. 'Brother to Celcha of the ganar. The enemy's willing tool, shaped by the plans of Mayland of the canith. He managed to covertly corrupt an assistant, by sowing the seed before the initial conversion.'

'I still don't understand what these ganar have against me and Evar,' Livira protested.

'The Exchange breeds and multiplies coincidence. It is part of its engine. The way it functions.' Yolanda shook her head. 'Surely you know this? Did you think such things end at the portals it delivers you through, or, like the illusions and translations, might also not follow you, entangling you with others to whom you are already connected?'

'I . . .' Livira let her silence answer.

Yolanda shook her head. 'The library's founder waits for us within. The enemy is with him. It is a time for choosing sides.'

'Irad and Jaspeth are in there?' Evar's eyes widened and he stared at the uninspiring grey lump of the Mechanism.

Yolanda shrugged. 'If you like.'

Stick-shot in the distance broke through the irregular crashes of the automaton's approach. Livira spun around in alarm, her expression fading from shock to something unreadable. 'I can't!' She started back towards the exit and the sound of their enemies. 'Oanold and the others . . . they're eating people. Our people! Gevin – they're eating Gevin! That's the evil here. Not Irad or Jaspeth. The library's not the problem. It's us. We're the evil, humans, it's us.'

Meelan, still holding his sister's hand, called out. 'Yute told us how many of them there are. Soldiers armed with 'sticks. They'll just kill us all, Livira!'

Livira looked towards him, her face tragic but determined. 'I'm scared too. I didn't say what I should have said. I was too scared to lose you all. Too selfish. But we can't not go back. We just can't. Or at least I can't. I wouldn't be able to look any of you in the eye. If I saved myself like that, I wouldn't be worth saving.'

'Livira!' Evar caught her arm. He wanted to tell her she shouldn't go, or couldn't go, that it was madness, that the monsters would kill her. The ones of her own kind. But he understood the look on her face now. Guilt. And he knew that anything he said to stop her would only erode whatever esteem she had for him. So, all he found to say was, 'I'll come with you.'

'No!' Yolanda's voice became a cold wind. 'By your own admission, you've given the greatest weapon into the hands of the greatest evil. That book is a flame of its own making and the fire that spreads from it may consume the library itself. Now you will stand before the powers that be and make an account of yourself. You will not throw away the lives of the only people who might yet undo the damage you have wrought!'

'Which people?' Evar asked, still holding onto Livira's arm, though whether he was her anchor in this storm, or she his, he couldn't tell.

'You two, of course!' And with that Yute's daughter strode towards the grey door of the Mechanism. The door became fog before her, and she passed through it, both arms clasped around the book she held over her chest. Nothing but the swirling of the mist marked her passage.

'Only one person can go in at a time?' Livira said weakly, looking at Evar for confirmation.

Evar nodded. 'That's what we were always told.'

'But today,' said Yute, going into the Mechanism after his daughter, 'we've been summoned by the ones that made the rules.'

A library may grow big enough to hold every
fact concerning the mechanics of the universe,
but truth itself is larger than any page.

The First Book of Irad

CHAPTER 41

Arpix

Arpix followed Yute through the mist of the grey door. He had heard Livira's many tales of the one Mechanism she knew about, but he had never visited. He put that reticence down to the fact that while nobody had told him not to enter it, the Mechanism was clearly a secret held close by the deputies and head librarian. When they wanted him to know about it, Arpix reasoned, they would tell him.

Another part of him whispered that this law-abiding excuse was just something he'd reached for gratefully, and that the truth was that it was fear which had held him back. Livira had told him how Evar and his siblings had been trapped within the device for whole lifetimes and more. Arpix had been wary of exposing himself to such risk and had ungenerously characterized the transportation Livira described as 'cheating'. He would, he said, rather absorb books through his eyeballs, and leave the rest of his anatomy out of the experience.

Even now as the grey mist swallowed Yute from sight, Arpix hesitated. Behind him, Jella paused too. 'You don't have to.'

Arpix nodded to himself. He didn't have to. But Clovis would. Jella would. All the people he loved would. All the people he had left in the world. He made fists of his hands, telling himself that he was tired of his dried-up, tight-wrapped existence, tired of himself, and ready for change. And with that, he stepped into the mist.

From the stories Livira had told him, Arpix was expecting to step into another world of light and colour and fascination. Instead, a darkness enfolded him, a darkness so profound that it devoured ideas as small as up and down, and took with them any notion of a floor beneath his feet. It consumed even time itself. This was the void that had held Evar Eventari until the bones of his parents had become dust along with those of generations to follow.

Two points of light hung in the Mechanism's night, and Arpix wondered if they had always been there, and he had somehow failed to see them until now. They became closer, brighter, larger, resolved by his attention into two thrones, each in its own pool of light, a great space between them as if at opposite extremes of some vast dais.

In the same way that the lights had entered Arpix's mind, each throne now held an occupant who might have been there all along. A man on each throne, somehow conveying an impression of great size despite the fact that there was nothing here to offer scale.

The man on the left sat upright, a regal gravitas to the planes and angles of his face that was never present in King Oanold's, not even in the flattery stamped upon the realm's coins. Dark hair curled from beneath a silver circlet to frame his features. The blade of his nose reminded Arpix strangely of Carlotte. A librarian's robe wrapped him, the same grey as the Mechanism, and across his lap lay a large black book.

The man occupying the other throne lounged in his seat. He shared sufficient similarities with the librarian that he might be a younger brother. The same dark curls, though longer and unkempt. The same prominent nose and dark, watchful eyes, though with a glint of humour. The stubble on chin and cheeks might, with another week, constitute a beard. In place of the other's robes he wore a motley of browns with flashes of crimson. The garb of a traveller, perhaps. The staff leaning against his throne looked more suited to walking than to ceremony.

Arpix looked for the others, Livira, Clovis, Yute, Evar . . . but if the void held them, it did not reveal them. The men on the thrones seemed to be focused on the far distance and neither deigned to acknowledge his presence.

'Hello?' Arpix's voice came out more timidly than he would have liked. It seemed almost a crime to break the silence.

'Ah,' the older man rumbled. 'It has come to this now?'

The younger man looked at Arpix with mild interest. 'Arpix Reed. A true son of the library if ever there was one.'

'Might I enquire . . .' Arpix started again. 'You have me at a disadvantage. Your names?'

The older man cleared his throat. 'I have read enough books to know that saying I have many names would be an awful cliché. Call me Irad. My brother is Jaspeth.'

Arpix made an awkward bow. 'And I am here . . . because?'

'We asked for you and you came,' Jaspeth said.

'You're here to decide the library's fate.' Irad bowed his head.

'You're here to settle a bet.' Jaspeth grinned, white teeth in the darkness of his face.

'Just me?' Arpix stammered a little.

'All of you.' Irad waved a hand as if Arpix were part of a sizeable audience. 'All of you who have become part of this tangle.'

Arpix gathered his courage. 'Forgive me, but the library spans worlds and time. Surely its fate can't depend on my friends and me?'

Jaspeth sat forward in his throne, reaching for his staff. He eyed Arpix as if he might agree with his assessment of his lack of consequence, then shrugged. 'Every crack has to begin as the smallest of things, even if it grows to split away some vast tonnage of ice, or to divide a planet. Even the shattering of reality must begin with a hairline fracture.' He looked over at Irad. 'My family has a poor history with fratricide. We invented it. This gathering – this delegation – is our answer to the irreconcilable views we've been gifted. We will abide by the outcome of your efforts and thereby avoid violence between us. Whether you can do the same is a question for you.'

Irad folded the fingers of one hand through those of the other. 'There will be a time of choosing. Sooner than you think. Sides must be picked and taken. The decisions made here matter. They will echo through time. I invite you to choose the vision I have laid out. The library as it would have been had my brother not opposed me. Every work that has ever been committed to record by any species made available to all, without the barriers of language or distance. A library with so many doors that it will never be out of reach. A place where all opinion, discovery, and imagination can be summoned in a comprehensible form without delay. Immortal memory to counter the fragility of flesh. A ladder by which intelligence may ascend. With such a gift any species could hardly fail to reach nirvana.'

Jaspeth, who had been shaking his head slowly, now focused on Arpix and the intensity of his stare felt as if the noon-day sun were blazing upon him.

'Many poisons taste sweet. Much that is deadly proves pleasing to the eye. My brother's gift is such a thing. Wisdom is difficult to write down, harder to find amid the ocean of the unwise, and, when found, next to impossible to learn from a page. The wisdom to use knowledge must be earned rather than given. That takes time. Lifetimes. Millennia. Knowledge without wisdom is fire in the hands of children. You know this.

'There *is* a ladder to the heavens, but there are no shortcuts when it comes to scaling it. When you fall you must start afresh, without the fear of falling that memory will bring, without the fatal distance that memory will place beneath you as it lifts you back to the highest point that any have reached so far. My brother's library presents itself as wings with which you might fly, but in truth it shackles you in ways that are difficult to see. A clean slate is the real freedom. Fresh innocence. *Tabula rasa.*'

'And the third way?' Arpix dared to speak into the pause after Jaspeth fell silent. They had, after all, summoned him and spoken of choices.

The mouths of both brothers quirked in disapproval but in that same moment a third figure appeared, standing between the thrones, dwarfed by them, confirming Arpix's previously unfounded belief that Irad and Jaspeth were as tall as houses.

Yute stood there, tiny and pale. 'There are many other paths.'

Irad looked down at him, frowning. 'I fashioned you from nothing. Just as the creator made his angels from light and void.'

'And some of them still fell.' Yute studied his hands. 'Some fell as far as I have. Perhaps lower still.' He looked up, staring in Arpix's direction, though Arpix now understood that he was more than a hundred yards away and if Yute could also see a hidden audience then maybe his gaze had found another to settle on. 'I offer compromise. The library has, for many cycles of men, canith, and countless others, existed under this compromise—'

'And it has failed to prevent disaster a thousand times,' Jaspeth interrupted without heat.

'It has.' Yute bowed his head. 'But unlike your solution, Lord Jaspeth, or Lord Irad's, compromise has many forms. It can change, adjust, seek new solutions. That is my only defence of it. That is my plea to any who will join me and avoid absolutes.

'Believe me when I say that whatever choices you make in this matter, you will not be my enemy. Irad and Jaspeth are – forgive me, my lords – archetypes. Neither is inherently wrong, neither is evil, and those who follow them deserve neither credit nor censure for that choice.

'Evil, such as it is, is found far closer to home. It is found among humans, among canith, and in every other form of intelligence. What follows us in the library is as close to evil as I've seen.

'King Oanold has in his possession, though he doesn't yet know it, a weapon to put all others to shame. A weapon forged by the unwitting trespass of a human and a canith. Some of you will have heard me speak of the fire-limit. The level of technology a people are able to reach before they burn their world down with it. Sometimes the fire is the hot flicker that consumes cities and eats through library shelves. Sometimes the fire is of a more advanced kind that can scour bedrock and poison the skies. Sometimes it will even shatter worlds. But with the book that Livira and Evar have created, King Oanold has reached a fire-limit where the flames are of the sort that can reduce the laws of nature to ash and burn the very substance of the library rather than merely the books within it.'

Jaspeth stood from his throne. 'Compromise is a cancer, a rot that destroys what it touches. At least my brother's vision is clear. It has purity to it. It's wrong, but there is nothing soft or corrupt to it, nothing hidden to be revealed later.' His dark gaze swept the void and Arpix felt the tingle of it on his skin. 'Let us see the place where compromise took my brother's fallen angel.' He stamped the heel of his staff on whatever invisible ground he stood upon.

Where Yute had been Arpix saw another Yute. Blood and panic covered the face of this new man. The vision showed only him and his immediate surroundings, a place that burned with the library's light. Stacks of books taller than Yute moved in and out of the vision, fading away at the edges as he hurried through a forest of the things.

Sounds reached out from the scene, distant shouts, muffled cries of pain, screaming.

The scene widened. Behind Yute and to the left dozens of the stacks had been toppled and books carpeted the floor. In one place a hand reached out, the fingers unmoving and stained with crimson. Yute hurried on, stepping around the bloody corpse of a child. A canith child. He avoided the body of an old female, grey-maned, no mark of violence visible upon her.

The scene widened again to show the trail of Yute's red footprints leading back through the bookstacks to a circle of crops where Livira's old friends, Gevin, Katrin, Neera, and a score of others from the city milled about in confusion, shock on their faces, the greenery trampled around them. At their backs stood a pool of dark water, its surface rippled and unquiet.

Another two canith bodies lay among the plants. The humans steered clear of them.

The focus returned to Yute. He reached a soldier, one of Oanold's veterans who had skirmished with canith out on the Dust for years before they rolled over Crath City's walls in a grey wave. Her uniform was marked with soot in places and with blood spatters.

'No! Stop!' Yute caught her sword arm as she made to skewer a canith on the ground who might or might not be dead.

The woman shook Yute off with minimal effort. An elbow to the stomach sent him staggering back, gasping for breath. She ran the length of her steel through the body at her feet, then looked back at Yute, frowning, shook her head and moved on, hunting for survivors.

Yute's voice returned as a whisper, then a croak. 'Come back. You have to stop this . . .'

Arpix knew that Yute came through the portal last, to ensure that nobody who left the library with him used any of the other portals. It seemed clear, though, that he hadn't known what would be waiting for them on the other side of the doorway. He arrived last, and the soldiers were already exacting what they considered vengeance upon what looked to be a largely unarmed community of canith living in the library.

Arpix, who was already sickened by the cruel aftermath of the slaughter, suddenly had a bad feeling about who these canith might be. It was the way of the Exchange, when left without instruction, to link things, to bring together causes and effects, wants and desires, to fit one piece to another.

The void in which he hung allowed no sounds other than those from the vision Jaspeth was sharing, but somehow, rippling under the quiet between the fading sounds of murder among the stacks, Arpix could feel the silence shaking with Clovis's howling.

Yute moved on, one arm across his stomach, half a run, half a stagger. His path took him past the bodies of a score of canith, most cut down from behind. Two soldiers lay dead, one with a missing throat, the other's head smashed against the floor. Their weapons had already been salvaged. He passed the entrance to one of the reading rooms. A tall figure stood beside a shorter, fatter man who was in the process of placing a grey wig upon his bald head. A dozen soldiers flanked the pair, most staring where the tall man's singular gaze was directed: down the corridor.

'Algar! Stop this madness! These aren't—'

'When you find cockroaches in the kitchen of your new home you stamp on them.' The fat man turned around as a soldier helped him into a robe of purple velvet lined with ermine. 'You don't say, "These are different cockroaches, let us give them a chance to prove themselves."' King Oanold faced Yute, the remnants of his disguise – the dress and shawl of some older noblewoman – on the floor beside him.

Yute saw soldiers at the far end of the corridor running as if in pursuit of someone. 'We have to leave. Now! We need to go back and try another door.'

Algar exchanged a look with the king. 'Our soldiers seem to like it here. They're doing an excellent job of driving back the sabbers.'

'Driving them back?' Yute's outrage loaned rare colour to his words. 'They're slaughter—'

'Did we not just leave my city in flames? My library?' Oanold roared. 'This is justice! It's mercy compared to the retribution that the law demands.'

Yute stared from the lord to the king. He straightened and drew his untidy robes around him. 'In the chambers beyond this one these people maintain armies that dwarf the one which invaded our city. Consider this a peaceful village surrounded by fortresses. I have unwittingly helped you to bypass their defences, but if we don't leave now, by the same route that brought us here, their kin will come in numbers so great . . .'

Distant cries of pain and fear rattled down the corridor from the reading room. Human voices. The sounds of a tide turning, of an advance becoming a retreat.

'. . . perhaps it has already started,' Yute said.

Knowledge is a deadly weapon, but for those
too lazy to wield such a blade, simply hand it to
your foe and let them destroy themselves.

Attributed to Jaspeth

CHAPTER 42

Livira

Livira hung in the void and watched as Irad and Jaspeth spoke to an audience that might be millions strong or might just be her. Somewhere deep inside her she knew that, like the Exchange, what this place was showing her was coloured by her expectation. It had patterned itself to fit with a mythology she knew. The library and its creators were both larger than any one mythos, and what Irad and his brother truly were she could not imagine. If they owned singular selves and revealed that truth to her, perhaps she would be unable to comprehend it, or she might burn up in the light of their divinity.

They spoke of her as the author of a crack that had been written into the world. Something that could spread and destroy. She had never meant to do harm. Maybe that was the only way in which the indestructible could fail and the immortal come to their ends: through the work of the ignorant. Structures that could withstand any assault might, in the end, fall to mistakes and to the random actions of those not seeking to bring them down.

Yute was summoned from the void to stand between the two gods, one a deity of memory, the other of oblivion, and Livira's heart went out to him. He looked too small to bear the weight of everything that lay between the two brothers.

Even as Yute spoke, Livira saw the battle he had to fight. The brothers each offered a pure vision, something grand, a statement easily made and easy to line up behind. Yute's stained compromise came fraught with grey edges, too much choice, too little clarity, every boundary open to endless discussion and debate.

Even so, Jaspeth seemed threatened by him, enough to stand from his throne and replace Yute with a vision of a past Yute whose actions might speak louder than his words and might linger in memory long after his arguments were forgotten.

It took Livira longer to understand what she was seeing than she felt it should have. The realization that she was looking at the sabber raid that had slaughtered Evar's people hit her like a blow to the stomach. Her people, Jons – the soldier who had, with Malar, brought her from the Dust – were part of that massacre. Even those from the Dust merely stood and watched, not seeking to intervene.

Lord Algar, whose enmity had plagued her ever since childhood, had broadened his wickedness to genocide. King Oanold at last had the canith he had always wanted, a people untutored in war, ripe to fall before the scythe of his bitter veterans.

But Yute – Yute had been the key to it. How had he forgotten so much of his past power? He had been an assistant and the library had been an open book to him. But a millennium of city life had left him little more equipped to navigate the Exchange than she'd been on her first visit.

It hadn't been his fault. Not exactly. He'd balanced the harm that might be done by loose humans in the Exchange against the seemingly small chance of trouble occurring in the small gap between the first refugees passing through the portal and his own arrival. It seemed as if that delay had been longer than it should have been, though. Even given the size of the party. Had something kept him in the Exchange longer than he had planned? Or was it perhaps an artifact of the way time flowed at different speeds inside and outside the wood?

Either way, Jaspeth had made a shrewd play. However guiltless Yute might be, the canith would now hear the screams of their ancestors behind all of his arguments. And the rest of them would see that his attempt to navigate unknown waters had caused great harm. How could such a man sail the far more hostile seas that lay between Irad and Jaspeth's shores?

As the vision of Yute's past deeds began to fade, Livira felt a pull and recognized its source. Yute's recollection of his time as an assistant might have been wiped clean by the passage of centuries and the difficulty of any timeless knowledge finding space in a mind caught within the flow. But Livira's experience lay little more than a day behind her, and her memory had been a thing of legend among the librarians. The pull was the Mechanism at work. They were being ejected. They would stumble from its doors, over a score of them, back into the dangers that had chased them into the reading room, and straight into the fire of the argument that Irad and Jaspeth had lit beneath them.

'Evar.' Livira spoke the word into the void. 'Evar Eventari!' She wanted time with him and him alone. She wanted to speak without an audience. She wanted his attention without the competition of friends and enemies. '*Evar.*' And drawing on faint echoes of the Assistant's power, she made a space in which they both stood. A room of shadows and flame flickers.

'Livira?' Evar looked around him and came to her, arms reaching.

Livira wrapped her own arms around the canith, surprised once more by the size of him, the sheer physicality after being so long beyond touch, the smell of him, an animal scent, distinct, strong even, but provoking an undercurrent of excitement as she breathed him in. She buried her face in the hollow just beneath his sternum, her cheek subject to the innumerable soft prickles of the short fur there.

They stood in the embrace, neither of them willing to break the silence with questions or words of any sort, lest doing so might somehow invite a wider world and its problems into their moment.

At last, Evar shifted his hands until they were under her arms. She stood still, not knowing what to expect. When, without apparent effort, he lifted her until their faces were level and the best part of a yard lay beneath her dangling toes.

'I missed you.'

'I missed you too.' She had, if ached were another word for missed.

'Let's not lose each other again.'

'No.' Livira shook her head. If she had been in charge of the distance between them, she would have closed it immediately and repeated their first kiss.

Evar brought her to him, and pressed his face into her neck, nuzzling, a deep sound in his throat that sounded as if it came from a beast far larger than him, a northern bear perhaps, or a mountain ox. His mane engulfed her and with it that scent of his which filled her lungs with trembling desire.

'Where are we?' Evar lowered her to her feet, and she found her legs less willing to hold her up than they had been just a short while before.

'A place . . . I made.' Livira wasn't sure how to say it. 'A pause between the world's breathing. Time won't notice we're gone, but I don't know how long I can keep us here.'

Evar sighed. 'Yute brought the killers to my home.'

'He didn't know. It's Oanold that deserves the blame.' Livira hesitated, unsure. It *was* Oanold who deserved the blame, but surely all those others, the soldiers who had followed his order, deserved the blame too. Perhaps there hadn't been any order and the mere sight of canith without weapons had been enough to spur them into slaughter. It went deeper. The soldiers were just people. People given leeway, grievance, and a sharp edge to rebalance the scales. The canith were hardly saints. Every one of those trapped then killed in the chamber were descendants of the warrior and the priest who had come to Livira's settlement and watered the Dust with the blood of simple farmers. The same warrior and priest who had scaled Crath's walls and set the city on fire. 'There's a lot of blame,' she concluded, unhappy at the defeat in her voice. If she could hate one group or the other, she would at least take some comfort in the purity of that conviction. As it was, she feared that, if she allowed it, the world might one day bring her insights that would undermine her hate even for Algar or Oanold; she might come to understand them as products of weakness and circumstance rather than demons spat from a dark hell with motivations that were simple evil and nothing else. Livira shivered. For a moment it even seemed that Jaspeth might be right – too much information could drown you;

the world was simpler in black and white, more easily enjoyed, less fraught with guilt.

Evar studied her silence. 'Yute brought them. That's all Clovis will have heard.' He looked sad. 'Whatever happens, I am on your side, Livira. I won't arrive too late again.'

'Whatever happens.' Livira felt scared. She wasn't given to fear, though she had been so full of it when Oanold had her that she thought it might stop her heart. This fear was a different kind. A dread. The conviction that nothing would be right no matter how hard they might wish it. 'Whatever happens, we'll face it together.'

'Together.' Evar bent towards her, and the kiss came, sweeter and deeper than before, and closer to their final one.

*The wait for the world to tell you that you're
special can be a long and lonely one. Better to get
off your arse and let it know that you are.*

Blowing Your Own Horn: Lesson 1:
Pucker Up, *by Miles Smoly*

CHAPTER 43

Evar

Evar walked out of the Mechanism, blinking against the library's
light. He had seen the door as a bright rectangle in the void.
Distant at first but closer with each step. Until the moment he
escaped, a large part of him didn't believe that, even with Livira's
help, the thing would let him go. And yet, stepping out had been
as easy as stepping in. On the threshold, a strange anger suffused
him, as if he had wanted the Mechanism to acknowledge its
debt to him, as if he had wanted it to remember him as special,
not simply another visitor to be taken in and set free like any
other.

The scene that met his return blew those thoughts away like dust
before the storm. Strangers, screaming, struggling, harsh shouts. The
newcomers seemed all to be soldiers – just like those in the vision
that Jaspeth had shown them – only leaner and dirtier. Scores of
soldiers were wrestling Yute's people into submission, binding their
hands with cords, rope, or even strips of cloth. Those resisting were
being clubbed or punched. Evar spotted Arpix's long, skinny form
sprawled on the ground, unmoving, a bloody wound on his forehead,
hands tied behind his back.

Soldiers stood to either side of the Mechanism's door, waiting to seize everyone as they emerged. It seemed that the last in had been the first out. He was the first canith to return.

Perhaps Oanold's army had grown complacent as they overwhelmed unprepared civilians, some of them children or elderly. Maybe the appearance of a canith stunned them for a heartbeat. Or perhaps humans were just that slow. But even taken by surprise, Evar managed to strike the nearest soldier with a flat palm to the chest, hard enough to lift him from his feet. At the same time Evar pulled the man's sword from his scabbard with his other hand.

Evar spun, tumbling another soldier and driving his stolen blade to the depth of its hilt through the chest of the man who had taken hold of Livira. He would have done more. A lot more. But someone among his many opponents threw a grenade. The explosion was by far the loudest thing Evar had ever heard and smoke swept in behind the shockwave, so fast that it swallowed all and any carnage.

For several dazed moments Evar staggered about, arms out in front of him, hunting Livira. He was sure he was calling her name, but no sound reached his ears. Instead, they were filled with a great, pulsing silence that sang a single high note.

His confusion cleared long before the smoke did but, lacking sight or hearing, his mind had little to work with. Time and again he collided with bodies that came out of the surrounding cloud. He dealt with them more gently now, not knowing friend from foe, seeking Livira.

Another concussion hammered through the smoke, further away this time. He turned towards it and found his arms full of Livira. She recognized him and clung tight. Evar held her with one arm, rotating slowly to ward off any danger that might come out of the thinning smog.

'What in the hells?' Clovis emerged from the Mechanism, Kerrol at her shoulder.

Immediately Clovis went to one knee beside the soldier Evar had killed. In her right hand the white sword pointed towards potential attackers while with her left she rolled the man from his front to his back. A snarl twisted her face, exposing teeth from front to back.

The smoke hung thickest around the mouth of the corridor to the main chamber. Its retreat revealed a dozen and more of Yute's party, most huddled on the floor, some still struggling to free each other from the bonds they'd been secured with. None of the soldiers remained save the dead man and another hobbling into the smoke with a broken gait, bent around some agony.

'Arpix!' Evar looked around for the man who he'd come to realize was his first human friend apart from Livira. 'Arpix?'

Clovis stood sharply, stricken. 'Where is he?'

'They must have taken him,' Evar growled. 'They were going to take them all. I saw—'

'Keep them safe.' Clovis pulled the orb from her armour and tossed it to Kerrol.

'They'll eat him. They'll eat him alive!' Livira broke free of Evar's arm and started running towards the corridor. 'I've seen it.'

Evar caught her before she got ten yards.

Clovis passed them both at speed, aimed at the retreating smoke. The route Oanold and his soldiers had taken to reach this place and this period – the two steps they had taken through time – had picked those same marauders who had slaughtered Clovis's family when she was a small girl and placed them in front of her as a grown warrior. Their first jump in time had consumed most of the two hundred years that had always stood between Livira and Evar, and the second smaller jump had devoured the last decade or so, allowing Clovis the time to grow, whilst the soldiers' guilt still lay fresh upon their shoulders, the blood of Clovis's community still staining the uniforms of those King Oanold commanded.

Others of Yute's party crowded around them. Meelan, Leetar, Jella.

'They're saying they got Salamonda too. And Neera.' Angry sobs broke Livira's command of Evar's tongue so it became hard to understand her.

'And Yute?' she asked Meelan.

'No.' He shook his head. Evar's grip on the human's language remained weak but he understood that Yute had yet to return from the Mechanism.

Livira twisted free of Evar's hands. 'I'm going with her!' She pointed at Clovis's retreating figure, now barely visible through the smoke. 'To get Arpix.' She strode off without looking back.

Evar made to go after her, but Meelan grabbed his arm and stared up, locking eyes, speaking with great intensity. 'A hundred of them. Weapons. Arrow-sticks. Soldiers. You can't win.'

Evar looked down into the young man's pale, serious face. 'I have to try.' He twisted his mouth around the strange words.

Meelan bowed his head. 'We'll all go. Arpix would come after me.'

Meelan's sister grabbed his arm as he stepped forward, and Evar set a hand to his chest. 'Me and Clovis. You slow us down.' With that he turned to Kerrol. 'You know what's coming?'

His brother nodded, eyes sombre.

Evar sprinted after Livira and scooped her up, knowing she would hate him for it. Ignoring her screams and punches, he hurried back to Kerrol with her and handed her into the prison of his brother's arms. He fell to his knees before her.

'I am *so* sorry, Livira.' He bowed his head before her screams of frustration. 'I'm not strong enough to see you die.'

And with that he turned, racing after his sister, passing over the head and headless body of the first straggler before he caught her up as she navigated the chamber beyond.

In the main chamber, Evar and Clovis faced the forest of shelf-towers once more, each steel-cored and reaching hundreds of yards up to brace the ceiling. The huge ganar automaton had been making slow but steady progress. Thousands of the towers lay in twisted ruins behind it amid the clutter of their contents. But still it had advanced less than halfway across the floor's expanse and had half a mile to go before reaching the reading room.

Even so, the constant thunder of falling books, and the deep twang of metal fists striking steel columns, drowned out any cries from those the soldiers had abducted.

'There are a lot of them,' Evar said.

'They're just sabbers.' Clovis rolled her head, neck joints cracking.

'Humans,' Evar corrected.

Clovis pinned him with her fiercest look. 'Arpix is human, and I would face this danger for him alone. But the ones who took him are the sabbers I've been hunting my whole life. They're the ones who killed my father, killed my mother, killed my true brothers.' The fierceness faltered at this as if she might have taken a step too far in the matter of brothers that were true or false. 'You might take my war away from me with common sense and talk of where guilt ends and innocence begins. But *this* is *my* battle. The one I've waited for since the day they came. And here, somehow, lifetimes later, those same sabbers have delivered themselves to me and I will have my accounting with them. This won't end until the last of these bastards has bled upon my blade – the Soldier's blade: they killed him too, remember? I'm going to save Arpix, kill the king, and take this weapon, this book everyone's talking about. This won't end until every last one of these fuckers dies. And every kill you take from me I will hold against you, little brother.'

Evar bowed his head. He couldn't argue with her. He had wanted to rescue whoever could be rescued. Arpix, Salamonda, and Neera first since they were dearest to Livira's heart and to his own. If he came back with them then she would forgive him for leaving her in Kerrol's arms. He would have been satisfied with a rescue. But Clovis would have her slaughter to weigh against the slaughter of old and, right or wrong, Evar would not leave her to the task alone.

'Come on.' Evar took the lead. He wondered where the skeer warrior was. If it remained in the chamber, he hoped it found the soldiers first rather than him. Let them expend their ammunition on the insectoid.

The orchard layout of the towers offered many long avenues of sight that narrowed into invisible distance, but the soldiers could not be seen down any of them. Instead, Evar had to rely on the training Starval had given him. In many places tracking the band's progress was easy enough. Footprints in dust, spatters of blood, and dislodged books all told a tale. In other spots Evar's decisions hinged on the smallest of clues. Sometimes instinct or an educated guess served.

Before long though he could smell them and follow the charnel reek around every twist and turn. He came close enough to hear the tramp of feet, and glimpse figures hurrying along ahead of them only to be lost among the towers as the angles changed.

Evar's heart began to thunder both with anticipation and with dread. The dead man's blood still coated his stolen blade. Evar hadn't enjoyed killing him. He knew humans, ones that he liked and loved. Taking the lives of others – even the worst of them – was not something he wanted to become used to.

When Clovis's hand closed on Evar's shoulder, and brought him to an unexpected halt, the tension inside him almost swung his sword her way. 'Sorry!'

Clovis snorted as if the idea he might have hurt her was comical. 'We need to go up. Projectile weapons in straight aisles can defeat the best of us. It's how the Soldier – their Malar – died. And he was a fine warrior, even as a human.'

'You nearly killed him back in the Exchange that time without even thinking about it,' Evar protested.

'Focus!' Clovis punched his chest. 'We're not here to talk about that. We're here to do this.' She shook her head. 'And I *did* have to think about it. It might not have looked like it but that little human almost got me that time.' Clovis tapped the side of her head. 'Focus.' And in the next instant she was swarming up a shelf-tower.

Ten yards above the ground Clovis struck out after their prey. She ran, setting her feet to the tight-packed books first on one shelf then on a shelf at the same level but on a different tower further along. And in this manner, skipping along the narrow and unstable edges offered to her, Clovis danced through the air high above the soldiers' heads.

Evar followed, able to match her agility though delayed when one set of books betrayed him, spilling to the ground and leaving him lunging for the opposite tower to keep from falling.

The crash of books brought soldiers and their 'sticks swivelling in Evar's direction, yet still they didn't see him, their aim focused at ground level and on the dislodged tomes.

Clovis dropped among the enemy where they stood thickest. She spun, sweeping an arc that became a circle and, where the white blade went, bodies fell apart in crimson floods. She felled two more soldiers and was away, leaping from shelf-tower to shelf-tower, gaining elevation as if climbing a staircase that only she had the wit to see.

Evar closed his open mouth, aware that in the time Clovis had killed eight of the foe, he had done exactly nothing. Shouts went up among the dozens of troops scattered among the towers. A book close to Evar's head jerked into the air and plunged to the ground, leaving fragments of pages swirling in its wake. A bullet! It had been hit by a bullet!

Evar leapt for a different pillar, closing off the angle that the shot might have come from. Other projectiles buzzed through the air.

'There! Up there!' Another soldier spotted him, calling her comrades to her. Four of them charged towards the base of his tower, swords drawn.

If they weren't fighting him, they could be coming at Clovis from behind while she fought others. He needed to play his part.

Evar leapt into their path. He landed as Starval had taught him, rolled beneath their blades, bowled three of them over, half decapitated the fourth. Then he was moving, dodging this way and that, coming swiftly upon new enemies and leaving them behind him, stunned, wounded, or dead.

Every stride placed Evar at the centre of another set of avenues radiating out along the compass points and the diagonals, a set of lines down which anyone with a 'stick might sight their weapon. He kept moving, jinking left, jinking right, relying on his speed to gain the initiative in every encounter.

A man slid from Evar's blade. Another flew back as Evar shoulder-charged him, sending him crashing into the nearest shelves with a sickening crunch. From time to time Evar glimpsed his sister crossing the line of his vision. More often he found her victims, their bodies ruined by sword blows. Always he heard her roaring rage, her shattered howls ricocheting among the towers.

Ahead of him Evar saw a group of soldiers and the first of the humans not wearing a uniform. The man stood taller than the five around him, though he was less broad than the rest. For a mad moment Evar thought he'd found Arpix, but as the man's head turned his way Evar saw that in place of Arpix's rags he wore a fine cloak, and that he was older, with a crimson eyepatch.

Evar raised his sword in challenge, the edge blunted by the work already accomplished. He moved to close the distance and make his attack but found himself on both knees. The small red hole in his jerkin just below his pectoral muscle confused him, as did the fact that he was keeling.

Two of the soldiers advanced cautiously on him, blades levelled, the one-eyed man just at their backs. Evar still had things to learn about human expressions but felt confident in saying that the man's smile promised nothing good.

Footsteps approached from behind too, and Evar, understanding at last that he had been shot, struggled to get up. He only made it to one knee.

'It's a shame it can't understand me,' the man said. Evar thought he must be the Lord Algar that Livira had written of in her books. 'Look at his eyes, though. He knows this is going to hurt.' Algar glanced around. 'Haven't they caught the others yet? I hope this isn't the only one we take alive.'

One of the soldiers stepped forward, arm raised for the killing blow.

'Stop, you idiot!' Algar snapped. 'Just tie it up. We'll let the circle heal it, and then see what punishments the king has in mind.'

'Good eating on one of these,' a female grunted behind Evar. Some of the others laughed. Algar made no response, but his single eye burned with a hunger that was about more than food.

One of the soldiers behind grabbed Evar's arm, and he found himself too weak to stop them. His struggles merely brought another man to the task.

'Put his eye out.'

The words were spoken quietly and took a moment to register with the soldiers.

'What?' the woman asked, though it seemed she must have heard.

'His eye,' Algar said. 'It won't kill him. Indulge me. The pain might help keep him alive until we get him back to the circle.'

The woman shrugged and drew a short, broad-bladed knife of a sort used for tasks rather than combat. An arm snaked under Evar's chin from behind, controlling his head. Evar tried to bite the woman as she moved the steel point towards his right eye. She jerked her hand back.

'Kemmit, hold his head.'

A hefty, black-bearded man approached, pulling on thick leather gloves. Evar understood in that instant both the weight of fear that Livira must have felt at the mercy of these creatures, and the limitless bravery she had shown in her insistence that she go back.

Evar had said that he wasn't strong enough to see her die. He was glad now that she would not see his death.

Strong hands knotted in his mane and the knife point glimmered back into his vision. He roared and twisted but the bullet had taken more out of him than the blood filling his lung; and neither terror nor rage would put it back.

When the hot gore splattered across his face it took Evar a while to understand that it wasn't from him. Not until the bodies started to fall around him did he understand that Clovis had arrived.

'What are you doing?'

Clovis had taken hold of Evar's jerkin, grabbing it at the back by the collar, and was dragging him away.

'I'm dragging you away.'

It made sense, but this was Clovis and these were the sabbers she'd ached to revenge herself upon since she was a small girl. 'You're letting them go.'

'I'm not letting you go.'

Evar's heels traced two bloody tracks across the library floor as Clovis pulled him back the way they'd come.

'Clo, I'm dying anyway.' He coughed up a red splutter to prove it. 'Go save Arpix.'

Clovis's snarl came so loud and loaded with anguish that it sounded as if it should have burst from her in a shower of blood. A larger one than had accompanied Evar's cough. The snarl wavered, gained strength, strayed towards a howl, then stumbled into words. 'I can't leave you.'

'Clo—'

'There are healing circles. Arpix and the others aren't going to die in the next hour. You will. I can go back . . .'

'You can't open the door.'

'There will be a way.'

The anguish in her voice hurt Evar more than the hole in his chest did. He knew Clovis bitterly wanted to exact revenge on the soldiers who had – just weeks ago in the humans' experience – slaughtered her people. Canith blood still stained their uniforms. But more than this, he knew that particular desire was not the heaviest thing weighing against him in the scale upon which this decision had balanced. Clovis wanted to save Arpix. Even more than she wanted her vengeance. And despite those desires, both so strong that they might better be named requirements – here she was dragging him away from the battle she had dreamed of for half a lifetime.

Evar let his head loll to the left. 'And that thing's coming. It's me it wants.' The automaton's crashing advance was louder and closer. Evar caught glimpses of the destruction down every diagonal.

'It'll have to come through me,' Clovis replied past gritted teeth, picking up speed as she aimed for the reading room. They had no chance of making it to the centre circle in the current chamber. Not if the automaton had them in its sights. They'd be intercepted before they got there.

'Leave me.' Evar coughed. 'You can come back with the others.'

'We still have time.' With a grunt Clovis reached a half-jog.

The automaton paused from tearing at the forest of bars still blocking its progress. It began to back away, the clang of metal feet on library stone managing to get an echo even from a chamber two miles across.

'It's backing up,' Evar muttered.

'That's not good.' The reading-room entrance loomed ahead of them and Clovis broke free of the shelf-towers.

Livira, Kerrol – who no longer held her – Meelan, Jella and many of the others were standing at the start of the corridor and rushed forwards as soon as they spotted Clovis.

A crowd bore Evar towards the reading chamber, speeding Clovis's effort. Behind them, back in the main chamber, the automaton's steady retreat turned into a rapidly accelerating advance, the tempo of its many-ton footfalls rising towards a roll of thunder.

'Hurry!' Clovis shouted over the approaching storm.

They didn't stop until they reached the reading room and as they carried him Evar wondered if the Mechanism might not be the way for Livira and the others to escape what was coming.

Clovis finally laid him before the Mechanism and Livira fought to his side. The anger on her face melted as she understood the seriousness of his injury. 'We need pressure on the wound, front and back!' She took his knife in a trembling hand and started to cut strips from her robe; Evar tried to apologize again for his weakness, but could only cough, speckling Livira's now-pale face in crimson.

Others reached them. Clovis stalked around Evar as Livira and Jella fussed at the holes the stick-shot had left in him. Evar let his head loll and observed proceedings, strangely distant both from his pain and from his fear. Only concern about Livira still ached within him, the rest he could slip away from – he could fall through the floor like when he was a ghost, leave it all behind him. But her tears would fall, and he would feel them no matter how deep he sank.

The Mechanism had released Yute and his daughter, but more than that it had given up two others who had presumably answered the summons before Evar's party arrived. Standing on the opposite side of the Mechanism's white door to that chosen by Yute and Yolanda were Mayland and Starval, one tall and golden, the other short, dark, and watchful.

If Yute and Yolanda held any enmity for the canith who had murdered their wife and mother respectively, none of it showed on their faces. Yute looked sad rather than vengeful. His daughter appeared pensive and, like Starval, watchful, though her focus seemed to take in more than just what might be visible to others.

Many from Yute's party had gathered around him at the Mechanism. Evar knew they would be telling him that the automaton was coming, burdening the white almost-human with their fears, seeking reassurance. Evar doubted Yute had any to give.

Starval came the other way rapidly, elbowing Livira aside to reach

Evar. He snapped a sharp glance up at Clovis. 'What have— How could you let this happen?'

Clovis made no reply, her own gaze fixed on Yute, the person who had sent Oanold and his followers to her chamber. Evar let his head roll back and took her in. Even from this unusual angle he could see the fury rising through her. Oanold's troops were the bullet that had torn through her life, but the finger on the trigger had been Yute's.

Starval tapped Evar's chest. 'The lung's flooded.'

A sudden lancing pain made Evar gasp and choke. He looked down, thinking he'd been stabbed, only to discover that he was right. Starval had thrust between his ribs what looked like a thin silver rod.

'It's draining the blood?' Livira snarled, her mastery of their language drawing a surprised look from Starval.

'Yes.'

Evar saw that the rod was a tube. He doubted that Starval carried it to save lives, but there was a crimson stream at the far end, and whilst it seemed that as a general rule blood should be kept on the inside, in this instance it did seem to be helping Evar catch his breath.

Clovis stopped her pacing. 'I should go.' She looked at him and Evar saw her conflict. 'I'm no good here. Arpix needs me.'

Evar would have told her that she was doing good. That she had saved him, and her presence made him stronger. But she was right. Arpix did need her. He managed a small nod and without another word Clovis was gone.

The pounding charge out in the main chamber ended in a huge crash, but one that didn't end as suddenly as it came. Instead, the initial collision became a prolonged rending of metal. The automaton had discovered that with sufficient run-up its momentum would carry it a considerable distance through the shelf-towers.

The tearing began to slow, but even if the automaton didn't reach them on this charge, it seemed likely that it might win through on the next effort.

'Will it save him?' Livira asked Starval as soon as her voice could be heard.

'No.' Starval looked towards Mayland. 'He needs a centre circle. Or a proper doctor. And soon.'

Starval's attention returned to Evar and, in a whisper, Evar asked the question that had been eating him ever since Mayland snapped the head librarian's neck. 'Why, brother? Why take Jaspeth's side? You want to destroy the library?' He coughed and less blood came up than before. 'Mayland killed that human. She was no threat.'

Starval raised an eyebrow in a show of surprise, though his dark eyes held something like hurt, shame even, as if the question was a blow he'd been expecting. 'You should understand, Evar. You more than anyone. They kept us trapped our whole lives, brother. You didn't even have that' – he pointed at the Mechanism without looking at it – 'for a kind of escape.' He shook his head. 'This place is an anchor around our necks. Around everyone's neck. Shouldn't we be allowed to forget? We have to be burdened by the memory of . . . everything?'

'And the librarian?'

'Have you tried omelette yet?'

Evar frowned his confusion.

'There's so much out there, Evar. Almost all of it good to eat. Eggs.' He shaped one with finger and thumb making an oval. 'Beautiful things. Perfectly designed. Full of slime that will turn into a bird if you let it. But break them and you can make an omelette, and if you'd tasted one, you'd be breaking eggs. That human—'

'She wasn't an egg, Starval.' The words hissed weakly from him, but Evar saw his brother flinch under their weight.

The automaton began another charge and conversation rapidly became impossible.

Kerrol looked towards the entrance and shouted over the din. 'It's going to be in here soon. Can we go back in?' He pointed to the Mechanism.

Evar couldn't hear what Yolanda said but he could see her shake her head. The audience was over; the rules were back in play. Starval patted Evar's shoulder and stood, turning as he did so. He ran back to Mayland and Evar watched the pair arguing for a moment before Livira seized his attention, literally. She took his mane in both hands, kneeling beside him, and steered his face towards hers, close enough that she didn't have to shout.

'You said you weren't strong enough to watch me die. Well, I'm not watching you die either, and I'm not looking away. So, that leaves you only one choice.' Her voice cracked. 'Don't die.' A tear fell. 'Please don't.'

Evar, surprised to find that he was now on his back, reached up and pulled Livira down, holding her to his good side. He felt curiously numb, slightly weightless. He decided that if he had to die this would be the way he chose, lying peacefully with the person he loved tight against him. If it weren't for how much he knew it would hurt Livira he would close his eyes right now, squeeze her to him, and sleep that sleep he needed so badly, a soft oblivion without dreams.

'Wake up!' Livira shook him.

Evar opened his eyes to see Mayland nodding slowly as Starval continued to remonstrate with him. Mayland stepped to the Mechanism's door and reached above it, placing his hand flat on the grey stuff of the structure. He bent his head as if in deep thought.

'Evar, what are you—' Livira broke off, following his gaze.

Mayland completed whatever he'd been doing and backed away. Heartbeats later the door melted into mist and an assistant stepped out from the blackness within. Maybe the same Hellet who had watched their arrival from beside the Mechanism.

From behind Evar came an awful ringing, the sound of metal columns hundreds of yards long being torn free, twisted, and sent flying to bounce against the chamber wall. The automaton had broken out of the shelf-towers. Evar caught sight of its gleaming bulk filling the corridor, coming forward, slowly now, trailing ringing steel. Before it, made tiny by its size, Clovis came running, blade in hand.

The assistant walked past Evar, past Clovis, past them all, heading towards the entrance. Up close, its white enamel had a faint ivory mottling hinting at what the library might consider impurities. The Soldier and the Assistant had shown similar signs, though Evar would never consider Livira's presence in the Assistant as something impure.

The newly arrived assistant and the huge ganar confronted each other at the entrance, the automaton hunched to fit within the corridor walls. Its metal body was dented and cut with bright scratches where jagged steel must have scraped across it. Breaking a path across the chamber had taken a toll on it where the years had failed to register.

'No.' The assistant held out a white hand, palm forward.

The mechanical ganar lunged forward with an awful silent fury. It hit an invisible wall and came to a dead halt, though Evar saw that the assistant was jolted back some fraction of an inch. Clovis came to a skidding halt behind him and lent her strength to keep his place.

The ganar recovered itself and pointed with one stubby finger. There was no ambiguity this time. The digit was aimed squarely at Evar.

His 'Why?' escaped him as a gasp.

Grace had always felt like a bystander in her own life.
She memorized names, and faces, and numberplates in
case she should ever be called on to give evidence. She died
peacefully, never regretting her decision not to take part.

Tanylorn Daily Press, Obituaries

CHAPTER 44

Celcha

To those who come and go by the doorways of the Exchange time becomes a fractured thing, best remembered as a collection of events that happened rather than something enumerated. Even so, Celcha had done her best to count the days she'd spent, some frittered away, some laid down to purchase things she had thought she needed. A hundred years was her best guess. A hundred years since the poisoning of Krath. A century of her own time, and, in the way of ganar, she was in her prime, the extremes of old age still the best part of two centuries ahead.

In the world's timeline, however, the years had raced by far more swiftly. Celcha's present lay a thousand years from the day of her birth. She had needed to let that millennium slide by, a century here, a century there, to allow her plans space to develop, allow the seeds she'd planted time to blossom.

As many had already discovered, knowledge is the most valuable and easily transported of all commodities. Pound for pound neither gold nor diamonds come anywhere close. Celcha became a trader, taking information from place to place, investing her profits.

She travelled widely, leaping decades in a single bound when required to outrun trouble or to wait for machinations to mature into materiel. In her time Celcha had been to both moons, seen her people rise and fall, rise again and fall again. She had wandered the habitable band of Attamast, commissioned wonders from the ganar at their heights, and commiserated with survivors at their lows.

On Attamast she finally found a place to set the nootki that had been pressed upon her as she left the Arthran dig. The tiny figurines sat within crystal in the palace of a great king and watched five centuries pass before war came and made new dust of all that had been built there.

Celcha never, in all those years, settled. She had been unsettled by the tragedy of her youth, and roots felt too similar to chains for her to want to sink any. She could have abandoned the Exchange, spent her years on Attamast, raised a family perhaps, and become a link in a different sort of chain. She did not.

Instead, she roamed. No matter how far she wandered, her old hurts drew her back, anchoring her to the darkest day she'd yet seen. Her understanding of the Exchange and its ways grew, but still she could never find Hellet and knew that he must be avoiding her for reasons of his own. Over the years she toyed with the idea of going back to the dig at the time when they had both laboured for Myles Carstar. She should, by rights, be able to speak to Hellet there. She could warn him about the other ghosts, and guide them both to a better future. But even before the rarest and best-hidden of the library's own books cautioned her against such madness, her own instinct saved her from that path. The library had been built to last, but obdurate as it was, even the stuff of the athenaeum could be undone by paradox.

Guilt pursued Celcha, a vast, unrelenting guilt. And although the facts bound little or none of it to her actions, the crime still owned her. She could have checked deeper, worried more, trusted less. Even the smallest sliver of responsibility for one hundred thousand lives places corpses at your feet, and lost lives could not be shrugged away, at least not by Celcha. The child, Lutna, the princess who had shown her kindness, walked with Celcha every day of her life through a hundred years and more, undaunted by distance, even to the moons themselves.

Celcha diverted what portion of that guilt she could into anger and revenge. Had she not she would have drowned in it. She spent her resources hunting the two ghosts who had picked out her brother from the obscurity of the tunnels, wound him up like a clockwork toy, and loosed him on the world. She knew, in her secret heart, that Hellet hid from her because she would ask him to show these two ghosts to her, and that he for his part had forgiven their crimes in the greater cause of bringing down the structure that had allowed such crimes and allowed their repetition in many ways and many places.

Celcha reasoned that in time her quarry would return to the library. To find someone in a place so large it pays to have many pairs of eyes watching for them. She commissioned hunters, great and small, fashioned in her image so that her enemies might know the source of their demise. She had her memory of that last day imprinted upon each of her avatars. The image of the canith male and human female dancing out their victory, kissing above the corpses of a multitude of ganar who had choked out their last breaths alongside those who had enslaved them.

The application of decades will blunt most sharp edges. The wounds that Celcha's guilt inflicted upon her grew less grievous; the flames of her rage guttered and died, though the coals remained hot as is the way of the ganar. Celcha's kind were slow to anger but slow to forgive. Hellet had been an anomaly in many ways where Celcha remained truer to the archetype.

The alarm, when it finally came, long after she had abandoned hope, reached her in the Exchange. It was carried in the person of a small messenger construct in her own likeness and borne on the currents of coincidence. She picked the head-sized metal creature out of the grass. It had been so very many years since she set the things loose in their thousands that for several moments she had no idea what it might be.

'Oh.' Memory returned. She pressed the construct to her forehead. 'They've been found!'

Celcha carried the construct into the nearest portal and let it guide her.

✦ ✦ ✦

'The past . . .' It had always been a risk. Celcha had had to advance through the years. Letting time flow by you is a means of accumulating power. Plant a seed; return a lifetime later to reap what you have sown. And now her constructs had found their prey, but the deed was already done and all that remained was for Celcha to watch it.

She ghosted through untold walls, following the direction and the purpose that had sustained her for so long in place of the life that Hellet might have wanted for her. When she finally came upon them it seemed that the pair had hardly aged from the day of their dance. That was a good thing. Her vengeance might have consumed her youth but for the authors of the great crime it would be a swift thing, hard on the heels of their victory, striking before they could enjoy the spoils.

She found them in a reading room distinguished only by the fact that it held a Mechanism. It took her a few moments to find them amid the crowd of humans and canith. When she finally found *her* canith and *her* human she was shocked to discover the canith lying amid his own blood, apparently mortally wounded, and his paramour kneeling beside him in distress.

This was not the vengeance Celcha had wanted. This was not the victory. She had always known time would claim them both as it claimed everyone. To see the deceivers die at the hand of chance made her feel cheated.

Celcha watched despite this, and as she watched she saw that the wounded canith's gaze aimed past his grieving partner to a pair of canith beside the Mechanism's door, one tall and looming over the other who might be the shortest canith she'd seen. Something about the pair disturbed her. Some sense of the familiar.

While Celcha stared and tugged at the threads of memory, the taller canith did something to the Mechanism's door and a moment later Hellet emerged. Not Hellet as she had known him, clad in the scars of past cruelty, but Hellet in the assistants' white. Even so, she knew him without hesitation, as if her still-cracked sight offered up the ghost of him surrounding the whiteness like the memory of smoke.

Even the clanging advance of some huge new threat behind her couldn't take Celcha's gaze from her brother. For his part, Hellet walked past her without a flicker of recognition. Celcha turned, calling his name, and saw emerging from the constriction of the corridor a vast likeness of herself, somewhat battered just as she now was, trailing twisted steel behind it in mockery of the chains that she still dragged through the years. A lone canith ran ahead of it, dwarfed by the avatar, underscoring the towering height of the thing.

Celcha stood amazed. She had forgotten how large some of the constructs had been. At the time it had felt justified, somehow scaled towards the size of her anger. Now it seemed excessive, but at least the former ghosts would know the author of their doom.

'No.' Hellet held out a white hand, palm forward.

The mechanical Celcha lunged forward with an awful silent fury. It hit an invisible wall and came to a dead halt, though she saw that Hellet was jolted back some fraction of an inch. The canith that had run from the avatar tried to brace him, as if her strength might somehow make a difference.

'Why?' Celcha shouted. 'Why, brother?' Why had he put himself between her vengeance and the ones who had tricked them into murdering a city?

The construct recovered itself and pointed with one finger, aiming its accusation squarely at the wounded canith and the human tending him.

'Why?' gasped the canith, no understanding on his face.

*Few conflicts can match the ferocity with which siblings
make war, their grievances born in the womb. The love that
can run between them is more rare but similarly deep.*

When Harry Met Morgan, *Nicholas Whitehall*

CHAPTER 45

Livira

'Why?' A shout.

Livira stood up, releasing Evar's too-cold hand. 'Why me?' she
shouted again. There had been nothing ambiguous in the mechanoid's aim. Its finger, scratched from tearing through a thousand
steel poles, had been aimed squarely at her heart.

'My sister made this,' the assistant answered. Grey veins spread
across him. 'Her name is Celcha.'

At mention of the name the metal beast hurled itself forwards,
this time pressing against the assistant's wall with untold force.

'I don't know any Celcha!' Livira shouted. 'I've never even seen
a ganar.'

*'Liar!' Celcha screamed the word at the girl's face, eliciting no
reaction, though at last Hellet's head moved a fraction to acknowledge her.*

'*She* saw *you* though.' A degree of effort trembled the assistant's
words. 'I suffered the same malady in my former life. When I was
her brother Hellet. Ghosts visited me most days.'

'Where did she see me?'

'When is more revealing.' Hellet looked over his shoulder at her and under the gaze of his white eyes Livira felt seized by a sense of vertigo. 'She saw you, Livira. You and Evar Eventari dancing above the necropolis she had helped me populate.'

'You did that? You killed all those people?' Even with Evar dying in her lap and a vast killing machine looming over her, Livira shuddered with the chill of that memory. The image of so many bodies lying silent and dead in their homes had never left her.

Hellet inclined his head and turned to focus on opposing the construct's efforts to reach them. A true assistant could have reduced it to dust with a wave of its hand, but Hellet's doubts were visibly corrupting the white flesh he wore.

'Dancing?' Livira remembered it. That first kiss. She'd drawn Evar into it. Her hand tightened in his mane and, weak as he was, Evar raised his own to cover hers.

Before the kiss they had danced into the sky, not knowing that a city of humans and canith lay poisoned beneath their feet. Livira lifted her face to meet the hot copper stare of the creature trying to reach them. 'But . . . we didn't know about the dead. We'd just arrived. We didn't mean to disrespect anyone.'

'Even now, even here at the end she lies!' Celcha had no control over her avatar: its purpose lay encoded in the lore that had been written through it. But if she had, she would have stamped the liar underfoot and silenced her falsehoods in one violent moment.

Hellet's words came strained with effort, spoken to the monster before him. 'She believed you were the ghosts who had paved my way to the library and schooled me in the arts of alchemy with a flawed book insufficient to the task.'

'Tell her we're not!' Livira said, shocked.

Hellet slid back several inches before strengthening his defence and bringing the ganar to a halt once more. 'This is not Celcha. She learned the ways of the Exchange better than you have and furnished herself with both education and influence.' Hints of pride and sorrow underwrote his voice. 'She seeded this part of the library with these agents of her revenge, skipping through the years in her hunt. She lies ahead of us now, unable to interfere in these events.

All we have is the anger she left behind – the hurt she imbued in this metal hulk. She is the unintended consequence of Mayland's manipulations. I' – he touched his chest – 'am the *intended* consequence. A fractured being so deeply wounded by the library that even when taken in as part of it I have worked for its destruction. I am the poisoned seed that he has sown.'

Mayland? Celcha tore one hand slowly down across her face, careless of the furrows her nails carved. Mayland? Maybe . . . She looked once more towards the canith at the Mechanism's door. One tall, one short. She had never seen Starve clearly. Never more than glimmers. An arm, a leg . . .

With a grunt, Hellet thrust forward and the construct went staggering back a dozen yards. He half turned from it, staring not at Livira but at something unseen, standing between them. 'Even understanding the wrong done to me by Mayland, I had to appreciate the elegance of the lesson, and the truth of it. The library places the power to commit vast crimes into the hands of those wholly unready for such responsibility. To fight it I took the white, and stepped out of time, losing who I was, losing everything save my intent.'

And although Livira was no longer sure the assistant was speaking to her she understood his meaning. She too had lost herself in the timeless white, rarely surfacing, and even then unable to explain herself to the mayfly lives flowering and dying around her.

Veins of ivory, old and almost yellow, were spreading across Hellet as he spoke. Grey fault lines showed themselves across his back. Livira knew the marks for what they were: the weakness and corruption that marred the assistant's perfection when the spirit within stepped out of the timeless clarity of its view and muddied itself with the now – with real emotions and desires.

'Hellet? Why did you let me . . .' But it wasn't true. He had asked her not to, and who knew how much effort those words had cost him? Words that Celcha had ignored. 'Those two?' She looked at the pair of canith beside the Mechanism. 'Maybe and Starve?' A

cold horror enfolded her, prickling every hair she owned. All her labours culminated here. A vast tonnage of steel-wrapped vengeance. Now poised to snuff out innocent lives, this Livira and this Evar, within view of the true culprits. 'No . . .'

The automaton lunged again and this time Hellet slid back several yards, throwing Clovis clear. Kerrol rushed to his aid, holding the orb ahead of him in both hands. He'd wrapped cloth about his palms, anticipating the heat that had come when Evar used it to ward off the smaller automaton. Already the orb was shaking, its edges blurring.

Clovis rolled to her feet and scrambled to guard Evar and Livira. She snarled up at the construct, showing bloody teeth as she crouched beside Evar, blade raised, her other hand on his shoulder. 'There was no time. I couldn't leave you to this thing, brother.'

'Wait!' Despite Evar lying so close to death that it chilled his flesh, despite the imminence of her own demise beneath the ganar's fists, Livira wasn't ready to concede the library's guilt. It seemed to her that this wasn't something random happening to them as they escaped Irad and Jaspeth's audience. This was the *same* argument, made flesh. 'Wait! If Celcha had known *more* she wouldn't have set this thing loose on us. If you had known *more*, you wouldn't have killed a city. Shouldn't you have known more, not less?' Livira turned to Yute's daughter, the white child, for support. 'That's why you never came back to your parents? They'd given up immortality for a dream you didn't share. You were truer to Irad's vision than his own angels were. They were part of the compromise, feeding knowledge out in dribs and drabs, through a filter. You left because you hated what they stood for but loved who they were – you thought opposing them would hurt them more than losing you?'

'She was wrong.' Yute's quiet voice reached her.

'Will it go?' Livira asked Hellet. 'If I let it have me?'

'There's Evar too.' Hellet's whole body shook with the effort it took to hold back his sister's vengeance. Small shards of him fell away, tinkling as they hit the ground. Behind him Kerrol leaned into the effort, pushing the orb's aura at the ganar while the cloth about his hands smoked and charred.

'Evar too? Can't she see he's dying!' Livira's breath hitched in her chest and a painful sob broke from her. 'Can't she leave him be?'

'Stop!' Celcha shouted it at her own creation with the same force she had screamed into Livira's face just a short while before. And it ignored her as completely as the girl had. Celcha threw herself at the metal leg and rebounded. The thing had been designed to see and track ghosts. Even to touch them. Celcha fell back, feeling the hatred that had leaked out in the brief contact now crawling across her skin. 'Stop!'

Livira set Evar's head gently from her lap and stood up, knowing that even if the chance that her death would satisfy the construct was slim, she would put it to the test and take that gamble. She walked steadily towards the huge automaton, not looking back even once since she knew the sight of Evar's face might halt her in her tracks.

'Stop!' Hellet shouted, though whether at Livira or his sister's creature was unclear. Assistants never shouted but this one had, and in the same moment the ganar-automaton swept him up, grabbing both his legs in one hand. The swing of Hellet's body sent Kerrol flying backwards, his hands on fire, the orb making a glowing red streak as it spun free.

A heartbeat later the automaton hammered Hellet into the ground like a fisherman might brain his catch upon a rock.

'No!' It had been a hundred years since Celcha last saw her brother. A hundred years since he'd failed her. But still she cried out as though his pain was hers, and as he cracked her heart did too. Had he seen where her vengeance would take her? Had he seen her now on the day he asked her to set it aside? With every ounce of her will Celcha tried to force her avatar to stop. But this day had already happened, and the past has never cared about regrets.

Assistants didn't shout and they didn't break. This one did both. Where he'd hit the library floor mother-of-pearl blood coated the stone. The automaton brought him crashing down again, this time aimed at Livira. She could see the fist and body descending from on high and knew herself to be the target. It seemed slow, as if she should easily be able to step to one side, and yet somehow, she could not. Instead, she stood stuck between heartbeats, waiting to be turned into a gory paste.

Something tumbled her away at the last instant. The thing turned out to be a person throwing her aside with their own weight and sending her to the floor where the outer curves of the metal fist came close enough to brush against her legs.

Again, the fist shot towards the ceiling, dangling Hellet's remains and leaving another splat of his strange blood, this time mixed with crimson. Of the person that had saved her there was no sign. Perhaps the scream that came from Leetar's mouth was a name, but heart-break made it an incomprehensible howl. Even so, Livira knew it had been Meelan who had knocked her clear.

Celcha might have carried the deaths of thousands upon her shoul-ders for a lifetime rightly or wrongly, but the human that vanished into a welter of her brother's blood beneath the blow struck by her avatar was so unequivocally her fault that at last the weight of her guilt took her to her knees.

The ganar-automaton stamped forward, one huge metal foot crashing down within arm's reach of Livira's head. It raised an arm to swing Hellet's dripping corpse at Evar, still helpless on the ground. The world slowed around Livira once more as she began to sit up. She stretched her arm towards Evar, his name on her lips, frozen in the tragedy of the moment.

Beside Evar, Clovis waited with her useless sword. Starval, moving so quickly as to make even canith look slow, whipped upwards with a broad strip of leather. The oversized slingshot released its stone at the height of its arc, and the still-smouldering orb shot out of Livira's view.

Hellet's body smashed down and broke into bloody pieces, missing Evar by a yard. The automaton staggered backwards, its feet crashing to either side of Livira. She turned and saw that fire filled its open mouth, as if the orb had rattled down its throat.

Two more backwards steps and a muffled detonation shook the automaton from head to foot. It fell slowly, venting white smoke from every joint, and hit the ground with the sudden speed of a rock falling from a great height.

Livira stood unsteadily. The automaton's steel and brass body blocked the room's exit and already the smoke was starting to obscure its remains. 'Evar!' She began to stumble towards him.

Clovis ran towards their fallen foe, seeking a path past its corpse to reach Arpix. The smoke drove her back, choking. She staggered away, eyes red, and rasped at Livira, 'Make sure my brother gets out of here. I have something to do.' So saying, the canith sheathed her sword then advanced, still coughing, on Yute, pushing aside the terrified civilians in her way. 'You!' It didn't look as if covering her blade was an act of peace – rather that she intended to rip the librarian apart with her bare hands. 'You . . .' It seemed no other word could get past her anger. The one who sent the sabbers among her people stood before her. She advanced on the author of her life story, the one who had written in the first line of it that her family would fall beneath invaders' swords, ending the soft days of her childhood in the space of one bloody hour.

The people Yute had saved from the death of their city scattered before the canith's wrath, leaving her a clear path. A path into which Wentworth stepped, eyes narrow, tail twitching, teeth bared, showing for once the face that must have been the last thing in life that ten times a thousand rats had seen. Also at least half a dozen cratalacs.

Clovis paused.

Livira fell to her knees at Evar's side and took his hand in hers. He smiled weakly and she smiled back through her tears. Behind her, Leetar's sobbing gave voice to her own heartbreak.

Yute spoke, addressing Clovis. 'In the past, when the ganar-automata were damaged beyond a certain level, they would explode. Oanold's predecessors took care to lead them to empty chambers before serious battle. I don't imagine we have very long before this room fills with jagged pieces of machinery flying faster than stick-shot in all directions.'

'I'll die with your heart in my hands then,' Clovis snarled.

Yute bowed his head. 'My mistakes have caused great harm. But would your time not be better spent getting your brothers to safety?'

'Safety?' Clovis frowned at him through the mist-like smoke. 'We're trapped in here with a bomb.'

Yute stifled a cough. 'Lord Irad said we would divide ourselves between three paths. I see three doors leading to three quests.' He pointed to the faintly iridescent pools of Hellet's blood, the three largest sufficiently big to admit even a canith into whatever worlds lay beyond their surface.

Mayland, who had been leaning almost nonchalantly against the Mechanism, shrugged himself forward and set a hand to Clovis's shoulder. She flinched beneath his touch.

'Looks like I'm Jaspeth's pick. Though I'd have torn this place down without him if he didn't exist.' He took his hand away. 'Leave this one to his floundering. He's been failing for centuries. There's no worse punishment for his kind. He'd welcome what you want to do to him, believe me.' And with that he went to join Livira, Kerrol, and Starval at Evar's side. Clovis glanced at his departing back, at Yute, at Wentworth, and then with a snarl she turned to follow him.

Yolanda went to stand by the pool that Leetar knelt weeping beside. 'Lord Irad has charged me with representing his cause. Any who wish to bring his true vision into being and replace this' – she waved her arm at the surrounding chaos – 'failed experiment in compromise between opposites with something pure and glorious should come with me.'

Yute stood alone by the third pool. He looked at his daughter and seemed suddenly old, the centuries piled upon him. 'I'm fluent in more languages than I can count, but in none of them can age speak to youth. I say compromise – you hear weakness and cowardice. I say wisdom – you hear blinkered thinking, you see me hidebound, afraid of change. I say that the solutions will be messy, unsatisfying, and may leave both sides feeling dirty. You hear the call of distant trumpets; you see the vision of a future glittering on some high hill, raised above the murky swirl of warring faiths.'

'Are you trying to get us all killed?' Yolanda returned the ache of his gaze with a cold glance. 'Go. Let's not stand here talking until we die.' And with that she stepped into the glimmer of Hellet's blood and was gone.

Clovis bent to take Evar with her through the pool Mayland had chosen. Livira glared up at her, tightening her grip on Evar.

'Go Sister. The girl and I will bring him.' Mayland nodded at Livira. Clovis showed her teeth, backed away from Evar and, without a backwards glance at Yute, she stepped into the pool, vanishing in an instant. Starval followed.

Kerrol, trembling with pain, his burned hands clutched to his chest, met Livira's eyes. 'All of these words are noise. The only role the brain plays in these decisions is to come up with the explanation after the heart has chosen.' Slowly he walked to join Yute.

'Kerrol!' Mayland called after him. 'Don't be an idiot.'

Kerrol didn't turn until he reached Yute's side.

'This isn't you!' Mayland shouted, flustered for the first time.

Kerrol sat and shuffled into the pool of light, his legs swallowed by the floor. 'It's all me, brother. But you won't understand it until it's written as history.' He gave a smile. 'Keep them safe.' With a final shuffle he was gone, swallowed away to some other place. Yute, looking around with a sad smile, kept his place as if hoping more would choose his path.

Evar seemed to be slipping in and out of consciousness. Mayland shook himself then bent to take Evar's shoulders. 'Get his feet,' he told Livira with a degree of irritation.

Livira did as asked.

'Help me get him in.' Mayland looked down at Evar. 'Brace yourself, brother.'

Evar opened his eyes, frowning confusion. 'Livira . . .'

'One. Two. Now!' Mayland heaved. Livira heaved.

Evar slid away through the light. 'Livira!'

Livira stepped forward to follow him, but Mayland's hand covered her chest, halting her as effectively as a door. He spoke in Livira's language. 'I've watched you, human. This is not your way.'

'Evar's way is my way.' She glared up at him, mind racing. A dozen different thoughts tried to cram themselves through her head simultaneously. Could she dodge past him? How could she not have seen this coming? Would he kill her like they said he'd killed Yamala?

How long until the automaton exploded? Behind all of that, though, there was the calming thought that the instant he was gone she would follow, regardless of the threats or consequence. 'He's my path.'

The fingers of Mayland's free hand twisted as if he were stretching out an ache or manipulating the air itself. 'You still have a lot to learn, Livira.' The tips of his fingers darkened rapidly, looking as if they had been dipped into tar. 'Who do you think made sure your book would find my brother? And do you really think you can stop the library from falling to the weapon that you forged between you?'

'I don't care about the lib—'

But before she could finish, Mayland had stepped back and dropped from sight, trailing his arm. She threw herself after him, but as the last of Mayland's arm was swallowed from view it was as if his black fingertips had snagged a piece of silk laid upon the floor. The whole of the pool swirled away – a width of cloth whipped through a small hole, gone into the ground, leaving only glimmers.

Livira fell to her knees, clutching at the last traces of the light as it shimmered on the floor. The denial she would have screamed escaped only as a gasp of anguish from a throat too tight to accommodate it. Smoke flowed across the floor like milk.

'Livira!' Yute called to her.

She turned heavily, coughing on the smoke which, despite its creamy flow, clawed at her throat and would have brought tears to her eyes were they not already wet.

'Watch my daughter for me,' Yute said.

'You're not going to tell me I should work with you? Find a middle way?' She didn't care if the explosion came. Evar would die without her, without saying goodbye.

'I don't recall ever talking you into anything.'

Livira walked to the other pool, guided by Leetar's weeping more than the dim, shifting lump of her, just visible through the thickening whiteness.

Other shapes began to move. Survivors from the city, many of them survivors of the Dust before that, some from her settlement. It seemed they had been waiting for her decision to free them from the paralysis thrust upon them by a battle wholly beyond their experience and outside their comprehension. Yute had gathered them and led them to this place but whatever loyalty those acts had earned him had been eroded by the experience.

Livira found herself beside Leetar, a hunched form on the ground, with a dozen others at her shoulders. She could no longer see Yute and if he had more to say it was lost in the coughing.

'Let's go.' It was all she could find to say. She took a firm grip on Leetar, and stepped forward, dragging her in too.

Celcha knelt alone as the smoke thickened about her. When the explosion came it shook her far less than what she had already seen. The blast wave, sewn with fragments of her avatar, left her untouched. The detonation didn't drive her to the floor – she chose to fall.

'Sister.'

Celcha turned her cheek from the unfelt ground. Hellet stood above her, holding out his hand, strong and wrapped in the scars of his subjugation just as he ever was in the labyrinth of her memories.

Celcha lifted herself from the ground and reached for the offered hand with her own trembling fingers, expecting to find nothing but the phantom of her needing. Instead, a firm grip pulled her to her feet.

'How is this possible?'

'I don't know.'

'You're a ghost too?'

'I am.'

'How do you feel?' Celcha looked up at her big little brother.

Hellet frowned, flexed his shoulders, pursed his lips. 'I feel . . . free.'

Celcha's throat constricted around her reply. Freedom had been all they ever wanted. She asked another question, 'Where's your body?'

'I don't know.' Hellet smiled that oh-so-rare smile of his, showing tombstone teeth. 'Shall we go and look?'

*Many books are taken from the shelves. None
are ever entirely returned to them.*

Overdue, *author unknown*

CHAPTER 46

The rain fell for forty days and for forty nights and it seemed as if
the world must drown in such a deluge. But the Dust's thirst had
grown and grown and grown again, across ages of men and canith.
The cracks on the hardpan ran deeper than history and each needed
to be slaked.

The last of the taproots, most ancient of their kind, opened new
leaves. The wind-weed stopped its endless turning and sank its
fingers into the ground. And on the thirtieth day the Dust declared
itself finally full.

Streams ran where no stream ever had. One joined hands with
the next until rivers were made, tumbling raw and white-mouthed
into the great lakebed. Slowly, slowly, the waters rose, and on the
thirty-ninth day the ancient basin lay full and brimming.

'It's beautiful.' Evar gazed out over the greening plains. His rain-
dark mane hung soaking around his shoulders. The sky ran in
rivulets across the hard muscle of his chest and belly.

'It is.' Livira held his hand. Soon there would be grass, and the
herds would come, bowing their heads to eat, renewing a cycle that
had been so close to broken that none could tell the difference.

She leaned against him, not needing his strength or his support
but enjoying it even so. The rain fell warm and its soft invasion had
reached every part of her. Thin robes clung like a second skin; her

hair ran in black streams to frame her face. Water dripped from her nose, from her fingers, ran down her legs.

'It's not too late. It can be saved.' Evar rumbled and the sound vibrated through the side of Livira's head pressed against his ribs.

'It's not too late?' Livira raised her face to watch him, water filling her eyes.

'Close to dead is not dead.' He looked down at her, veiled by the wet darkness of his mane.

'Come down here.' She reached up to draw him into a kiss.

Evar resisted with a grin. 'You come up here.' And he lifted her.

Livira wrapped her arms about his neck and her legs around his waist, resting her weight on his hips. His tongue had a taste to it, but she liked it: the boys she'd kissed before had tasted of nothing. It was rougher than a man's tongue and reached further, but its exploration was gentle.

She pulled back from the kiss, slightly breathless. 'How far do you think you could carry me like this?'

'How far would you like to go, librarian?' A wolfish smile.

'All the way.' She kissed his nose. 'To somewhere dry. With something soft to lie on.'

Evar squeezed her to him. 'I remember this story. It was always one of my favourites. Watching everything change.' His voice fell to a whisper. 'How am I here again? Is it because I'm dying?'

'Don't say that.' Fear made her fierce. 'This is my story. There's no dying in it. It's about coming to life.'

'How are we here then?' Evar lowered her reluctantly to her feet. Letting her slide slowly down the length of him. 'And why' – he looked at the northern horizon where brightness showed, the first after more than a month of rainclouds coming in a grey tide – 'why do I feel watched?'

A coldness infected the wind, and the rain grew chill. Shadows, which had been washed away by the endless downpour, returned, reaching to the south.

Livira stepped back, looking at the sky. Her brow furrowed; anger showed. 'This is *my* book!'

✦   ✦   ✦

'Remarkable!'

'Lord Algar?' Algar's bodyguard, Jons, looked away from his study of the aisle stretching before him to where Algar sat with his back to the shelves.

Algar rubbed the bridge of his nose, trying to squeeze away the spiking headache that had made him look away from the page. The vision in his single eye had grown blurry.

This is my book. It had almost been as if it had been written in the knowledge that he would read it. The pain and the blur had struck as he read those words.

It had been one of the soldiers who had pointed to the hairline crack that had followed them across the chamber with the shelf-towers and back into the room they'd been trapped in for so long by the skeer. Even her sharp eyes would not have noticed it but for the escape of a faint black mist.

Nobody had an explanation for the crack following them wherever they went. This omen, combined with the heavy losses caused by what seemed to have been a single pair of canith, meant morale had been low on their return. The damned things had nearly got him too. The swing of a white sword had left a shallow cut running between his collarbones. Had the blow been a fraction higher and deeper it would have made an end of him. Though minor, the wound still burned and wept blood, and the centre circle wasn't safe to return to.

Algar felt the weight of their situation bearing down on him. Black demons had driven them from the circle where they'd survived these past weeks. The chamber into which Yute's rebels had fled held threats as bad or worse than the skeer that seemed to have been driven from it.

Algar had sought distraction in the second of the books they'd taken from the Duster girl. The so-called librarian that Yute kept as a pet. She had blinded them with the first book. This second one showed no immediate magics to match the darkness springing from the first, but she must have kept it for a reason. He had wondered if its magics were written into it more deeply. They must be.

The rest of the king's war party was spread around the aisles, gathering themselves after the canith attacks, giving closer attention to hastily bound wounds, taking stock. The prisoners had been secured near the centre of the group. Algar closed the book and stood up. One of the captives appeared to be wearing librarians' robes. Old, weathered, and torn, but still just about recognizable.

Once he was on his feet, he saw with a stifled gasp that almost invisible cracks now radiated out in all directions from where he'd been sitting. Additional fractures even ringed the spot with several concentric circles as if a great hammer had struck the exact spot where he'd sat. Algar backed away in shock and faintly – so faintly – the library's silence cracked around him, a single hairline fracture tracing its way across the floor, arrowing towards his feet.

With a frown he moved the book left then right. The crack meandered after it, first one way, then the other.

The book! The book was the source. Algar considered handing it to Jons in case the thing might be harmful. But no, the girl had carried it with her. He barked a short laugh of surprise. Nothing in all the years of research under the king and his forefathers had ever made so much as a scratch on the stuff of the library. Nothing in the histories reported any different result from societies that had conquered the skies and built weapons that levelled not only cities but continents. Yet here in his hand, a simple, crudely put together book of aimless love stories was carving through it before his eyes.

Algar set off in search of the prisoners. Soon, muffled sounds of pain led him to them. The soldiers had a ritual they called 'tenderizing the meat'. A grand name for a beating meant to take the fight out of new captives, but it served a double purpose, hinting at the fate awaiting them.

Three troopers had a tall, skinny young man on his feet, hands tied behind his back. They took turns in landing blows on him, waiting for him to turn towards the source before striking from a different angle. A gag reduced his cries to grunts and gasps.

'Leave that man alone.' Algar strode towards them, relying on the resting soldiers who cluttered the aisle to move their legs before he reached them.

'My lord.' The trio around the man stepped back.

'Take his gag off.' Algar studied the prisoner who stood hunched around his pain. Skinny, sunburnt, dirty but not with the same grime that stained the king's men. His robe looked to have been worn thin by hard use, torn in many places. 'This is no way to treat a librarian.'

The shortest of the three tormentors, a swarthy man with a thick black beard, yanked the gag away.

'What's your name, young man?'

'A-Arpix.' Blood ran from the corner of his mouth and one eye was already swelling closed.

'Well, Arpix.' Algar smiled the smile he had used for his children when they were small. 'I want you to tell me all about this book.'

Acknowledgements

As always, I'm very grateful to Agnes Meszaros for her continued help and chapter-by-chapter feedback as I write. She's never shy to challenge me when she thinks something can be improved or I'm being a little lazy. At the same time her passion and enthusiasm made working on the book even more enjoyable. Under the pen name Mitriel Faywood, she is now an author – go check out her excellent debut, *A Gamble Of Gods*, for which I was a beta reader. It's one hell of a story!

I should also thank, as ever, my wonderful editor, Jane Johnson, for her support and her many talents, as well as Natasha Bardon, Vicky Leech Mateos, Elizabeth Vaziri, Millie Prestidge, Sian Richefond and the design, sales, marketing, and publicity crews at HarperCollins. And of course, my agent, Ian Drury, and the team at Sheil Land.

Additionally, I need to belatedly thank a bunch of people who pitched in after I'd written the first draft of book one to calm my nerves over having made such a departure from my previous work. The following good souls read and commented on *The Book That Wouldn't Burn*, allowing me to make final adjustments before publication. And not one of them mentioned the fact I'd forgotten to include them in the acknowledgements – I had to discover that by myself and seek to correct the oversight here.

All of them are authors of various stripes: Doug Hulick, Michael Fletcher, Courtney Schafer, Helen Mazarakis, Shauna Lawless, Saeed Ajaib, Romana Pop, and Kian Ardalan.